GHOSTS

RAINA TELGEMEIER
GHOSTS

WITH COLOR BY BRADEN LAMB

graphix

An Imprint of

📖 SCHOLASTIC

Library of Congress Cataloging-in-Publication Data

Names: Telgemeier, Raina, author, illustrator.
Title: Ghosts / Raina Telgemeier ; with color by Braden Lamb.
Description: First edition. | New York : Graphix, an imprint of Scholastic, 2016. | © 2016 |
Summary: Catrina and her family have moved to the coast of Northern California for the sake
of her little sister, Maya, who has cystic fibrosis—and Cat is even less happy about the move when
she is told that her new town is inhabited by ghosts, and Maya sets her heart on meeting one.
Identifiers: LCCN 2016004672 | ISBN 9780545540612 (hc) | ISBN 9781338801903 (pb)
Subjects: LCSH: Sisters—Comic books, strips, etc. | Sisters—Juvenile fiction. | Ghosts—Comic books,
strips, etc. | Ghost stories. | Moving, Household—Comic books, strips, etc. | Moving, Household—
Juvenile fiction. | Families—California, Northern—Comic books, strips, etc. | Families—California,
Northern—Juvenile fiction. | California, Northern—Comic books, strips, etc. | California, Northern—
Juvenile fiction. | CYAC: Graphic novels. | Sisters—Fiction. | Ghosts—Fiction. |
Cystic fibrosis—Fiction. | Moving, Household—Fiction. | Family life—Fiction. | California,
Northern—Fiction. Classification: LCC PZ7.7.T45 Gh 2016 | DDC 741.5/973—dc23
LC record available at http://lccn.loc.gov/2016004672

10 9 8 7 6 5 4 3 2   22 23 24 25

Printed in the U.S.A.   40
First edition, September 2016
Edited by Cassandra Pelham
Lettering by Jenny Staley
Book design by Phil Falco
Creative Director: David Saylor

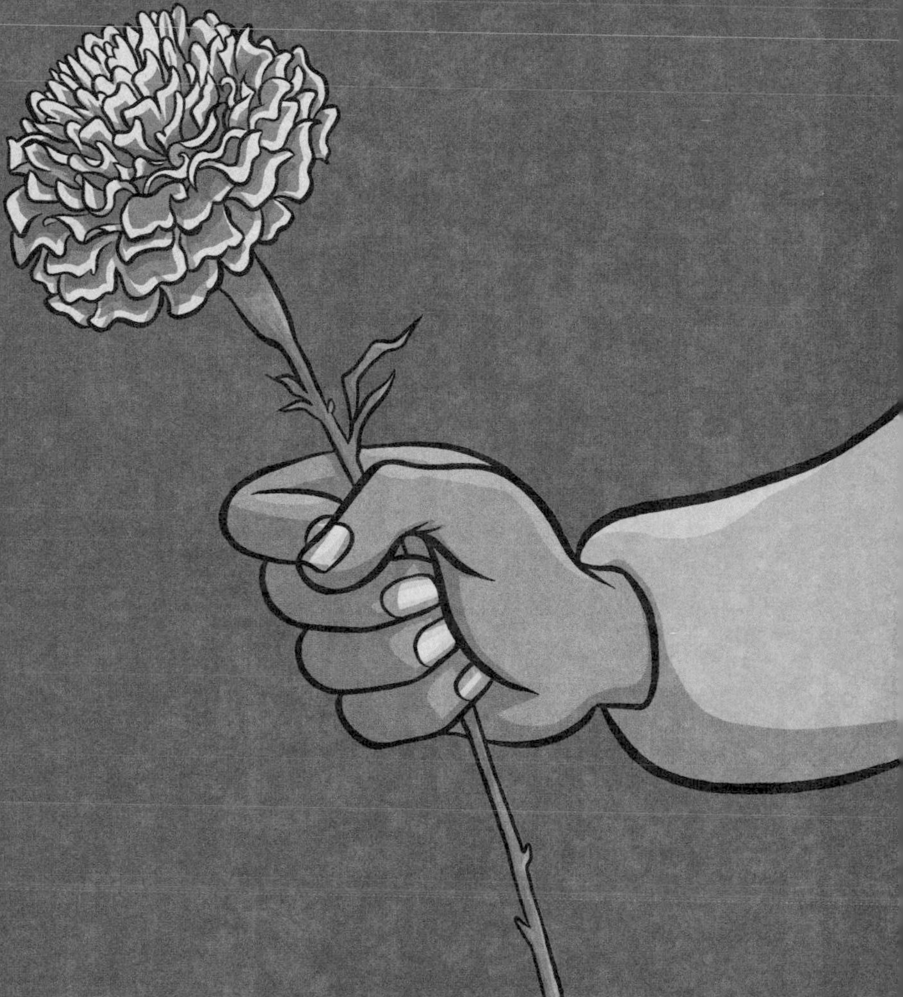

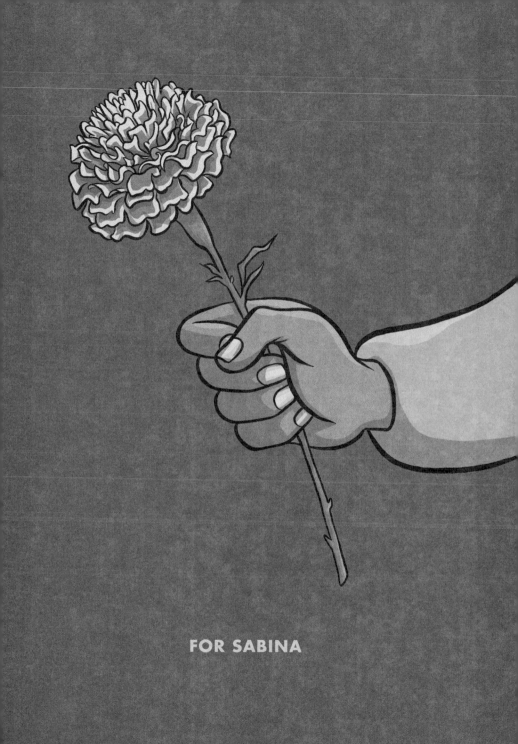

FOR SABINA

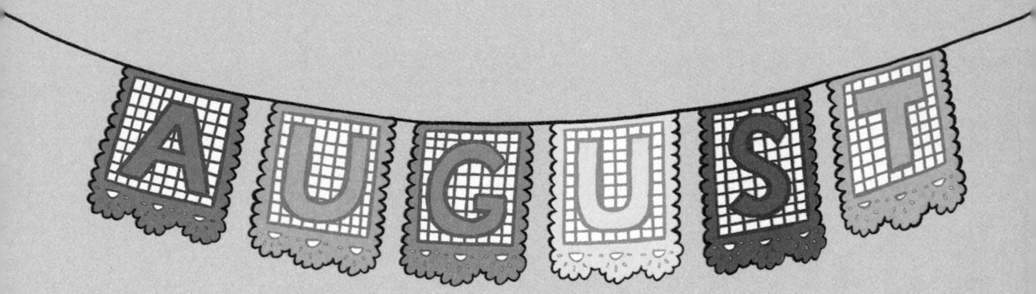
AUGUST

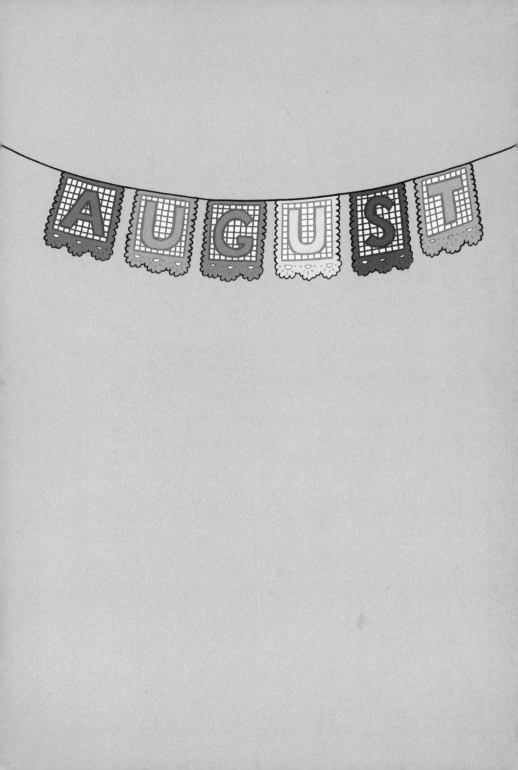

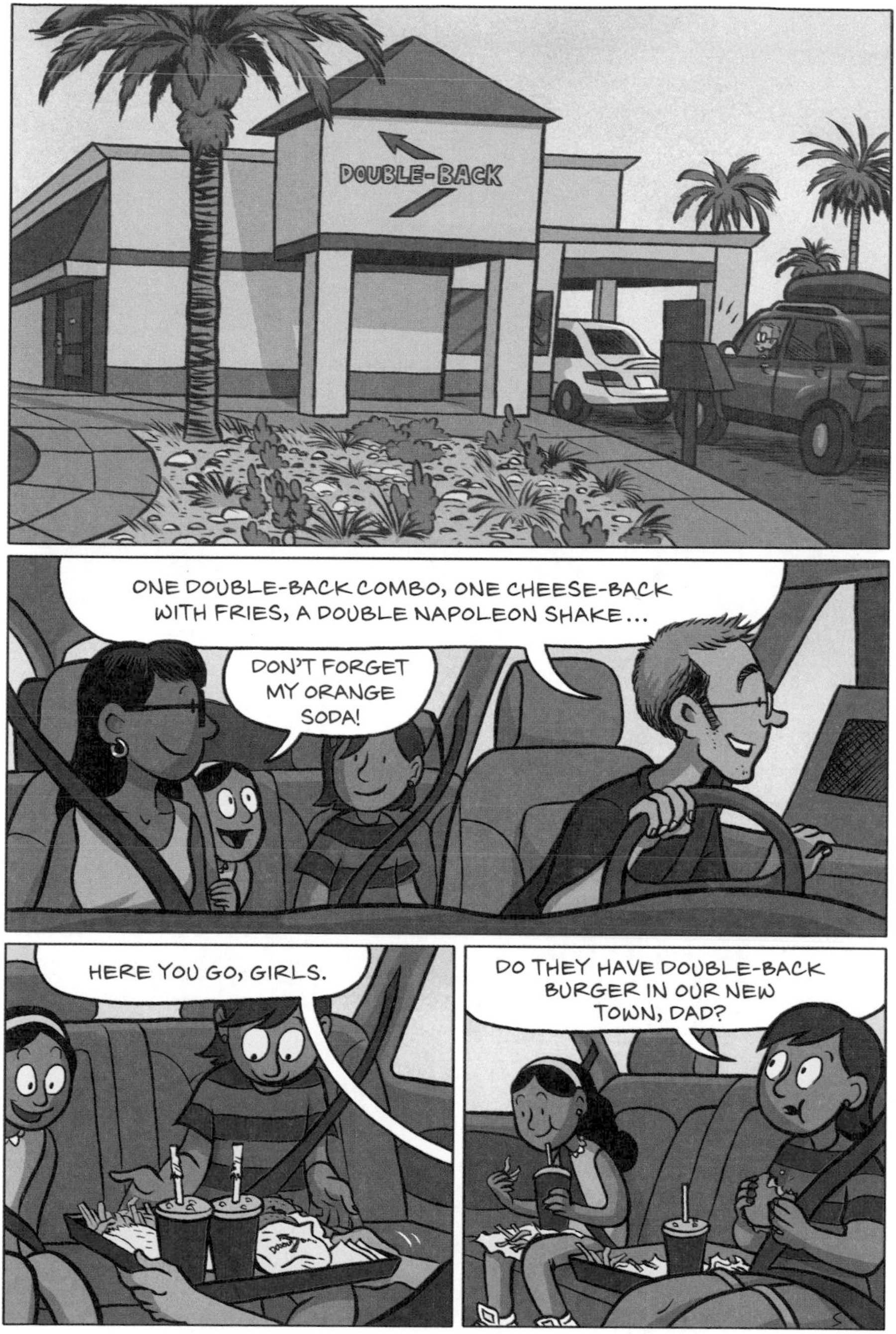
DOUBLE-BACK
ONE DOUBLE-BACK COMBO, ONE CHEESE-BACK WITH FRIES, A DOUBLE NAPOLEON SHAKE...
DON'T FORGET MY ORANGE SODA!
HERE YOU GO, GIRLS.
DO THEY HAVE DOUBLE-BACK BURGER IN OUR NEW TOWN, DAD?

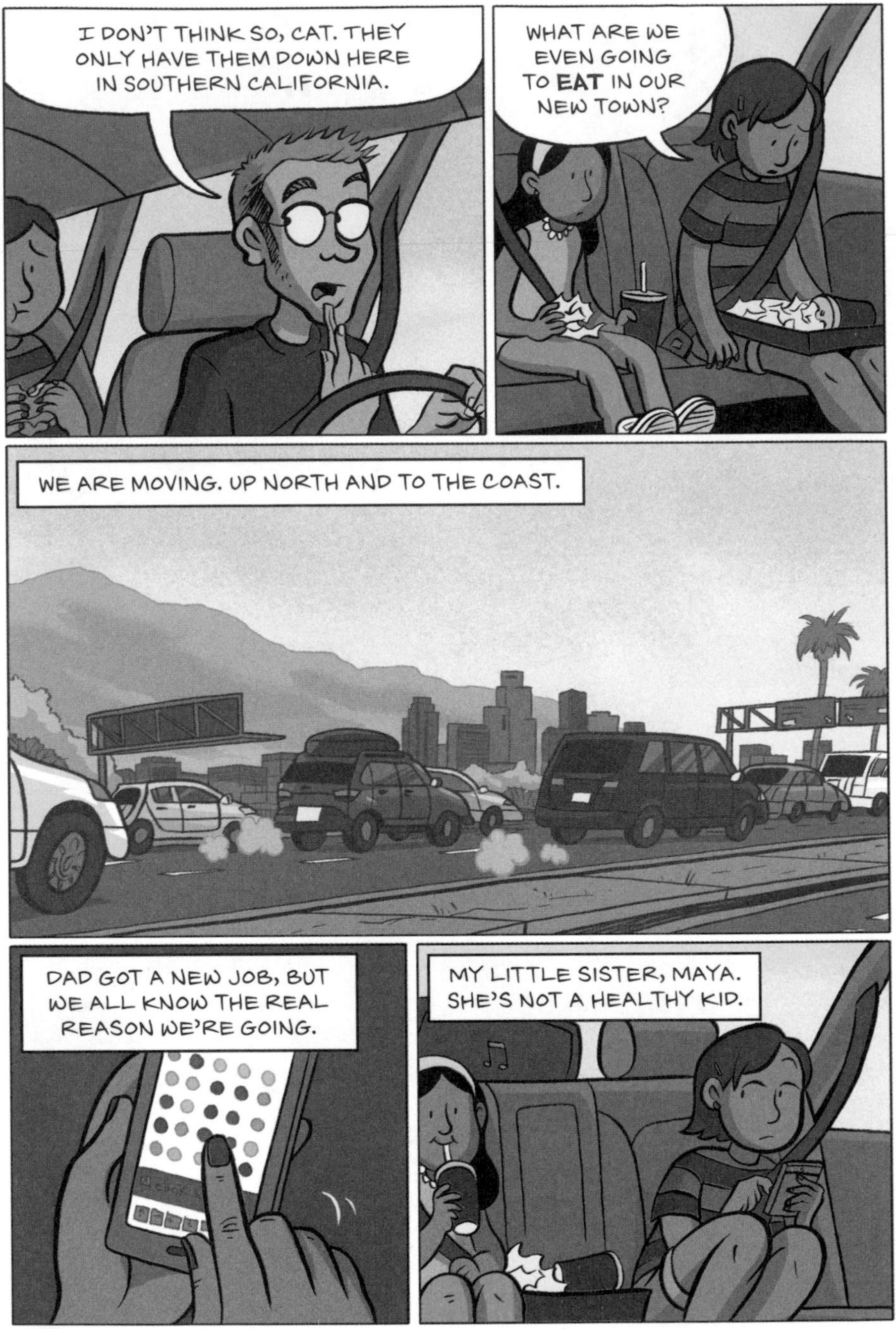
I DON'T THINK SO, CAT. THEY ONLY HAVE THEM DOWN HERE IN SOUTHERN CALIFORNIA.
WHAT ARE WE EVEN GOING TO **EAT** IN OUR NEW TOWN?
WE ARE MOVING. UP NORTH AND TO THE COAST.
DAD GOT A NEW JOB, BUT WE ALL KNOW THE REAL REASON WE'RE GOING.
MY LITTLE SISTER, MAYA. SHE'S NOT A HEALTHY KID.

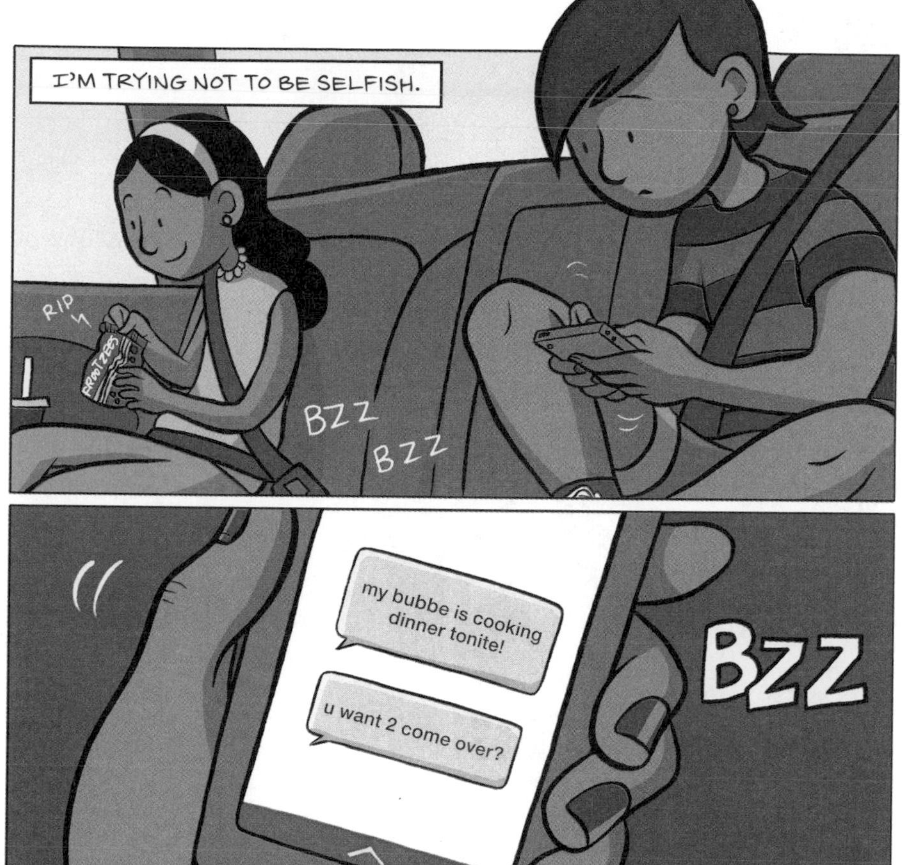
I'M TRYING NOT TO BE SELFISH.
RIP
BZZ
BZZ
my bubbe is cooking dinner tonite!
u want 2 come over?
BZZ
my bubbe is cooking dinner tonite!
u want 2 come over?
oh...right. i 4got. ☹
BZ
BUT IT'S HARD.

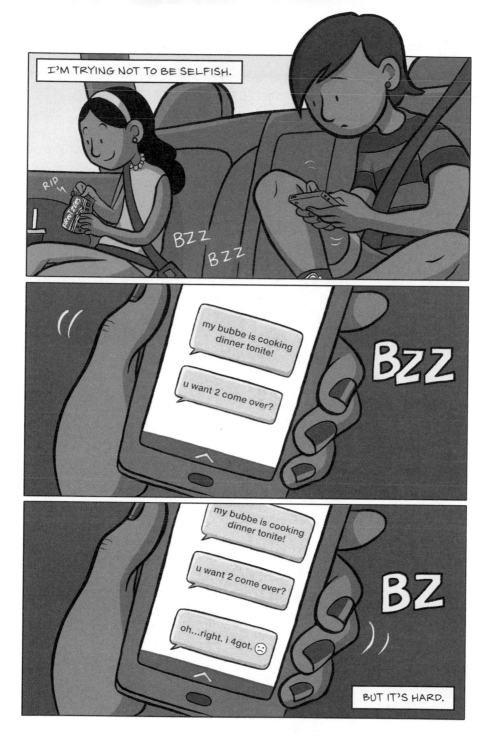

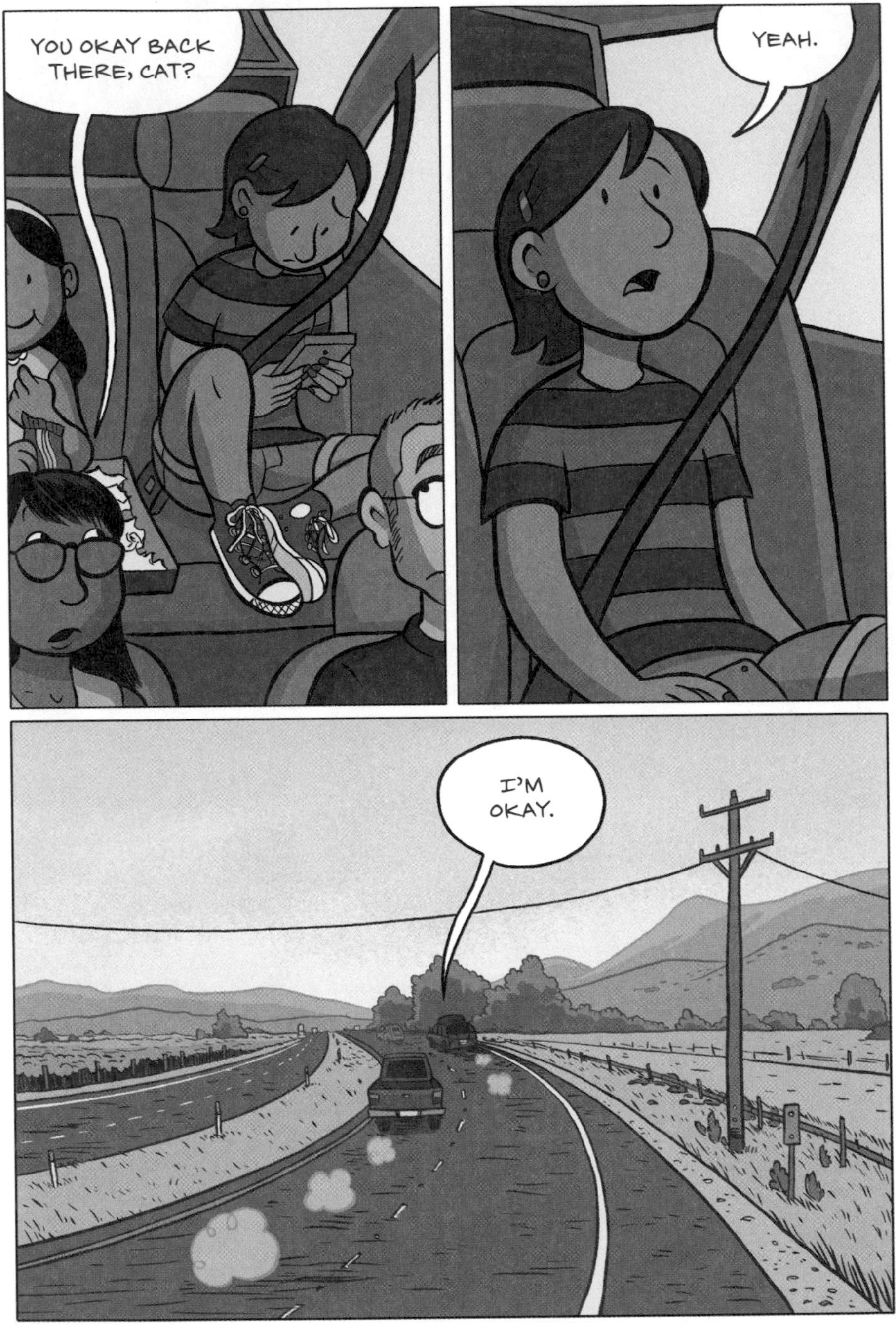
YOU OKAY BACK THERE, CAT?
YEAH.
I'M OKAY.

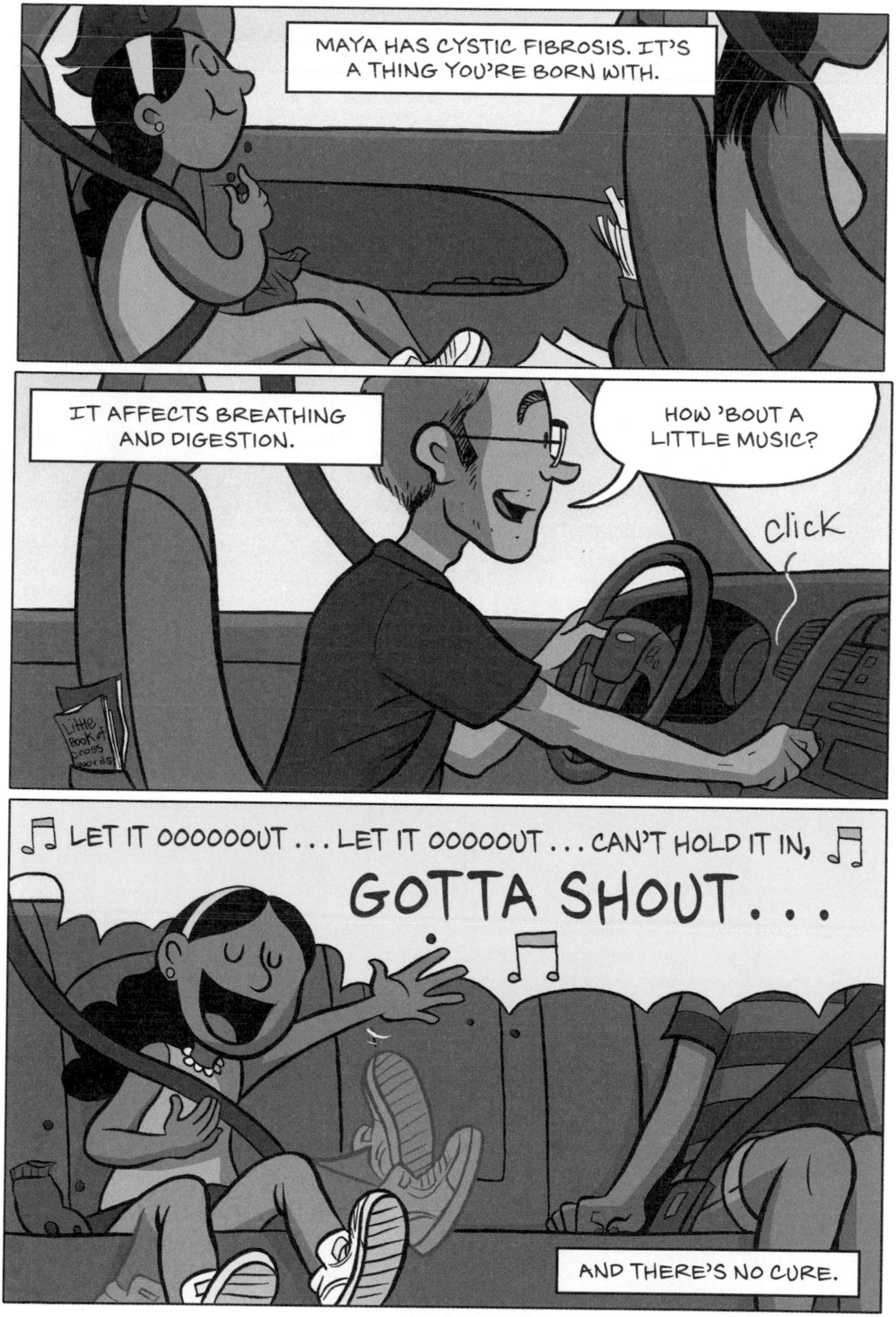
MAYA HAS CYSTIC FIBROSIS. IT'S A THING YOU'RE BORN WITH.
IT AFFECTS BREATHING AND DIGESTION.
HOW 'BOUT A LITTLE MUSIC?
Click
Little Book of Cross words
♫ LET IT OOOOOOUT . . . LET IT OOOOOUT . . . CAN'T HOLD IT IN, ♫
GOTTA SHOUT . . .
AND THERE'S NO CURE.

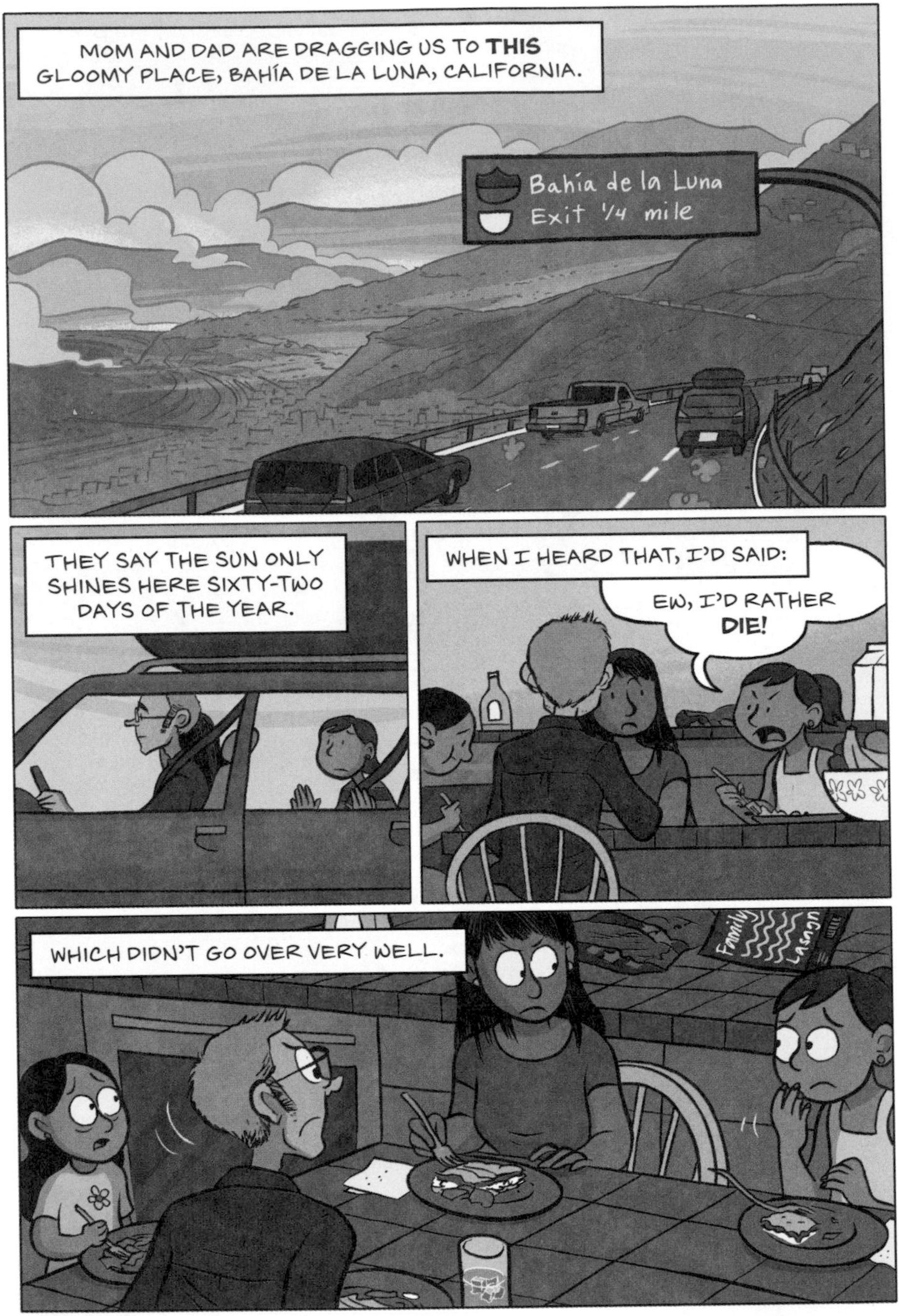
MOM AND DAD ARE DRAGGING US TO **THIS** GLOOMY PLACE, BAHÍA DE LA LUNA, CALIFORNIA.
Bahia de la Luna
Exit 1/4 mile
THEY SAY THE SUN ONLY SHINES HERE SIXTY-TWO DAYS OF THE YEAR.
WHEN I HEARD THAT, I'D SAID:
EW, I'D RATHER **DIE!**
WHICH DIDN'T GO OVER VERY WELL.
Family Lasagn

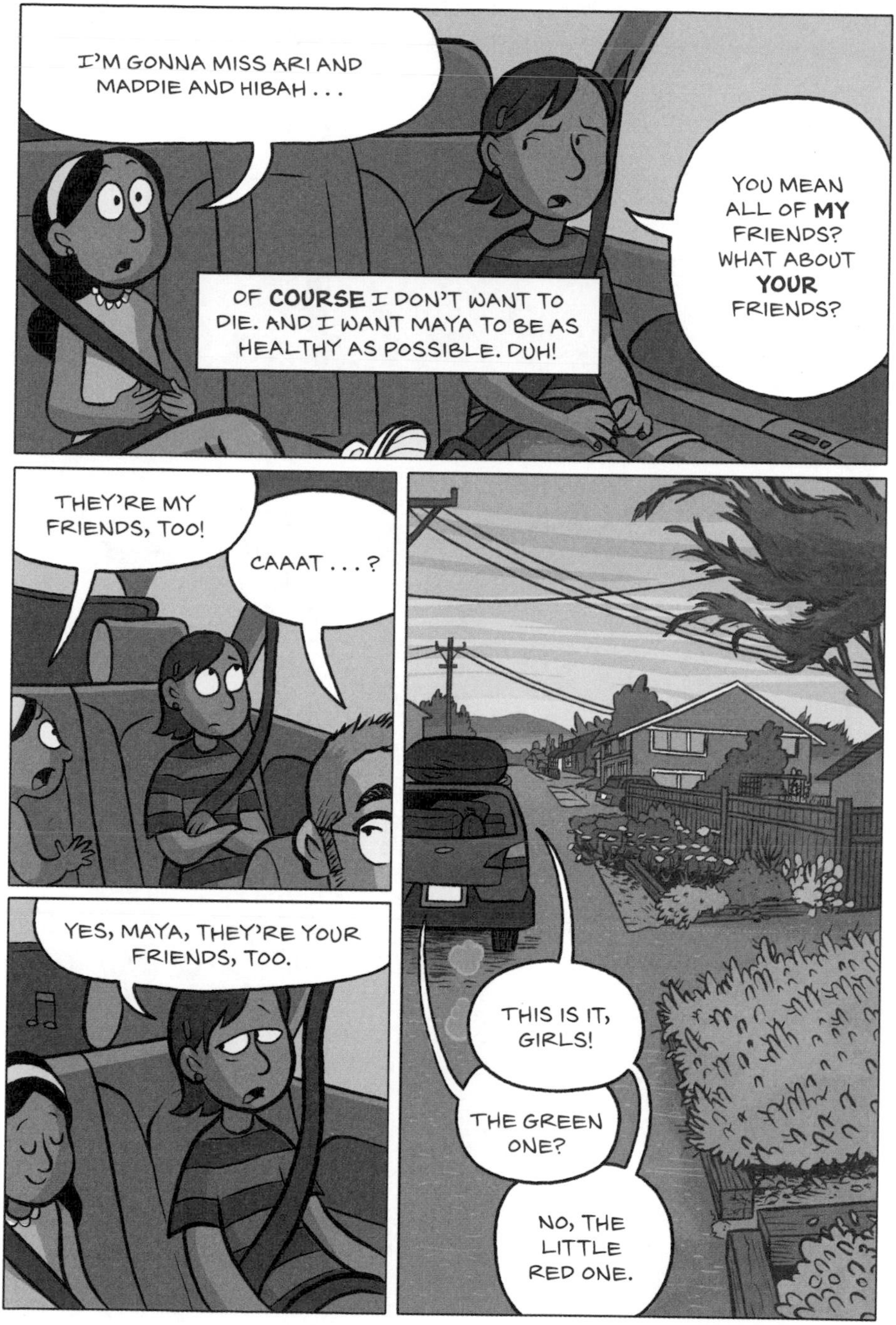
I'M GONNA MISS ARI AND MADDIE AND HIBAH . . .
OF **COURSE** I DON'T WANT TO DIE. AND I WANT MAYA TO BE AS HEALTHY AS POSSIBLE. DUH!
YOU MEAN ALL OF **MY** FRIENDS? WHAT ABOUT **YOUR** FRIENDS?
THEY'RE MY FRIENDS, TOO!
CAAAT . . . ?
YES, MAYA, THEY'RE YOUR FRIENDS, TOO.
THIS IS IT, GIRLS!
THE GREEN ONE?
NO, THE LITTLE RED ONE.

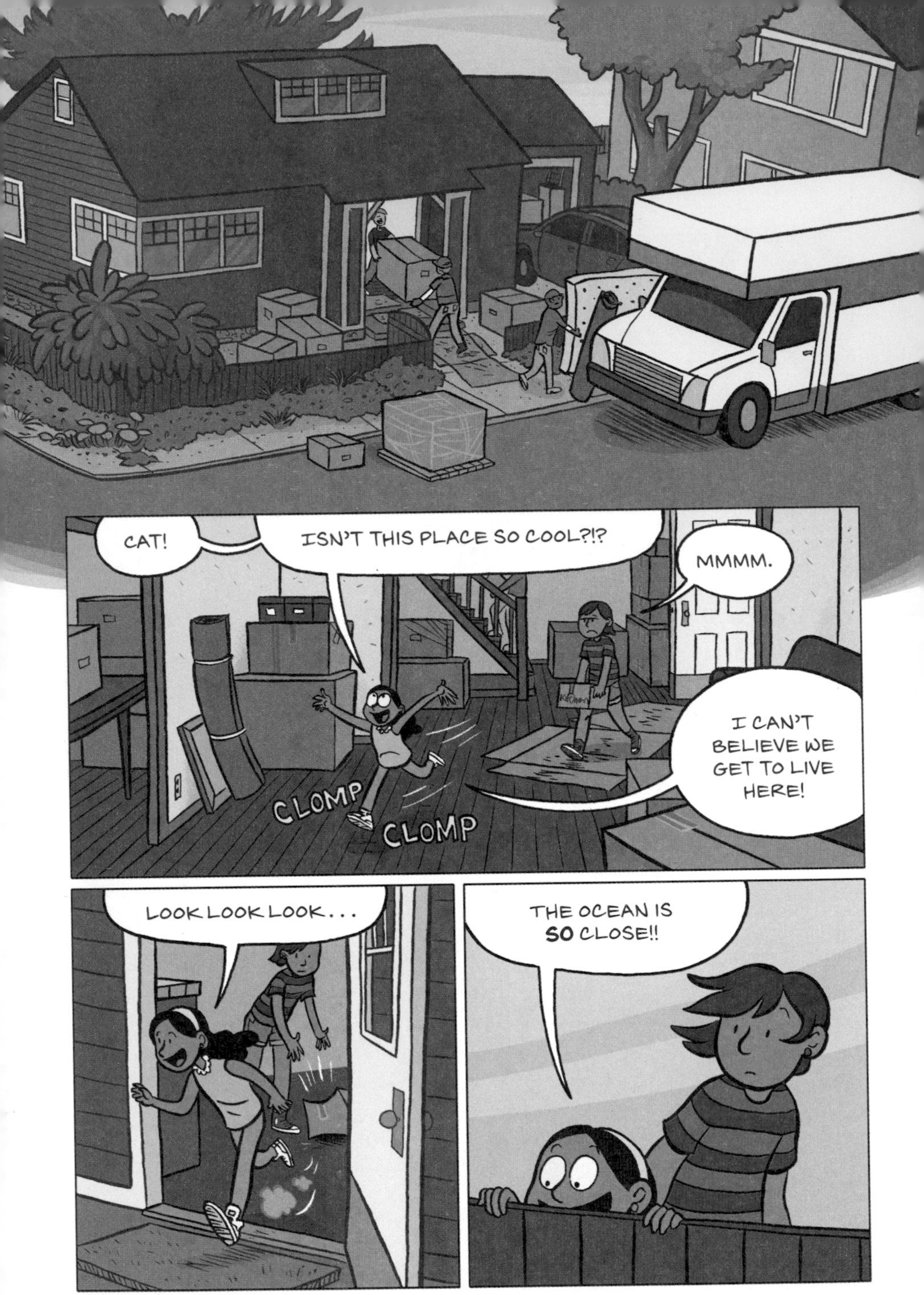
CAT!
ISN'T THIS PLACE SO COOL?!?
MMMM.
CLOMP
CLOMP
I CAN'T BELIEVE WE GET TO LIVE HERE!
LOOK LOOK LOOK . . .
THE OCEAN IS **SO** CLOSE!!

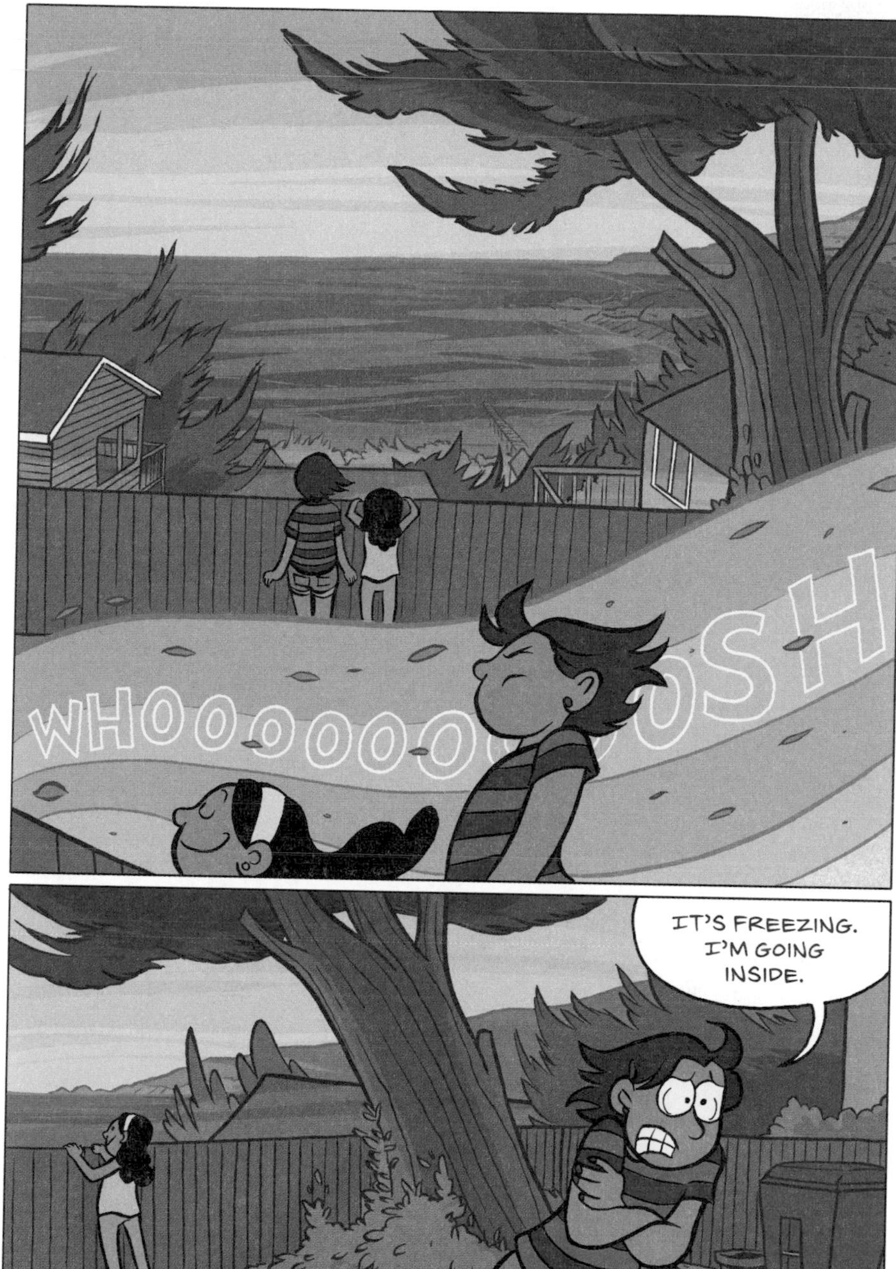
WHOOOOOOOOOOSH
IT'S FREEZING. I'M GOING INSIDE.

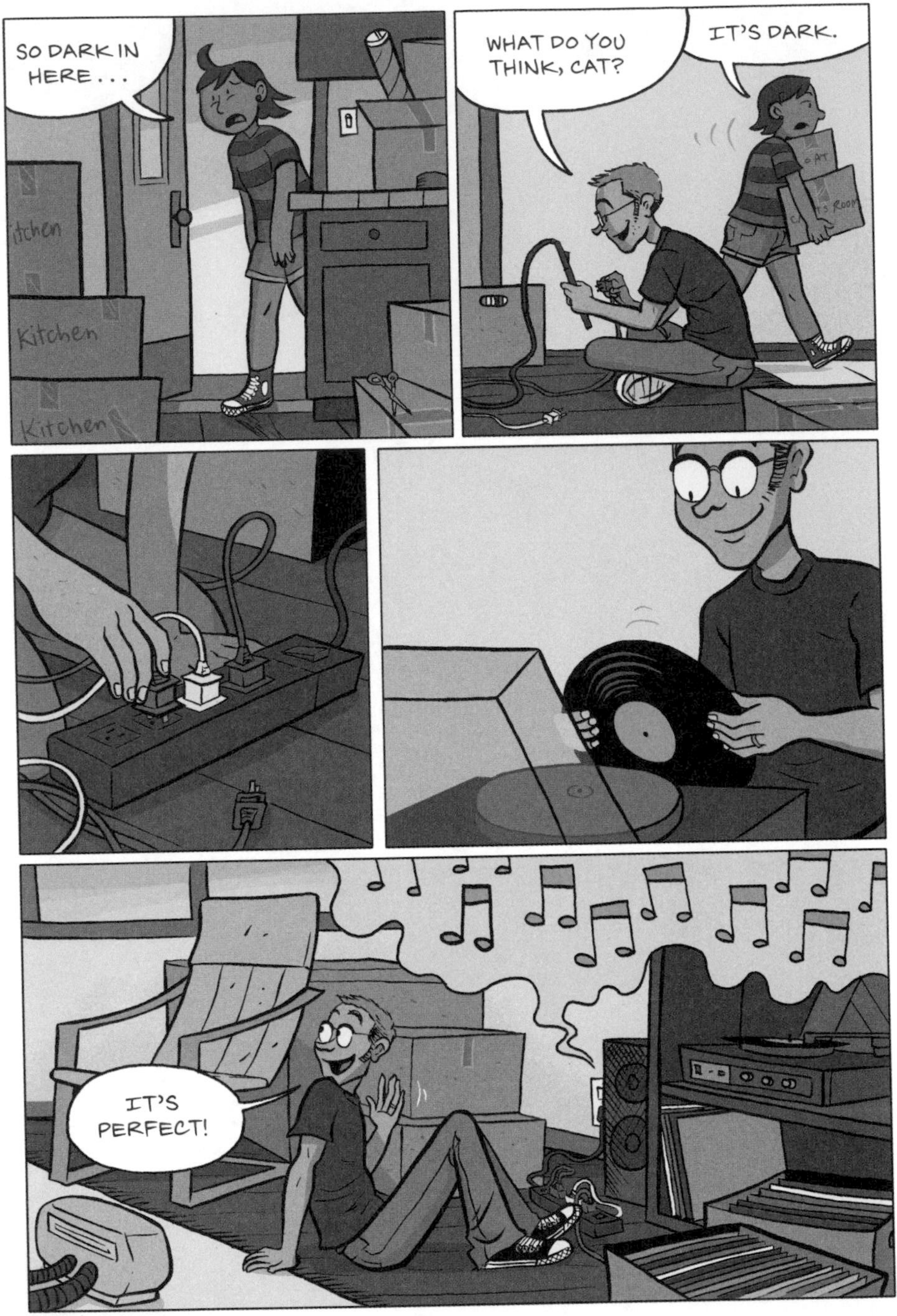
SO DARK IN HERE . . .
WHAT DO YOU THINK, CAT?
IT'S DARK.
IT'S PERFECT!

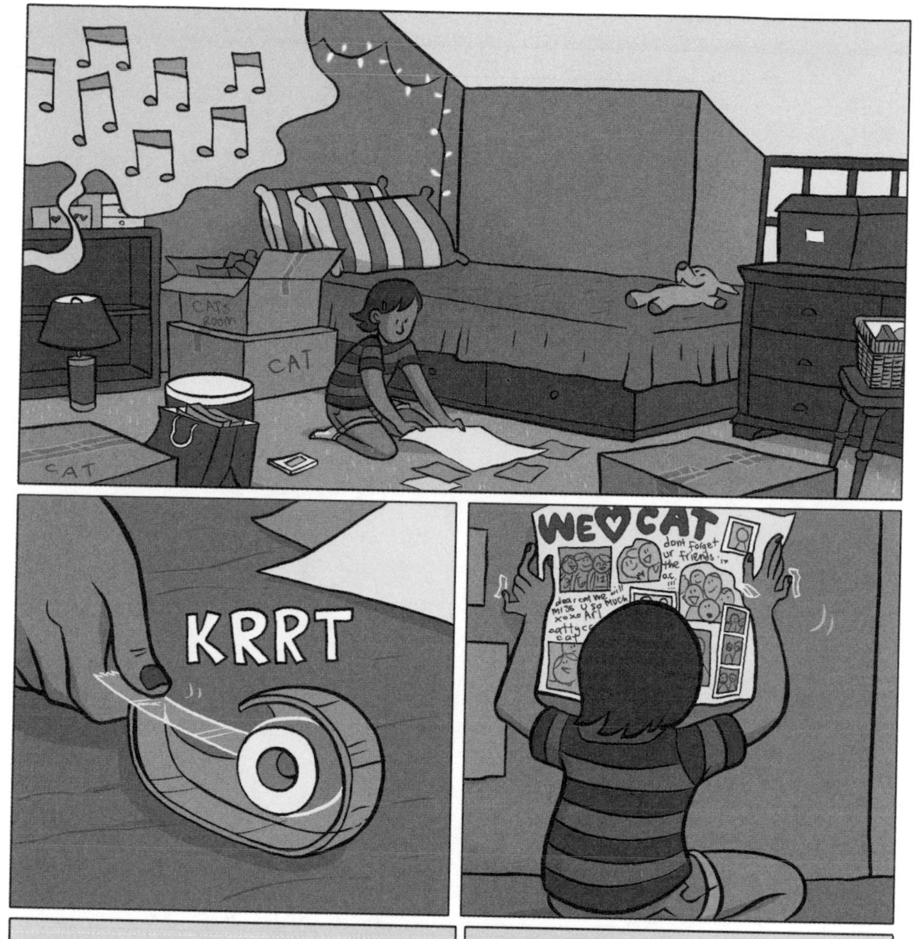
CAT'S Room
CAT
CAT
KRRT
WE♥CAT
dont forget ur friends in the o.c. !!!
dear cat we will miss u so much xoxo Ari
cattycat cat
SIGH.

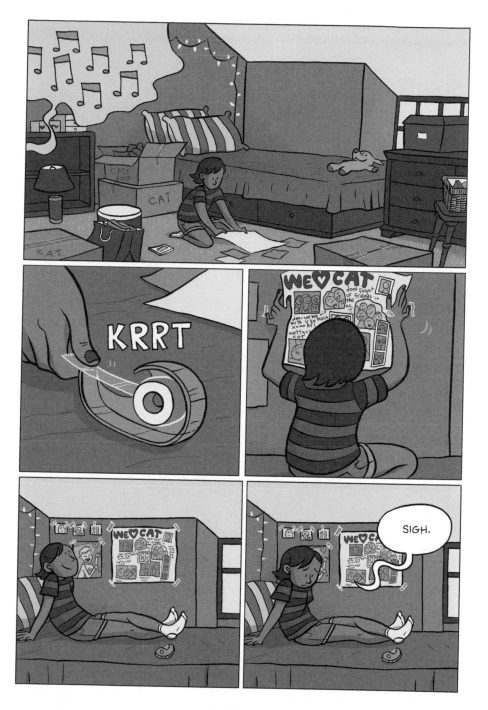

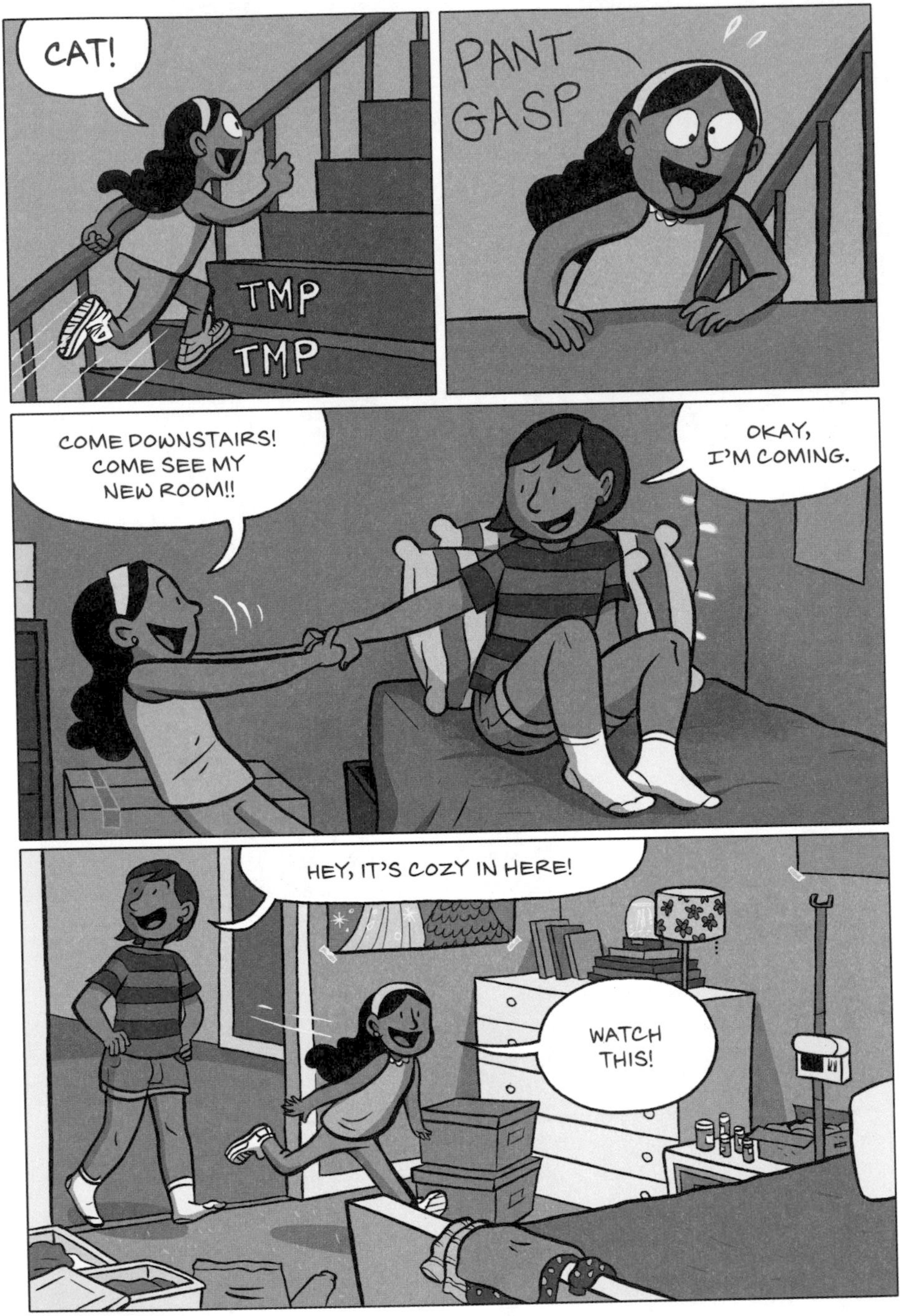
CAT!
TMP
TMP
PANT
GASP
COME DOWNSTAIRS! COME SEE MY NEW ROOM!!
OKAY, I'M COMING.
HEY, IT'S COZY IN HERE!
WATCH THIS!

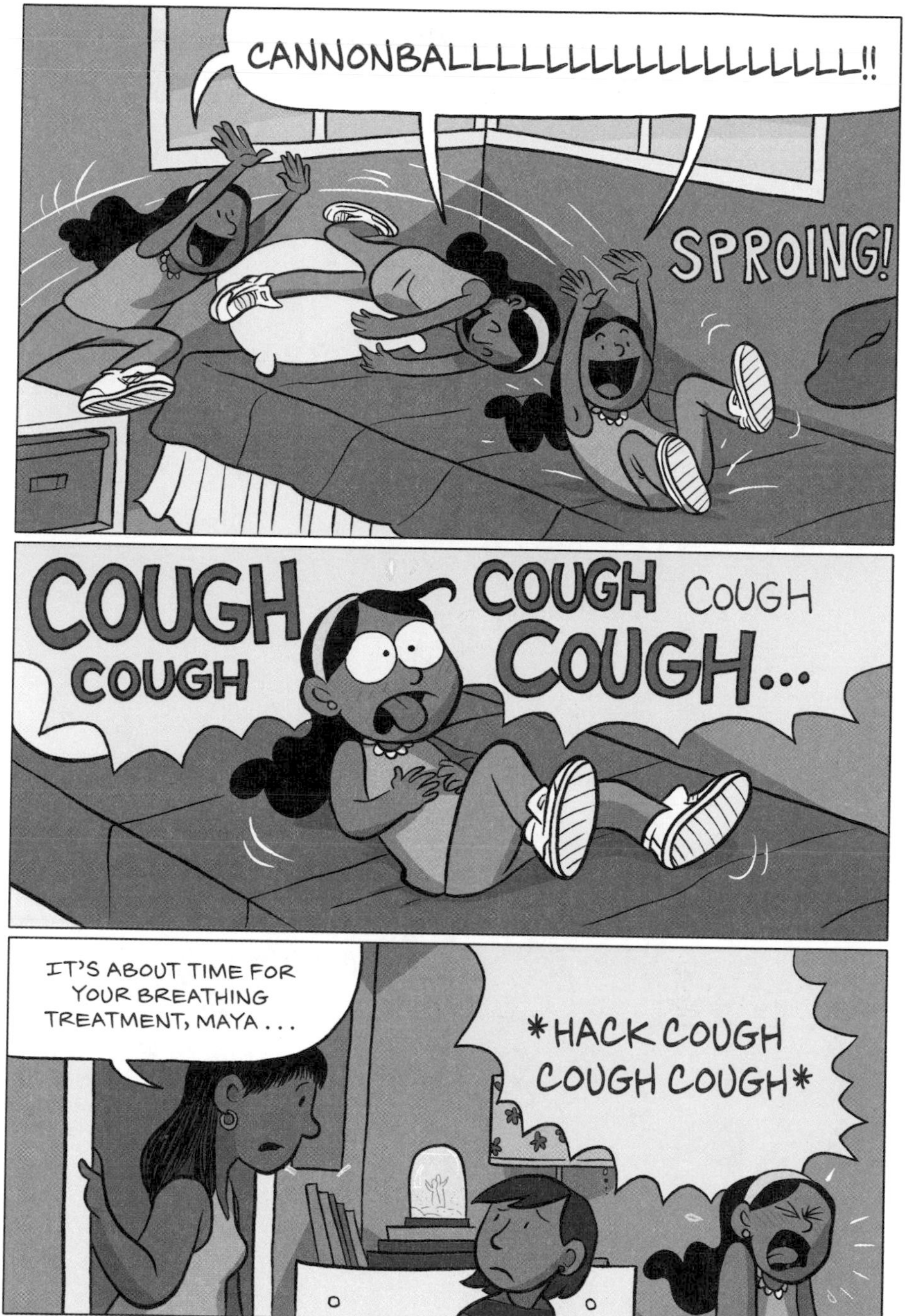
CANNONBALLLLLLLLLLLLLLLLL!!
SPROING!
COUGH COUGH COUGH COUGH COUGH COUGH...
IT'S ABOUT TIME FOR YOUR BREATHING TREATMENT, MAYA . . .
HACK COUGH COUGH COUGH

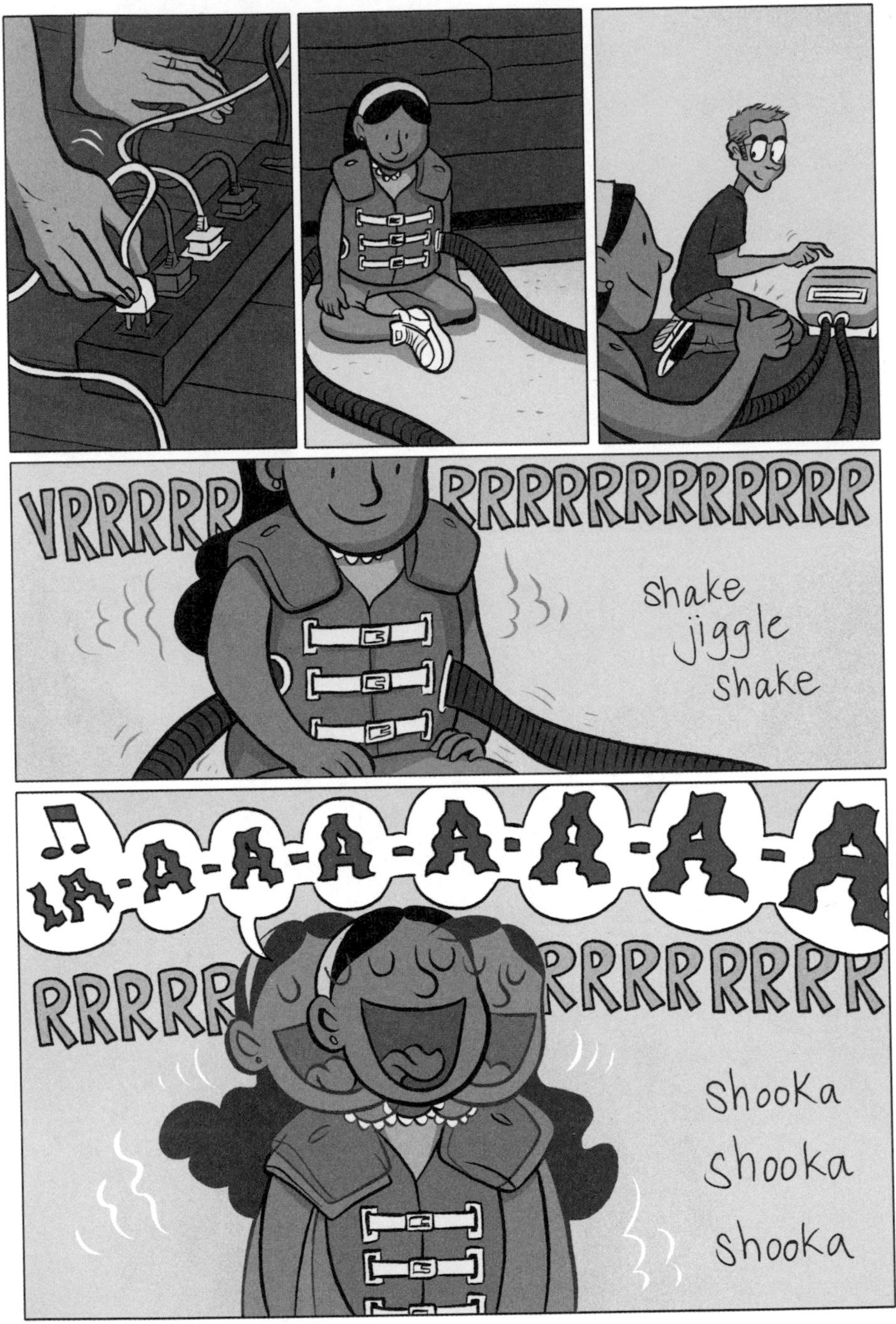
VRRRRRRRRRRRRRRRR
shake
jiggle
shake
♫ LA-A-A-A-A-A-A-A
RRRRRRRRRRRRR
shooka
shooka
shooka

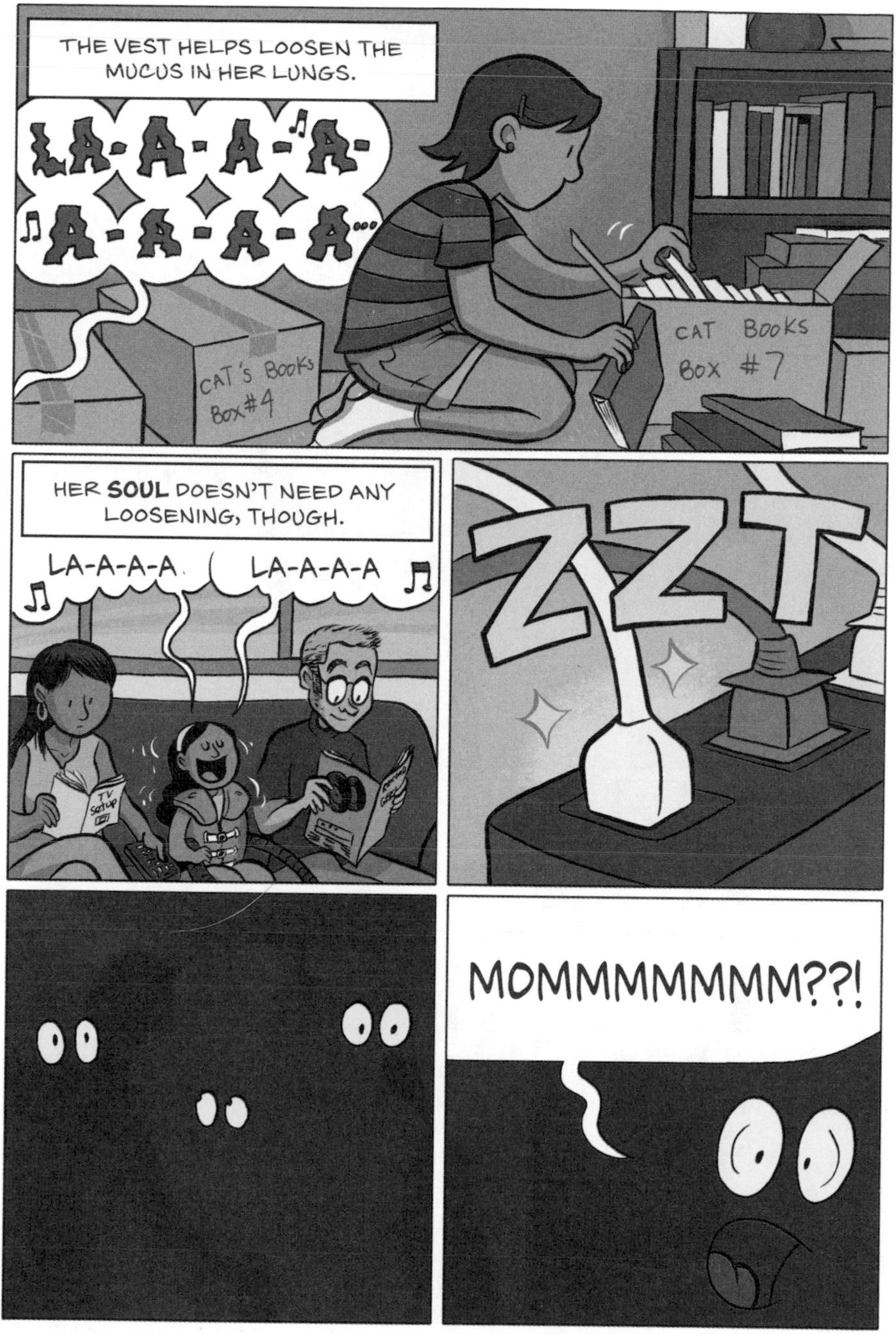

THE VEST HELPS LOOSEN THE MUCUS IN HER LUNGS.
LA-A-A-A-A-A-A-A...
CAT'S BOOKS Box #4
CAT BOOKS BOX #7
HER SOUL DOESN'T NEED ANY LOOSENING, THOUGH.
LA-A-A-A
LA-A-A-A
TV Setup
ZZT
MOMMMMMMM??!

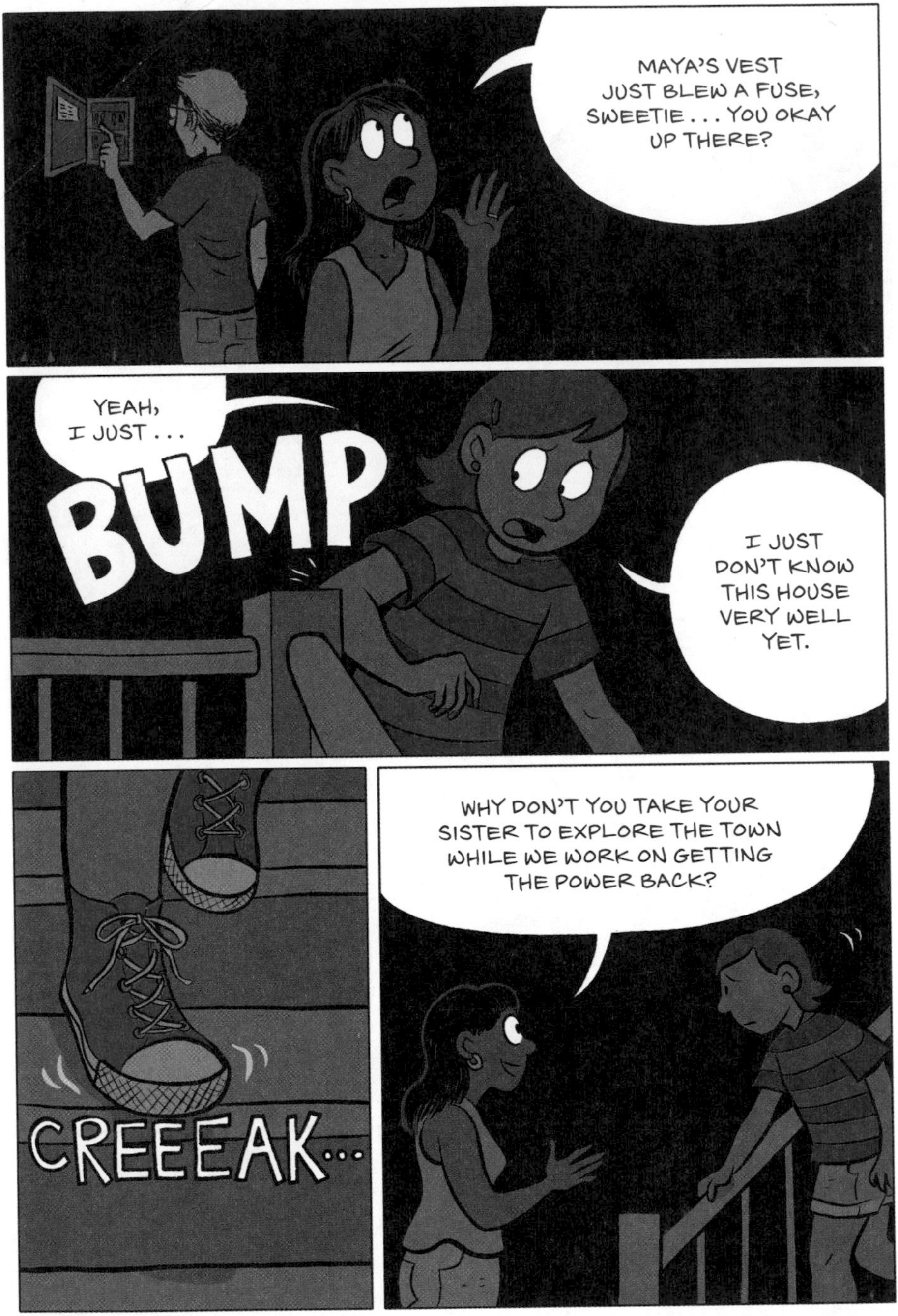
MAYA'S VEST JUST BLEW A FUSE, SWEETIE . . . YOU OKAY UP THERE?
YEAH, I JUST . . .
BUMP
I JUST DON'T KNOW THIS HOUSE VERY WELL YET.
CREEEAK...
WHY DON'T YOU TAKE YOUR SISTER TO EXPLORE THE TOWN WHILE WE WORK ON GETTING THE POWER BACK?

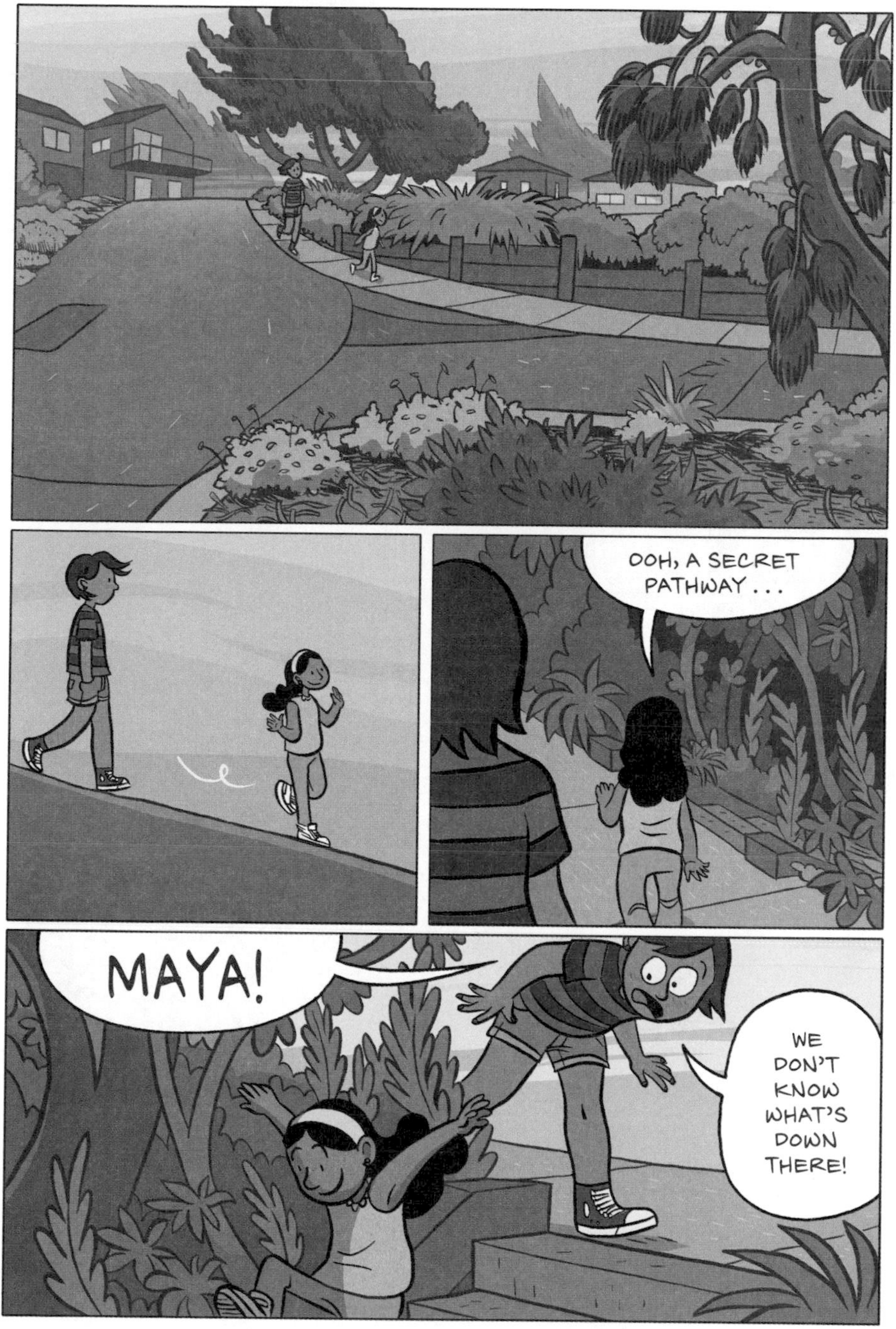
OOH, A SECRET PATHWAY . . .
MAYA!
WE DON'T KNOW WHAT'S DOWN THERE!

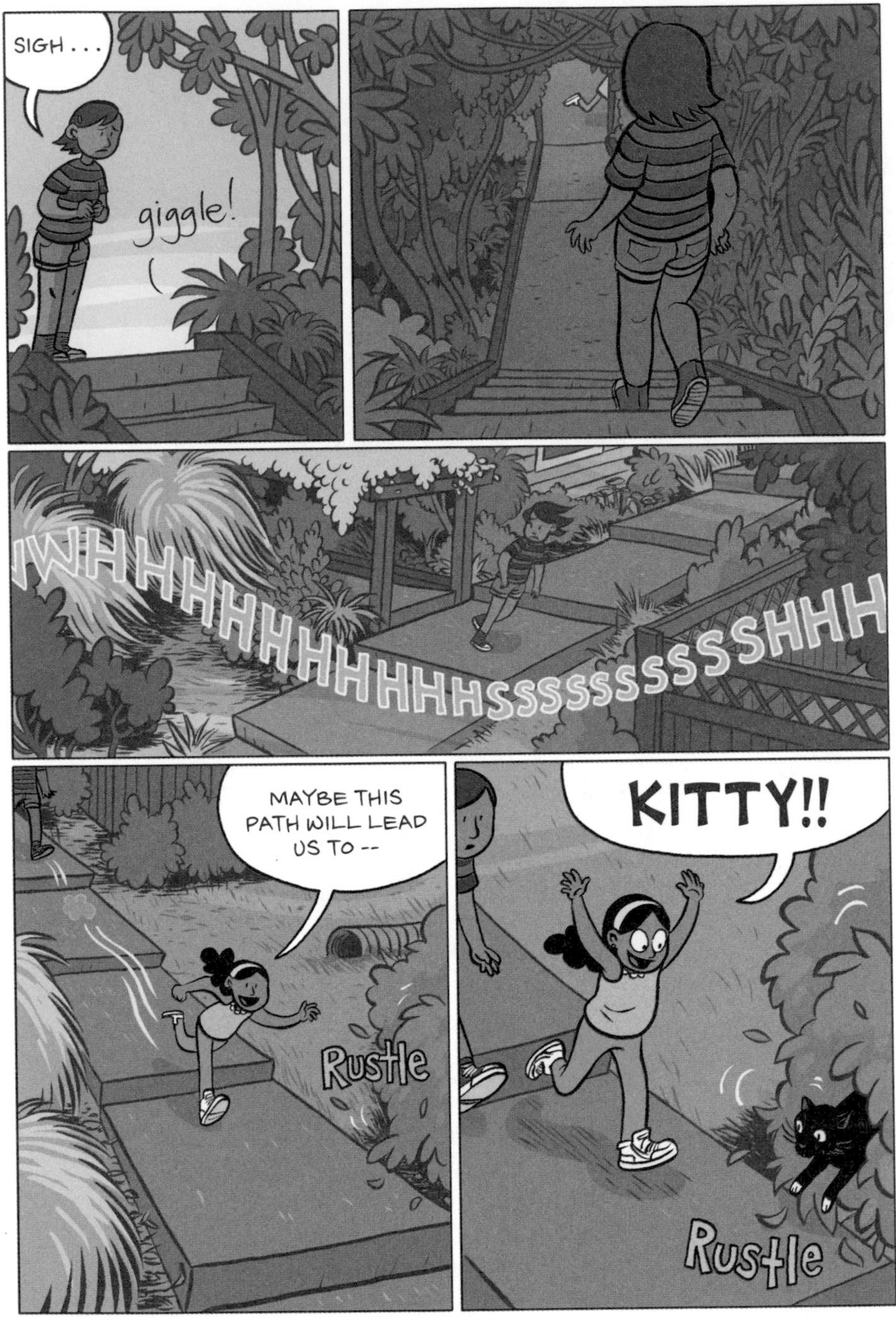
SIGH . . .
giggle!
WHHHHHHHHHHHHHHHSSSSSSSSSSHHH
MAYBE THIS PATH WILL LEAD US TO --
Rustle
KITTY!!
Rustle

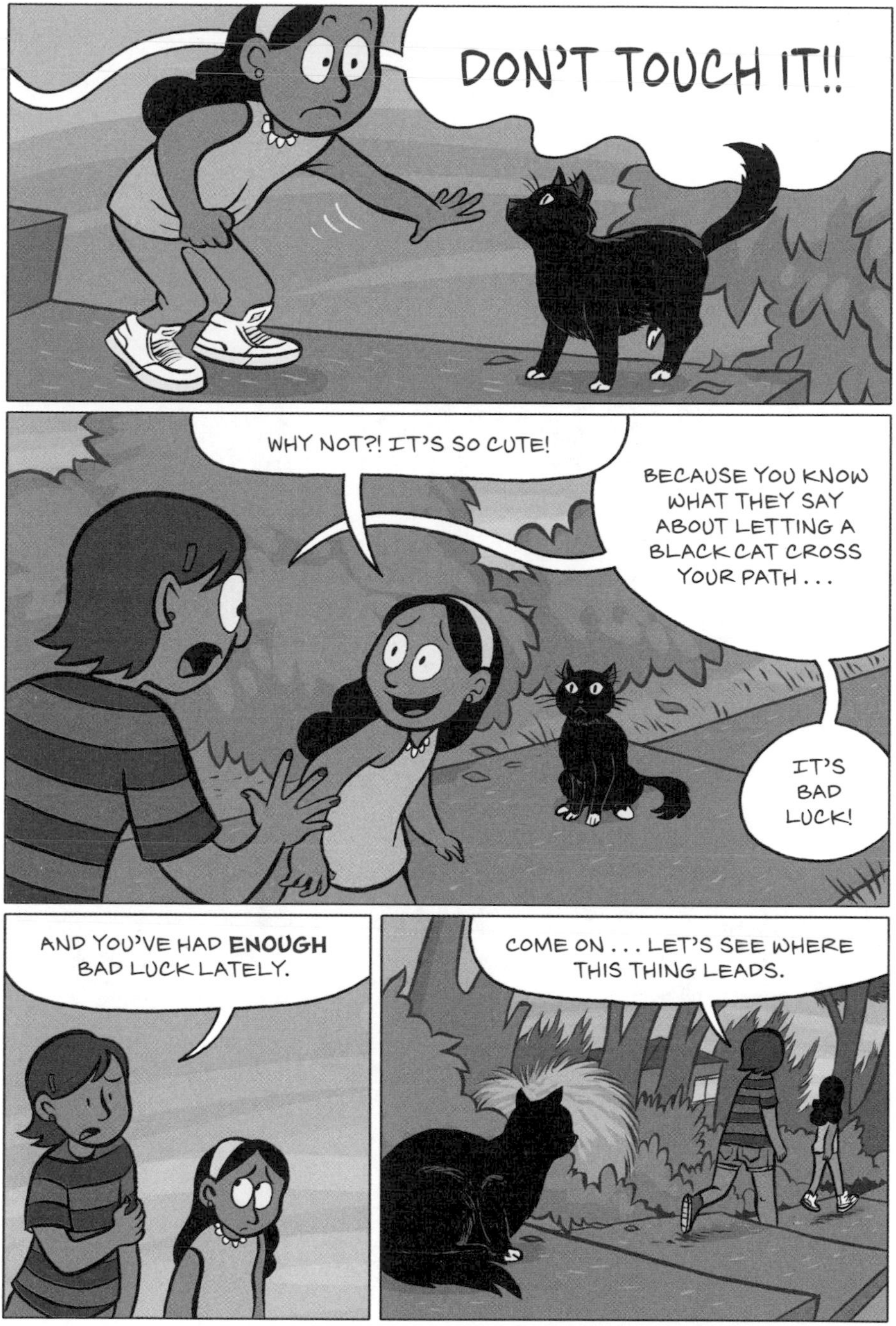

DON'T TOUCH IT!!
WHY NOT?! IT'S SO CUTE!
BECAUSE YOU KNOW WHAT THEY SAY ABOUT LETTING A BLACK CAT CROSS YOUR PATH . . .
IT'S BAD LUCK!
AND YOU'VE HAD **ENOUGH** BAD LUCK LATELY.
COME ON . . . LET'S SEE WHERE THIS THING LEADS.

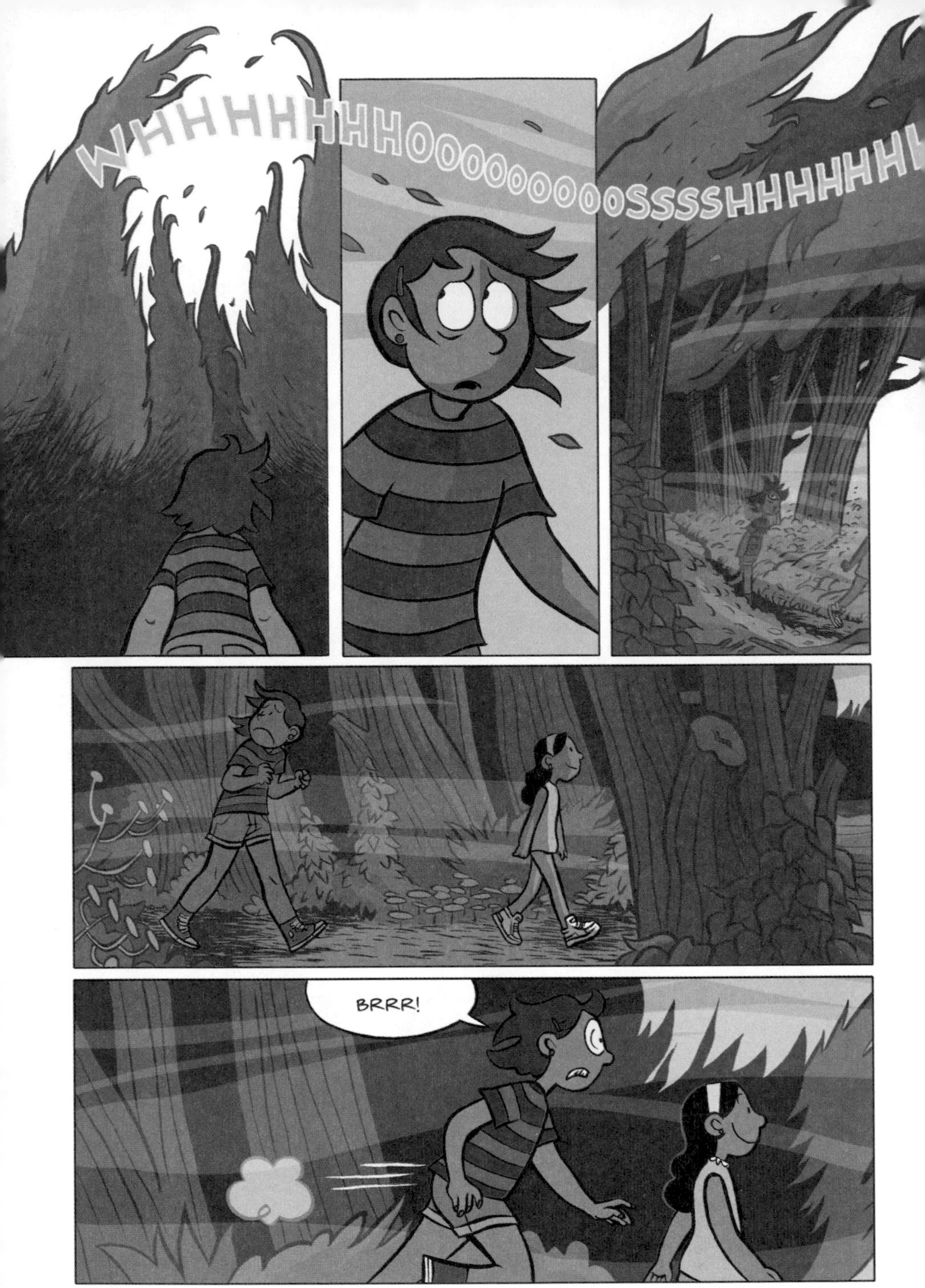
WHHHHHHHOOOOOOOOOOSSSSHHHHHHH
BRRR!

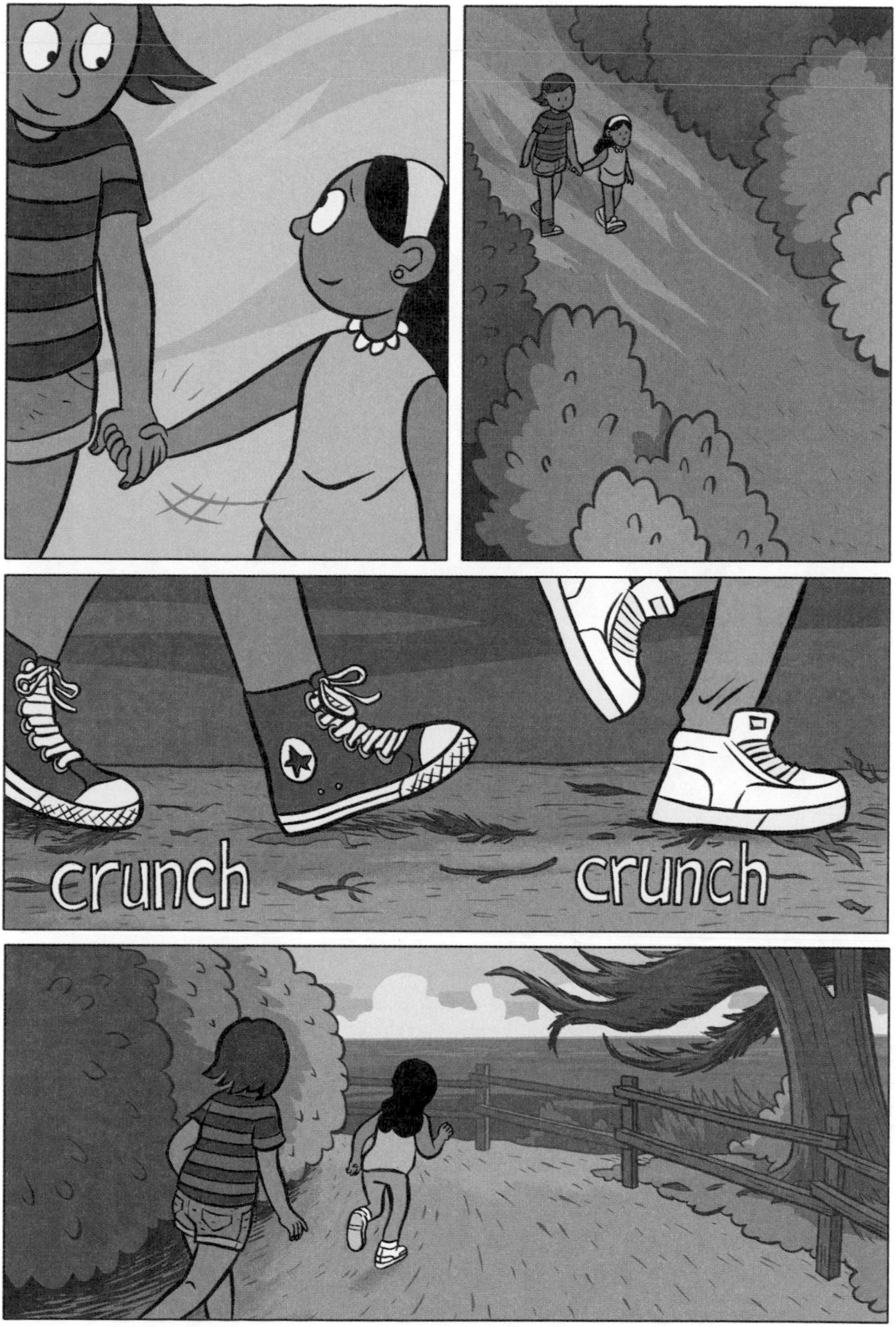
crunch
crunch

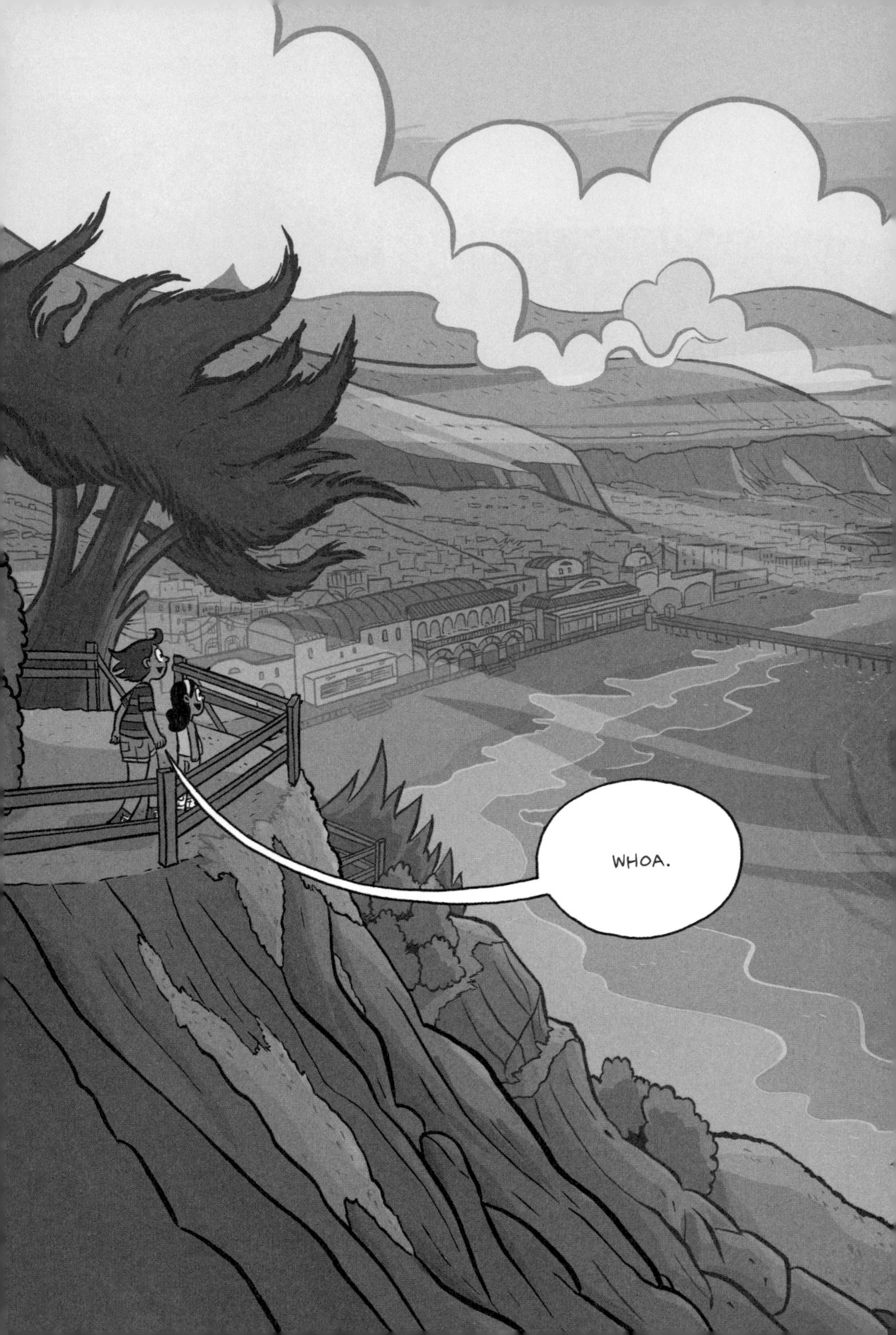
WHOA.

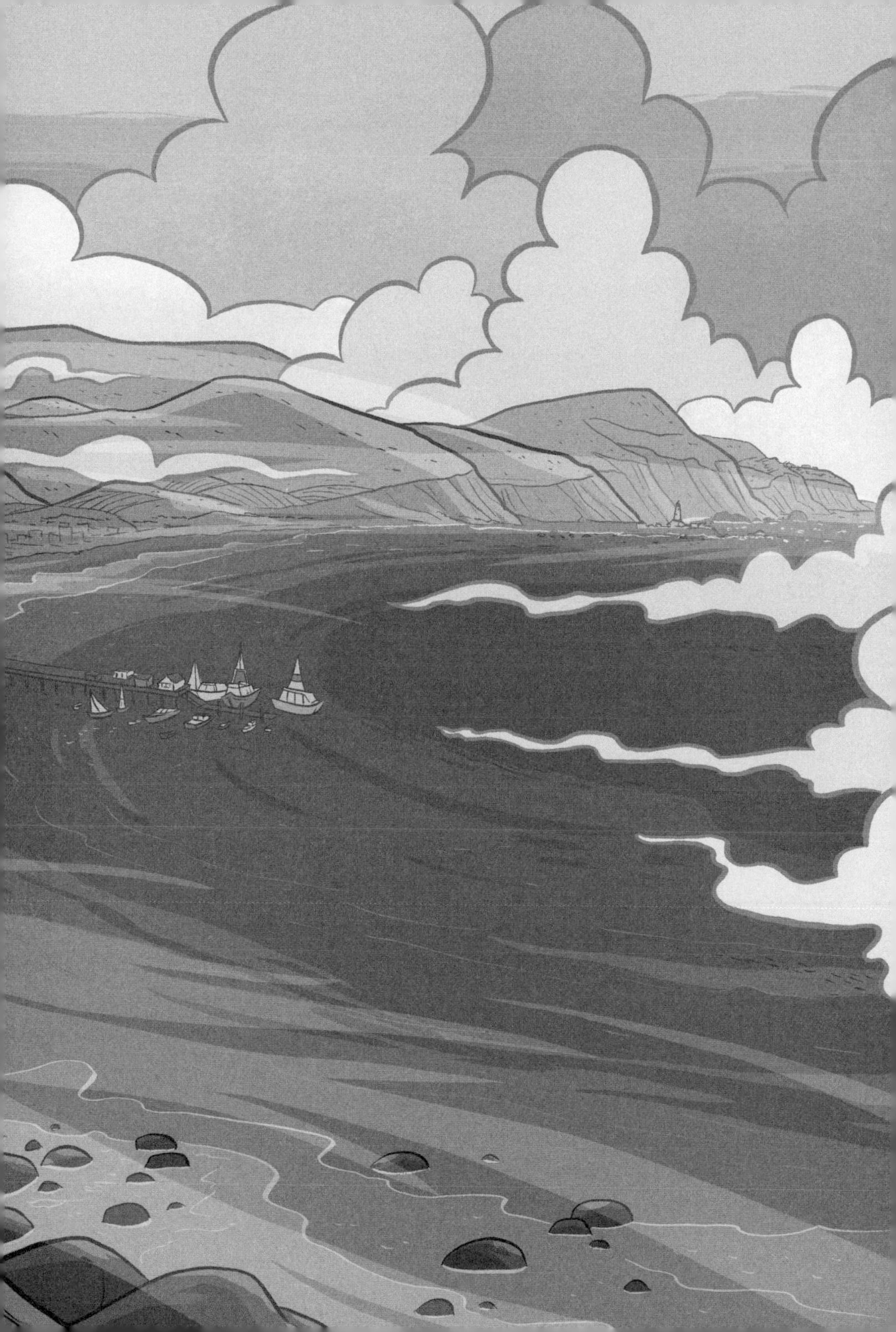

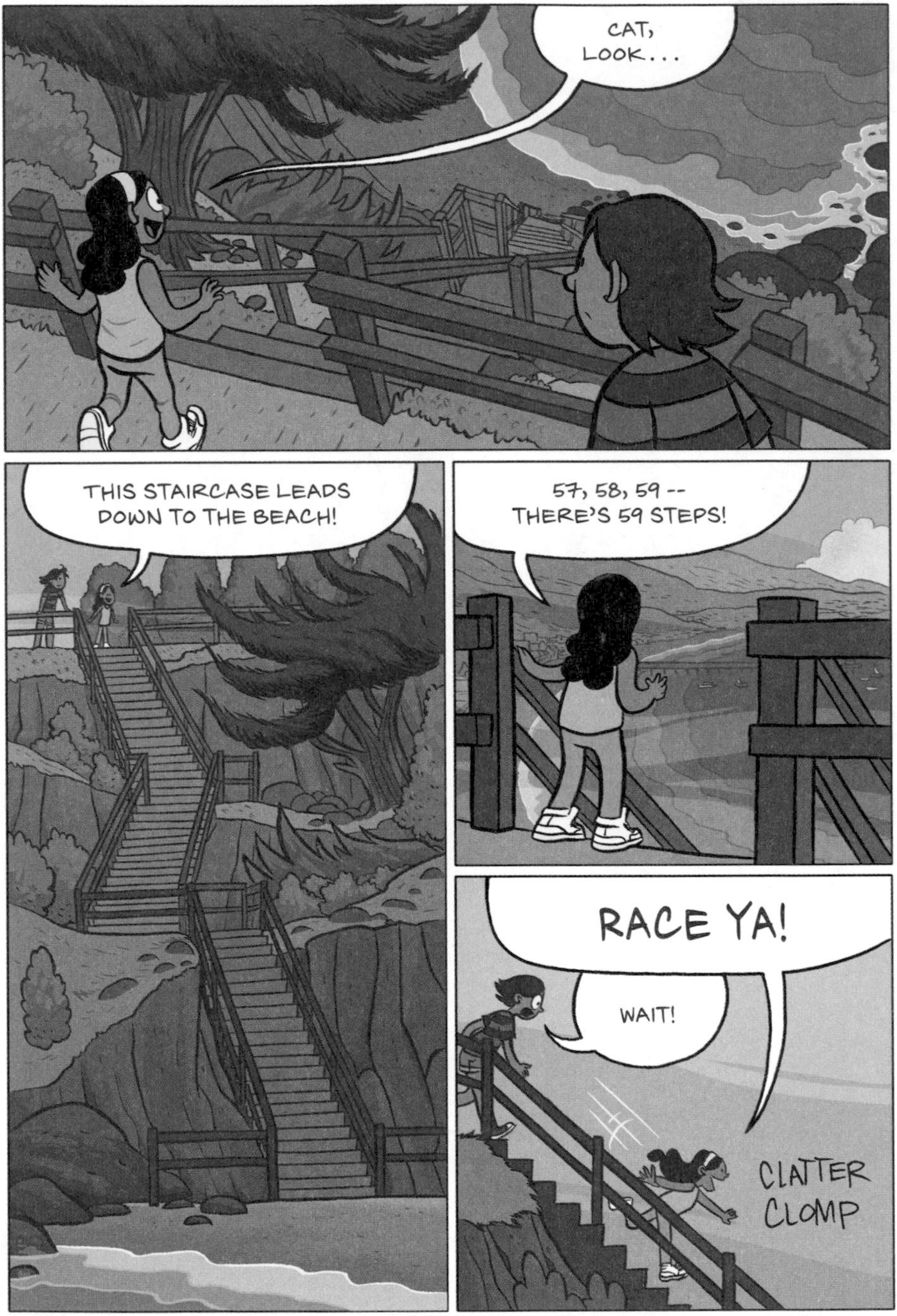
CAT, LOOK...
THIS STAIRCASE LEADS DOWN TO THE BEACH!
57, 58, 59 -- THERE'S 59 STEPS!
RACE YA!
WAIT!
CLATTER
CLOMP

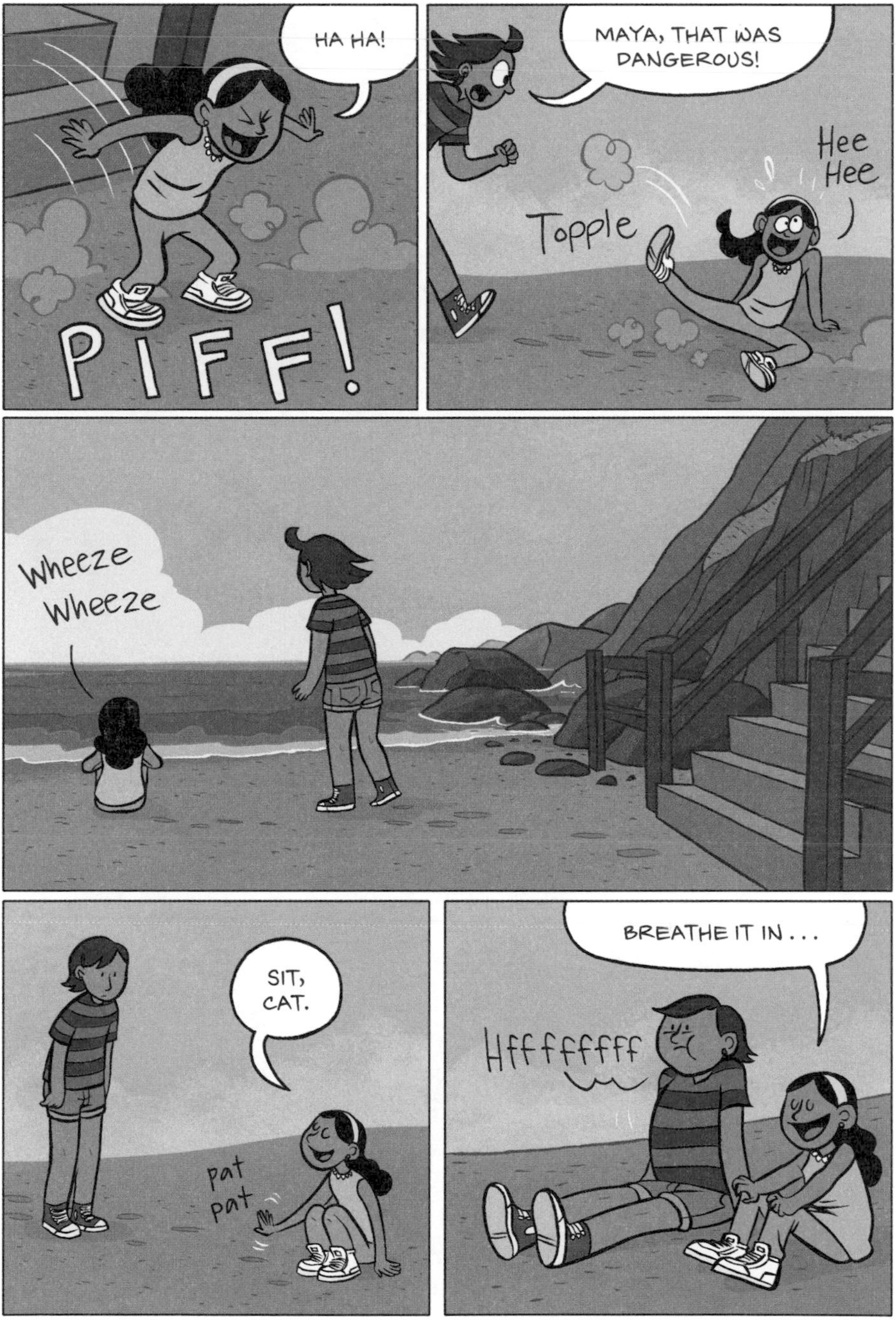
HA HA!
PIFF!
MAYA, THAT WAS DANGEROUS!
Hee Hee
Topple
Wheeze Wheeze
SIT, CAT.
pat pat
BREATHE IT IN . . .
Hffffffff

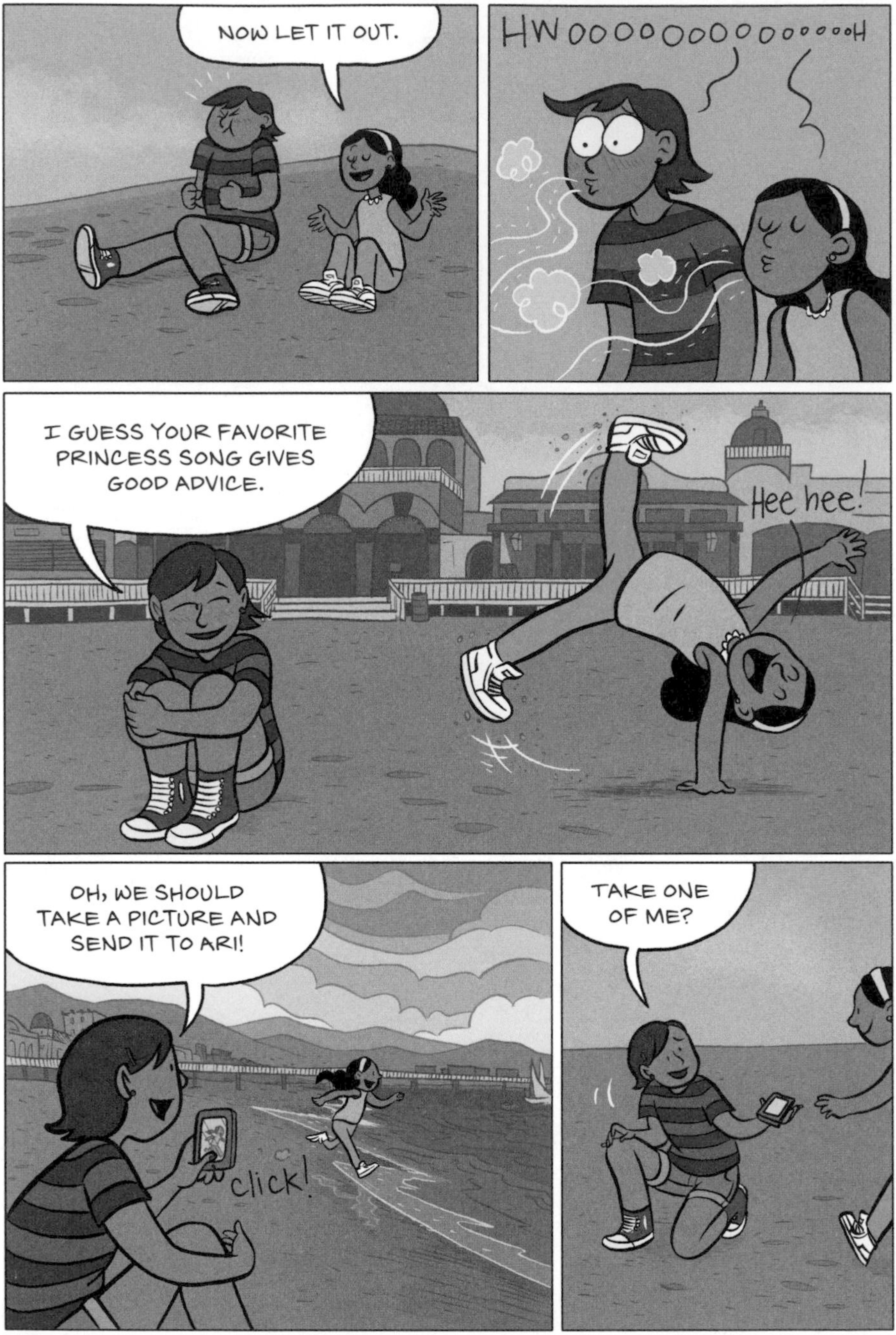
NOW LET IT OUT.
HWOOOOOOOOOOOOOOH
I GUESS YOUR FAVORITE PRINCESS SONG GIVES GOOD ADVICE.
Hee hee!
OH, WE SHOULD TAKE A PICTURE AND SEND IT TO ARI!
Click!
TAKE ONE OF ME?

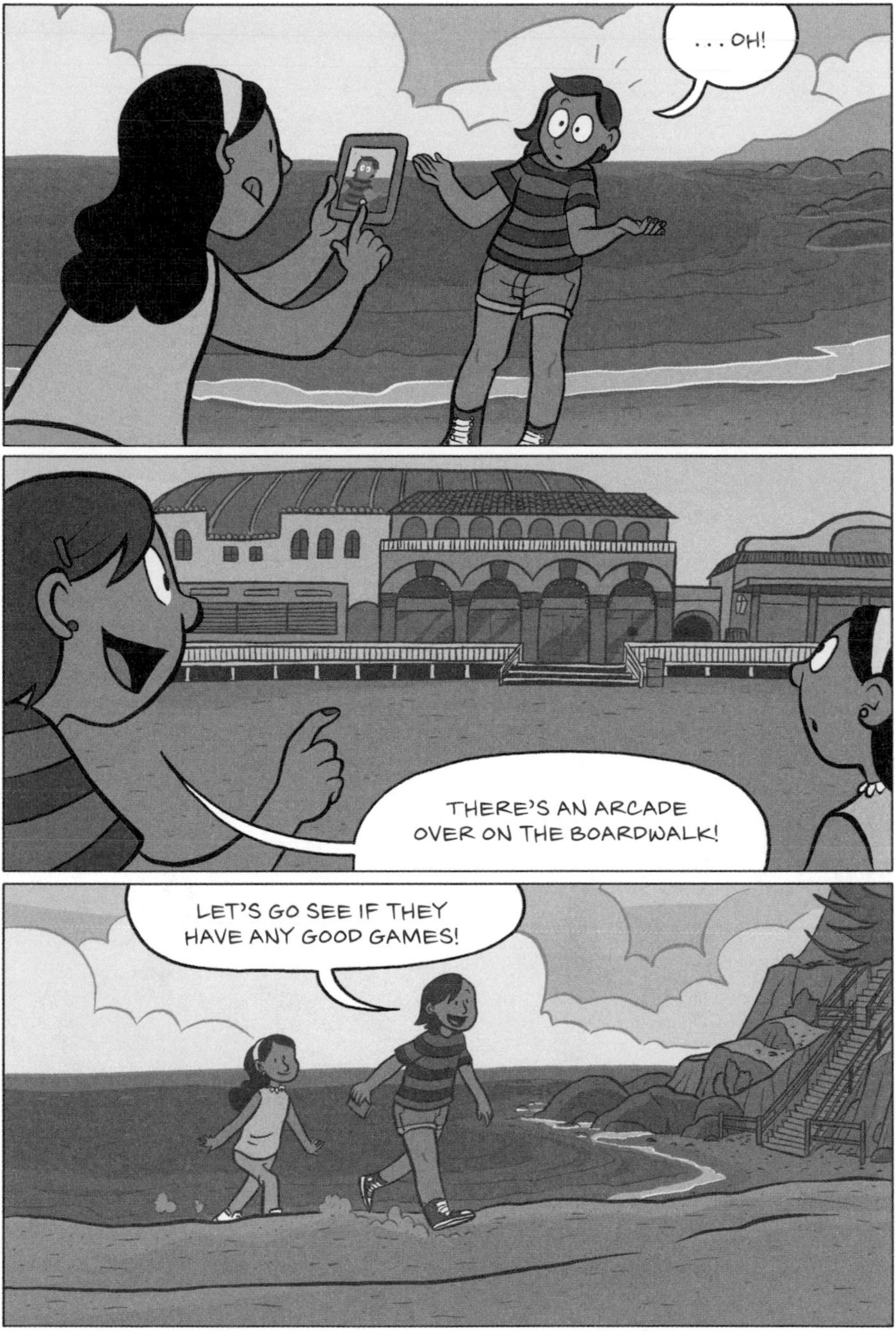
. . . OH!
THERE'S AN ARCADE OVER ON THE BOARDWALK!
LET'S GO SEE IF THEY HAVE ANY GOOD GAMES!

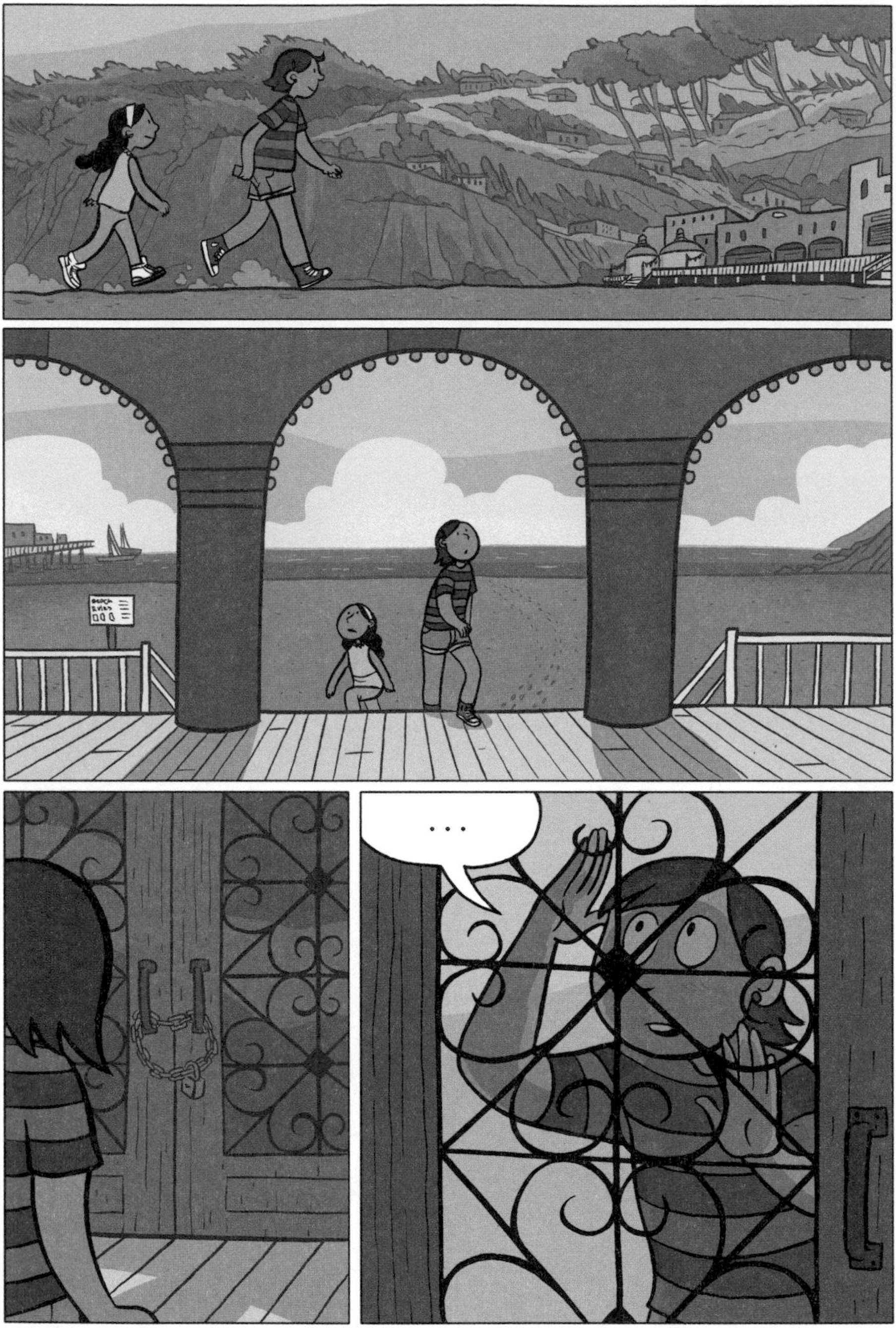
. . .

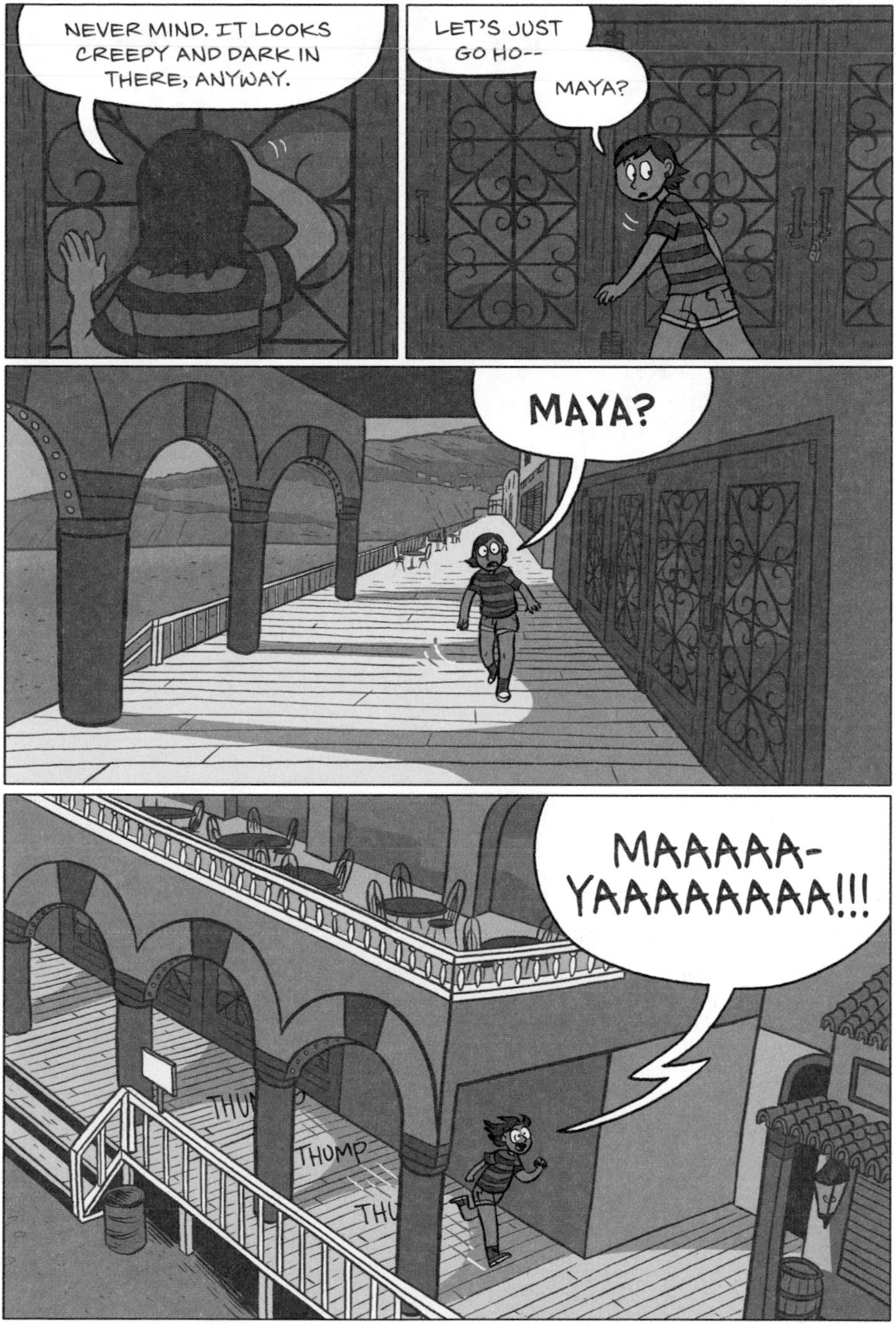
NEVER MIND. IT LOOKS CREEPY AND DARK IN THERE, ANYWAY.
LET'S JUST GO HO--
MAYA?
MAYA?
MAAAAA-YAAAAAAAA!!!
THUMP
THUMP

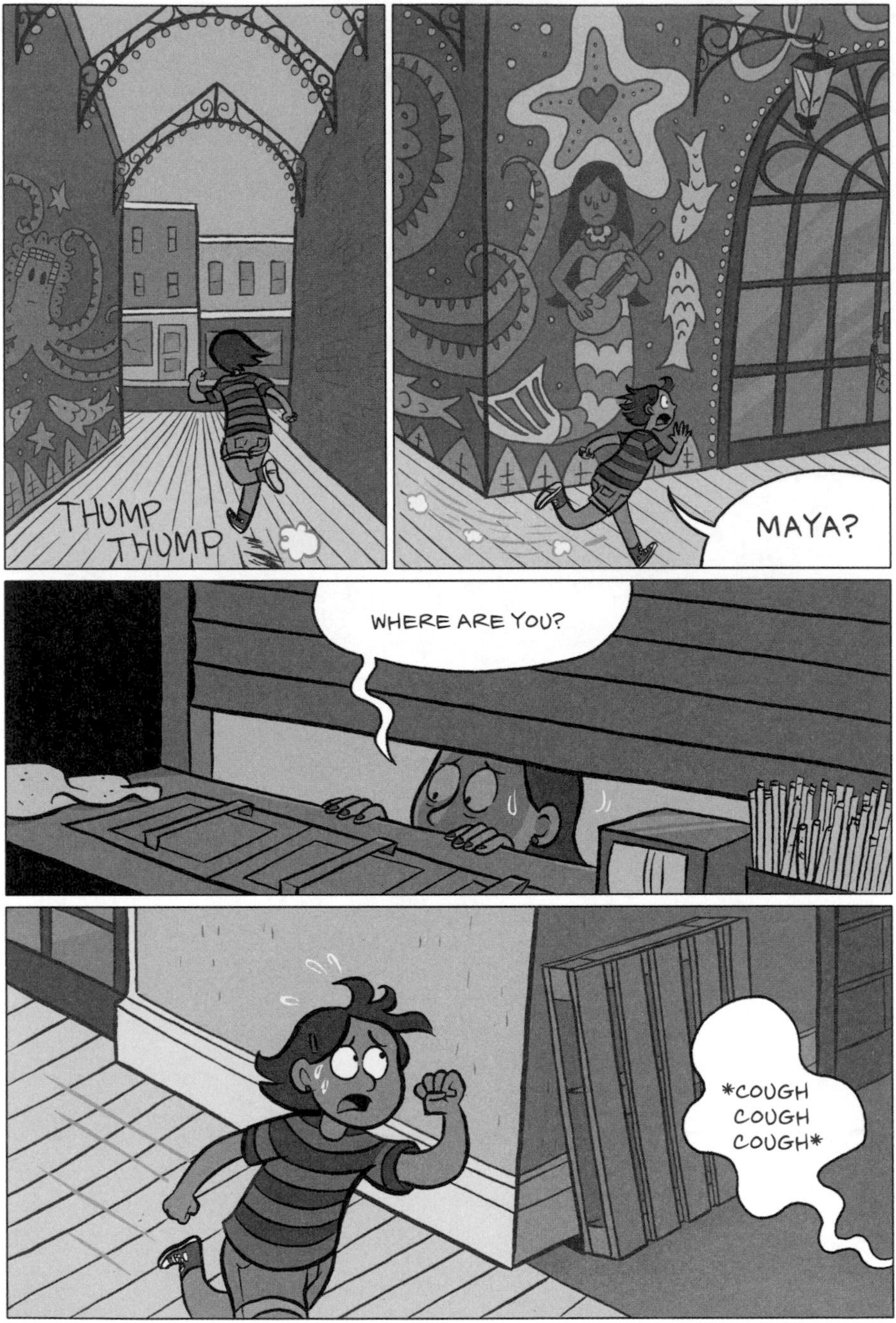
THUMP THUMP
MAYA?
WHERE ARE YOU?
COUGH COUGH COUGH

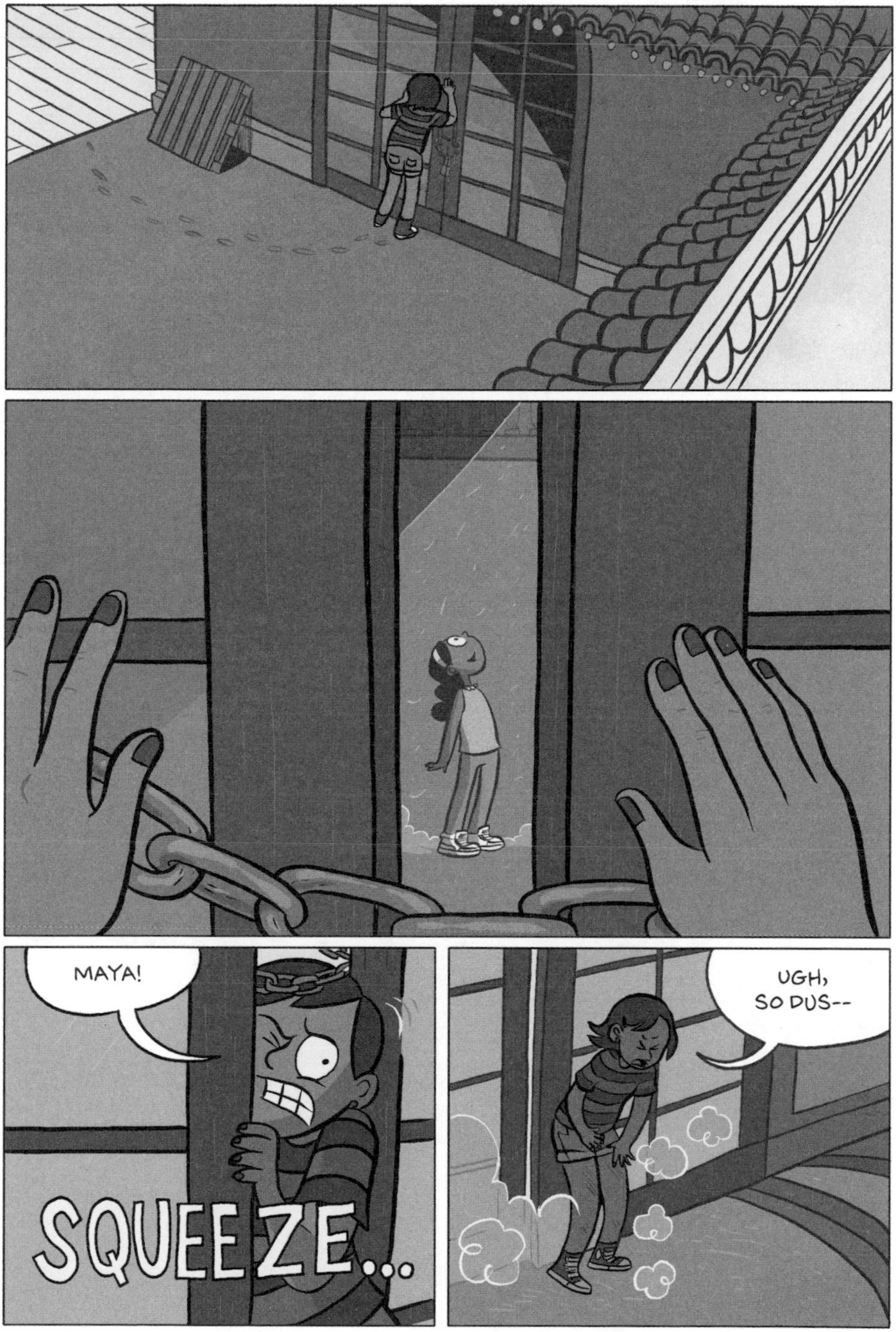
MAYA!
SQUEEZE...
UGH, SO DUS--

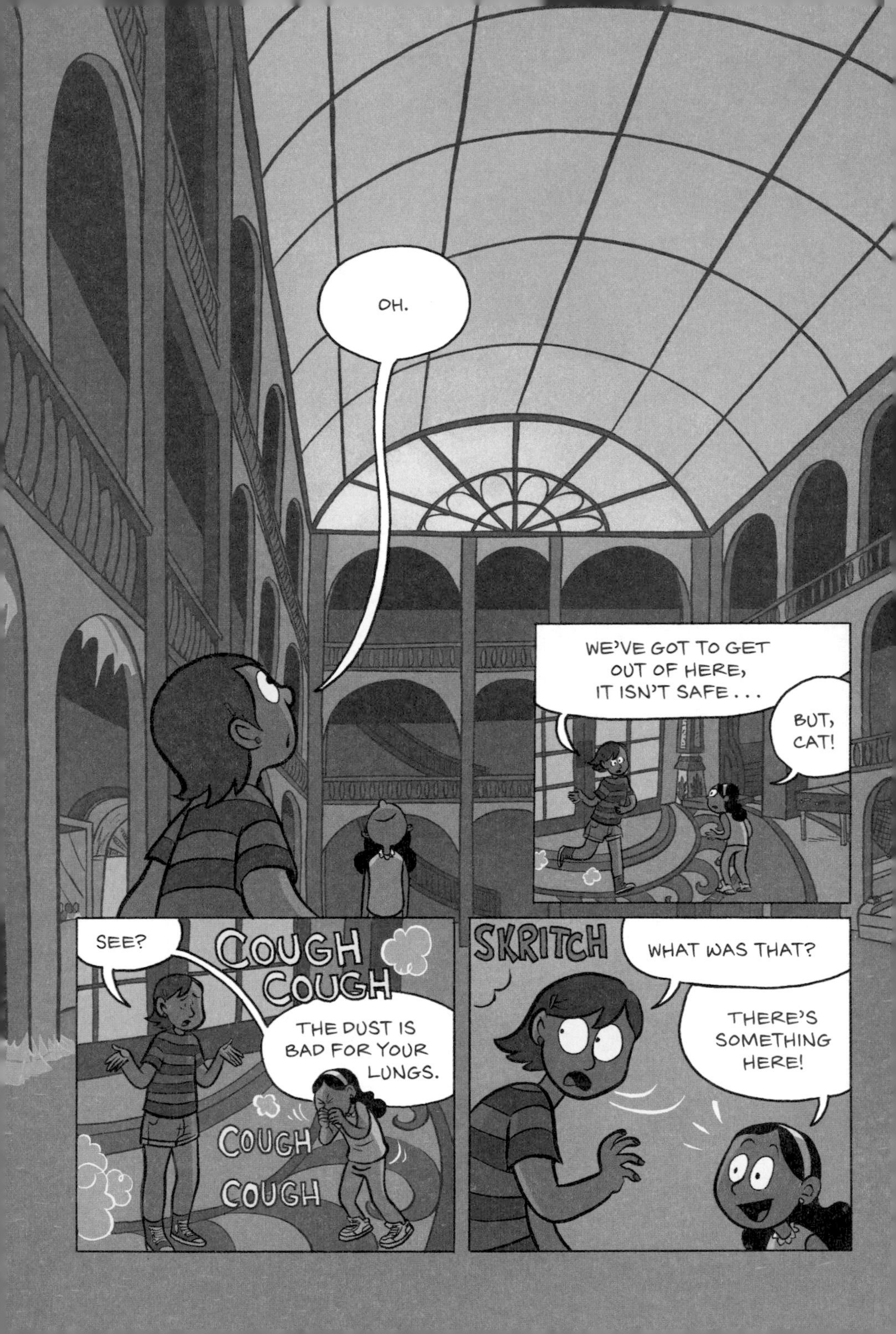
OH.
WE'VE GOT TO GET OUT OF HERE, IT ISN'T SAFE . . .
BUT, CAT!
SEE?
COUGH COUGH
THE DUST IS BAD FOR YOUR LUNGS.
COUGH
COUGH
SKRITCH
WHAT WAS THAT?
THERE'S SOMETHING HERE!

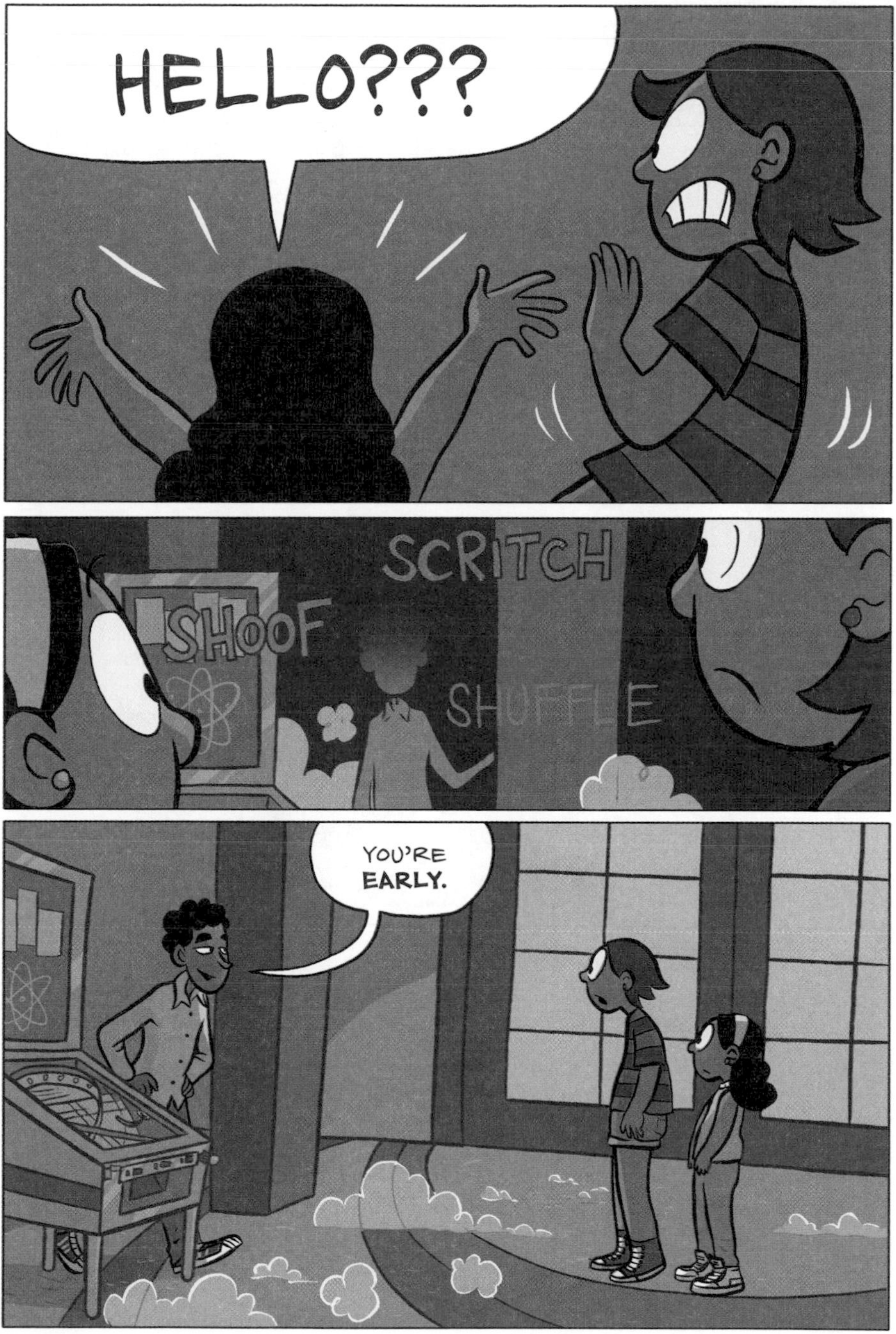
HELLO???
SCRITCH
SHOOF
SHUFFLE
YOU'RE EARLY.

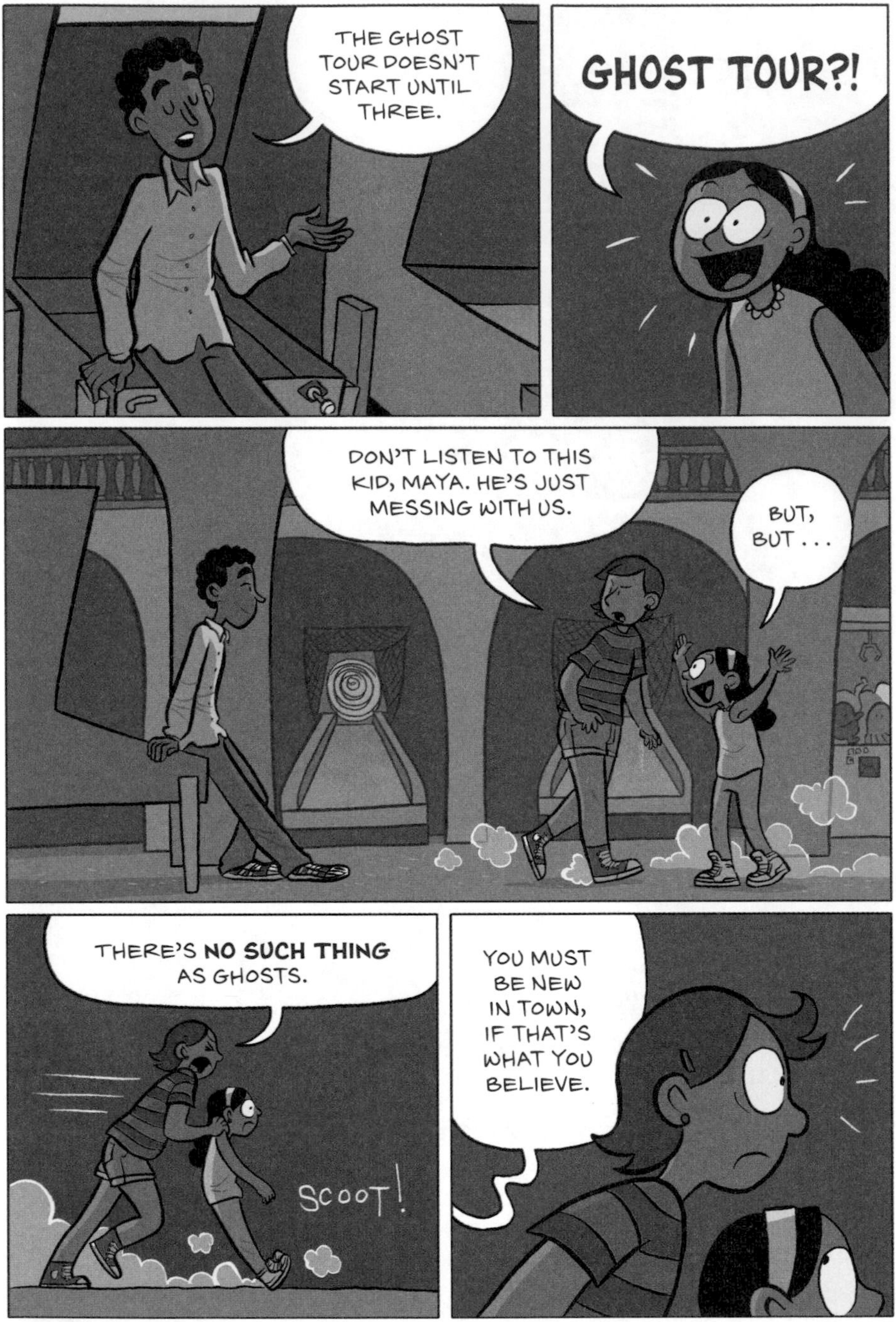
THE GHOST TOUR DOESN'T START UNTIL THREE.
GHOST TOUR?!
DON'T LISTEN TO THIS KID, MAYA. HE'S JUST MESSING WITH US.
BUT, BUT . . .
THERE'S **NO SUCH THING** AS GHOSTS.
SCOOT!
YOU MUST BE NEW IN TOWN, IF THAT'S WHAT YOU BELIEVE.

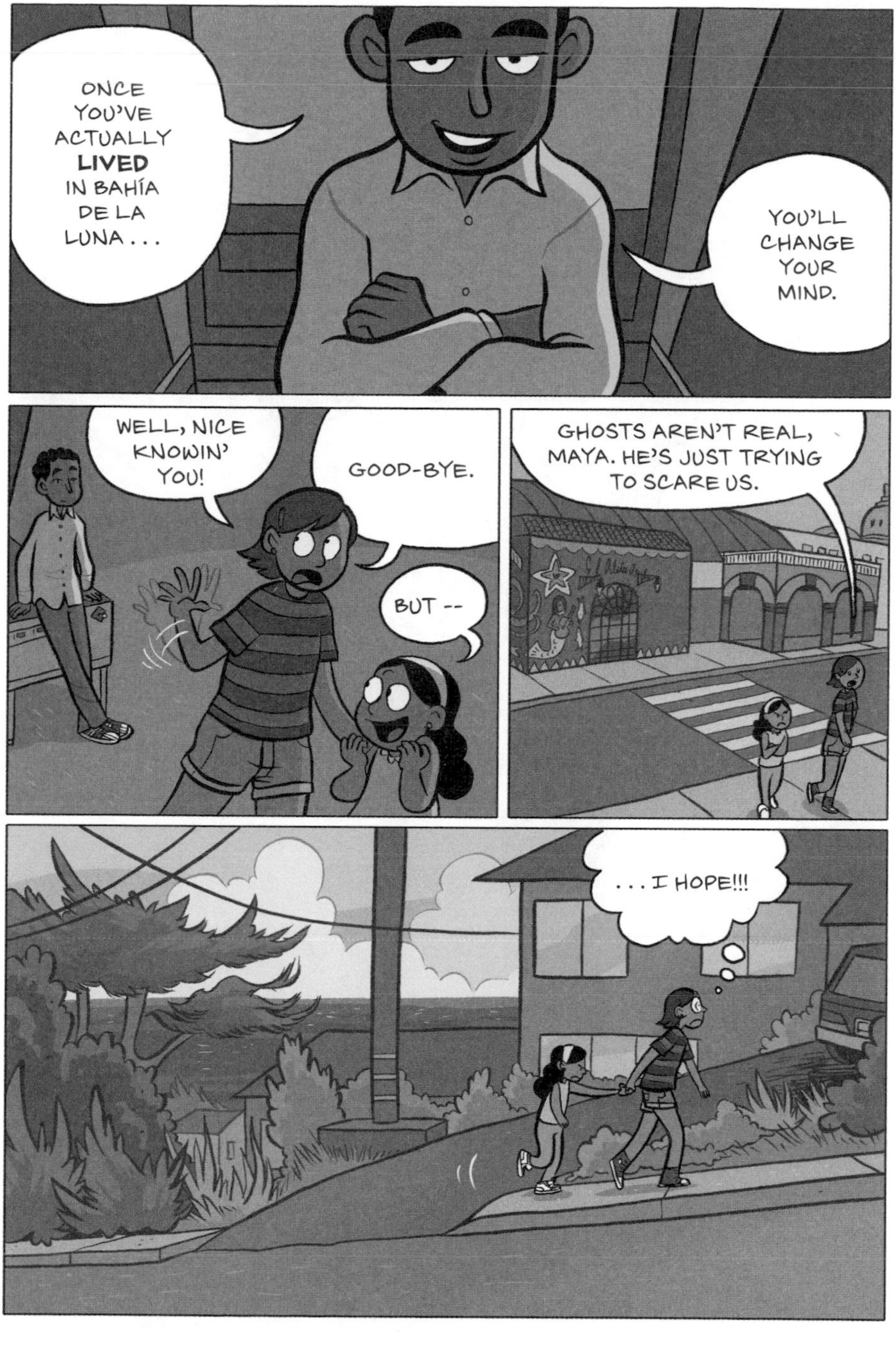
ONCE YOU'VE ACTUALLY **LIVED** IN BAHÍA DE LA LUNA . . .
YOU'LL CHANGE YOUR MIND.
WELL, NICE KNOWIN' YOU!
GOOD-BYE.
BUT --
GHOSTS AREN'T REAL, MAYA. HE'S JUST TRYING TO SCARE US.
. . . I HOPE!!!

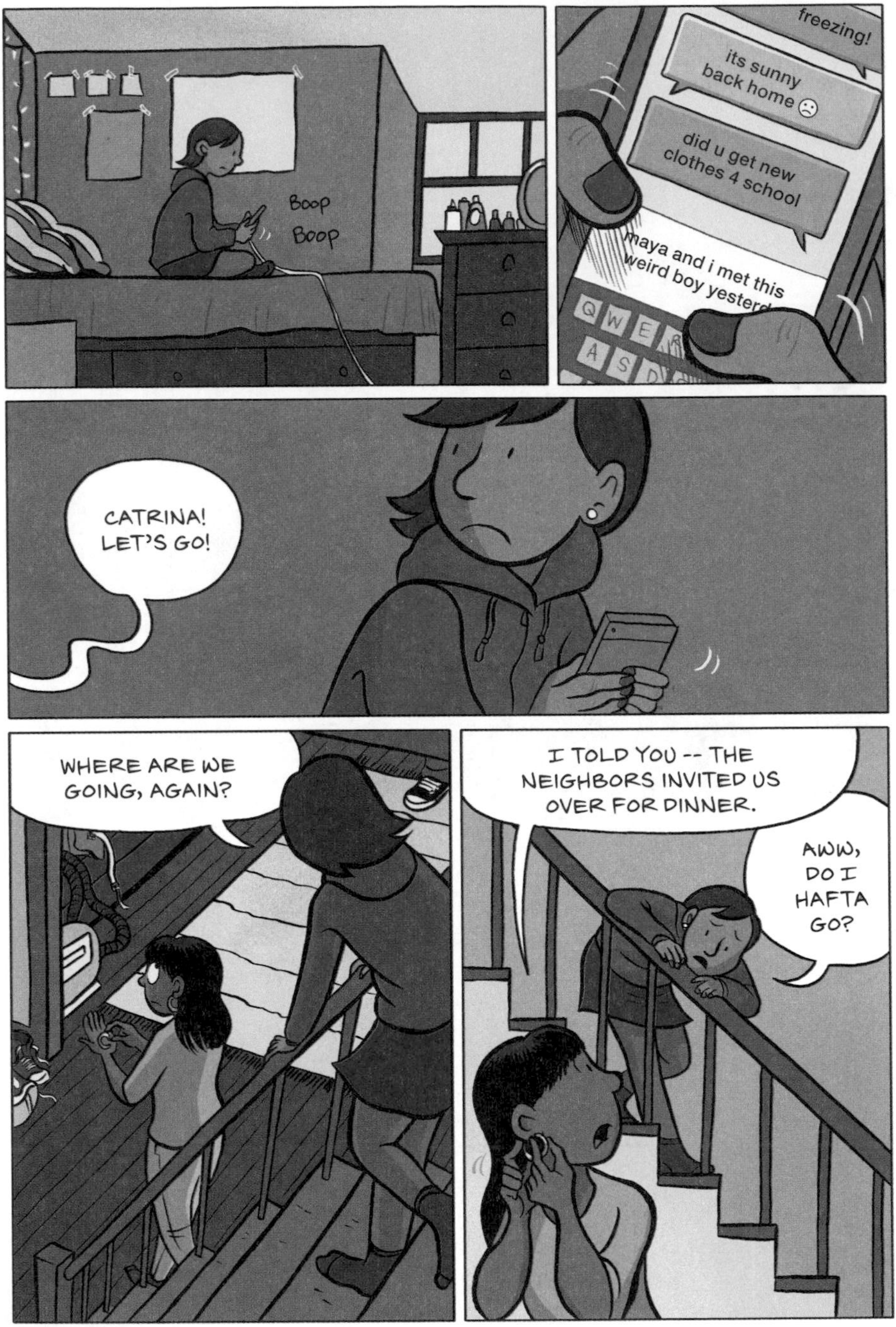
Boop
Boop
freezing!
its sunny back home ☹
did u get new clothes 4 school
maya and i met this weird boy yesterd
CATRINA! LET'S GO!
WHERE ARE WE GOING, AGAIN?
I TOLD YOU -- THE NEIGHBORS INVITED US OVER FOR DINNER.
AWW, DO I HAFTA GO?

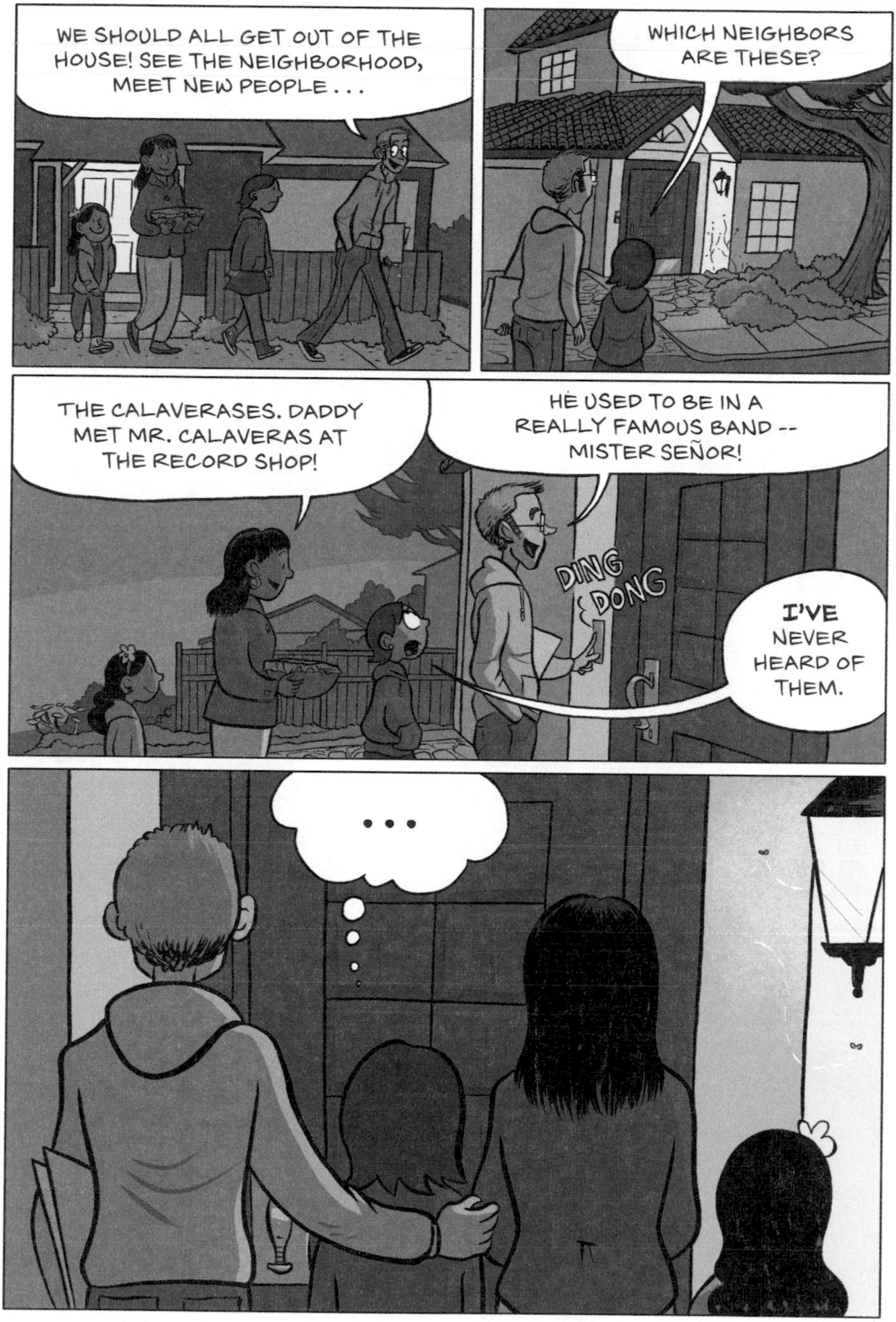
WE SHOULD ALL GET OUT OF THE HOUSE! SEE THE NEIGHBORHOOD, MEET NEW PEOPLE . . .
WHICH NEIGHBORS ARE THESE?
THE CALAVERASES. DADDY MET MR. CALAVERAS AT THE RECORD SHOP!
HE USED TO BE IN A REALLY FAMOUS BAND -- MISTER SEÑOR!
DING DONG
I'VE NEVER HEARD OF THEM.
. . .

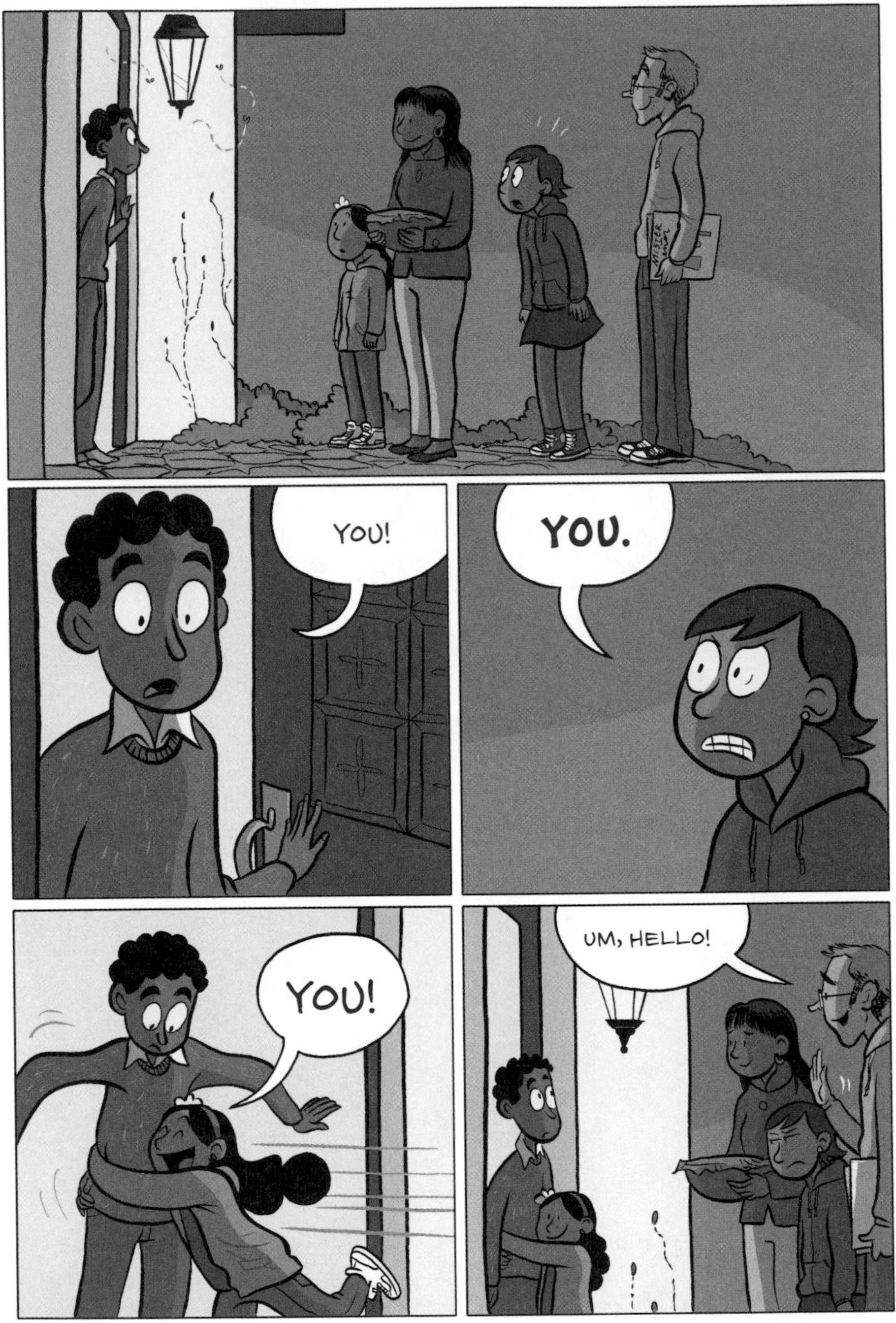
YOU!
YOU.
YOU!
UM, HELLO!

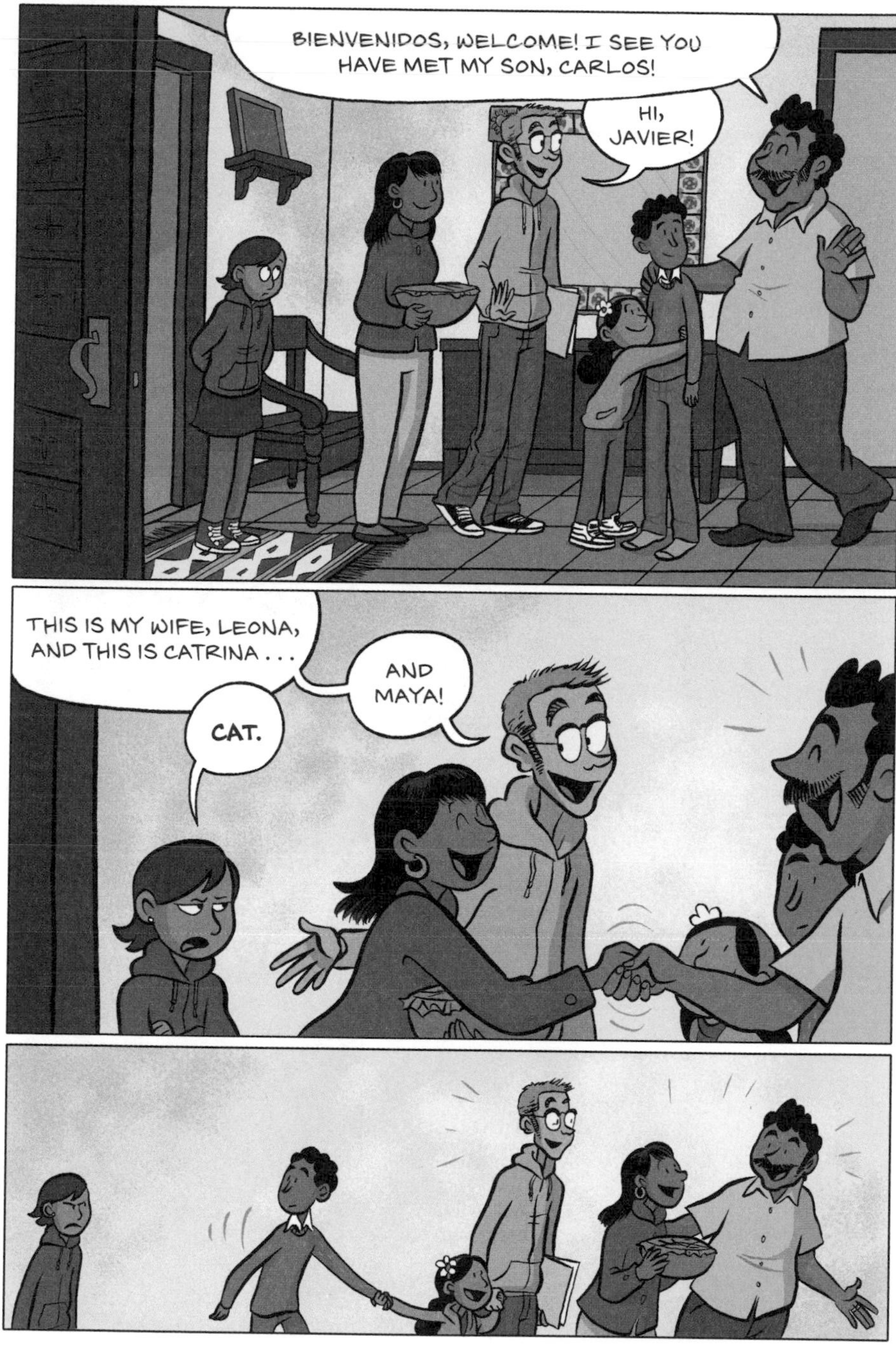
BIENVENIDOS, WELCOME! I SEE YOU HAVE MET MY SON, CARLOS!
HI, JAVIER!
THIS IS MY WIFE, LEONA, AND THIS IS CATRINA . . .
CAT.
AND MAYA!

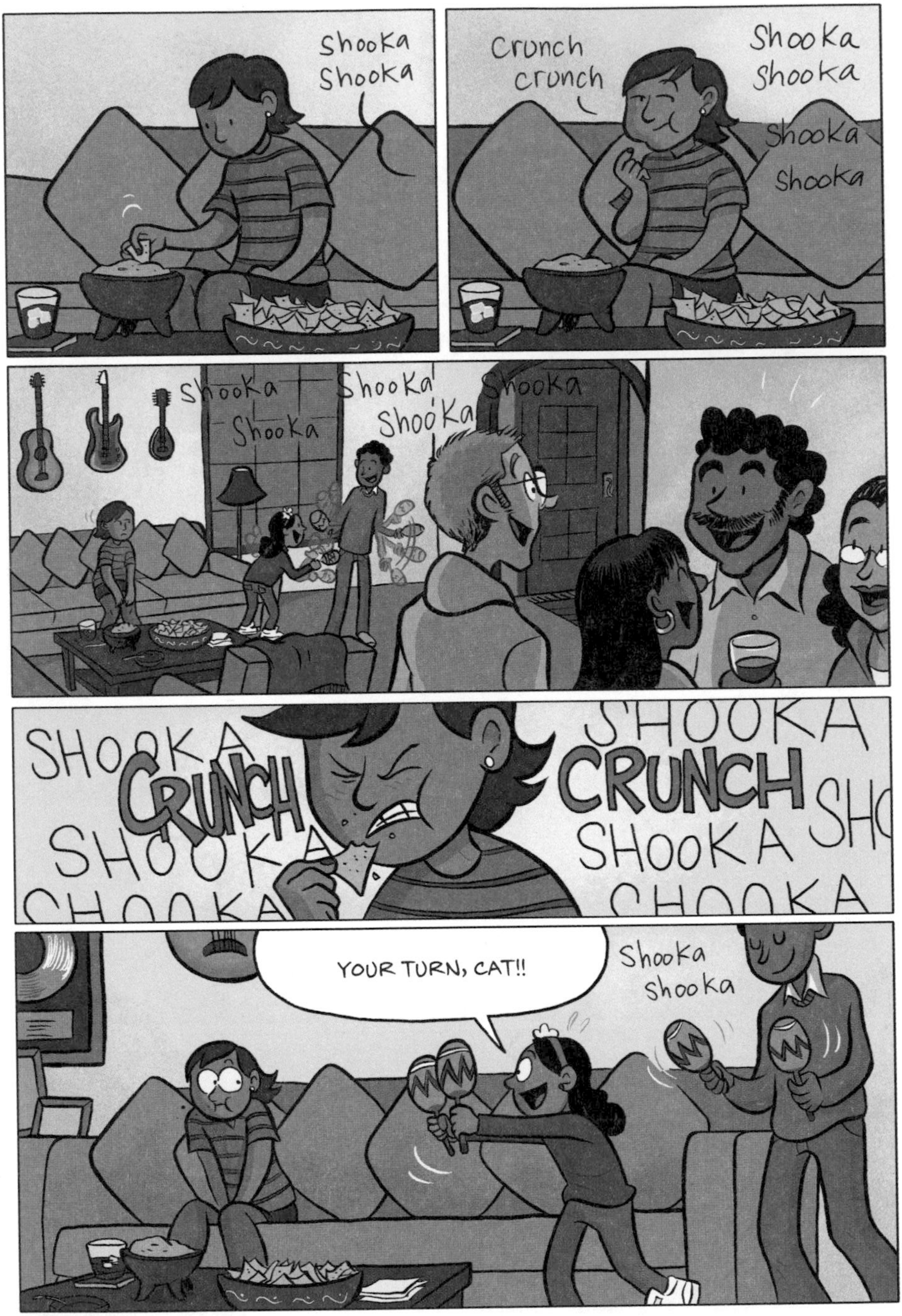
Shooka
Shooka
Crunch
crunch
Shooka
Shooka
Shooka
Shooka
Shooka
Shooka
Shooka
Shooka
Shooka
SHOOKA
CRUNCH
SHOOKA
SHOOKA
CRUNCH
SHOOKA
YOUR TURN, CAT!!
Shooka
shooka

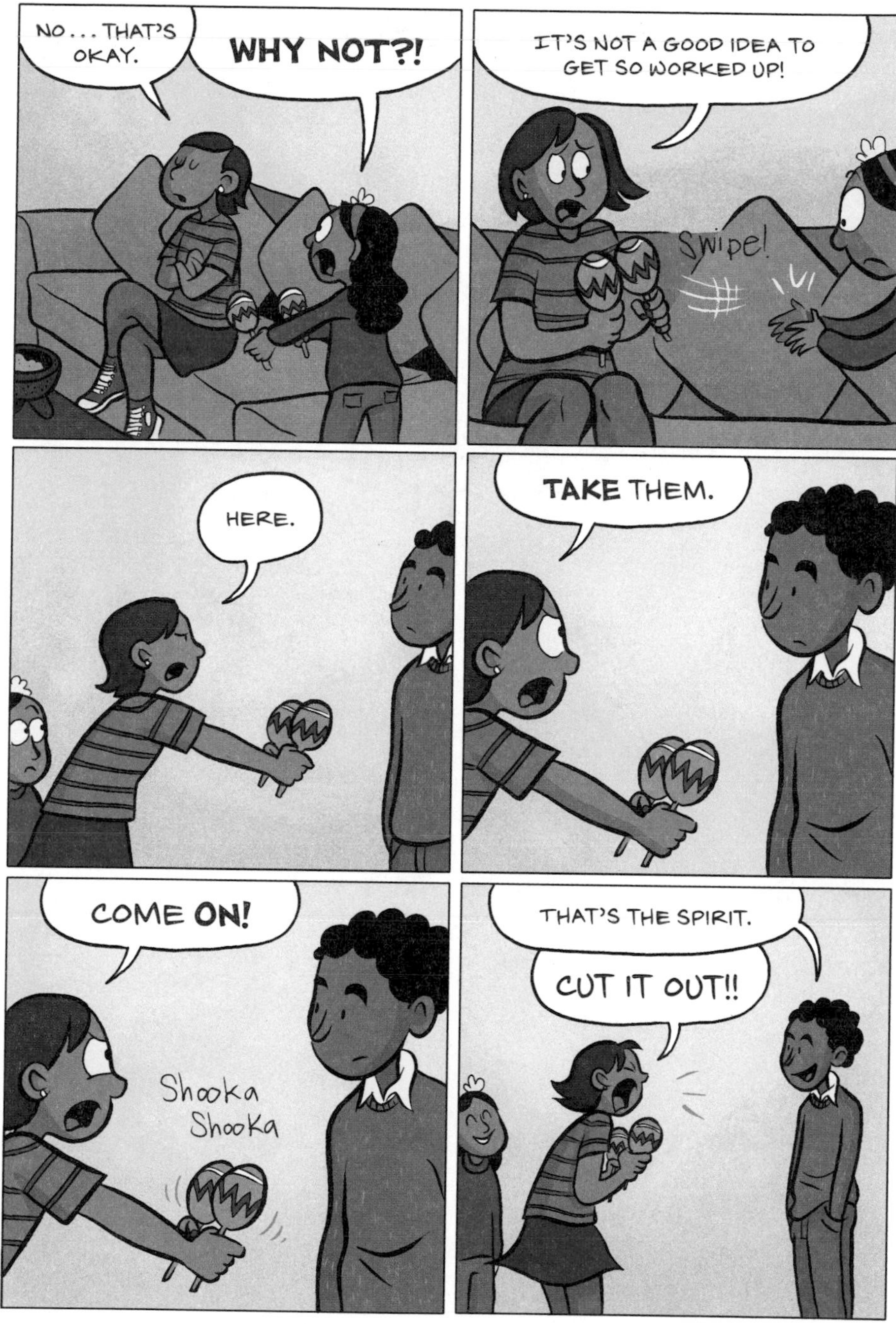
NO... THAT'S OKAY.
WHY NOT?!
IT'S NOT A GOOD IDEA TO GET SO WORKED UP!
Swipe!
HERE.
TAKE THEM.
COME ON!
Shooka Shooka
THAT'S THE SPIRIT.
CUT IT OUT!!

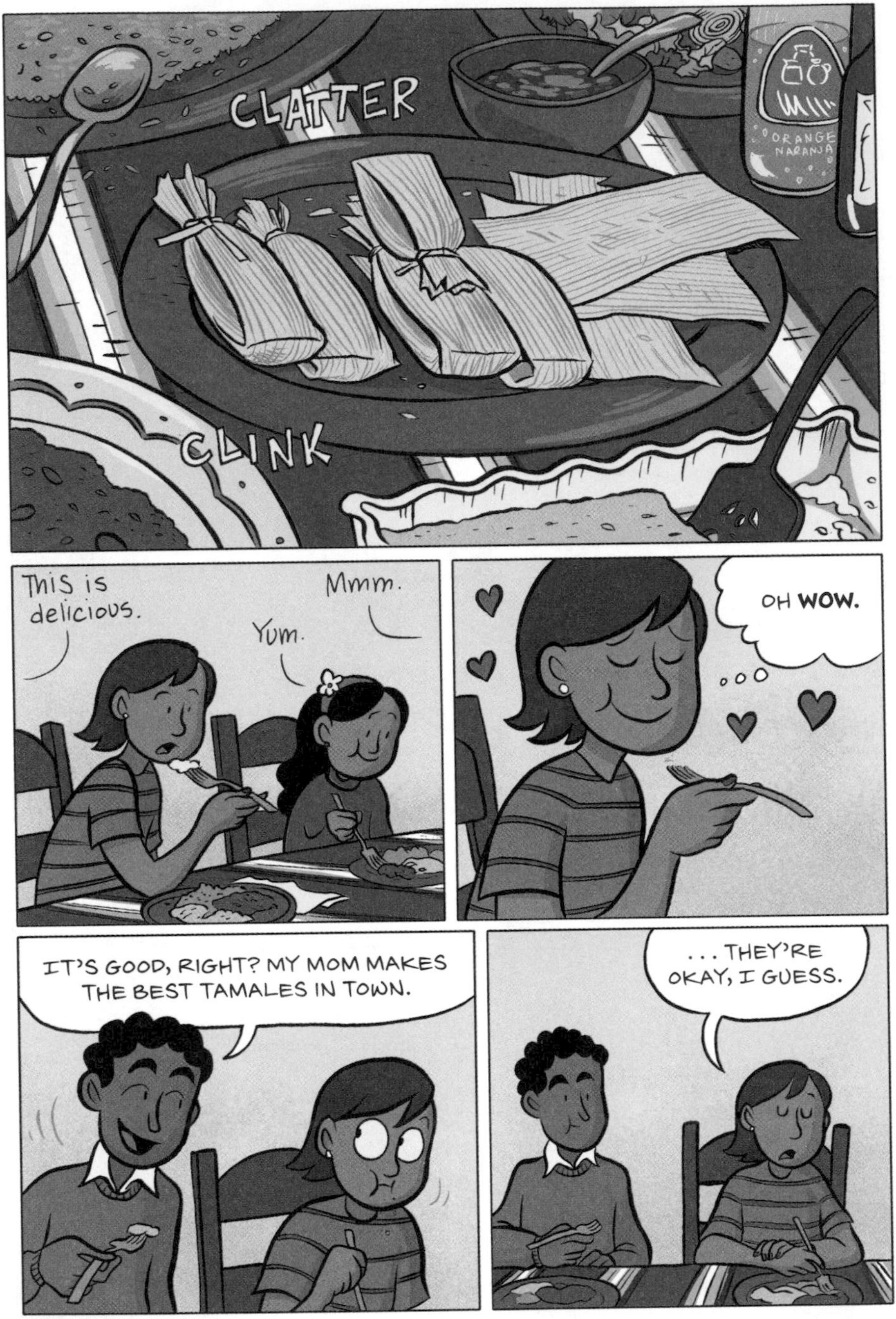
CLATTER
ORANGE NARANJA
CLINK
This is delicious.
Yum.
Mmm.
OH **WOW.**
IT'S GOOD, RIGHT? MY MOM MAKES THE BEST TAMALES IN TOWN.
. . . THEY'RE OKAY, I GUESS.

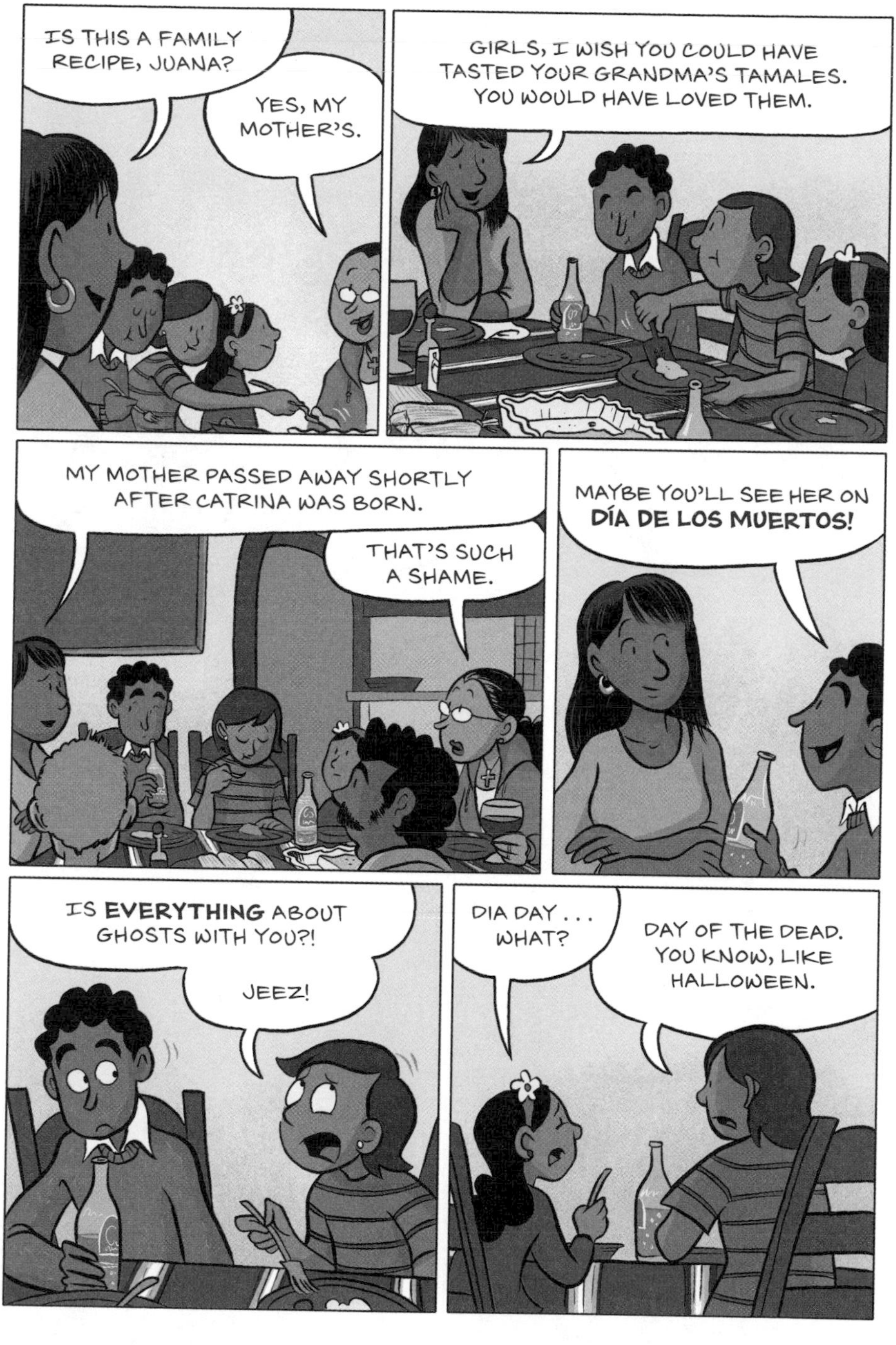
IS THIS A FAMILY RECIPE, JUANA?
YES, MY MOTHER'S.
GIRLS, I WISH YOU COULD HAVE TASTED YOUR GRANDMA'S TAMALES. YOU WOULD HAVE LOVED THEM.
MY MOTHER PASSED AWAY SHORTLY AFTER CATRINA WAS BORN.
THAT'S SUCH A SHAME.
MAYBE YOU'LL SEE HER ON **DÍA DE LOS MUERTOS!**
IS **EVERYTHING** ABOUT GHOSTS WITH YOU?!
JEEZ!
DIA DAY . . . WHAT?
DAY OF THE DEAD. YOU KNOW, LIKE HALLOWEEN.

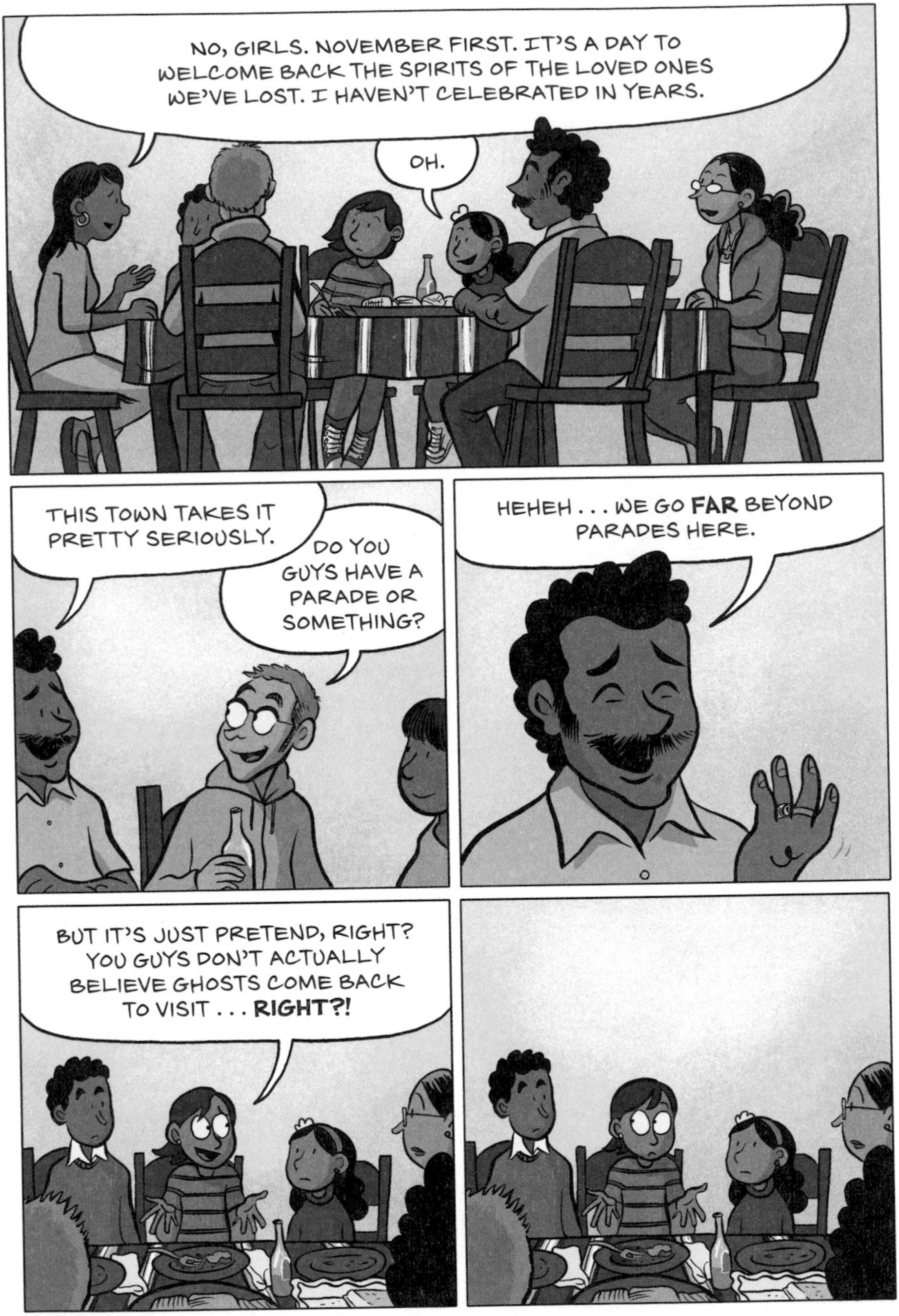
NO, GIRLS. NOVEMBER FIRST. IT'S A DAY TO WELCOME BACK THE SPIRITS OF THE LOVED ONES WE'VE LOST. I HAVEN'T CELEBRATED IN YEARS.
OH.
THIS TOWN TAKES IT PRETTY SERIOUSLY.
DO YOU GUYS HAVE A PARADE OR SOMETHING?
HEHEH . . . WE GO **FAR** BEYOND PARADES HERE.
BUT IT'S JUST PRETEND, RIGHT? YOU GUYS DON'T ACTUALLY BELIEVE GHOSTS COME BACK TO VISIT . . . **RIGHT?!**

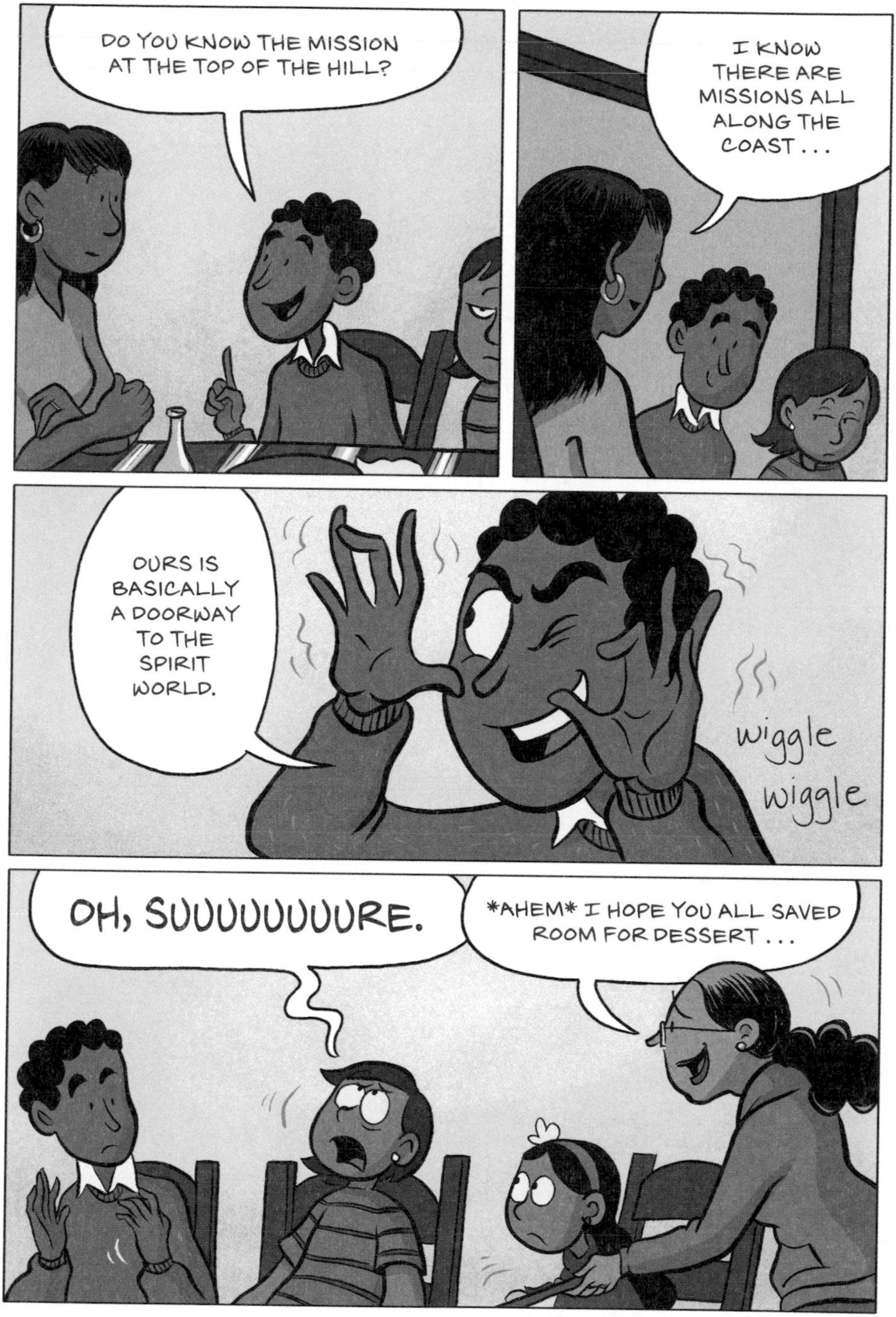
DO YOU KNOW THE MISSION AT THE TOP OF THE HILL?
I KNOW THERE ARE MISSIONS ALL ALONG THE COAST . . .
OURS IS BASICALLY A DOORWAY TO THE SPIRIT WORLD.
wiggle wiggle
OH, SUUUUUUUURE.
AHEM I HOPE YOU ALL SAVED ROOM FOR DESSERT . . .

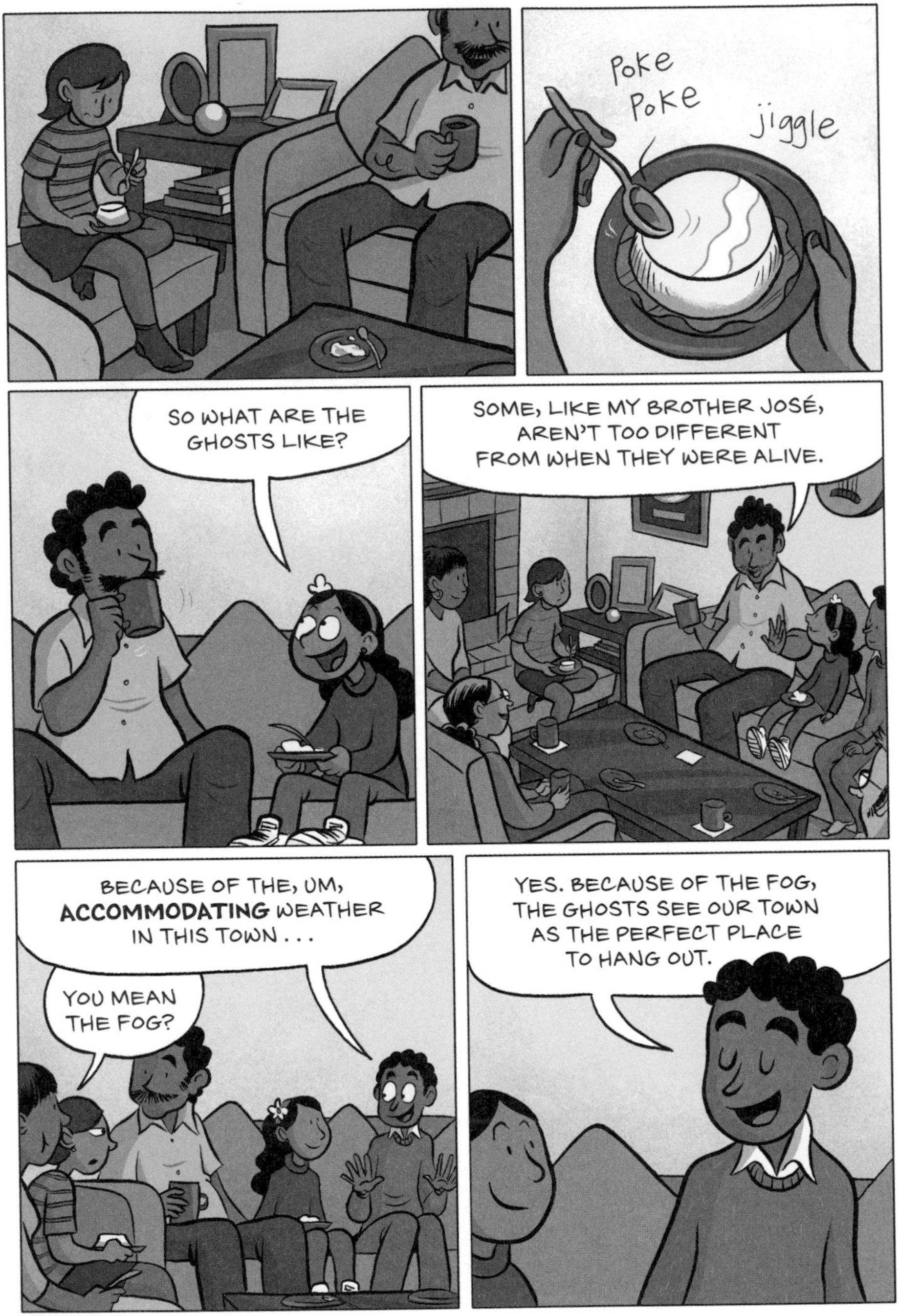
Poke
Poke
jiggle
SO WHAT ARE THE GHOSTS LIKE?
SOME, LIKE MY BROTHER JOSÉ, AREN'T TOO DIFFERENT FROM WHEN THEY WERE ALIVE.
BECAUSE OF THE, UM, **ACCOMMODATING** WEATHER IN THIS TOWN . . .
YOU MEAN THE FOG?
YES. BECAUSE OF THE FOG, THE GHOSTS SEE OUR TOWN AS THE PERFECT PLACE TO HANG OUT.

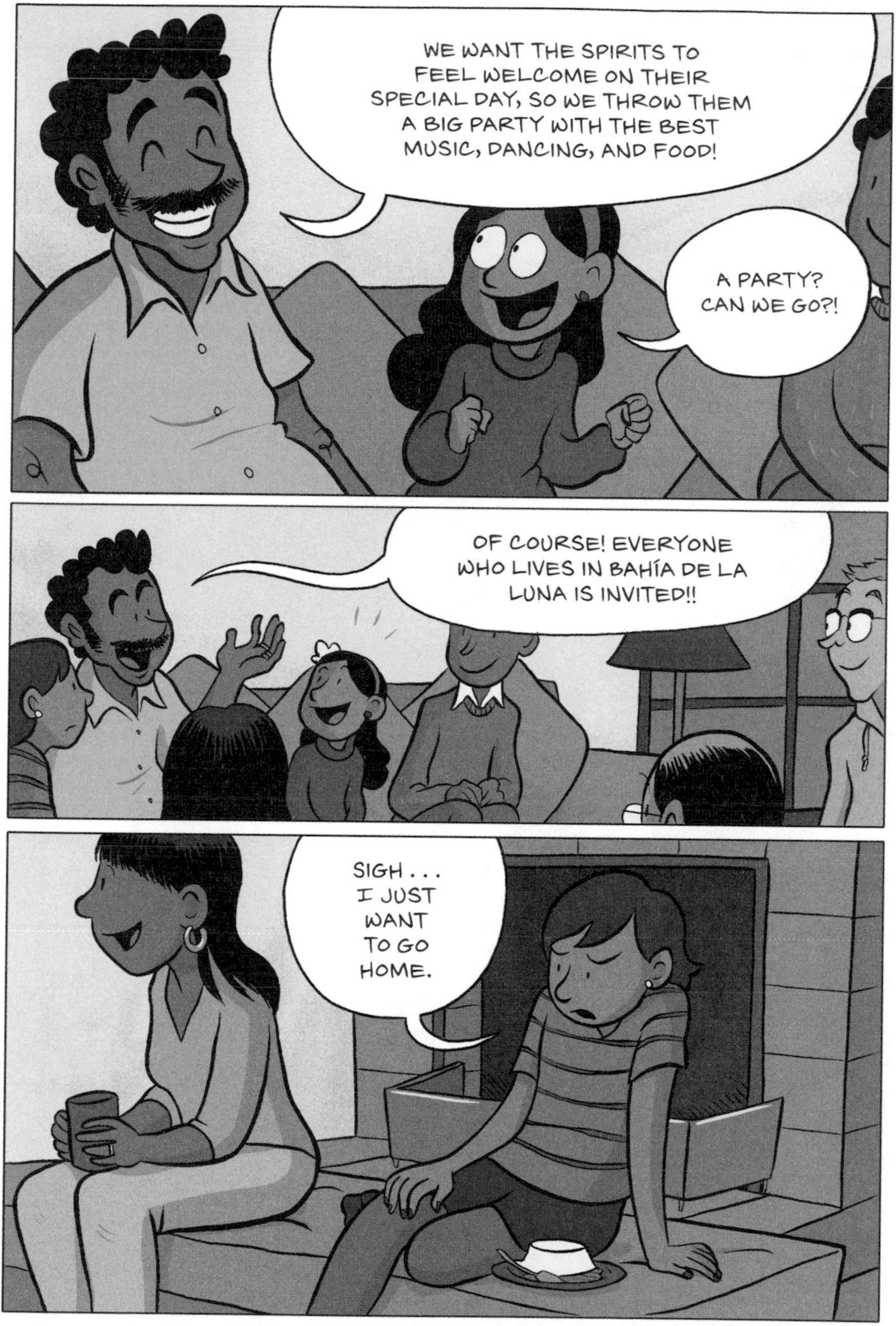
WE WANT THE SPIRITS TO FEEL WELCOME ON THEIR SPECIAL DAY, SO WE THROW THEM A BIG PARTY WITH THE BEST MUSIC, DANCING, AND FOOD!
A PARTY? CAN WE GO?!
OF COURSE! EVERYONE WHO LIVES IN BAHÍA DE LA LUNA IS INVITED!!
SIGH . . . I JUST WANT TO GO HOME.

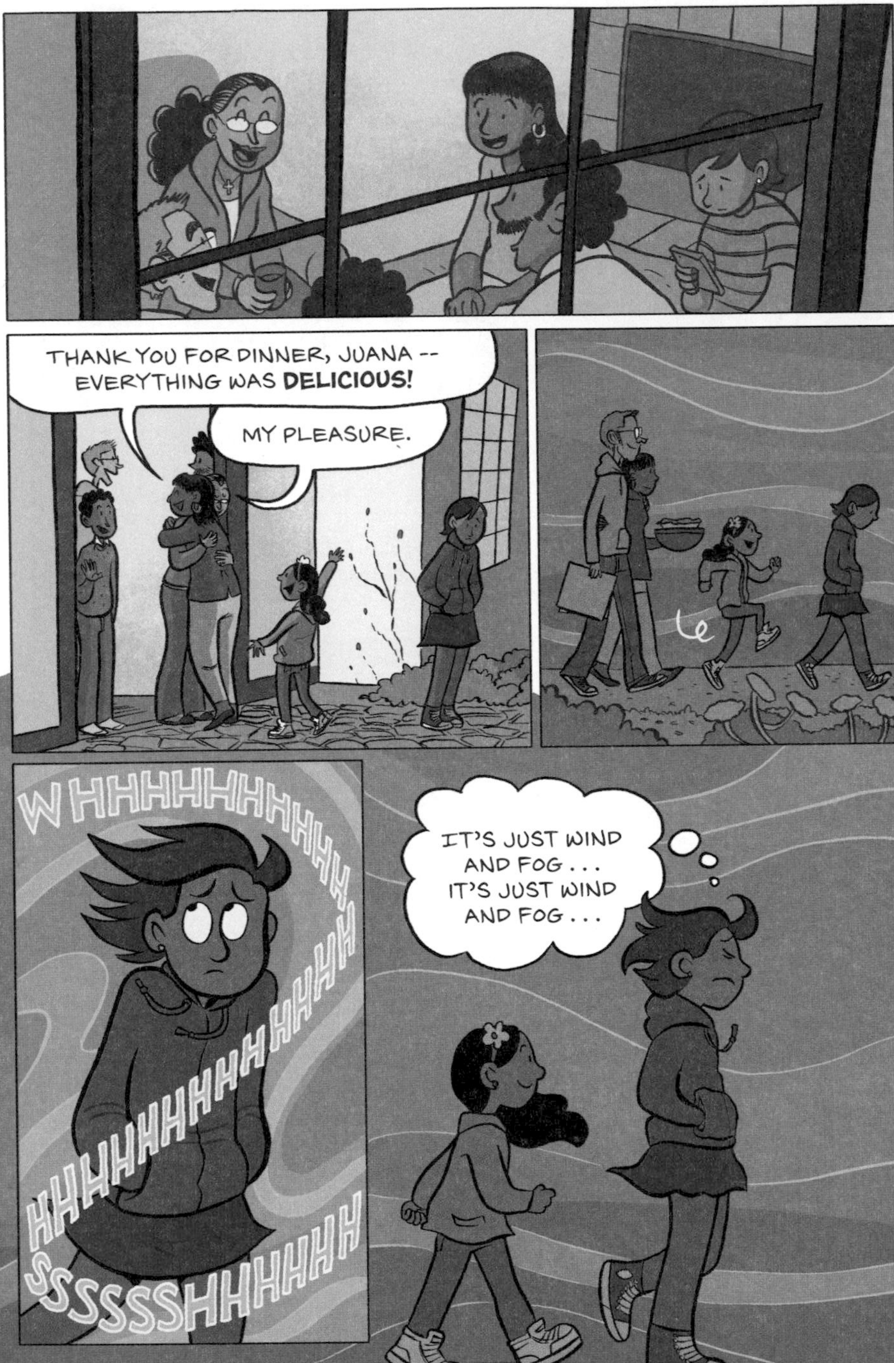
THANK YOU FOR DINNER, JUANA -- EVERYTHING WAS DELICIOUS!
MY PLEASURE.
WHHHHHHHHHHHHHHHHHHHHHHHHHHHHHHHHHHHHHHHSSSSSHHHHHH
IT'S JUST WIND AND FOG . . . IT'S JUST WIND AND FOG . . .

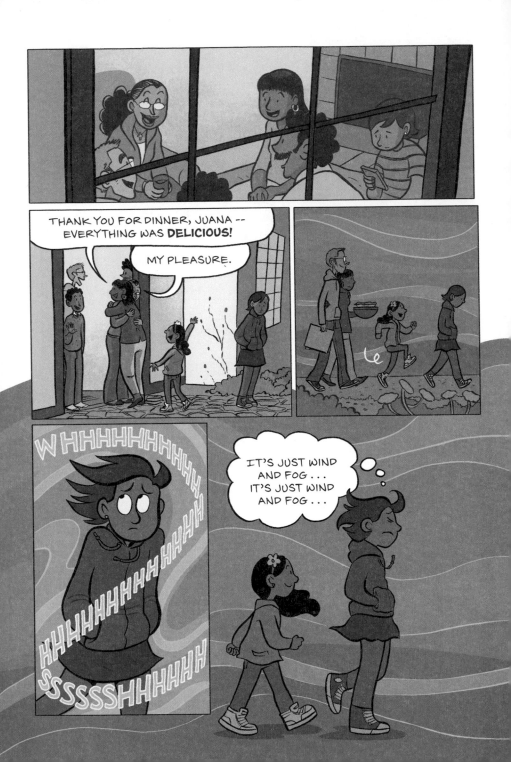

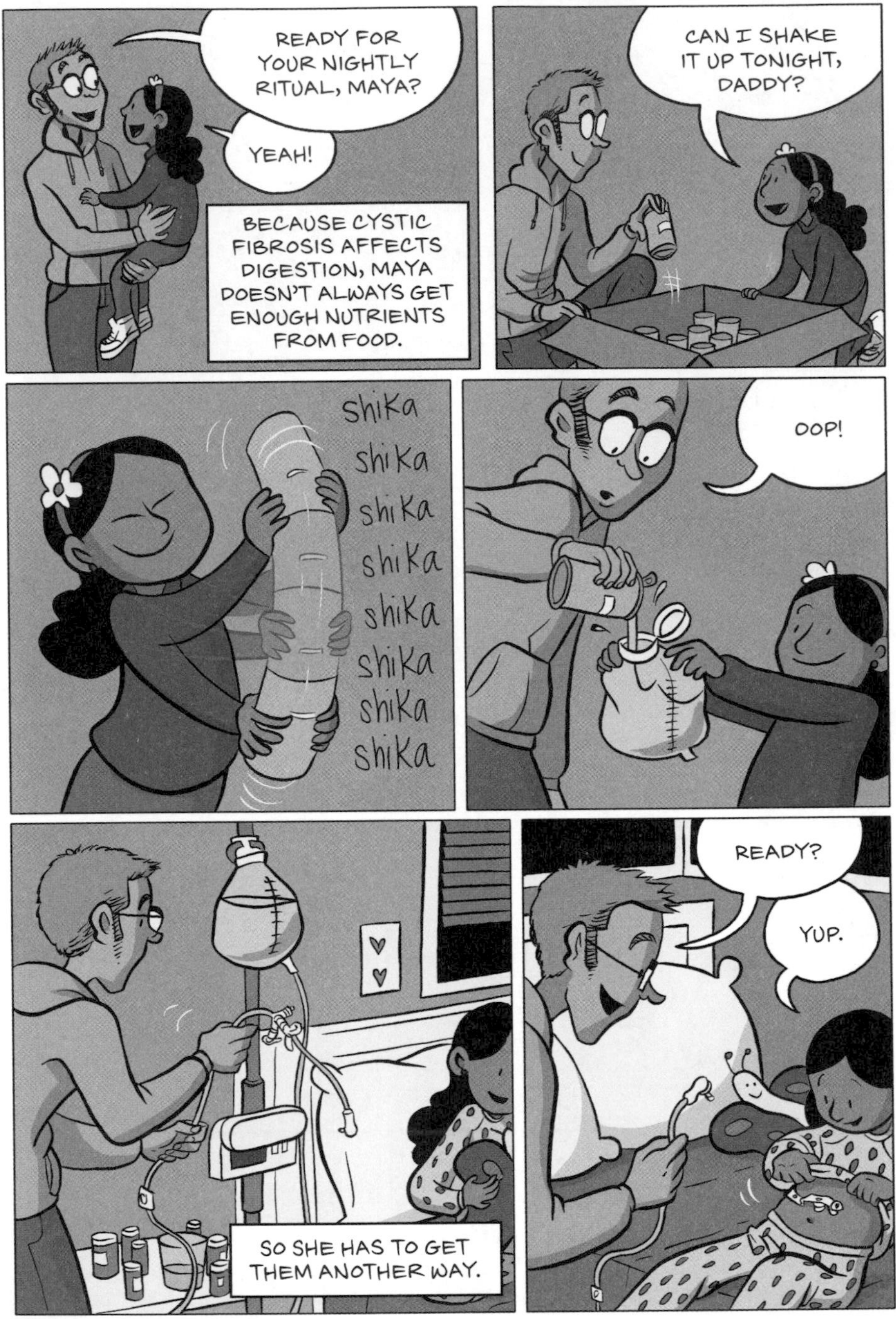
READY FOR YOUR NIGHTLY RITUAL, MAYA?
YEAH!
BECAUSE CYSTIC FIBROSIS AFFECTS DIGESTION, MAYA DOESN'T ALWAYS GET ENOUGH NUTRIENTS FROM FOOD.
CAN I SHAKE IT UP TONIGHT, DADDY?
shika shika shika shika shika shika shika shika
OOP!
SO SHE HAS TO GET THEM ANOTHER WAY.
READY?
YUP.

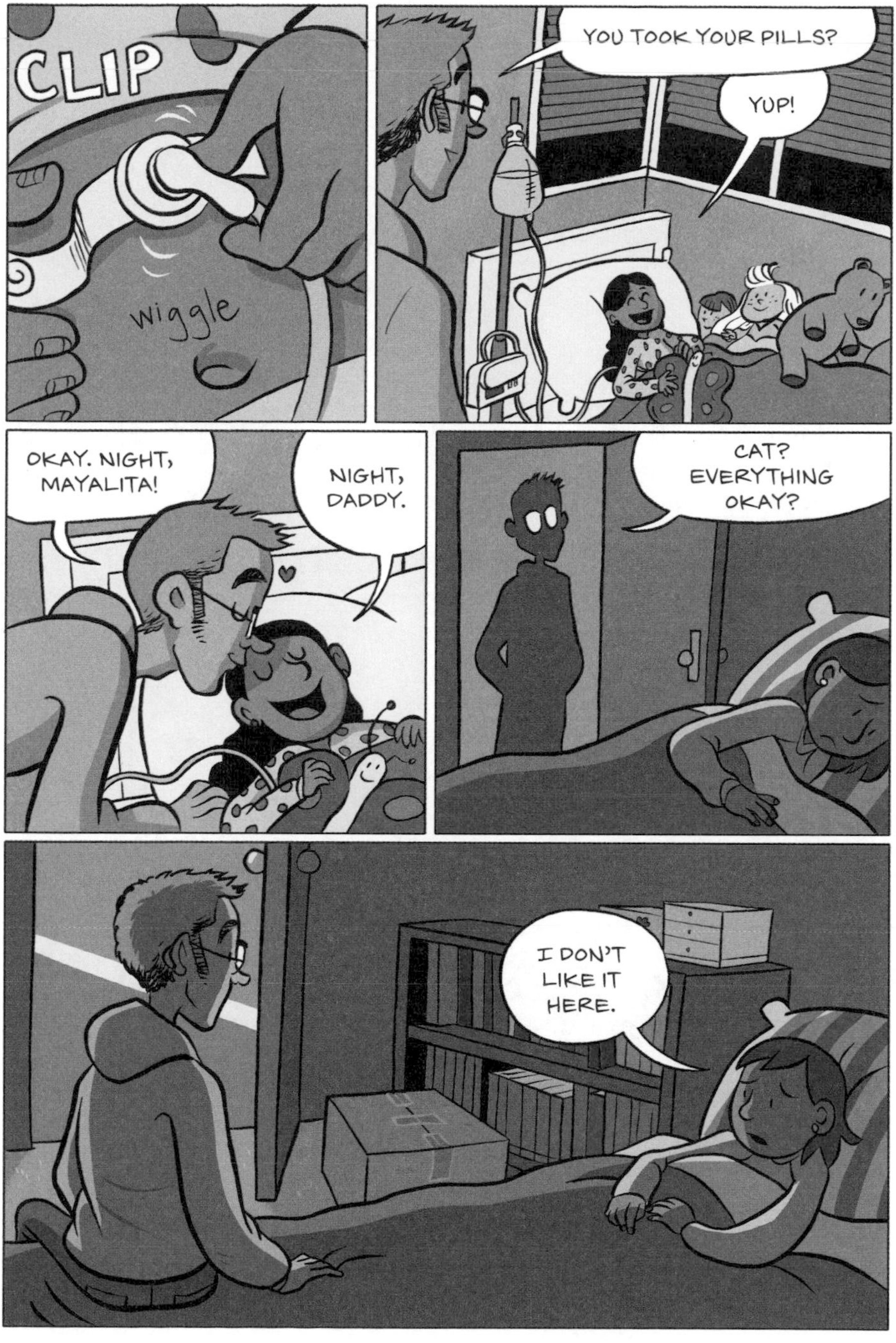
CLIP
wiggle
YOU TOOK YOUR PILLS?
YUP!
OKAY. NIGHT, MAYALITA!
NIGHT, DADDY.
CAT? EVERYTHING OKAY?
I DON'T LIKE IT HERE.

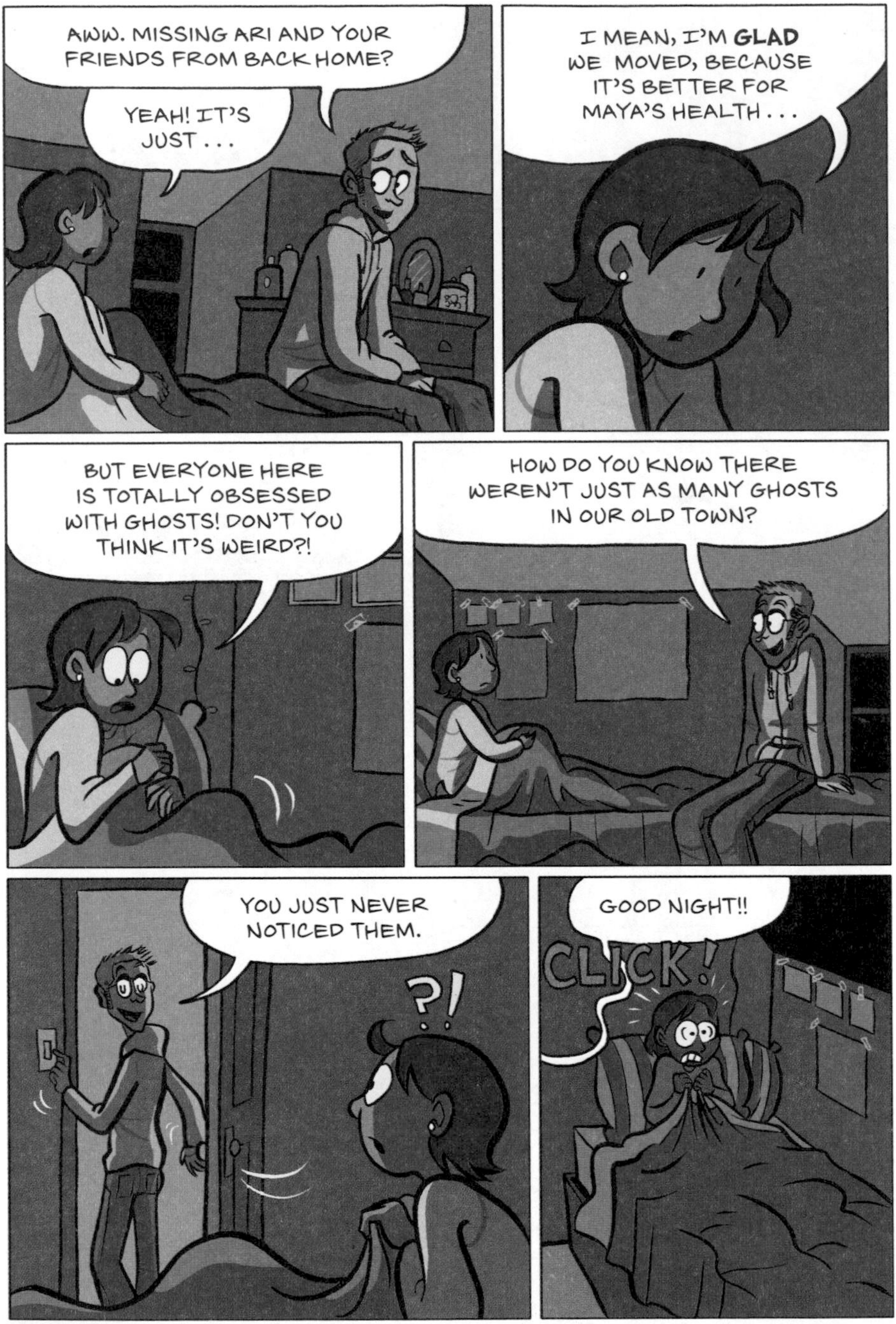
AWW. MISSING ARI AND YOUR FRIENDS FROM BACK HOME?
YEAH! IT'S JUST . . .
I MEAN, I'M **GLAD** WE MOVED, BECAUSE IT'S BETTER FOR MAYA'S HEALTH . . .
BUT EVERYONE HERE IS TOTALLY OBSESSED WITH GHOSTS! DON'T YOU THINK IT'S WEIRD?!
HOW DO YOU KNOW THERE WEREN'T JUST AS MANY GHOSTS IN OUR OLD TOWN?
YOU JUST NEVER NOTICED THEM.
?!
GOOD NIGHT!!
CLICK!

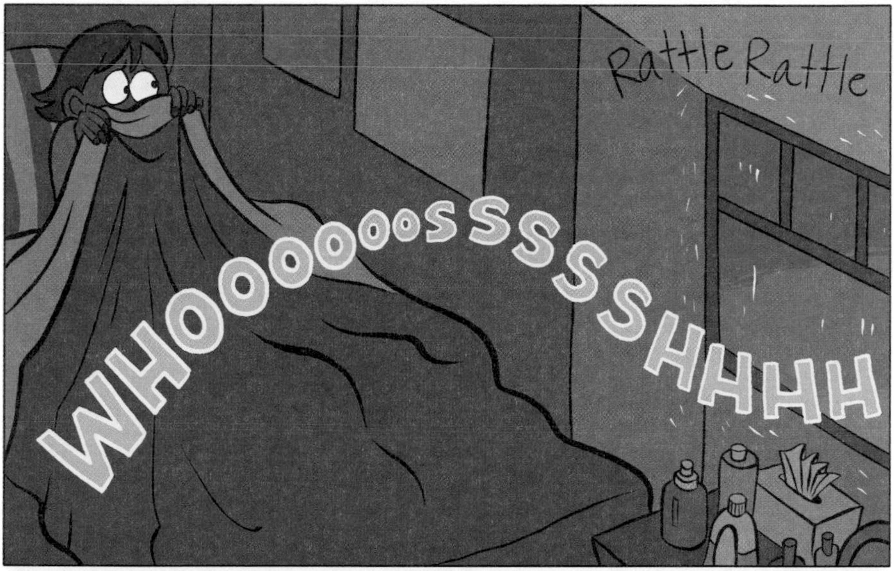
Rattle Rattle
WHOOOOOOOOSSSSSSHHHH

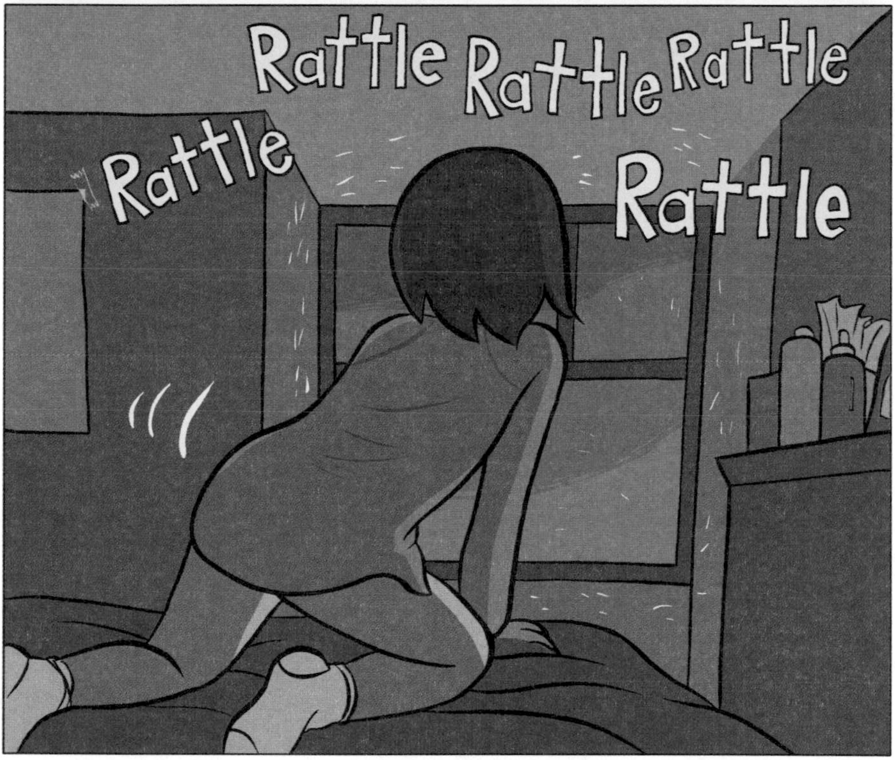
Rattle Rattle Rattle
Rattle
Rattle

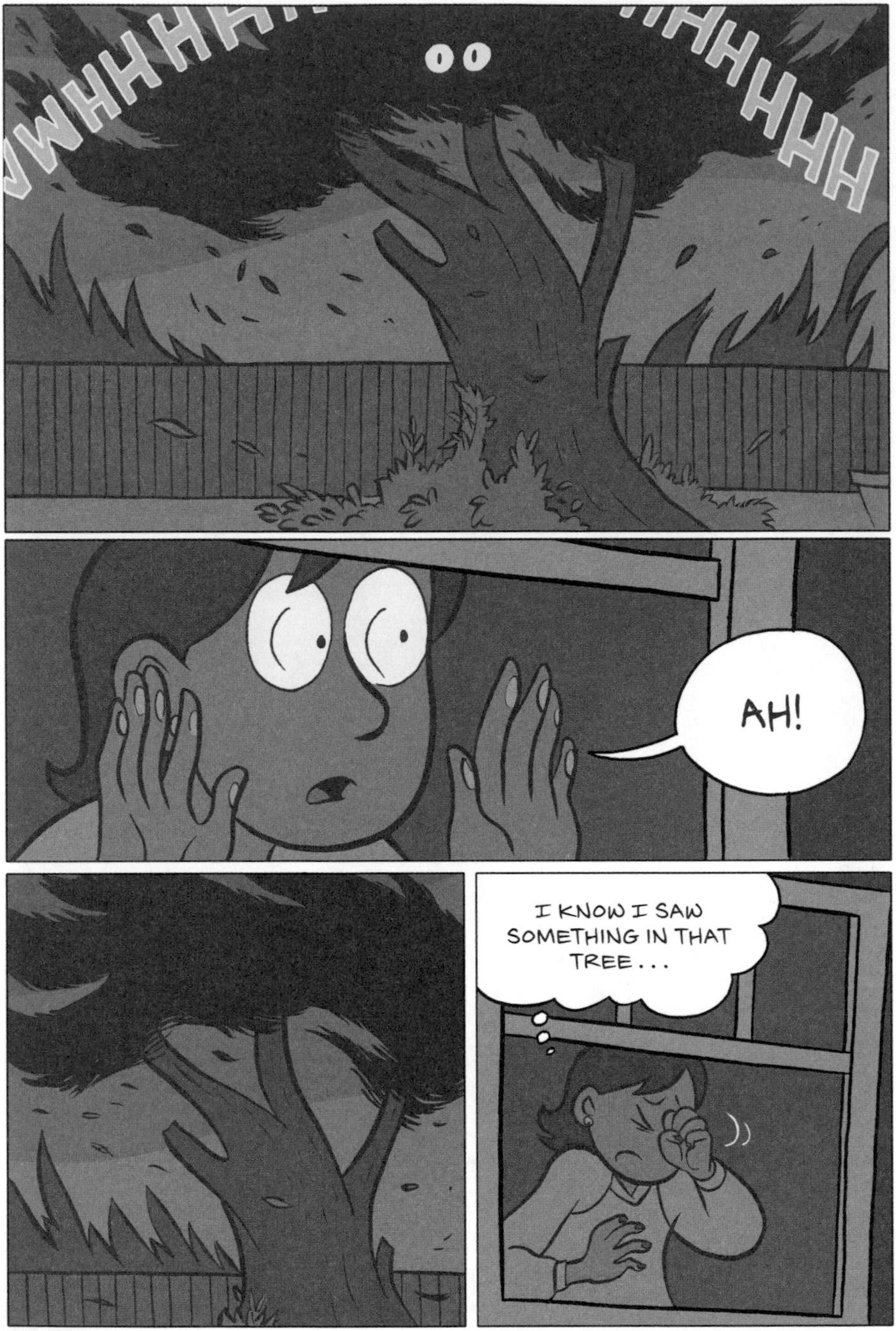
WHHHHH
HHHHHHH
AH!
I KNOW I SAW SOMETHING IN THAT TREE . . .

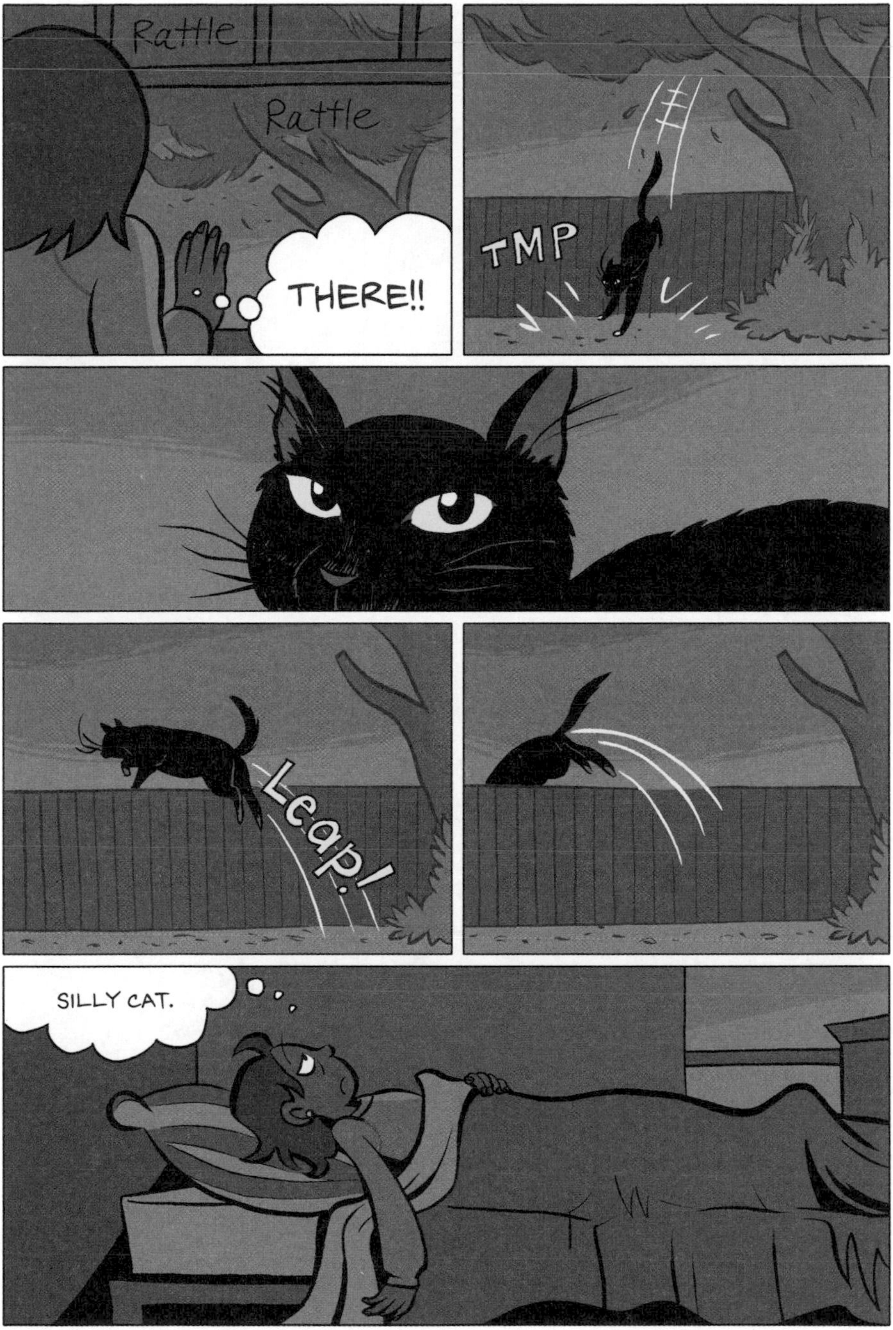
Rattle
Rattle
THERE!!
TMP
Leap!
SILLY CAT.

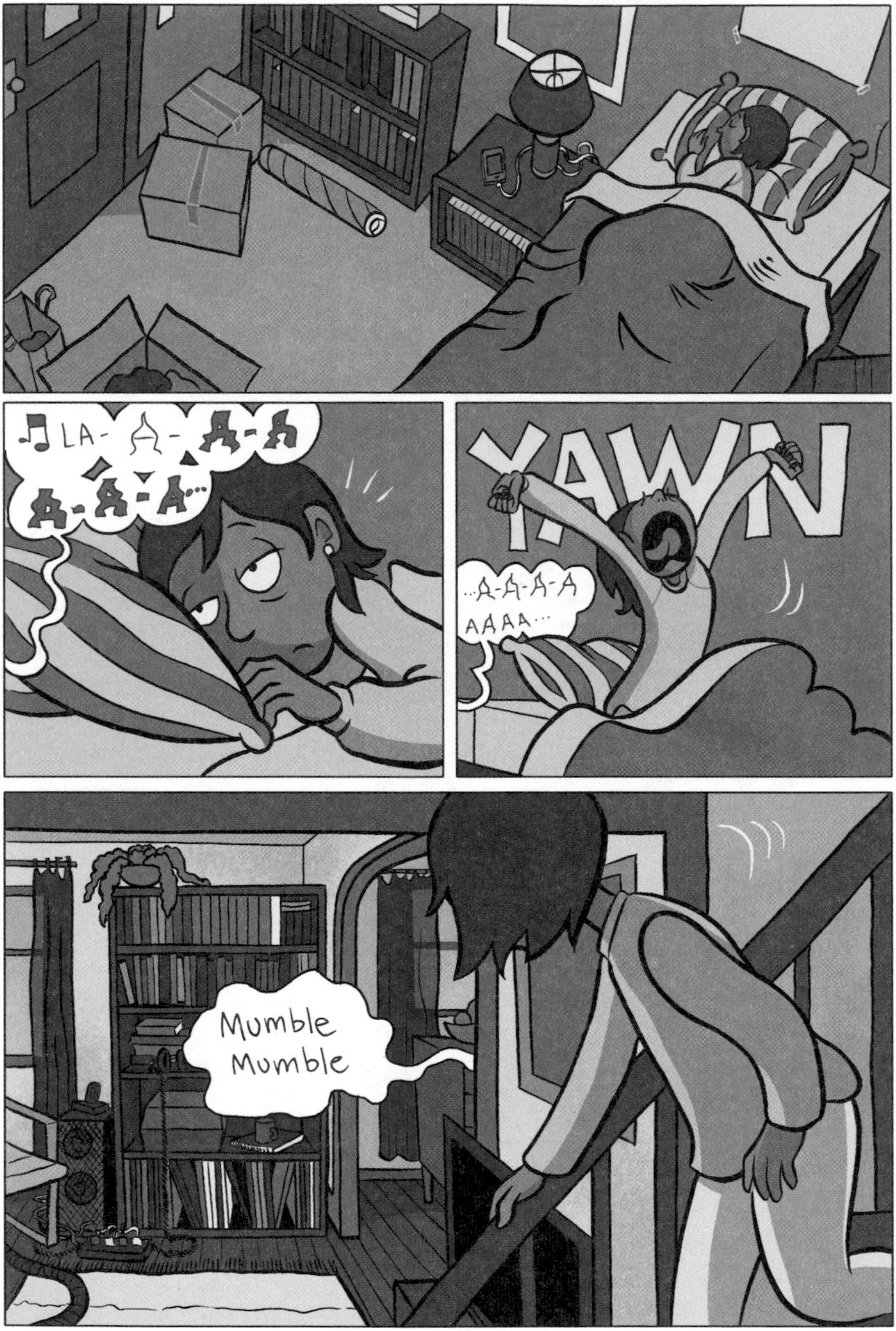
♫ LA- A- A-A
A-A-A...
YAWN
...A-A-A-A
AAAA...
Mumble
Mumble

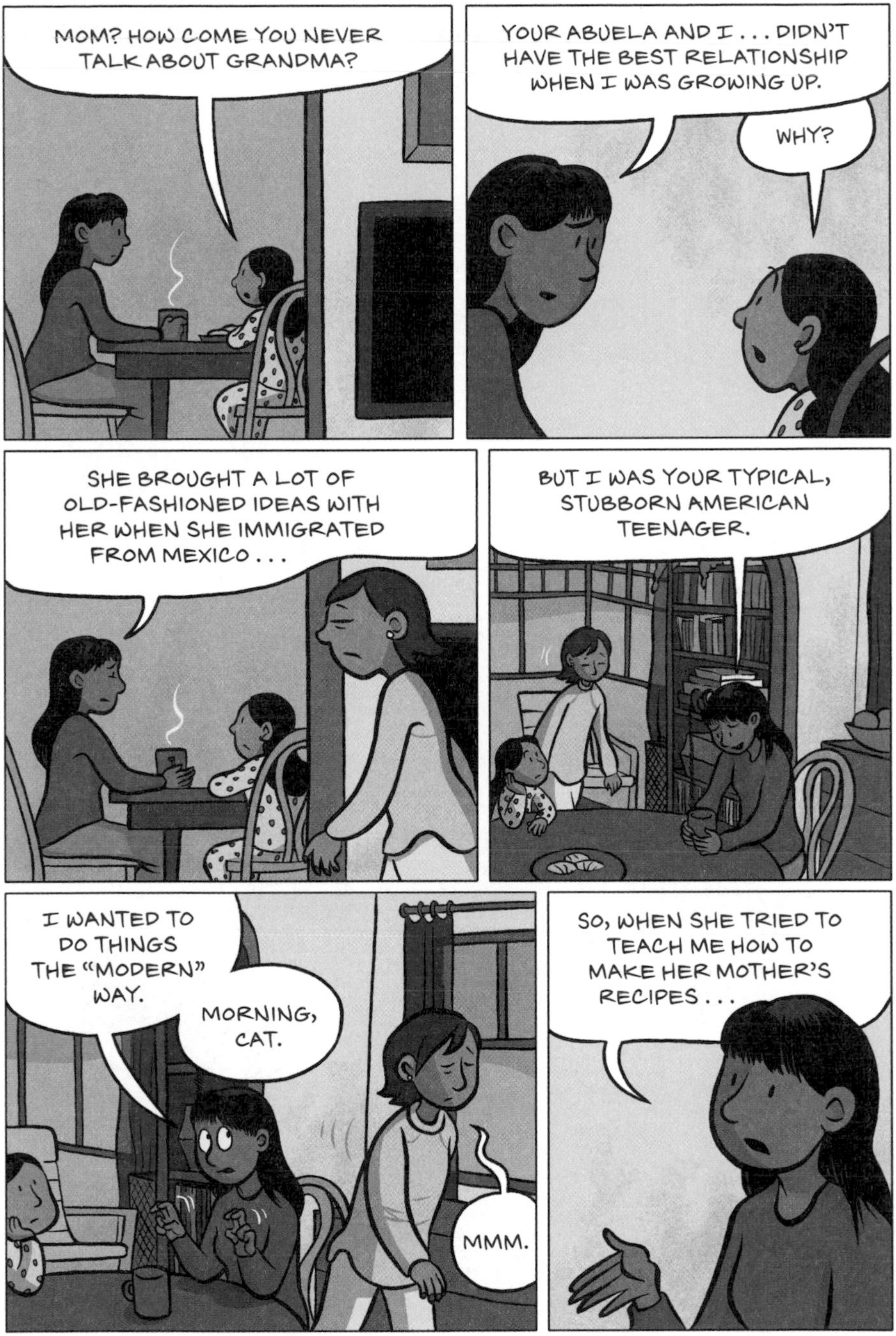
MOM? HOW COME YOU NEVER TALK ABOUT GRANDMA?
YOUR ABUELA AND I . . . DIDN'T HAVE THE BEST RELATIONSHIP WHEN I WAS GROWING UP.
WHY?
SHE BROUGHT A LOT OF OLD-FASHIONED IDEAS WITH HER WHEN SHE IMMIGRATED FROM MEXICO . . .
BUT I WAS YOUR TYPICAL, STUBBORN AMERICAN TEENAGER.
I WANTED TO DO THINGS THE "MODERN" WAY.
MORNING, CAT.
MMM.
SO, WHEN SHE TRIED TO TEACH ME HOW TO MAKE HER MOTHER'S RECIPES . . .

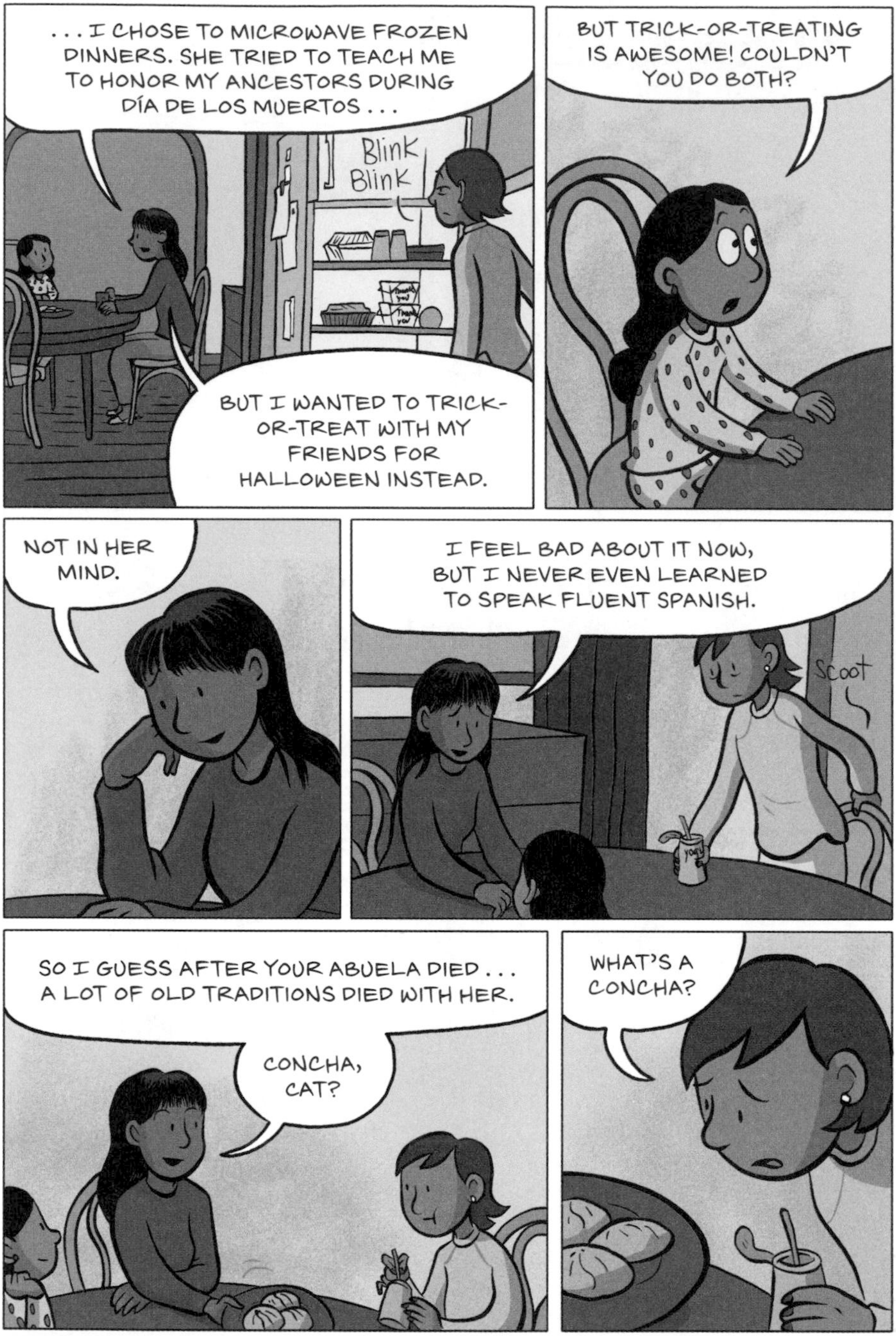
. . . I CHOSE TO MICROWAVE FROZEN DINNERS. SHE TRIED TO TEACH ME TO HONOR MY ANCESTORS DURING DÍA DE LOS MUERTOS . . .
Blink Blink
BUT I WANTED TO TRICK-OR-TREAT WITH MY FRIENDS FOR HALLOWEEN INSTEAD.
BUT TRICK-OR-TREATING IS AWESOME! COULDN'T YOU DO BOTH?
NOT IN HER MIND.
I FEEL BAD ABOUT IT NOW, BUT I NEVER EVEN LEARNED TO SPEAK FLUENT SPANISH.
Scoot
SO I GUESS AFTER YOUR ABUELA DIED . . . A LOT OF OLD TRADITIONS DIED WITH HER.
CONCHA, CAT?
WHAT'S A CONCHA?

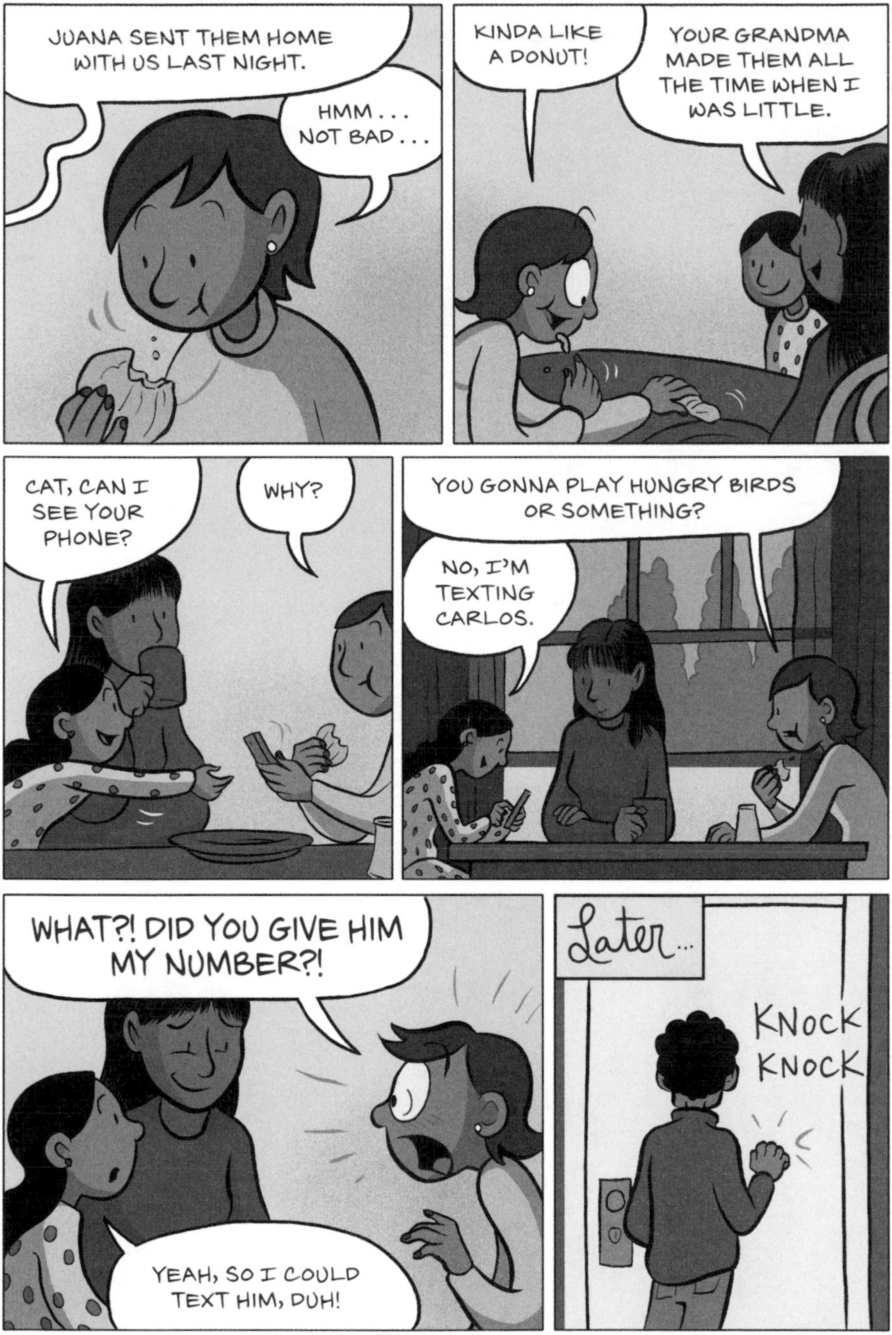
JUANA SENT THEM HOME WITH US LAST NIGHT.
HMM . . . NOT BAD . . .
KINDA LIKE A DONUT!
YOUR GRANDMA MADE THEM ALL THE TIME WHEN I WAS LITTLE.
CAT, CAN I SEE YOUR PHONE?
WHY?
YOU GONNA PLAY HUNGRY BIRDS OR SOMETHING?
NO, I'M TEXTING CARLOS.
WHAT?! DID YOU GIVE HIM MY NUMBER?!
YEAH, SO I COULD TEXT HIM, DUH!
Later...
KNOCK KNOCK

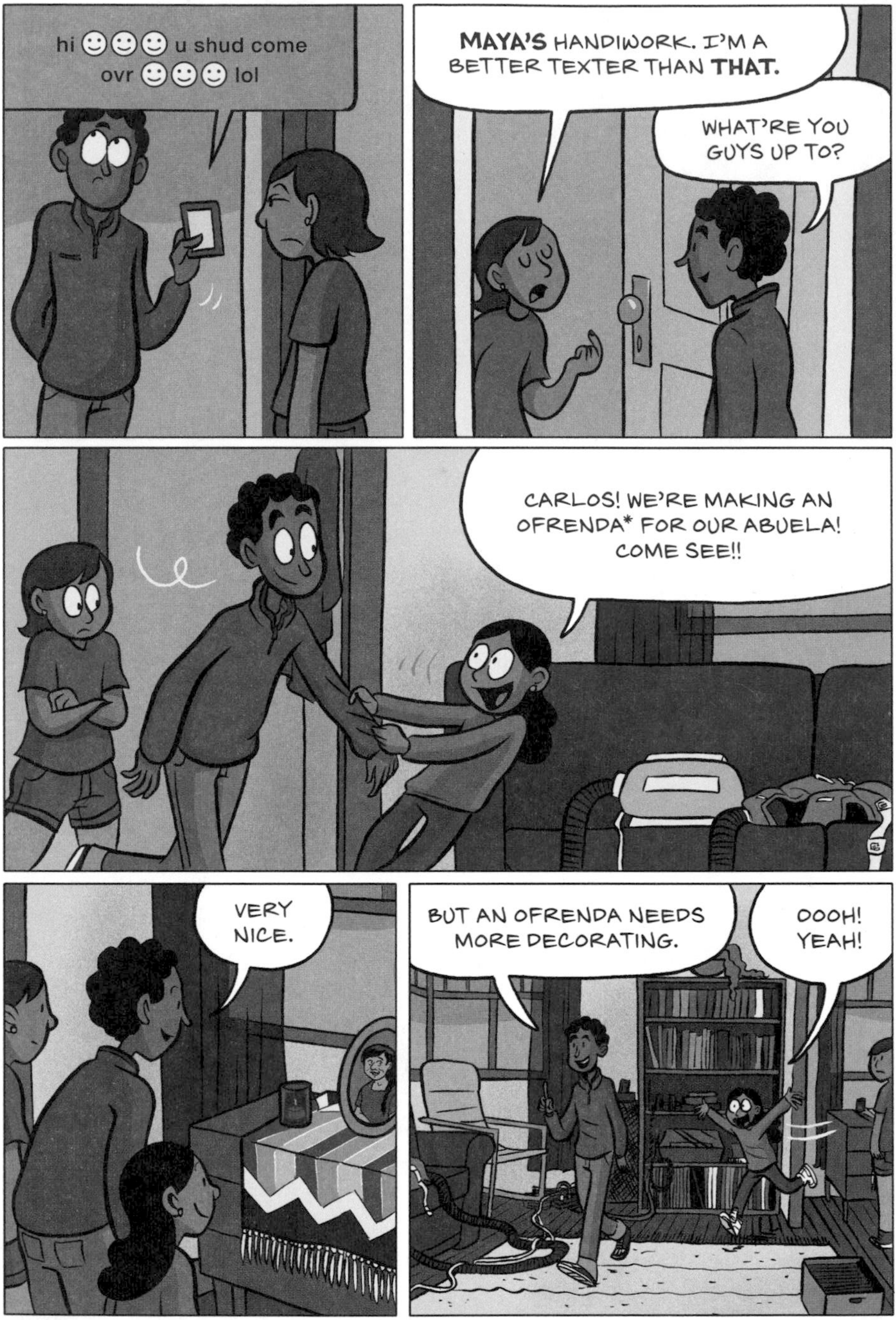
hi ☺☺☺ u shud come ovr ☺☺☺ lol
MAYA'S HANDIWORK. I'M A BETTER TEXTER THAN THAT.
WHAT'RE YOU GUYS UP TO?
CARLOS! WE'RE MAKING AN OFRENDA* FOR OUR ABUELA! COME SEE!!
VERY NICE.
BUT AN OFRENDA NEEDS MORE DECORATING.
OOOH! YEAH!

*AN ALTAR FOR A DECEASED RELATIVE

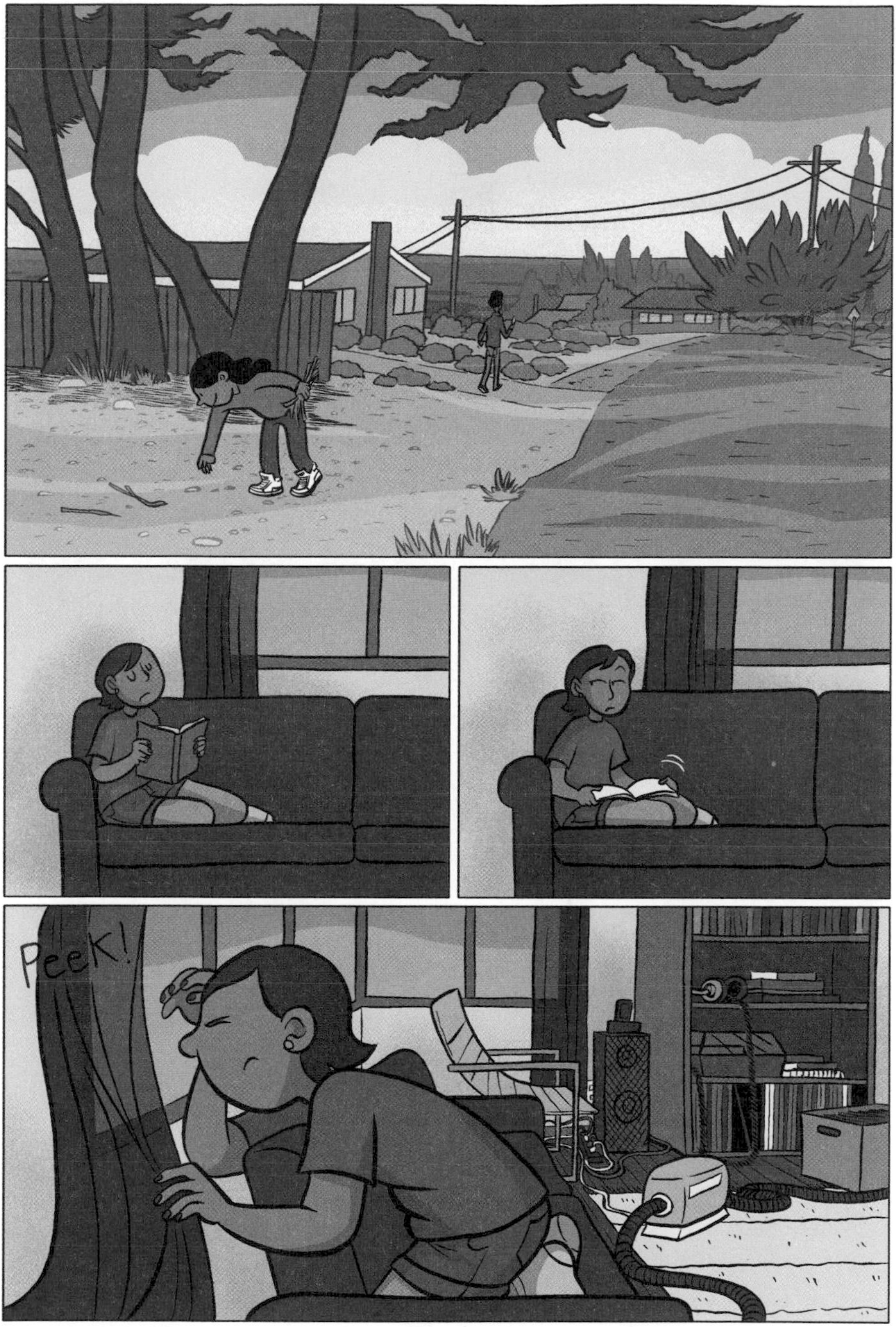
Peek!

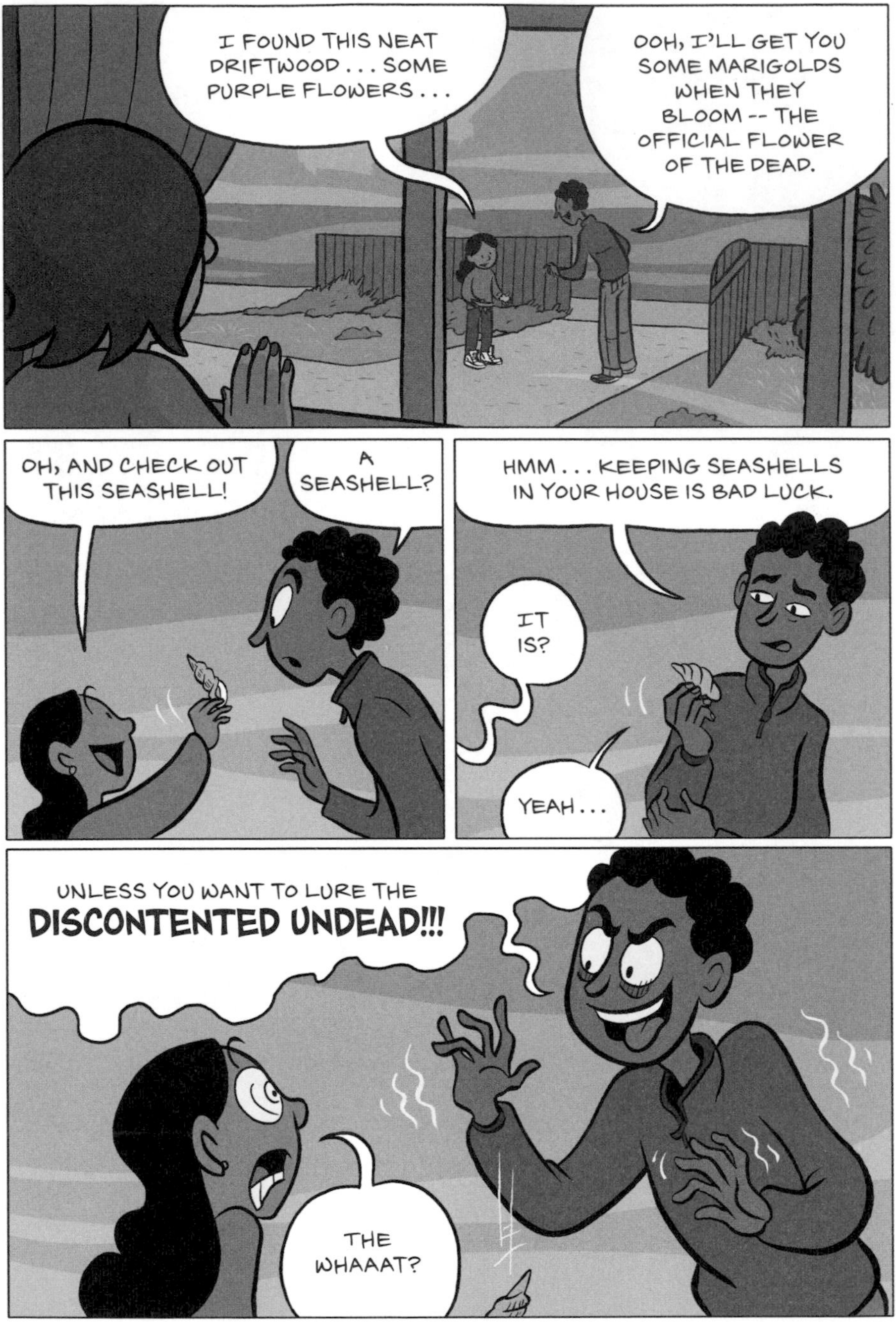
I FOUND THIS NEAT DRIFTWOOD . . . SOME PURPLE FLOWERS . . .
OOH, I'LL GET YOU SOME MARIGOLDS WHEN THEY BLOOM -- THE OFFICIAL FLOWER OF THE DEAD.
OH, AND CHECK OUT THIS SEASHELL!
A SEASHELL?
HMM . . . KEEPING SEASHELLS IN YOUR HOUSE IS BAD LUCK.
IT IS?
YEAH . . .
UNLESS YOU WANT TO LURE THE **DISCONTENTED UNDEAD!!!**
THE WHAAAT?

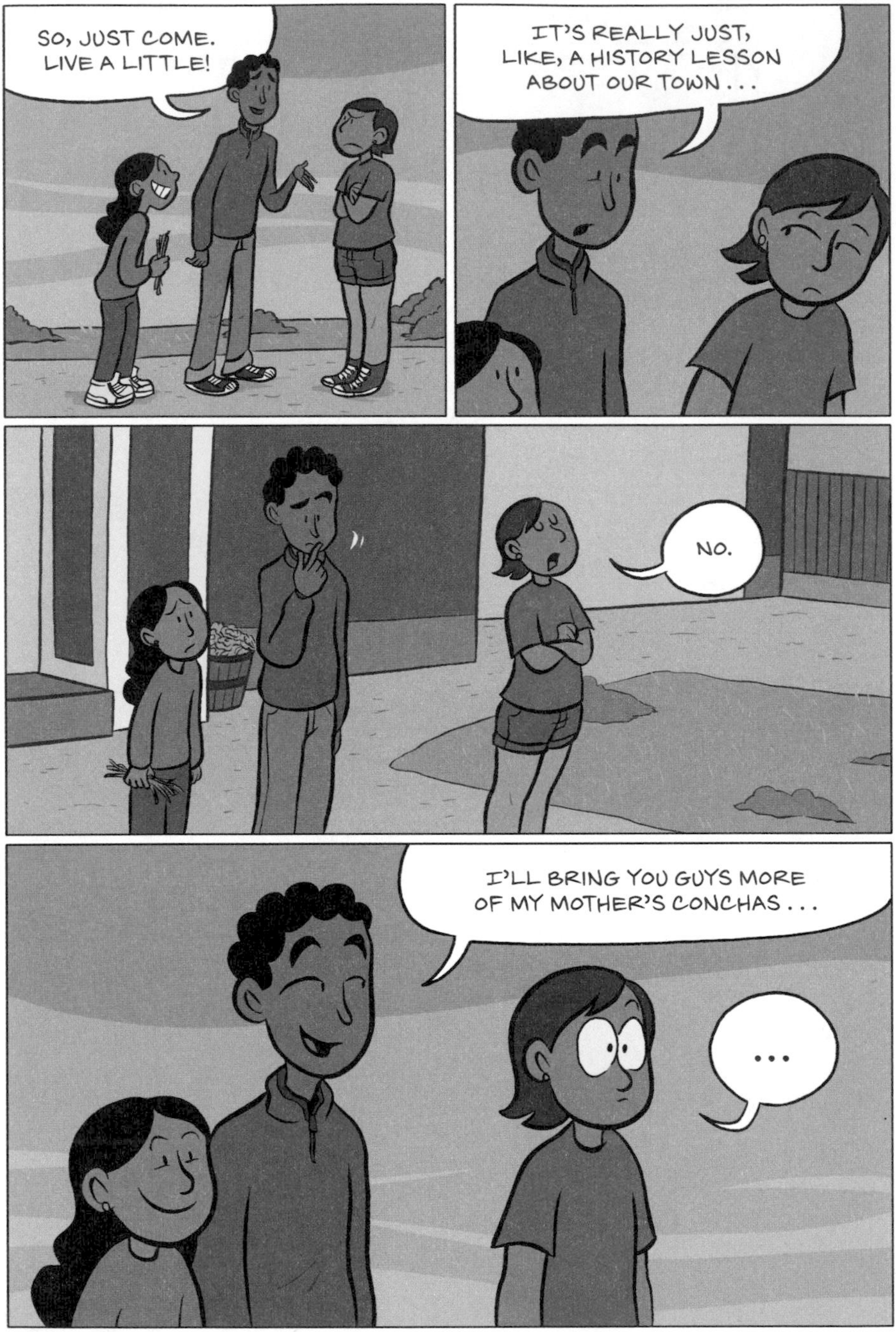
SO, JUST COME. LIVE A LITTLE!
IT'S REALLY JUST, LIKE, A HISTORY LESSON ABOUT OUR TOWN . . .
NO.
I'LL BRING YOU GUYS MORE OF MY MOTHER'S CONCHAS . . .
. . .

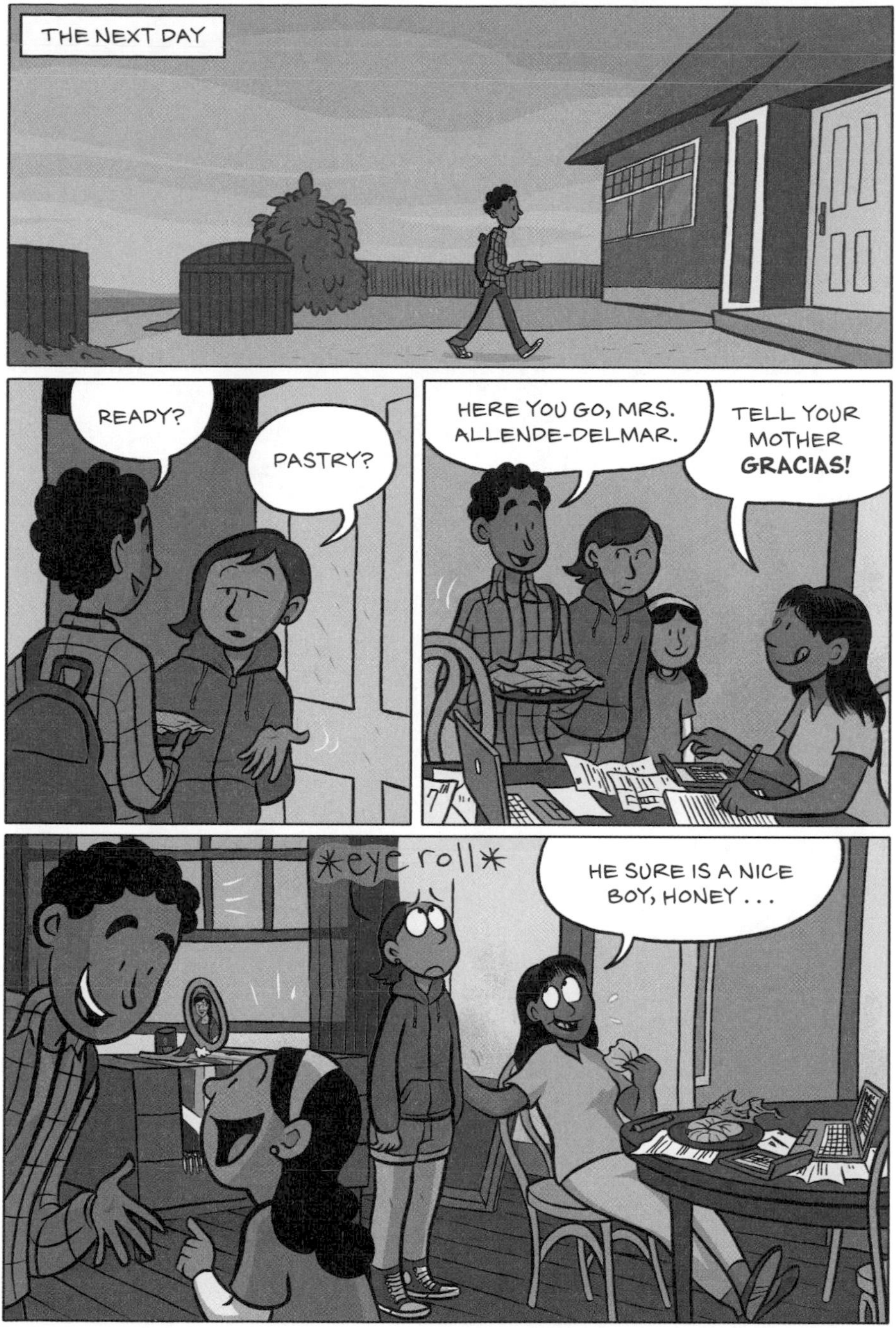
THE NEXT DAY
READY?
PASTRY?
HERE YOU GO, MRS. ALLENDE-DELMAR.
TELL YOUR MOTHER **GRACIAS!**
eye roll
HE SURE IS A NICE BOY, HONEY . . .

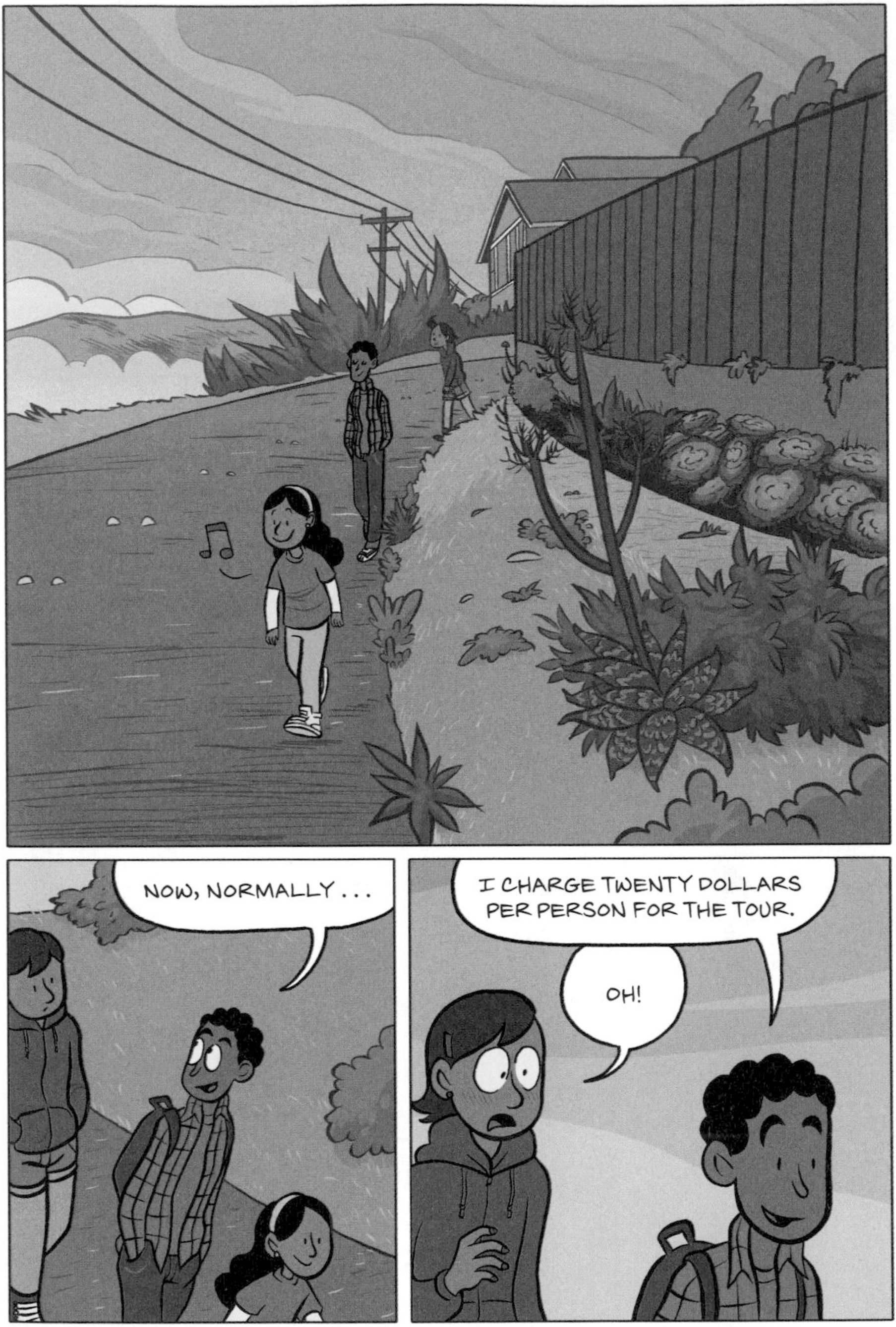
NOW, NORMALLY . . .
I CHARGE TWENTY DOLLARS PER PERSON FOR THE TOUR.
OH!

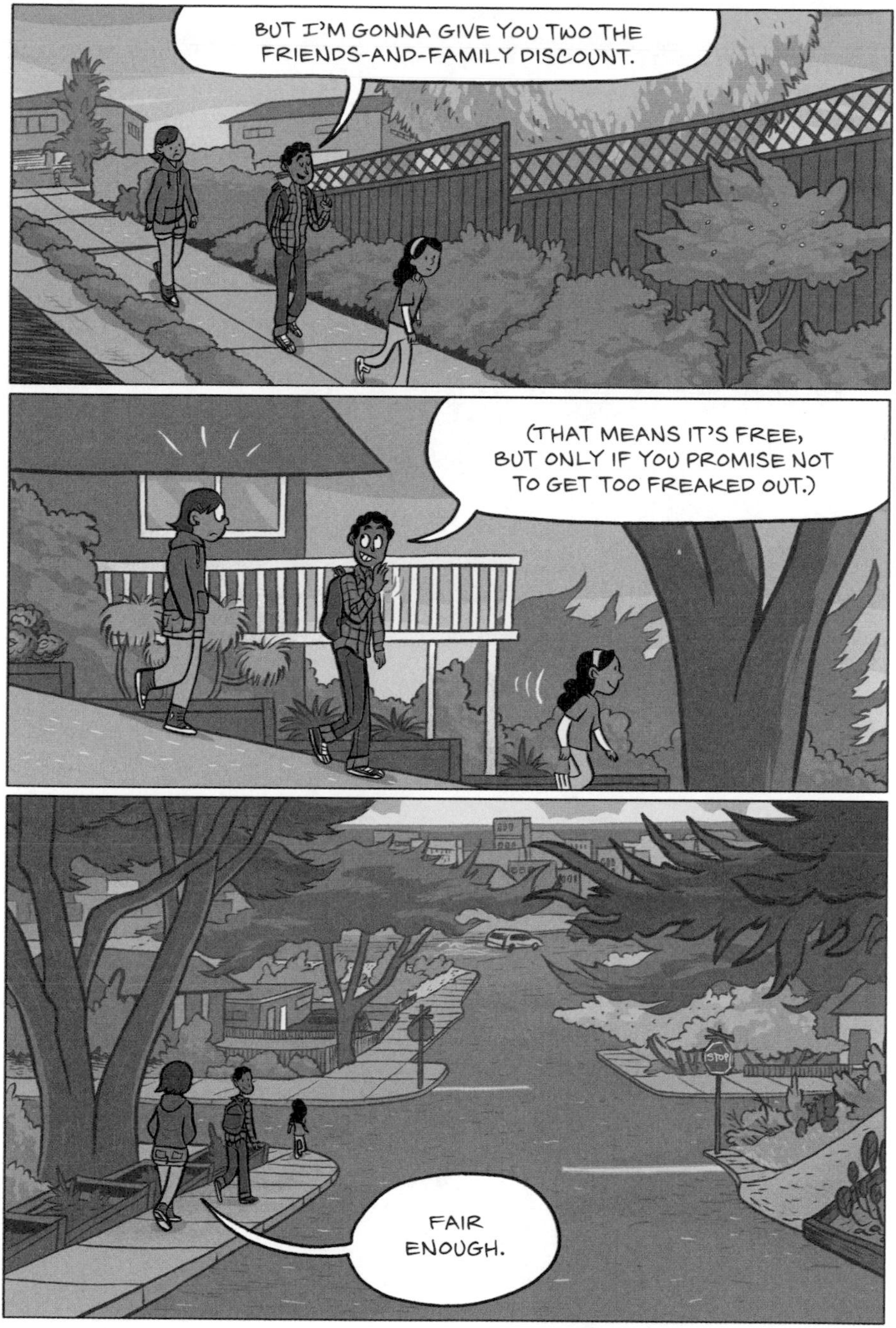
BUT I'M GONNA GIVE YOU TWO THE FRIENDS-AND-FAMILY DISCOUNT.
(THAT MEANS IT'S FREE, BUT ONLY IF YOU PROMISE NOT TO GET TOO FREAKED OUT.)
STOP
FAIR ENOUGH.

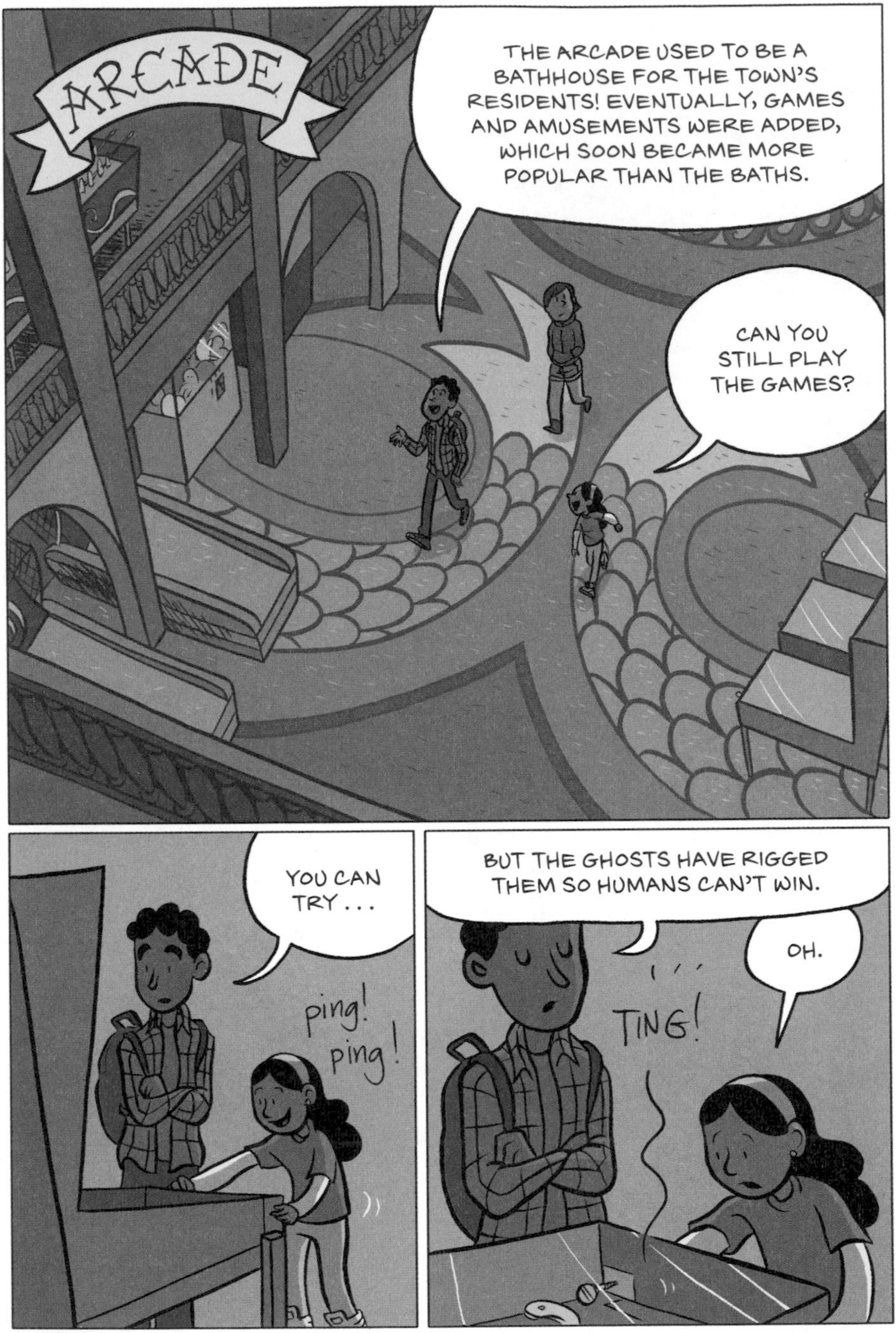
ARCADE
THE ARCADE USED TO BE A BATHHOUSE FOR THE TOWN'S RESIDENTS! EVENTUALLY, GAMES AND AMUSEMENTS WERE ADDED, WHICH SOON BECAME MORE POPULAR THAN THE BATHS.
CAN YOU STILL PLAY THE GAMES?
YOU CAN TRY . . .
ping! ping!
BUT THE GHOSTS HAVE RIGGED THEM SO HUMANS CAN'T WIN.
OH.
TING!

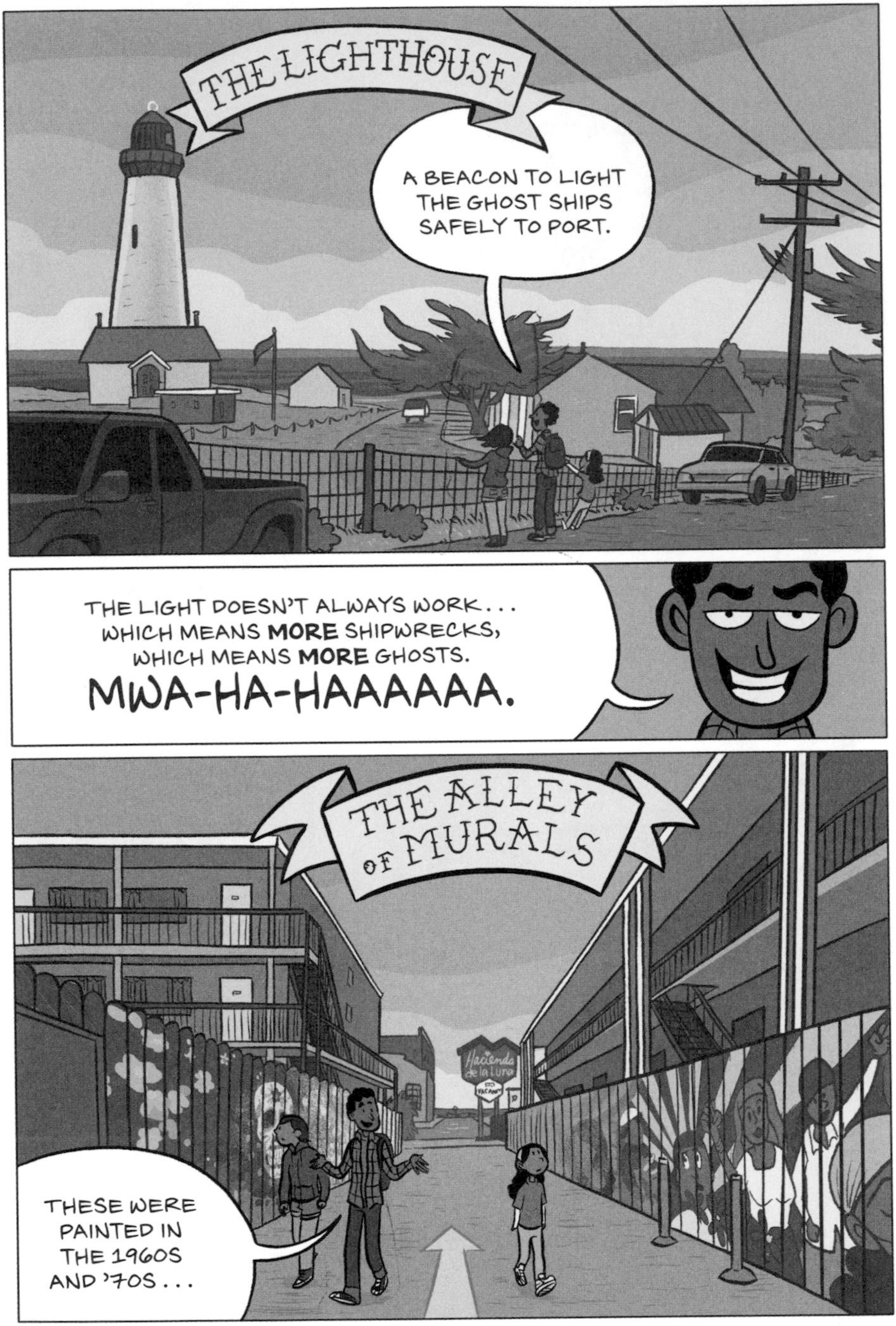
THE LIGHTHOUSE
A BEACON TO LIGHT THE GHOST SHIPS SAFELY TO PORT.
THE LIGHT DOESN'T ALWAYS WORK . . . WHICH MEANS MORE SHIPWRECKS, WHICH MEANS MORE GHOSTS.
MWA-HA-HAAAAAA.
THE ALLEY OF MURALS
Hacienda de la Luna
VACANCY
THESE WERE PAINTED IN THE 1960S AND '70S . . .

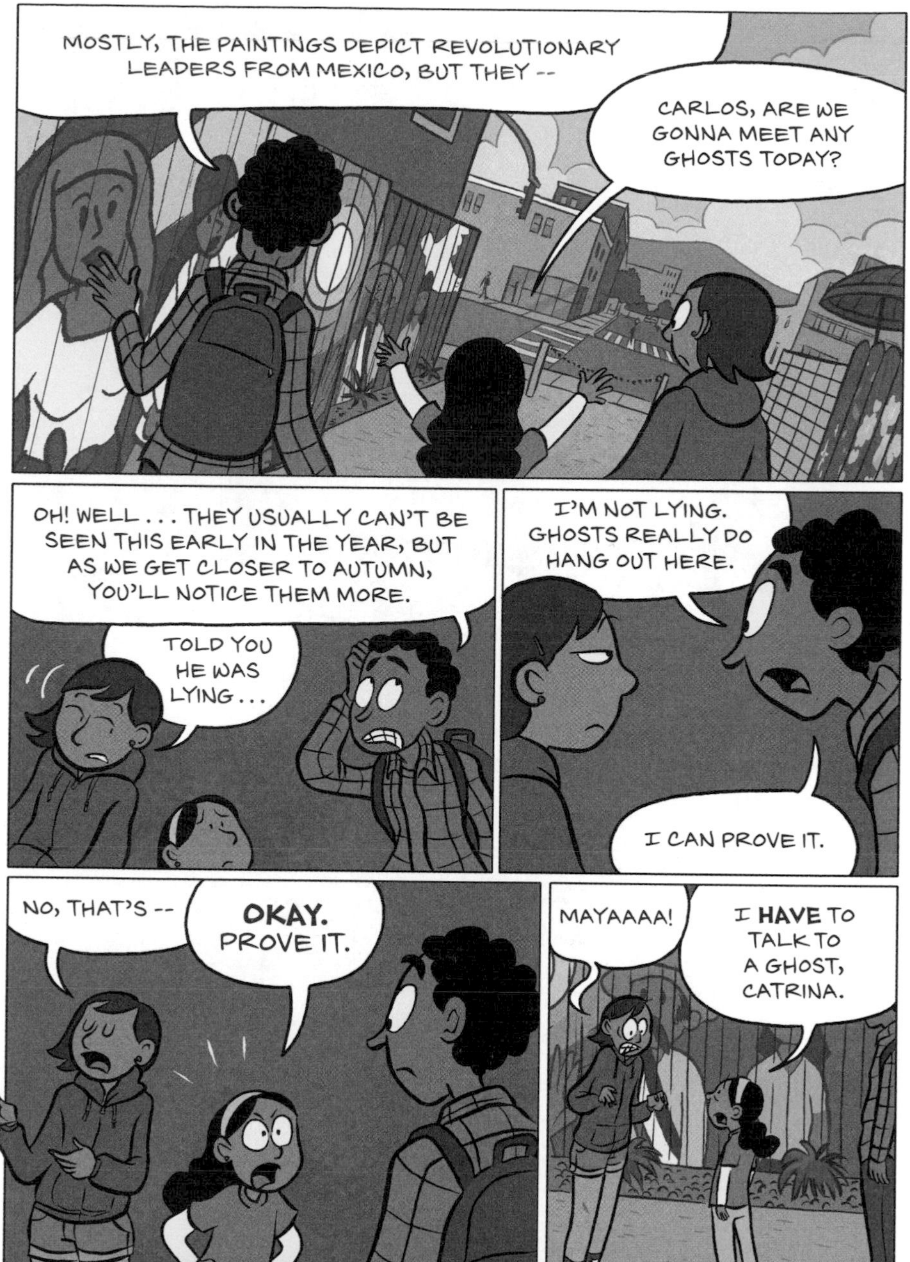
MOSTLY, THE PAINTINGS DEPICT REVOLUTIONARY LEADERS FROM MEXICO, BUT THEY --
CARLOS, ARE WE GONNA MEET ANY GHOSTS TODAY?
OH! WELL . . . THEY USUALLY CAN'T BE SEEN THIS EARLY IN THE YEAR, BUT AS WE GET CLOSER TO AUTUMN, YOU'LL NOTICE THEM MORE.
TOLD YOU HE WAS LYING . . .
I'M NOT LYING. GHOSTS REALLY DO HANG OUT HERE.
I CAN PROVE IT.
NO, THAT'S --
OKAY. PROVE IT.
MAYAAAA!
I **HAVE** TO TALK TO A GHOST, CATRINA.

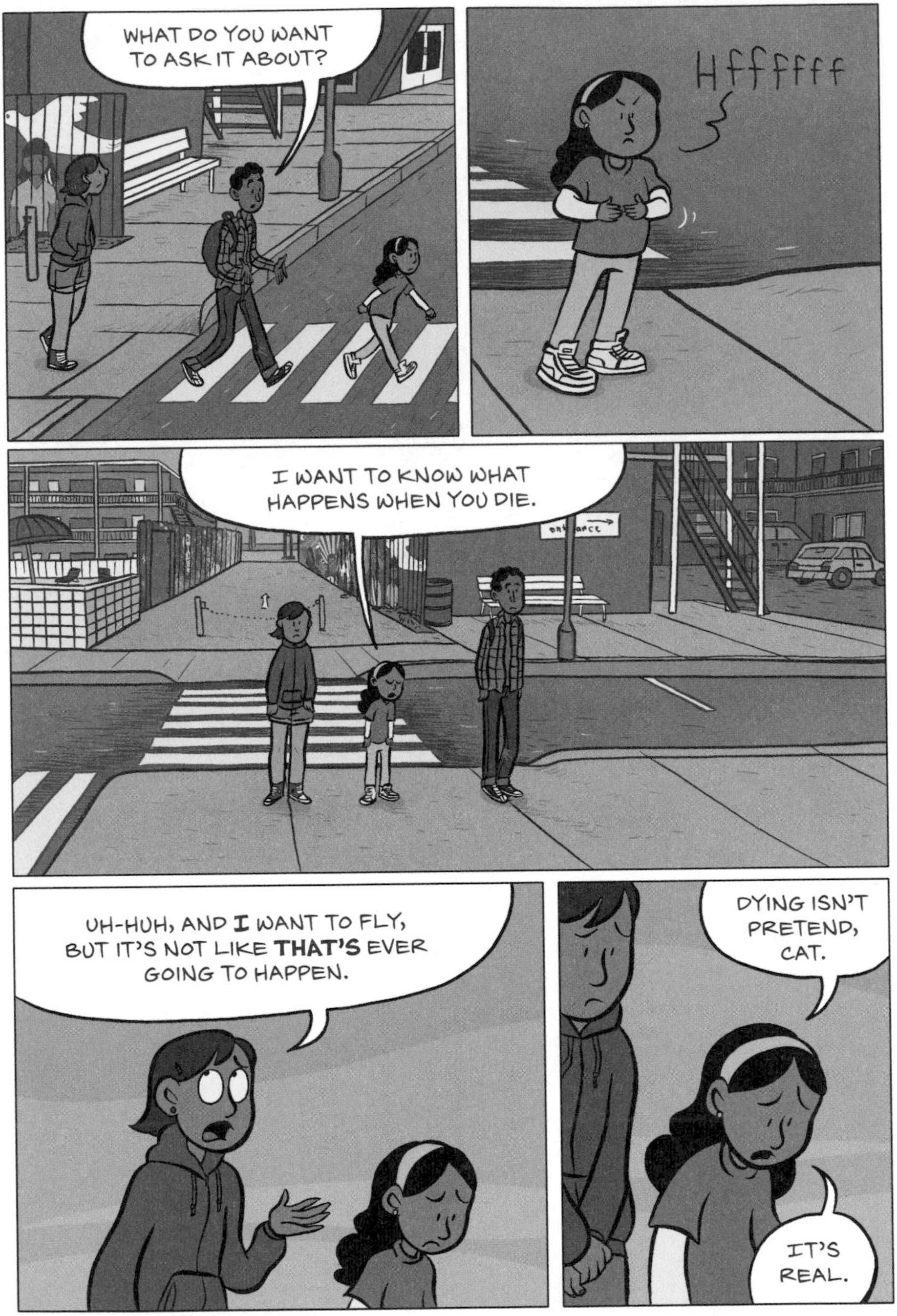
WHAT DO YOU WANT TO ASK IT ABOUT?
Hffffff
I WANT TO KNOW WHAT HAPPENS WHEN YOU DIE.
UH-HUH, AND I WANT TO FLY, BUT IT'S NOT LIKE THAT'S EVER GOING TO HAPPEN.
DYING ISN'T PRETEND, CAT.
IT'S REAL.

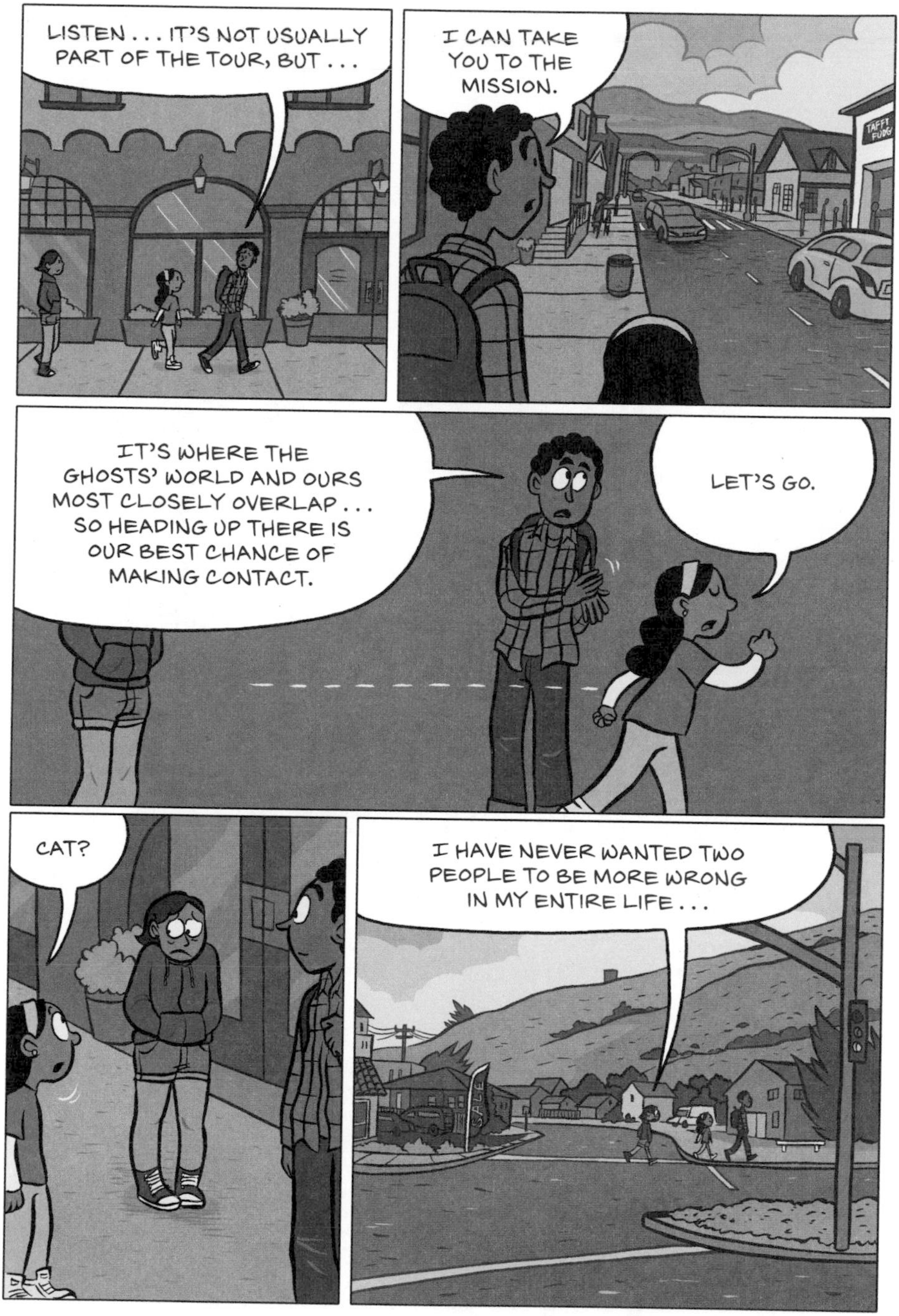
LISTEN . . . IT'S NOT USUALLY PART OF THE TOUR, BUT . . .
I CAN TAKE YOU TO THE MISSION.
TAFFY FUDGE
IT'S WHERE THE GHOSTS' WORLD AND OURS MOST CLOSELY OVERLAP . . . SO HEADING UP THERE IS OUR BEST CHANCE OF MAKING CONTACT.
LET'S GO.
CAT?
I HAVE NEVER WANTED TWO PEOPLE TO BE MORE WRONG IN MY ENTIRE LIFE . . .
SALE

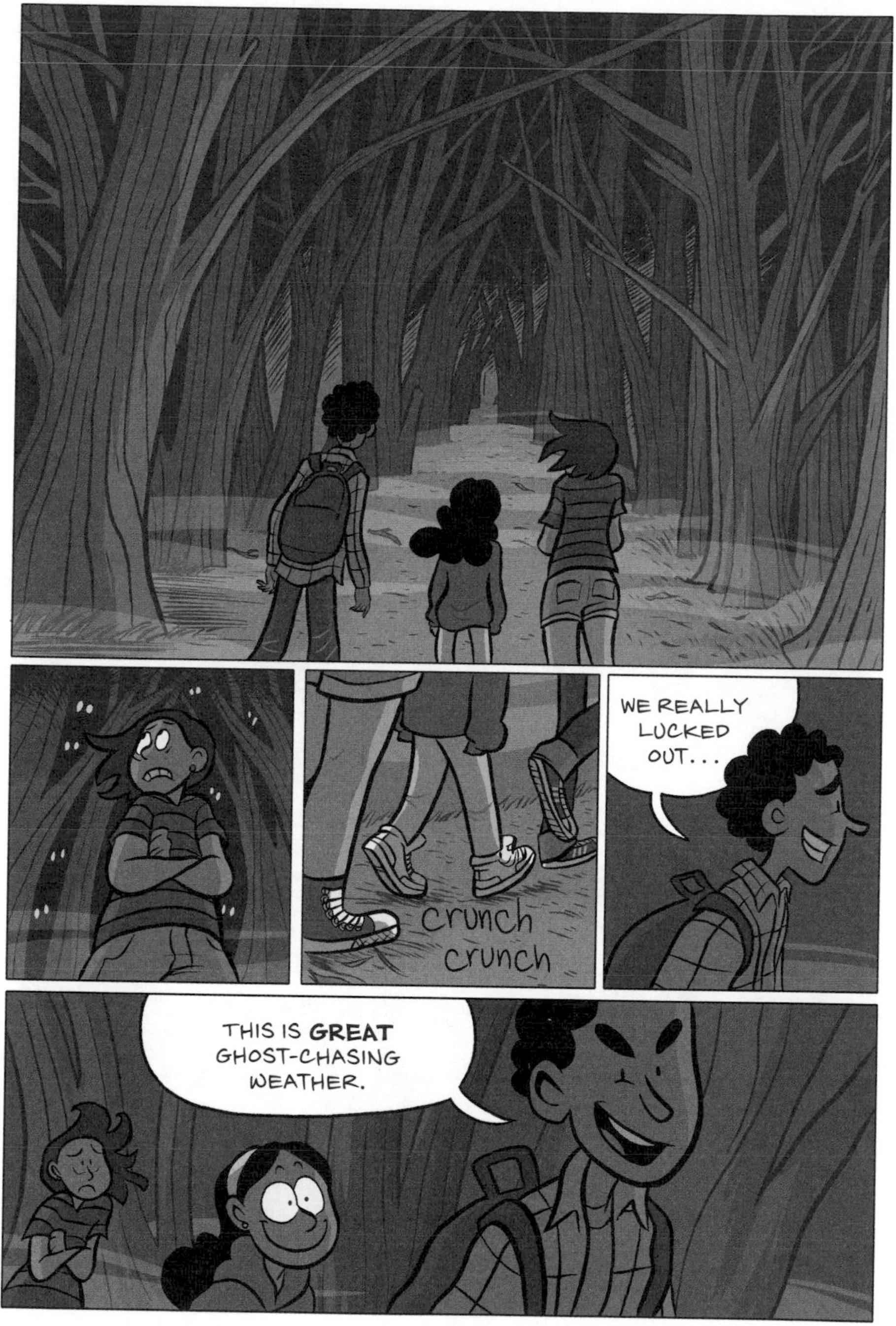
crunch
crunch
WE REALLY LUCKED OUT...
THIS IS **GREAT** GHOST-CHASING WEATHER.

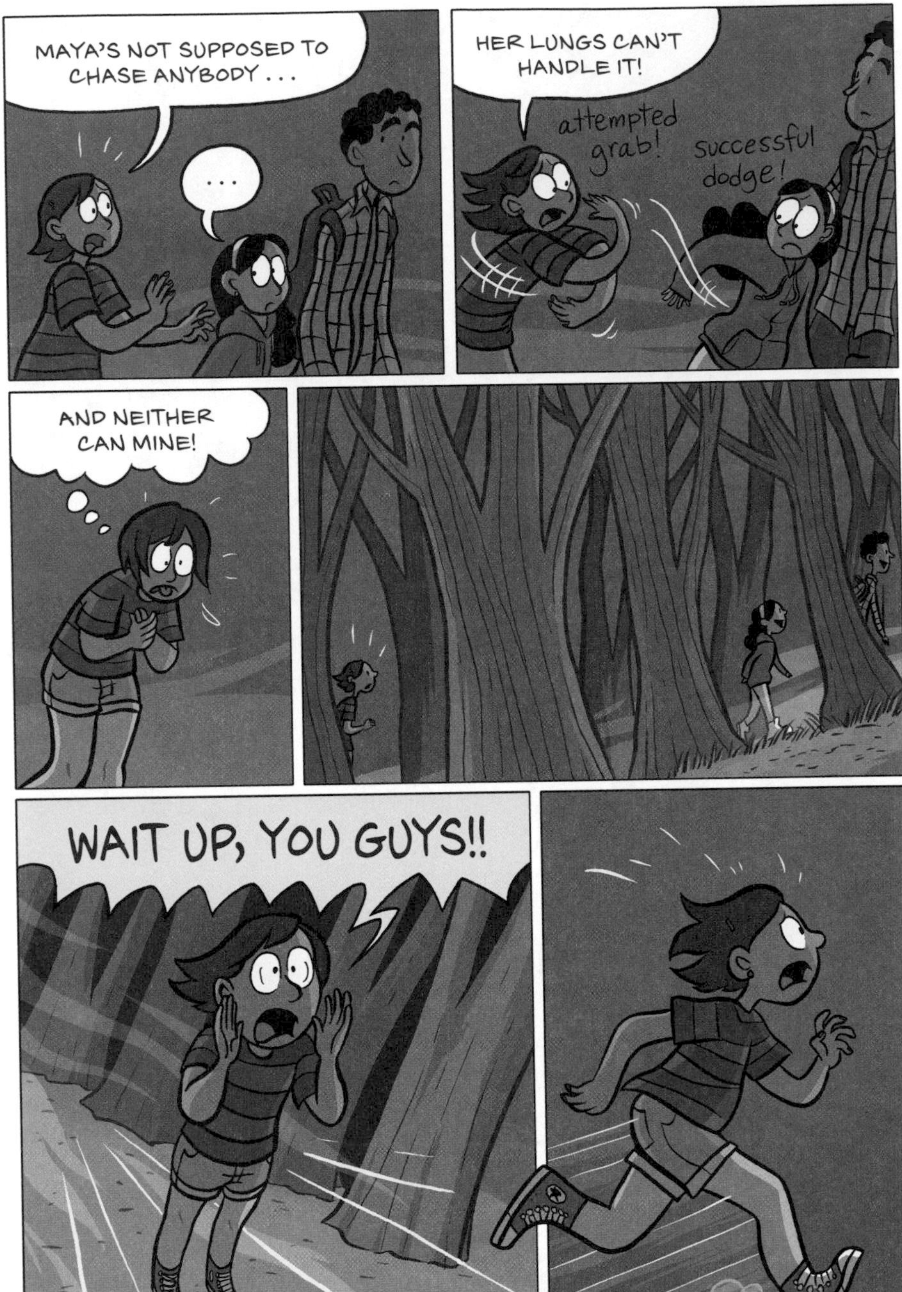
MAYA'S NOT SUPPOSED TO CHASE ANYBODY . . .
. . .
HER LUNGS CAN'T HANDLE IT!
attempted grab!
successful dodge!
AND NEITHER CAN MINE!
WAIT UP, YOU GUYS!!

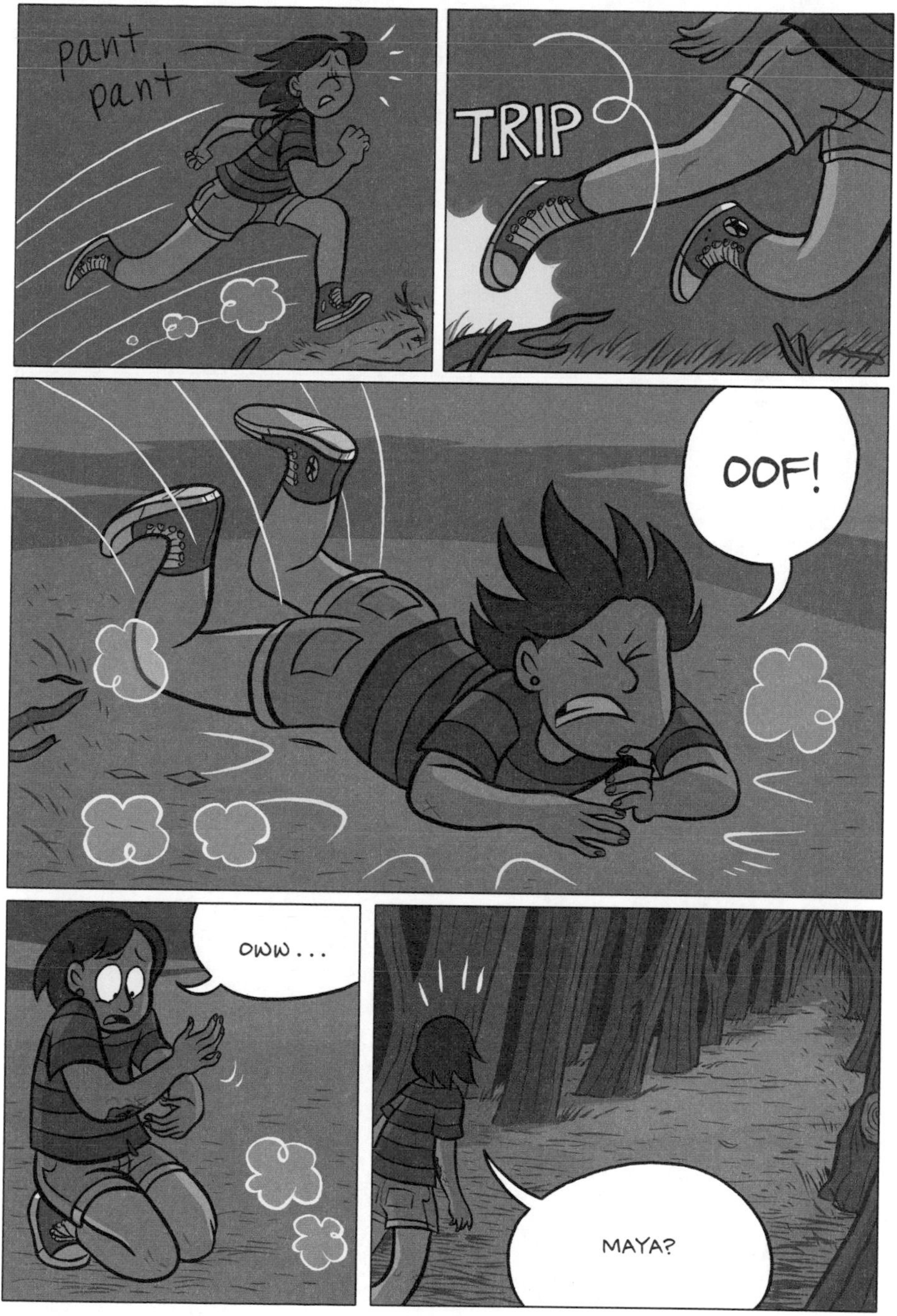
pant pant
TRIP
OOF!
oww...
MAYA?

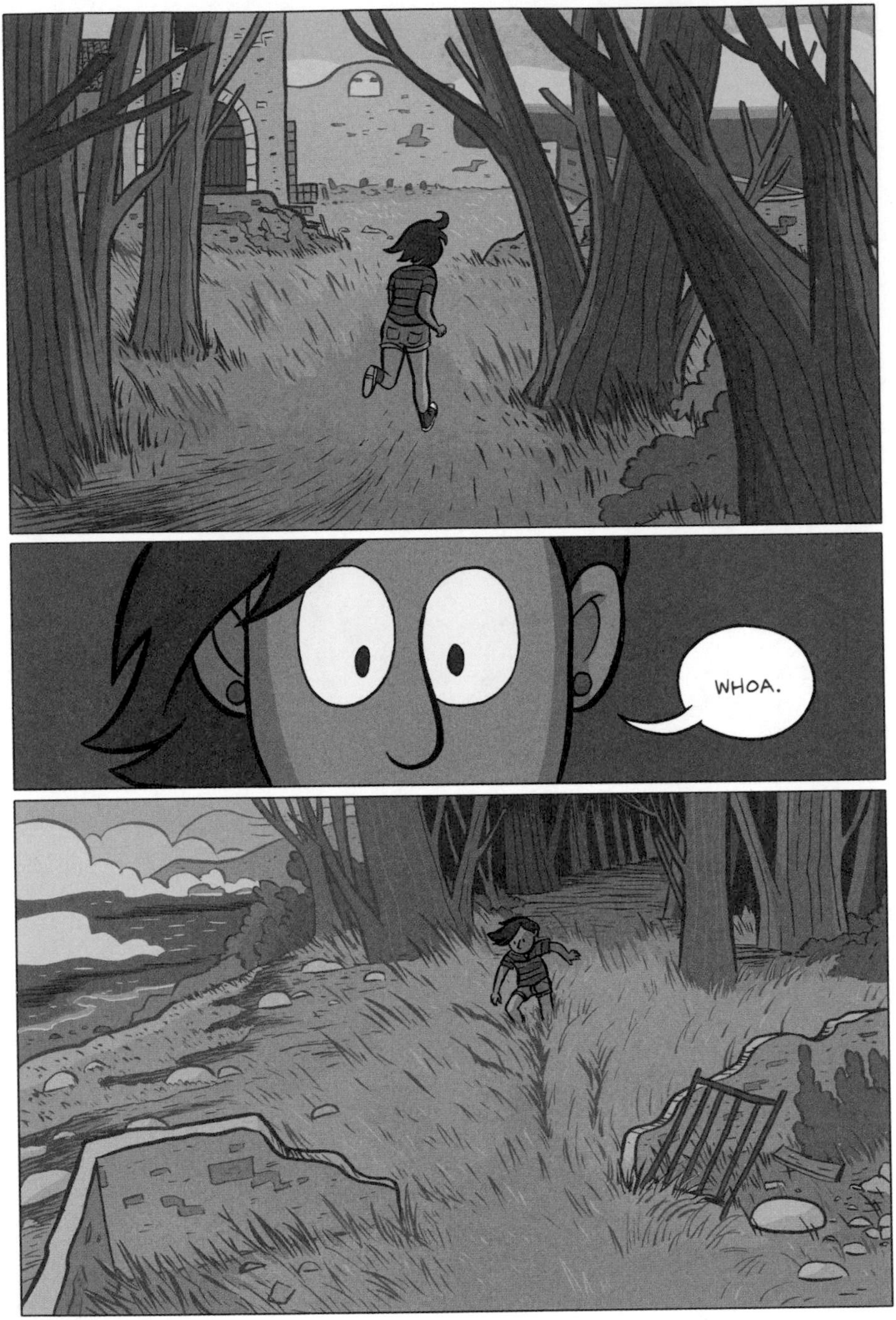
WHOA.

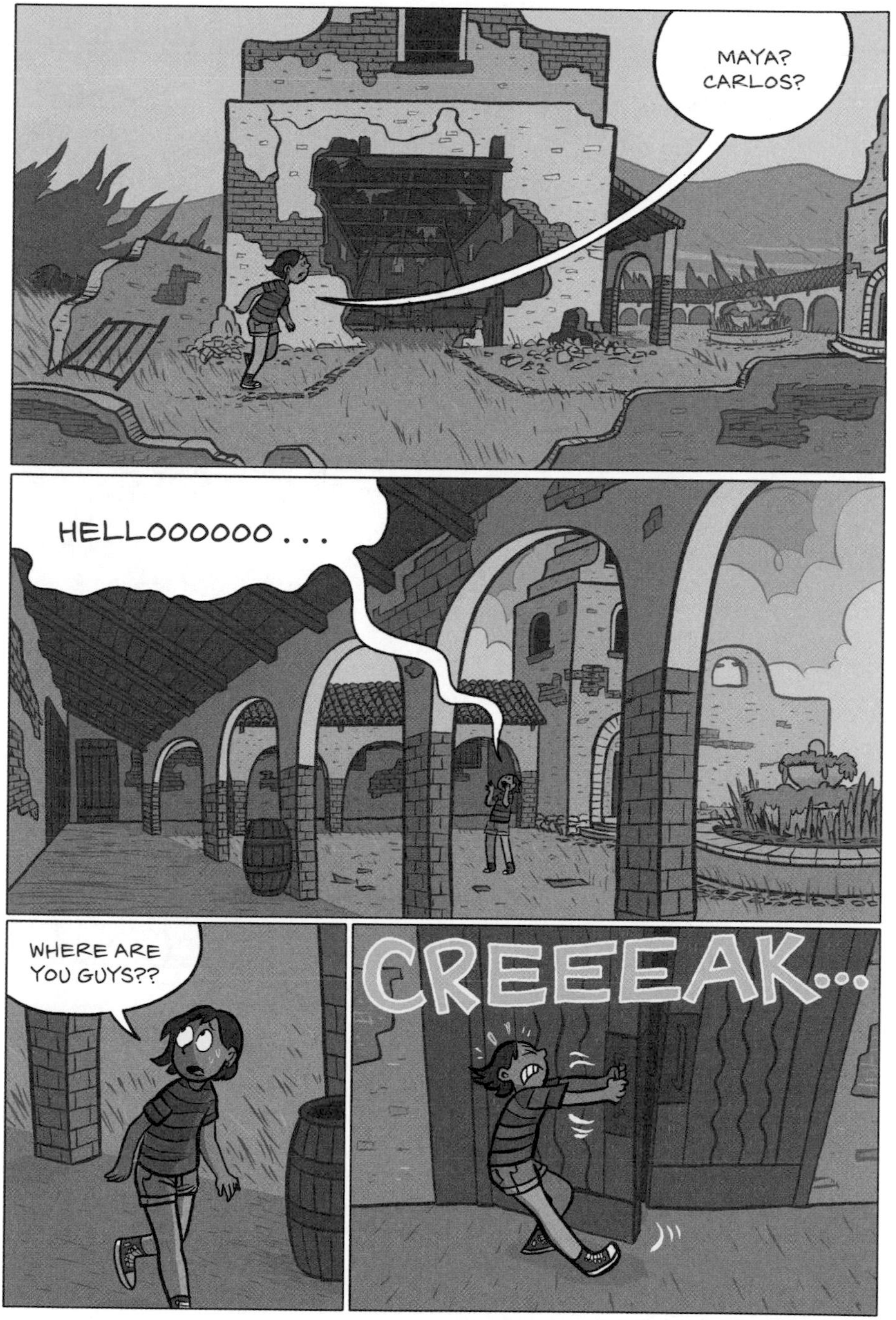
MAYA? CARLOS?
HELLOOOOOO . . .
WHERE ARE YOU GUYS??
CREEEAK...

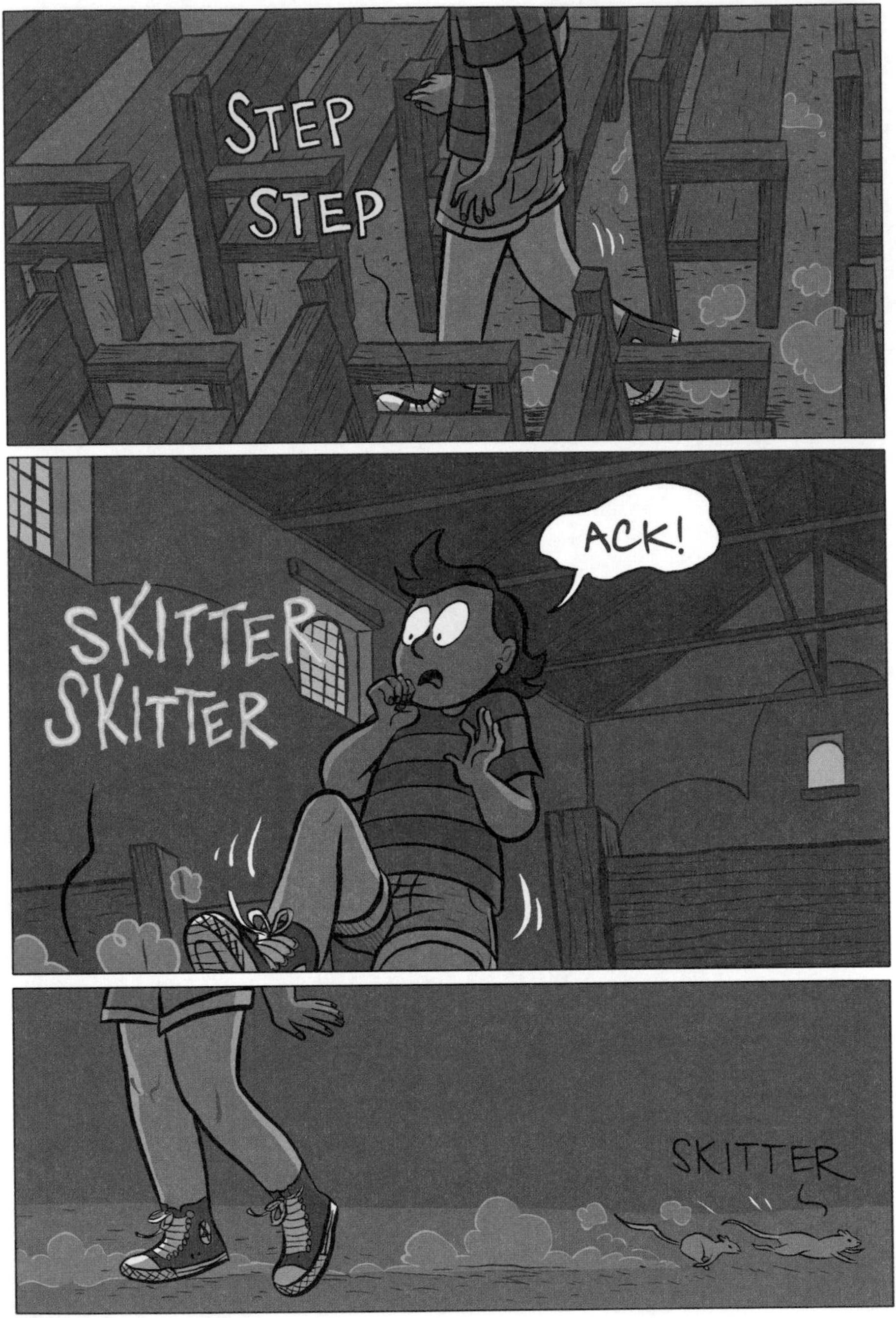
STEP
STEP
SKITTER
SKITTER
ACK!
SKITTER

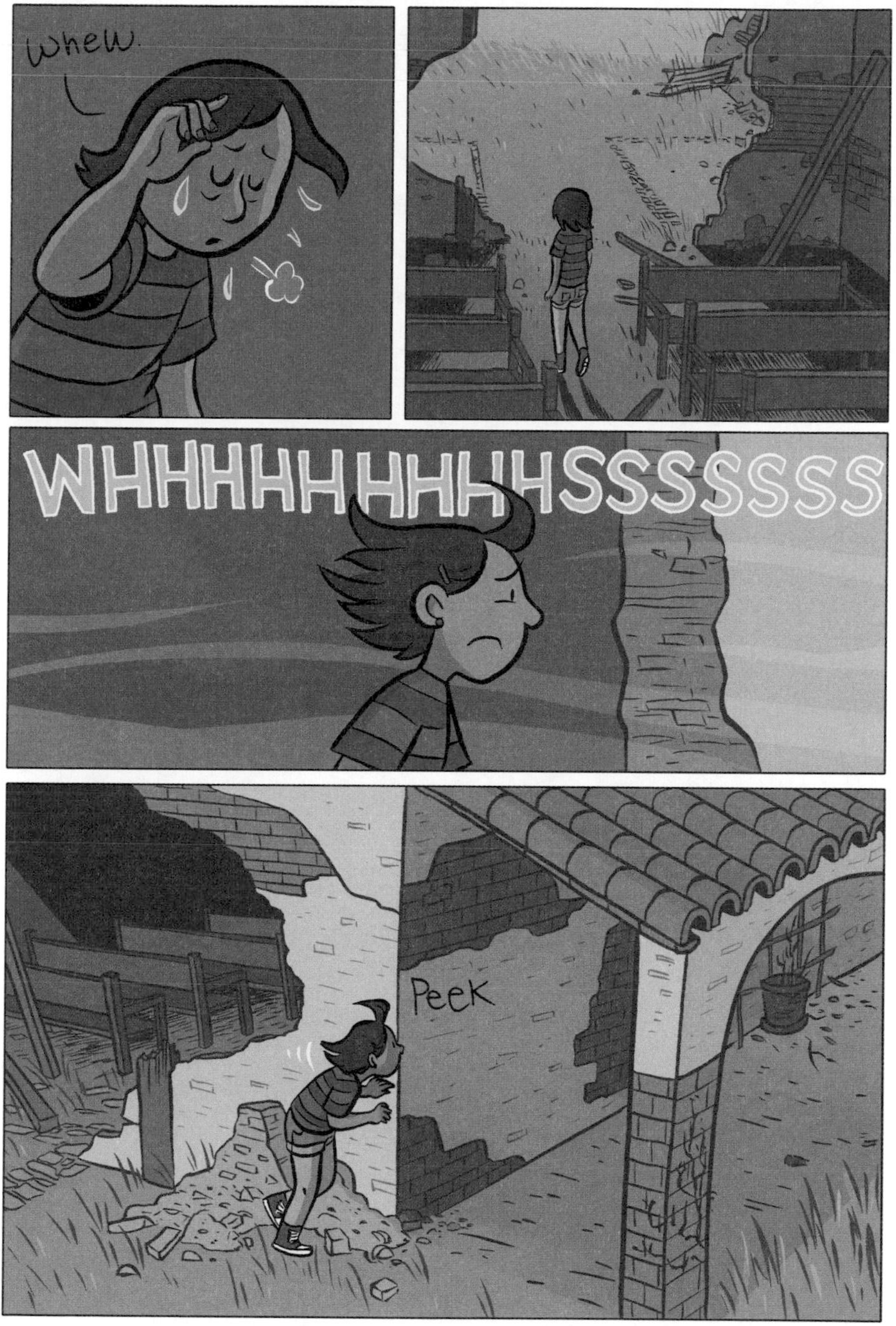
Whew.
WHHHHHHHHHSSSSSSS
Peek

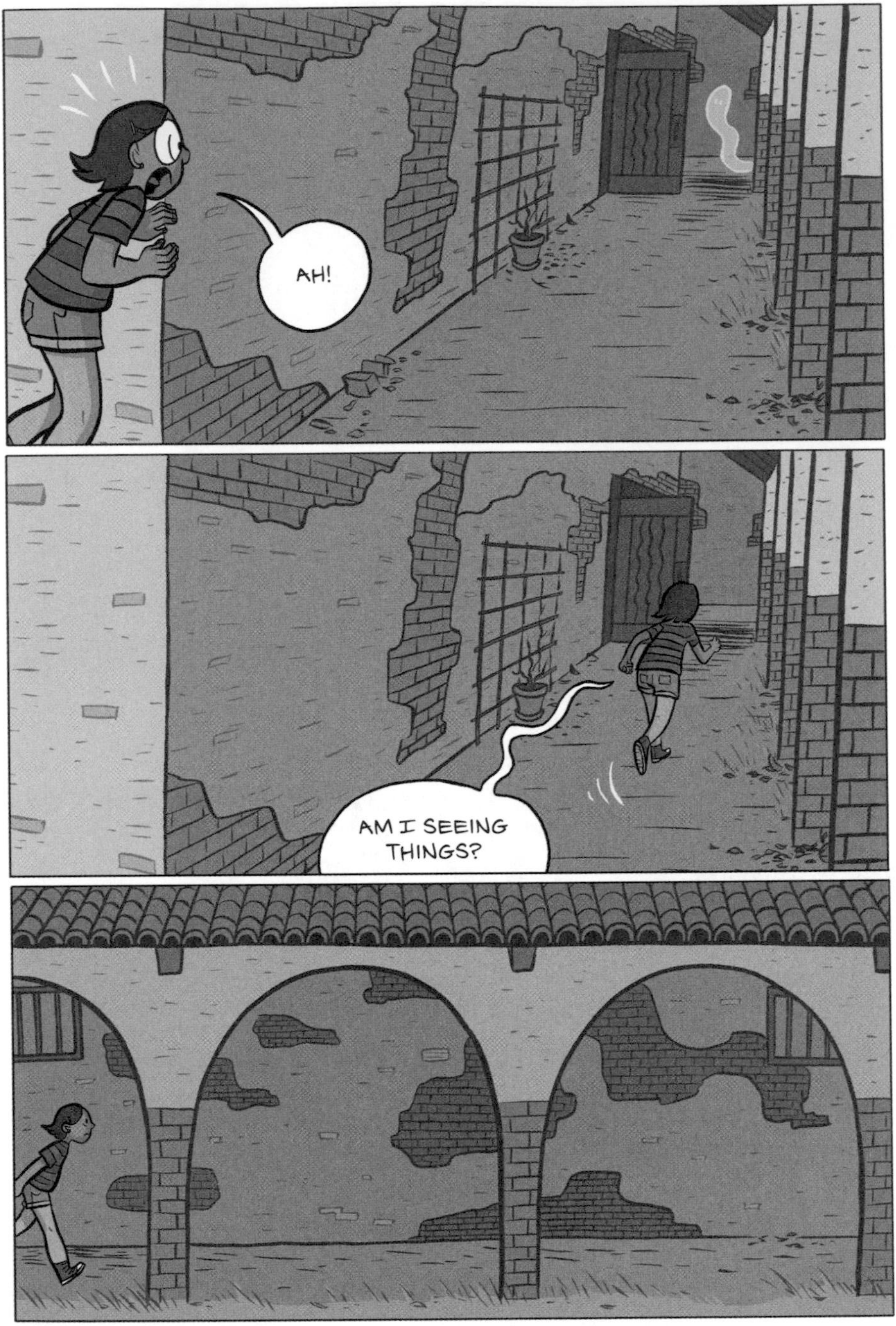
AH!
AM I SEEING THINGS?

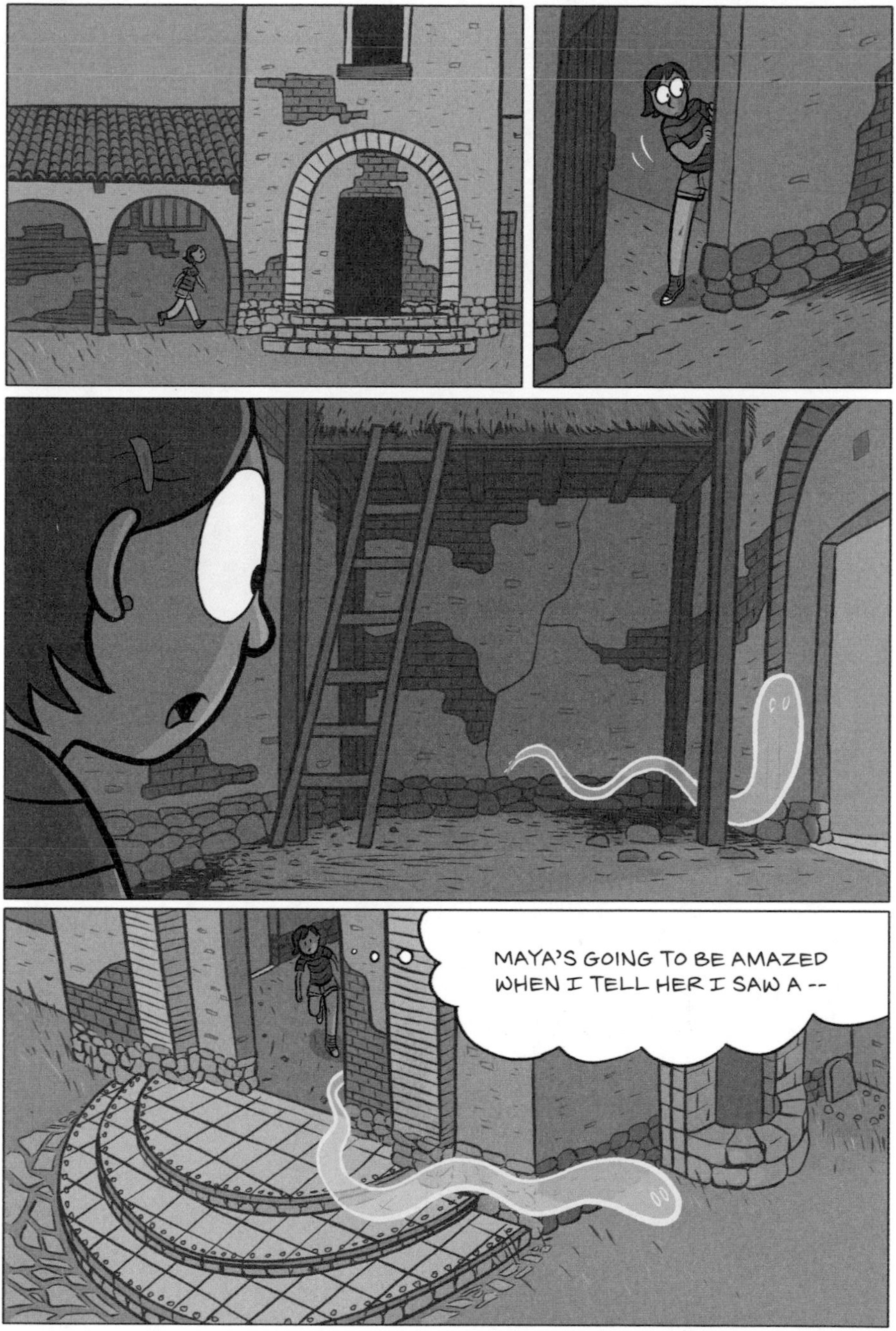
MAYA'S GOING TO BE AMAZED WHEN I TELL HER I SAW A --

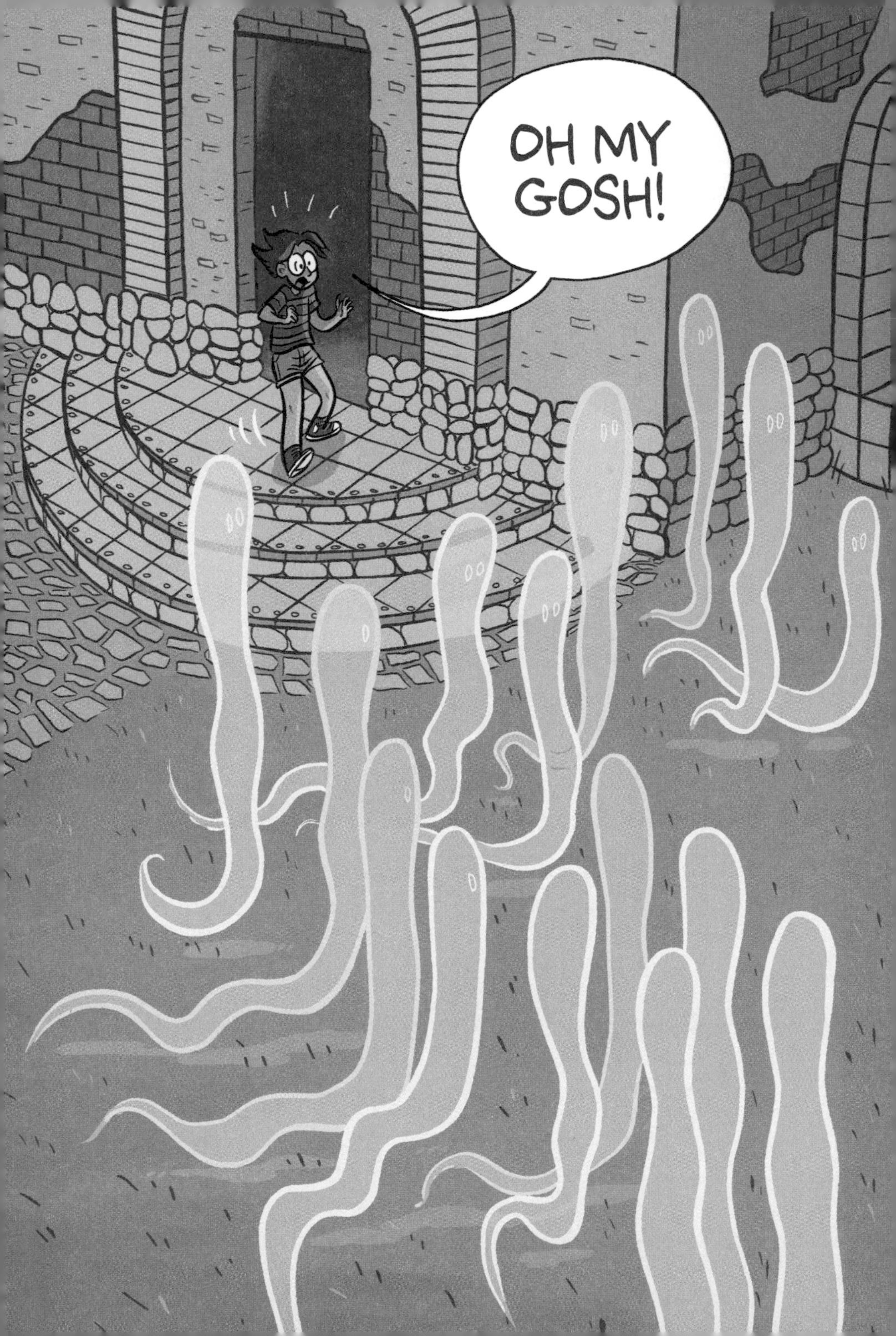
OH MY GOSH!

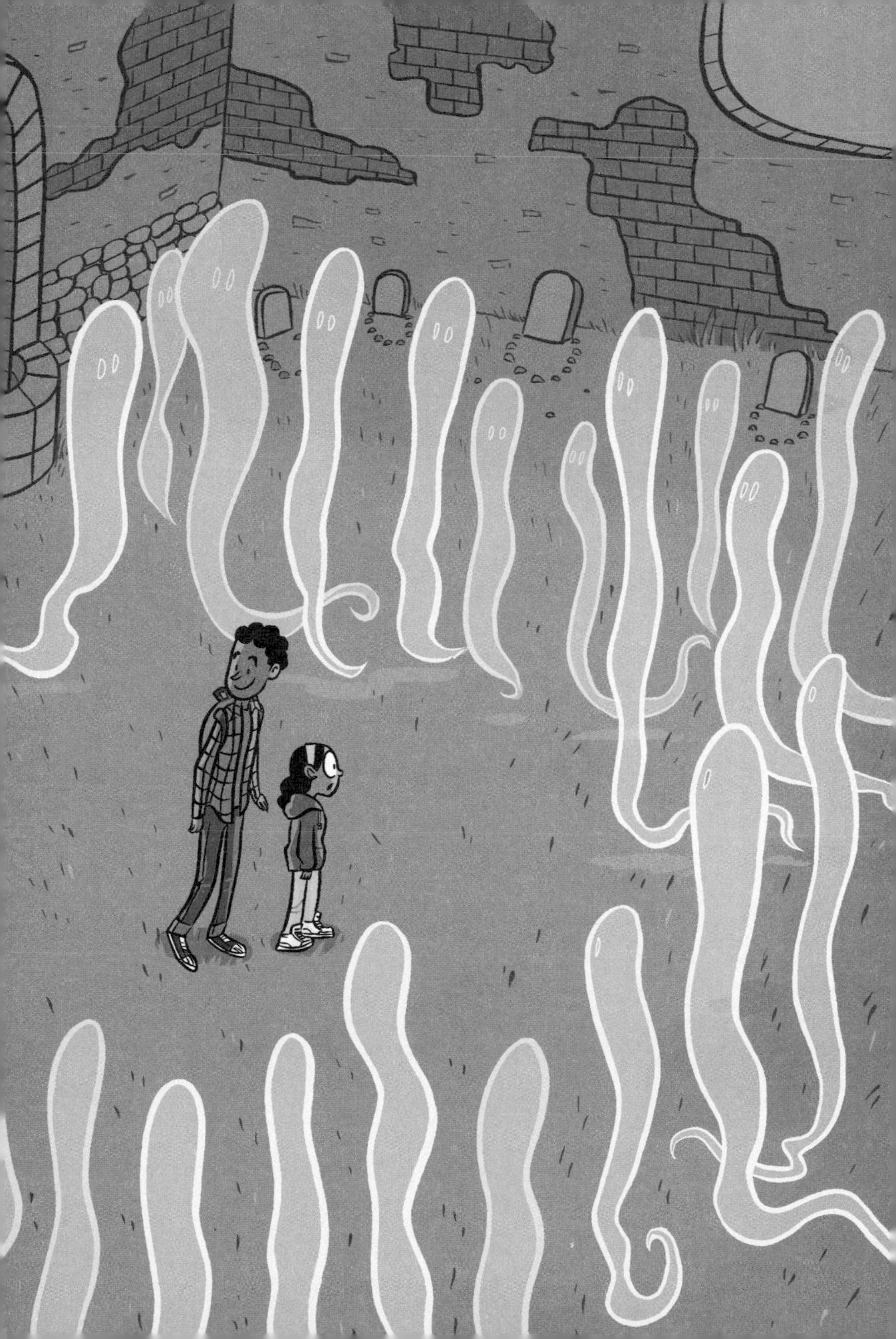

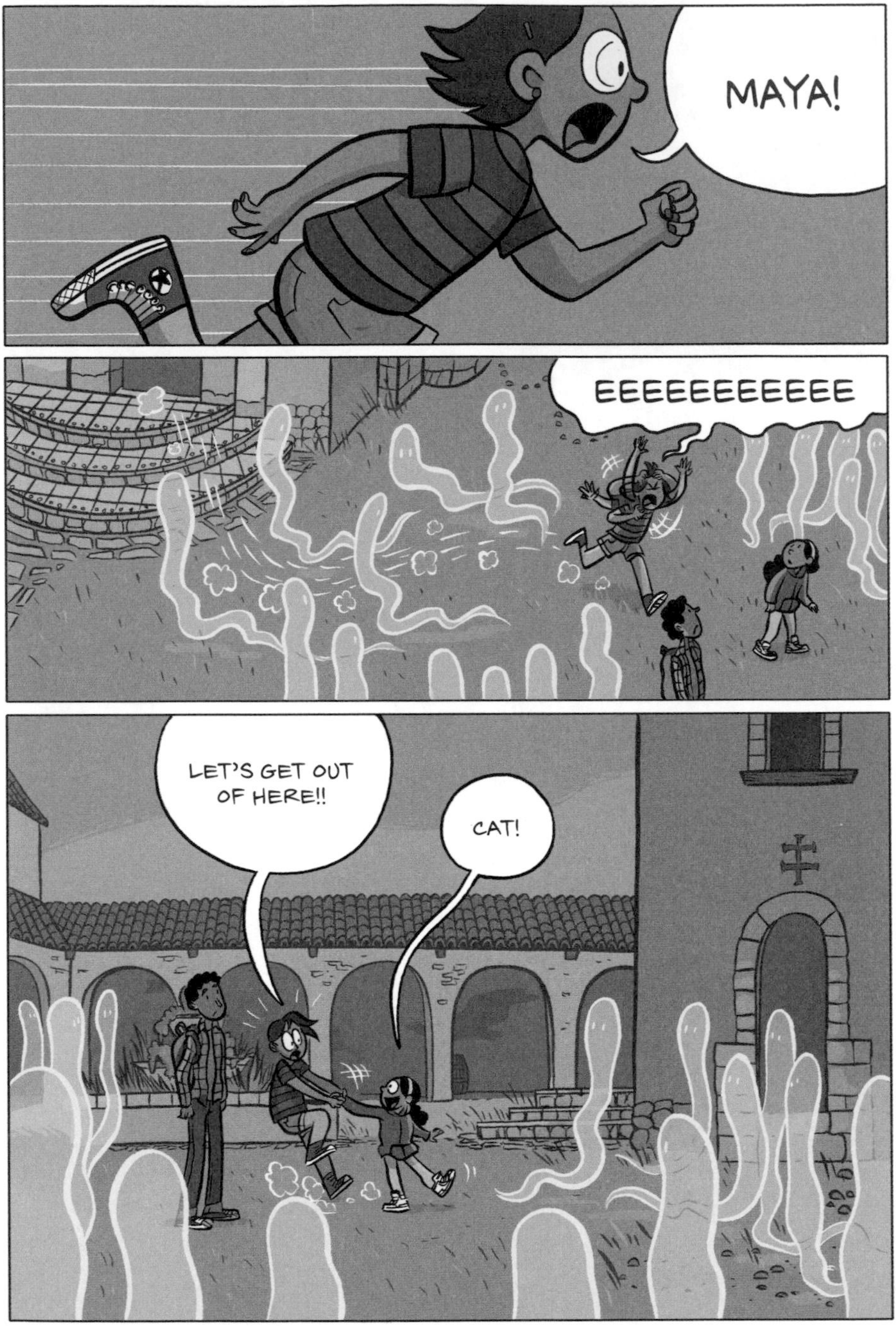
MAYA!
EEEEEEEEEEEE
LET'S GET OUT OF HERE!!
CAT!

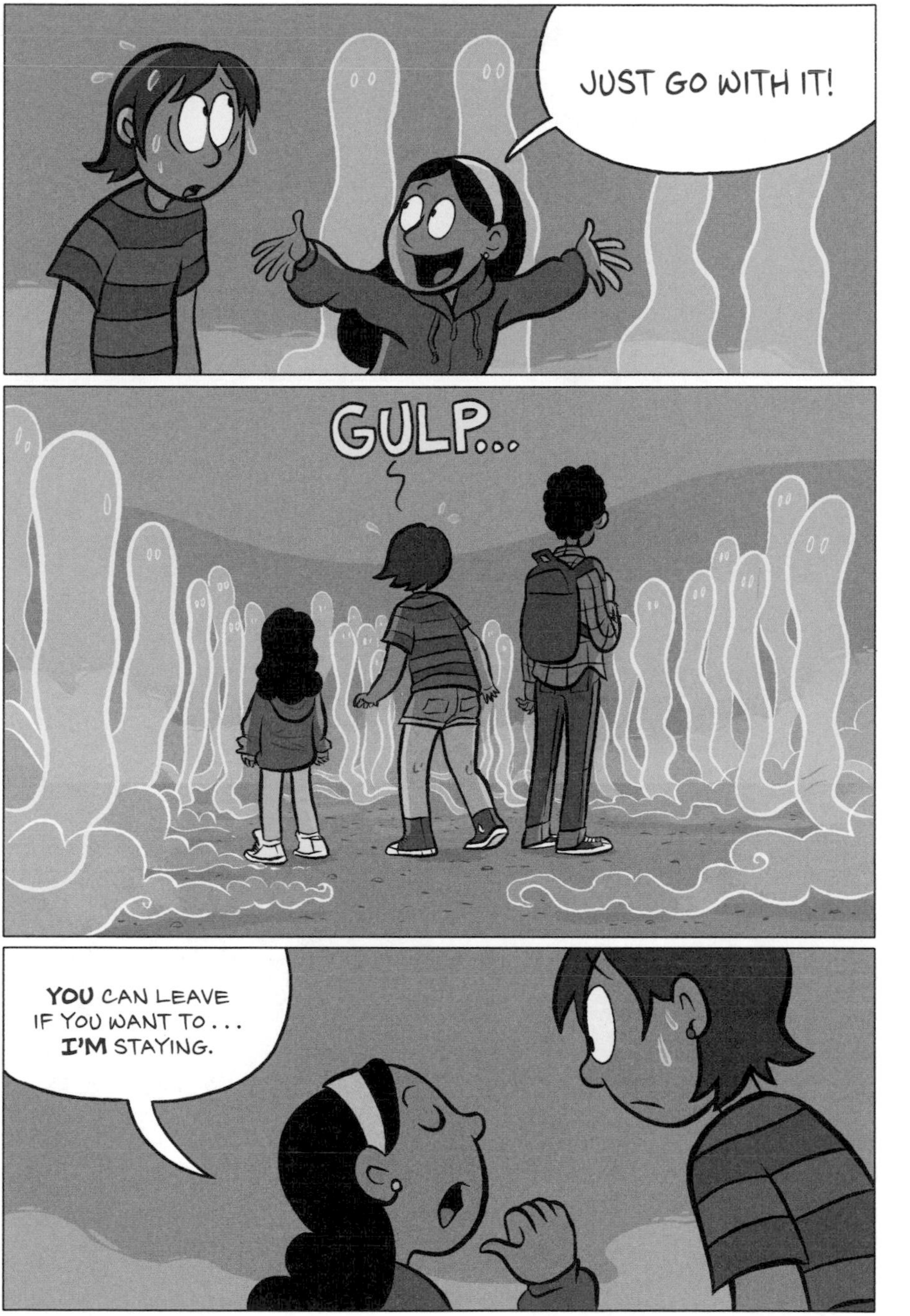
JUST GO WITH IT!
GULP...
YOU CAN LEAVE IF YOU WANT TO . . . I'M STAYING.

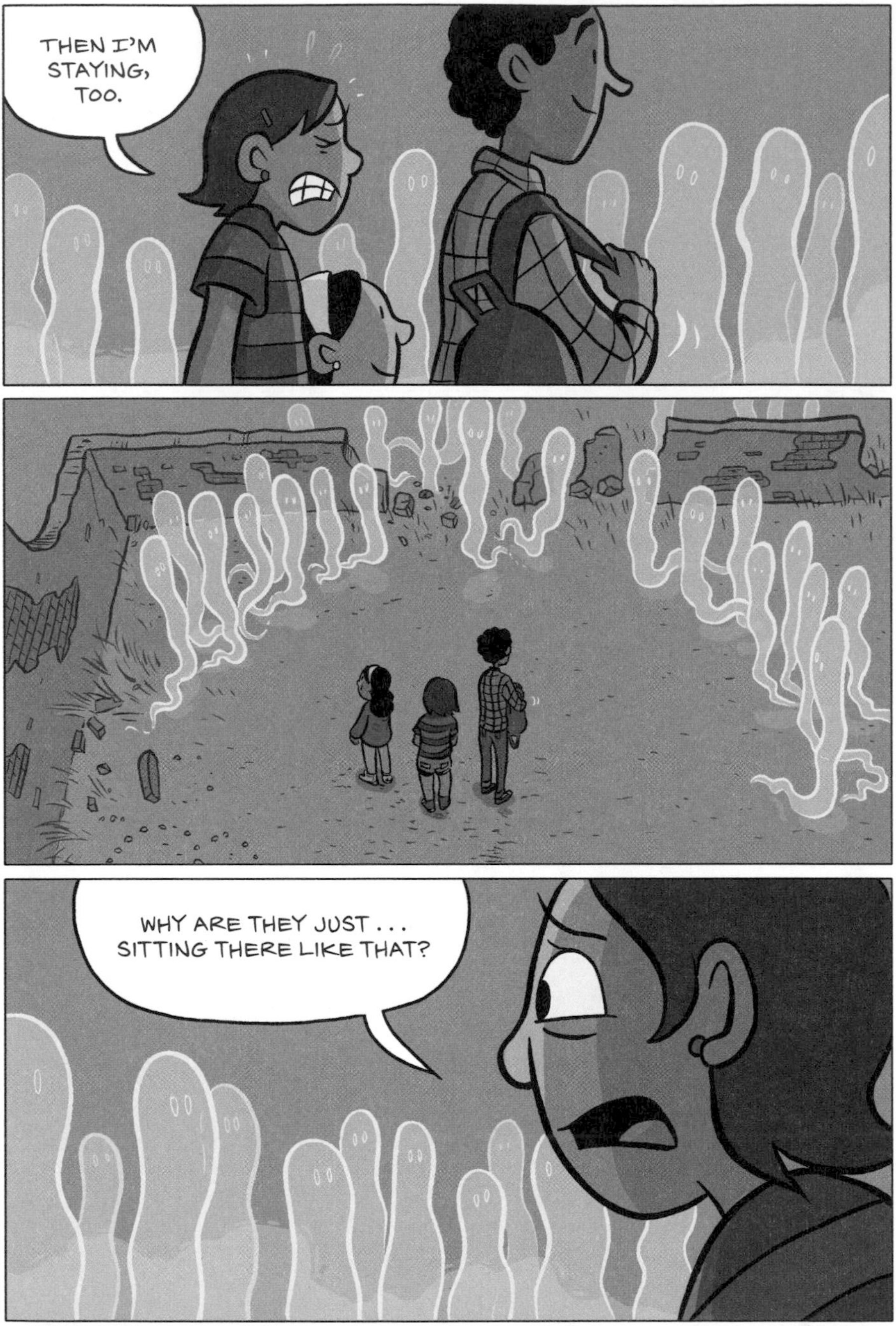
THEN I'M STAYING, TOO.
WHY ARE THEY JUST . . . SITTING THERE LIKE THAT?

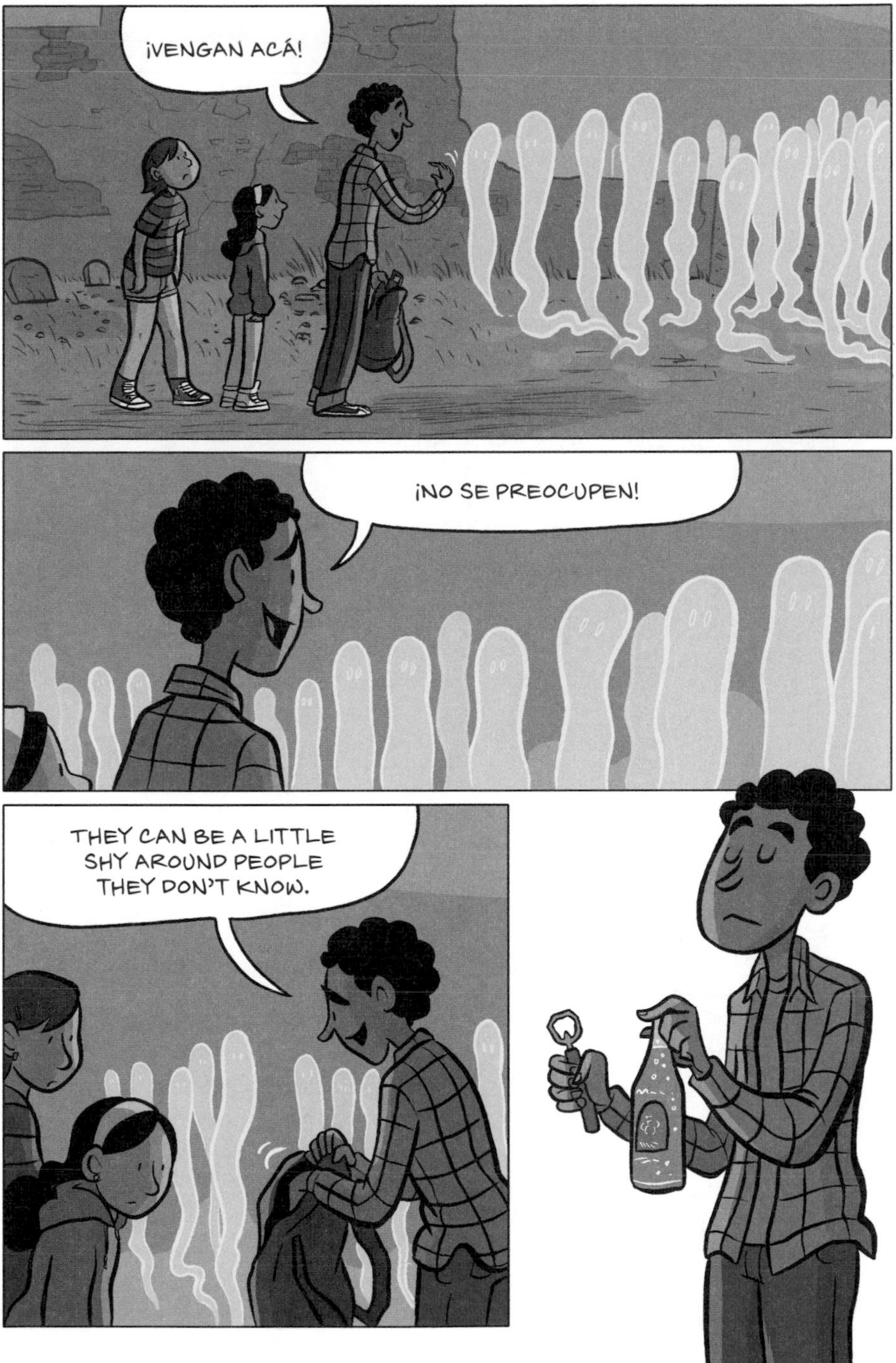
¡VENGAN ACÁ!
¡NO SE PREOCUPEN!
THEY CAN BE A LITTLE SHY AROUND PEOPLE THEY DON'T KNOW.

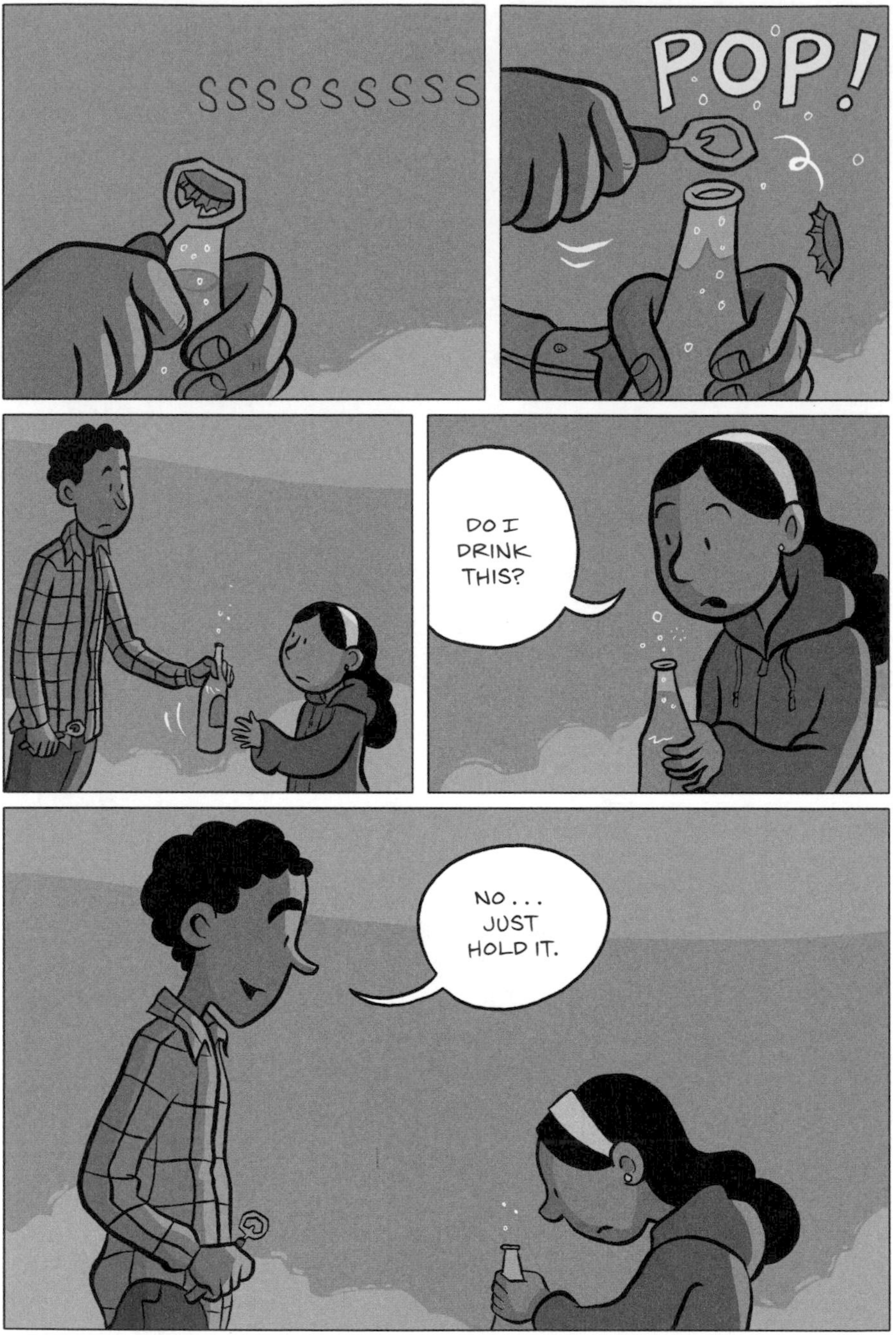
SSSSSSSSS
POP!
DO I DRINK THIS?
NO . . . JUST HOLD IT.

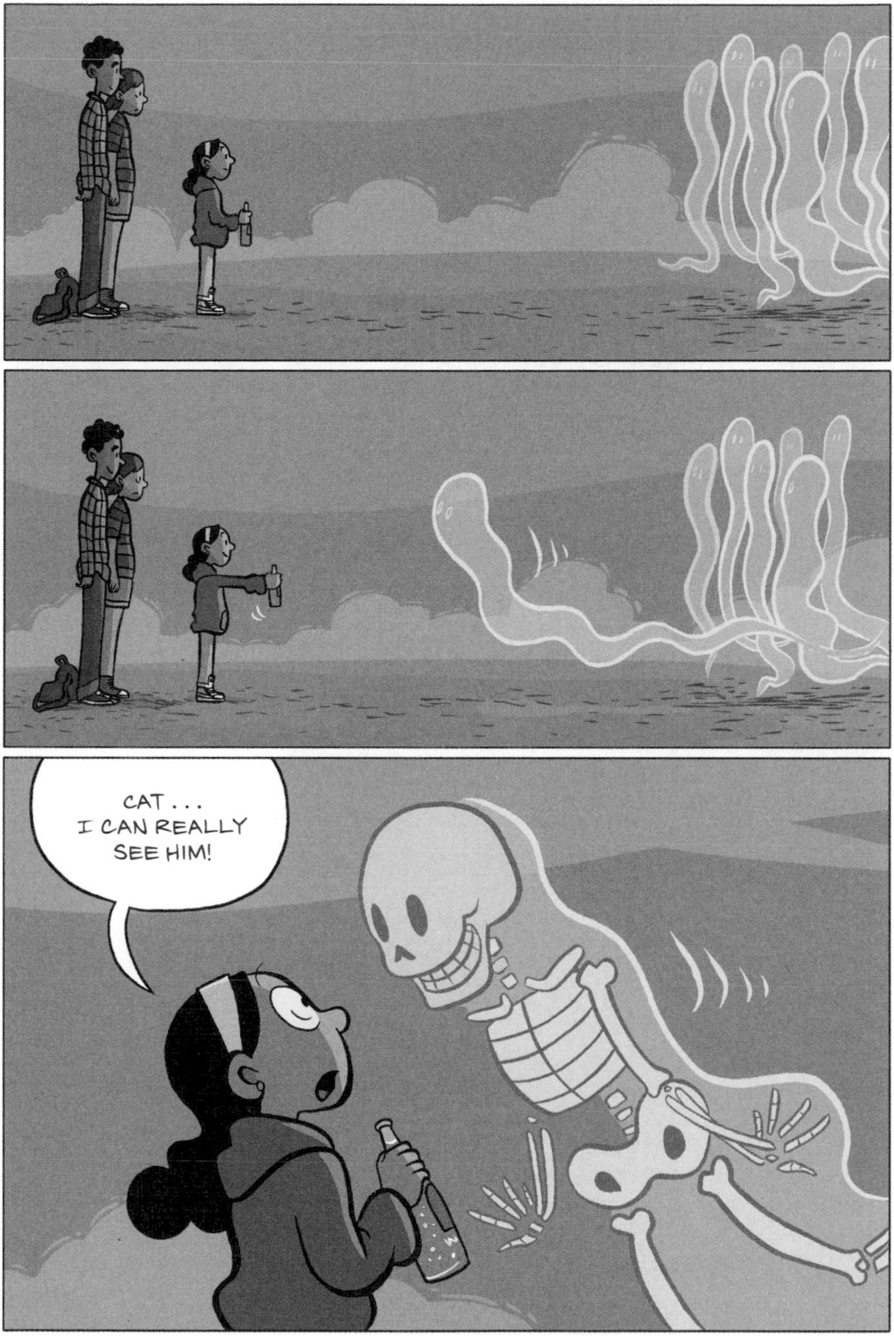
CAT . . .
I CAN REALLY
SEE HIM!

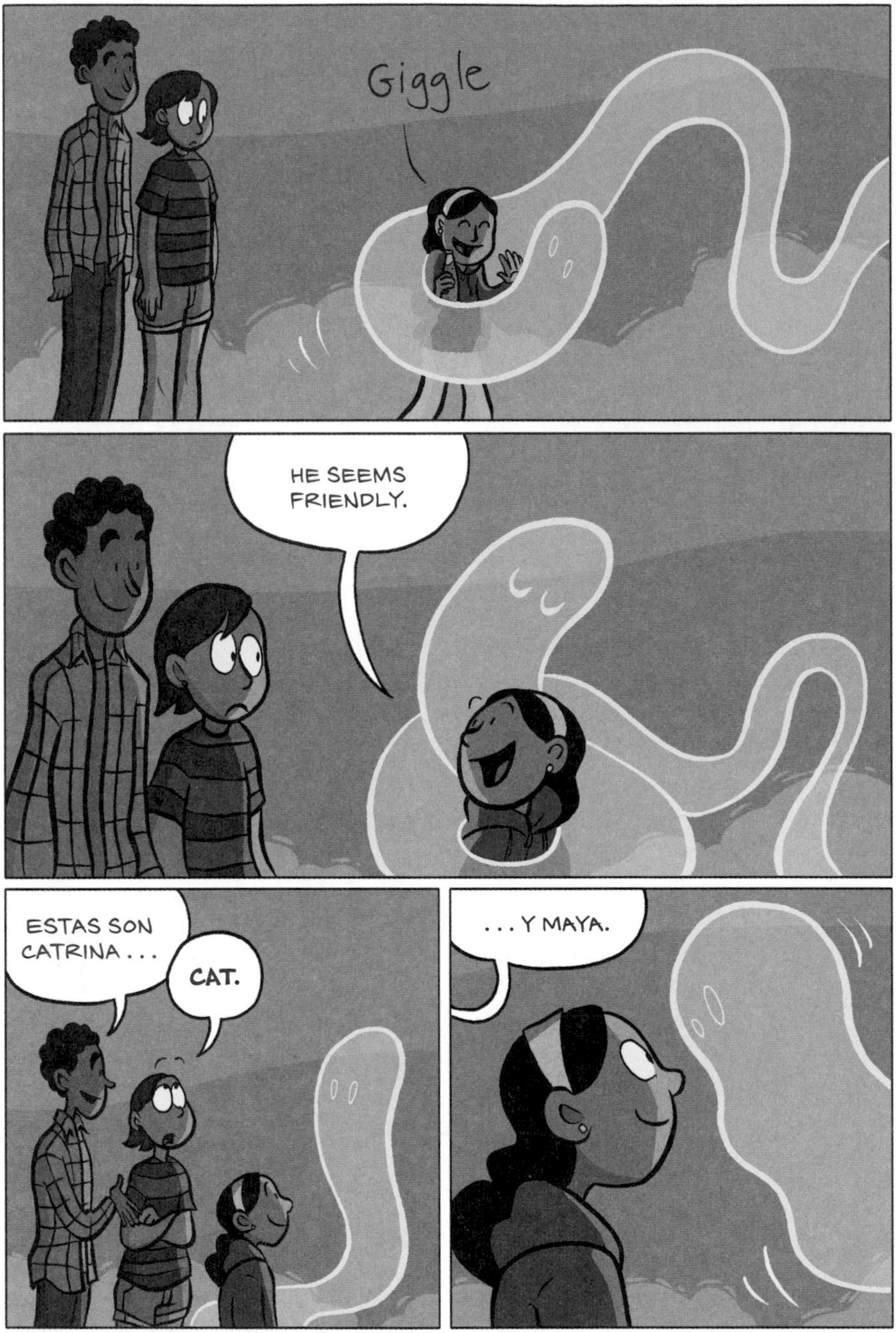
Giggle
HE SEEMS FRIENDLY.
ESTAS SON CATRINA . . .
CAT.
. . . Y MAYA.

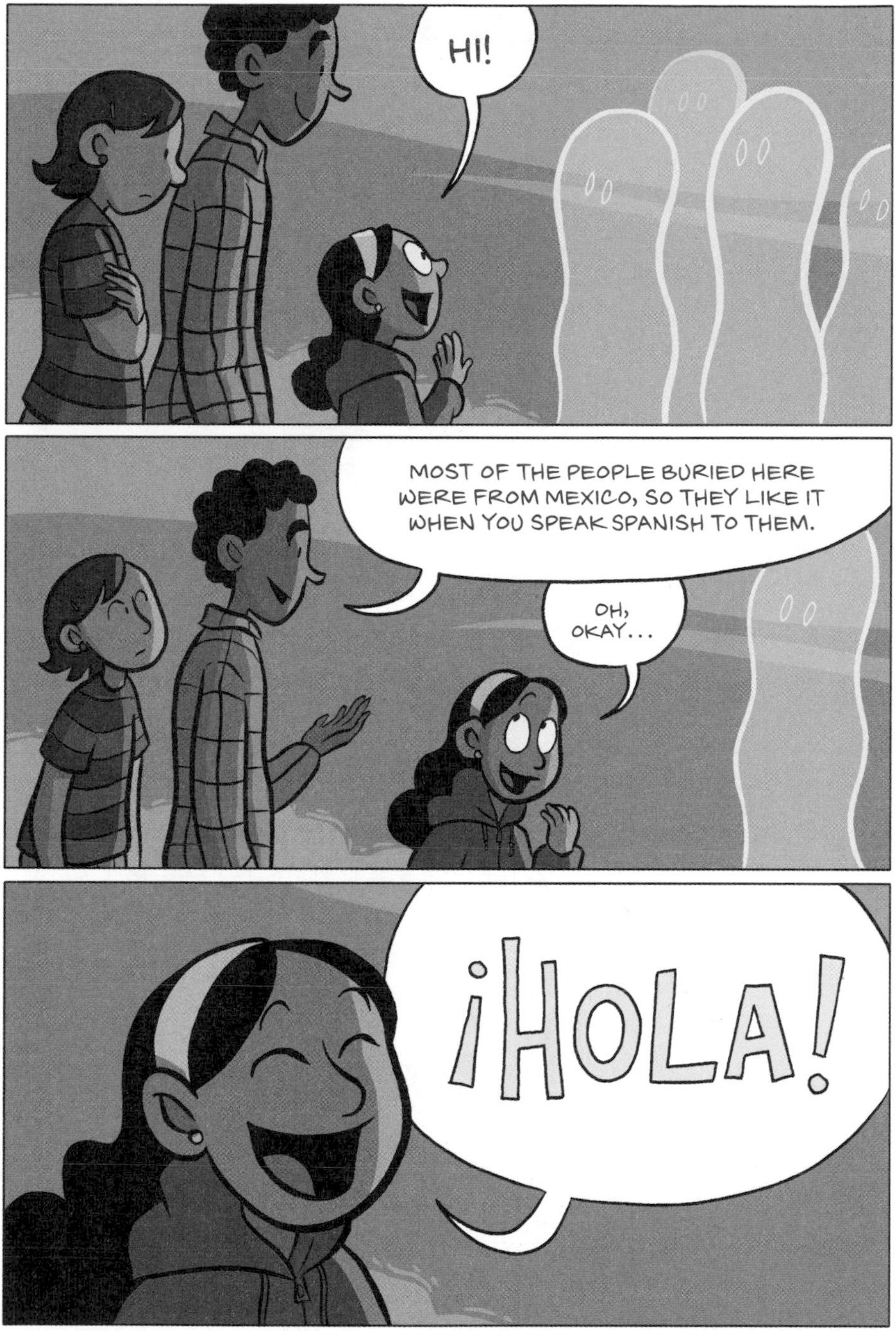
HI!
MOST OF THE PEOPLE BURIED HERE WERE FROM MEXICO, SO THEY LIKE IT WHEN YOU SPEAK SPANISH TO THEM.
OH, OKAY...
¡HOLA!

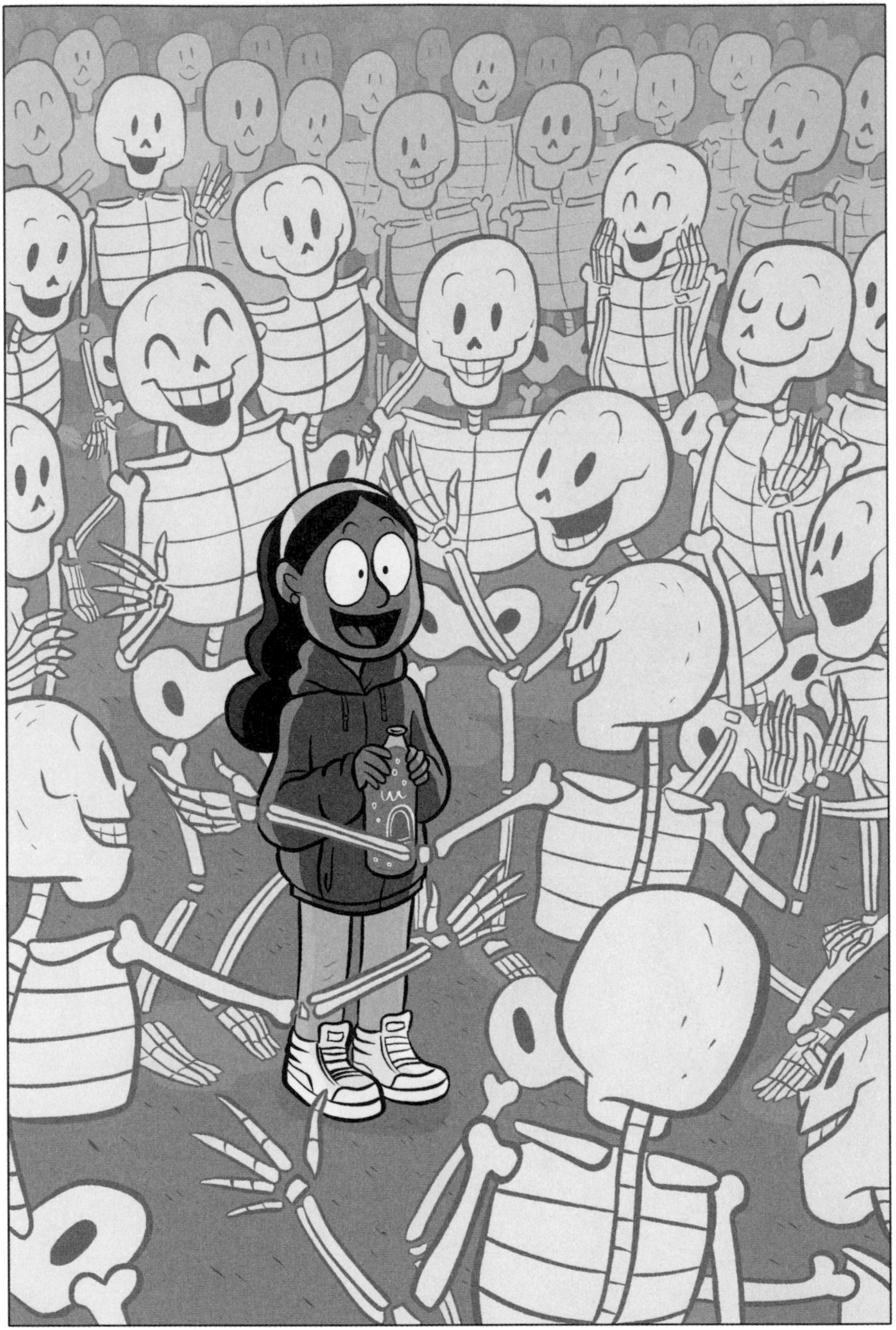

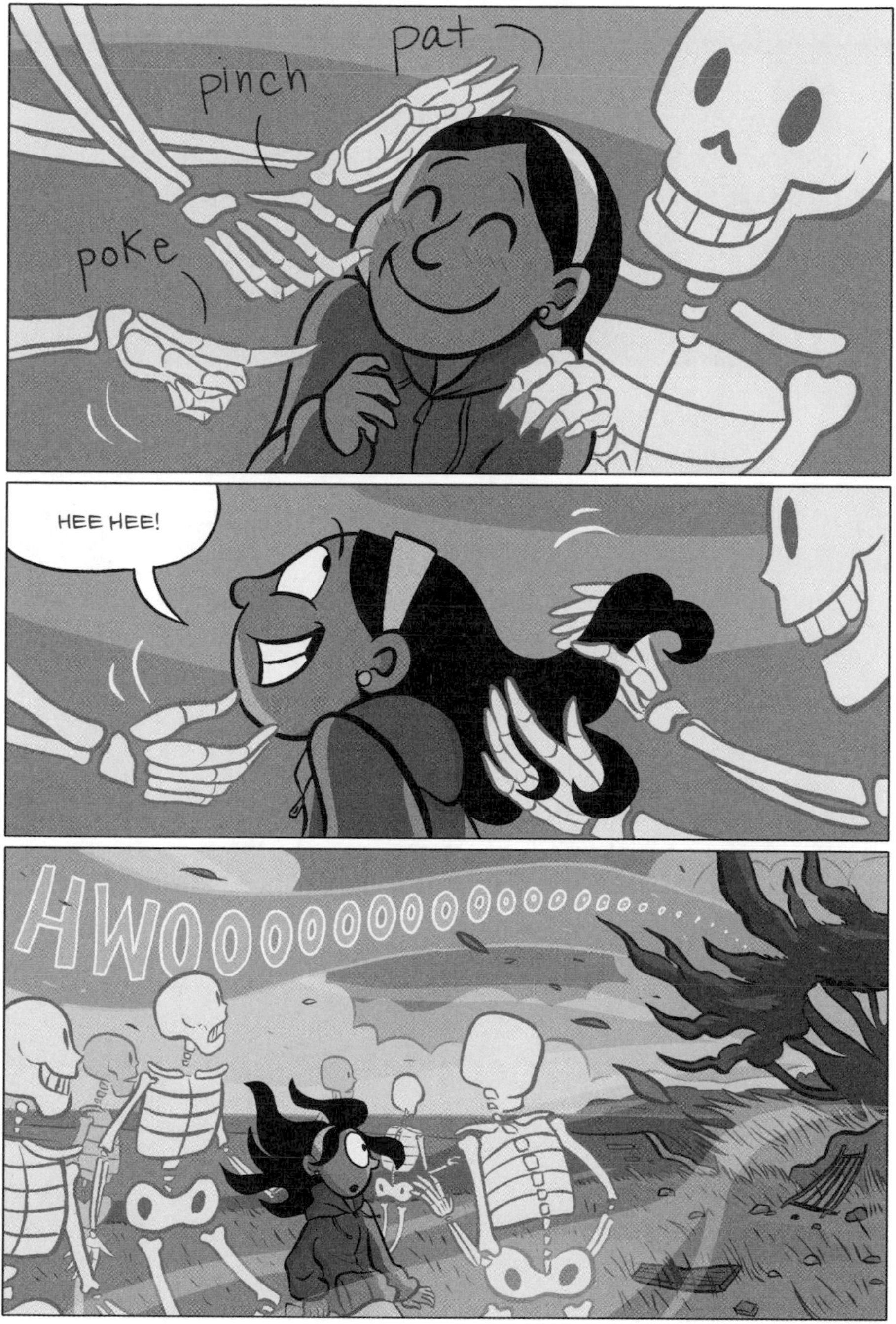
pat
pinch
poke
HEE HEE!
HWOOOOOOOOOOOOOOO...

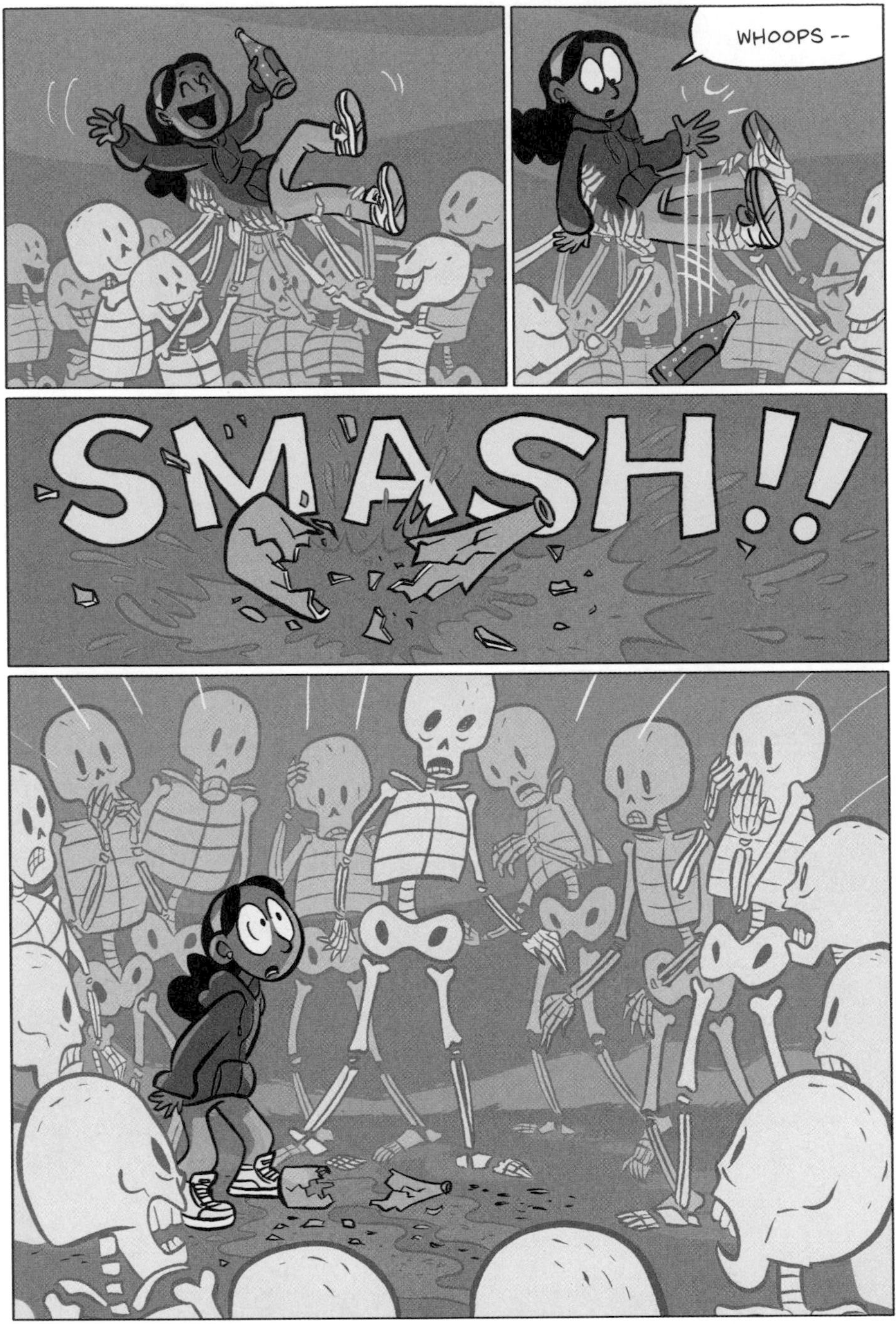
WHOOPS --
SMASH!!

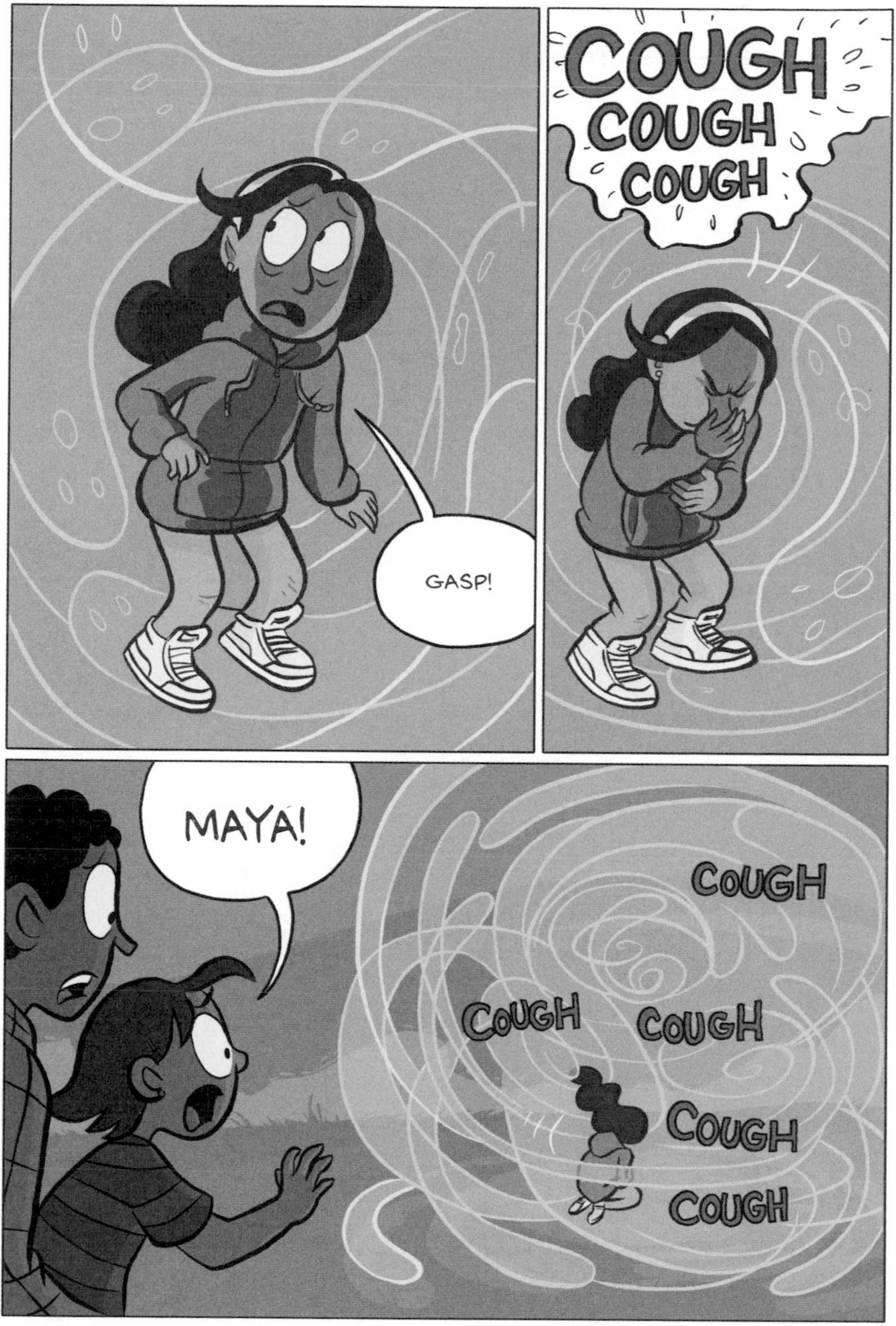
GASP!
COUGH
COUGH
COUGH
MAYA!
COUGH
COUGH
COUGH
COUGH
COUGH

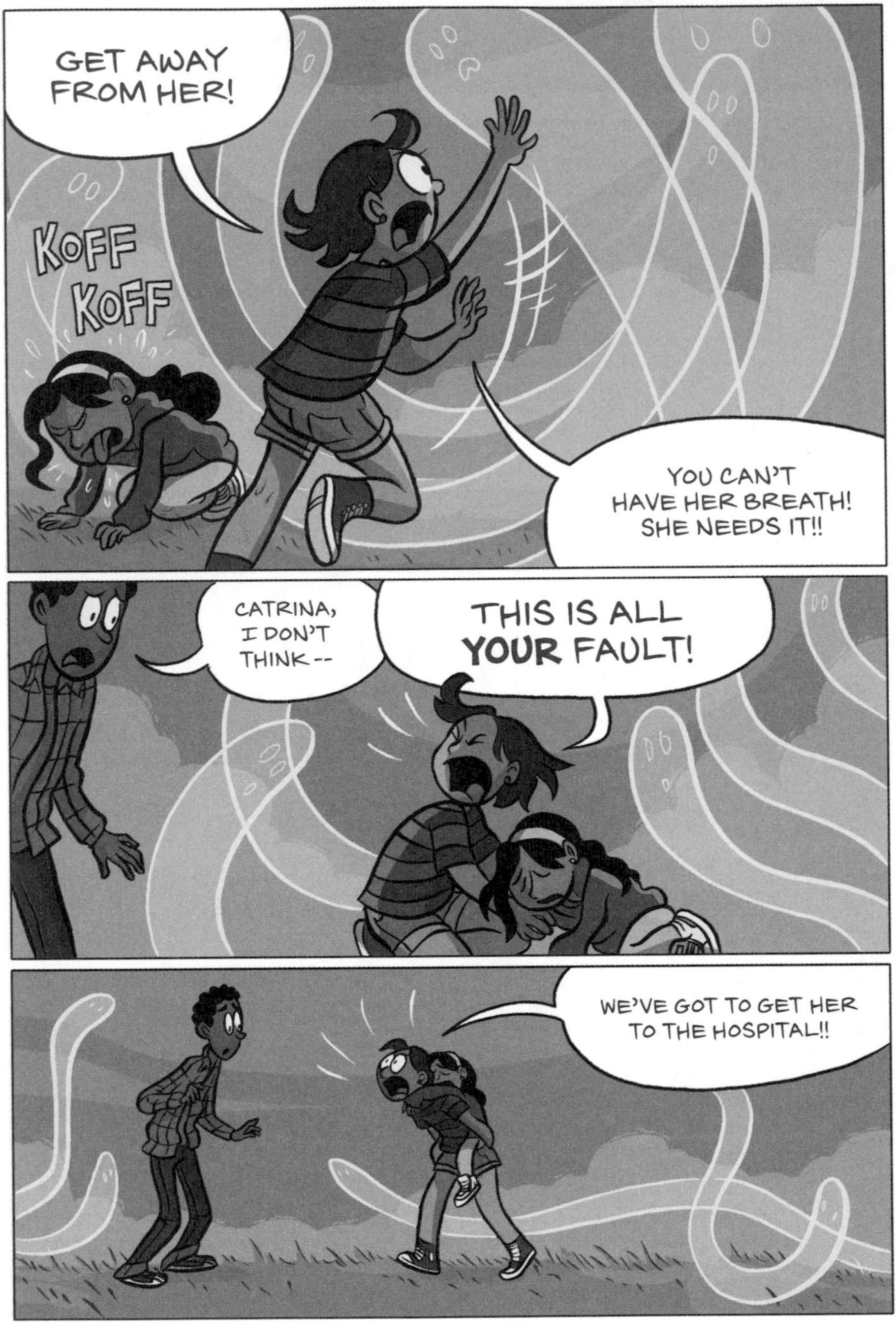
GET AWAY FROM HER!
KOFF KOFF
YOU CAN'T HAVE HER BREATH! SHE NEEDS IT!!
CATRINA, I DON'T THINK--
THIS IS ALL **YOUR** FAULT!
WE'VE GOT TO GET HER TO THE HOSPITAL!!

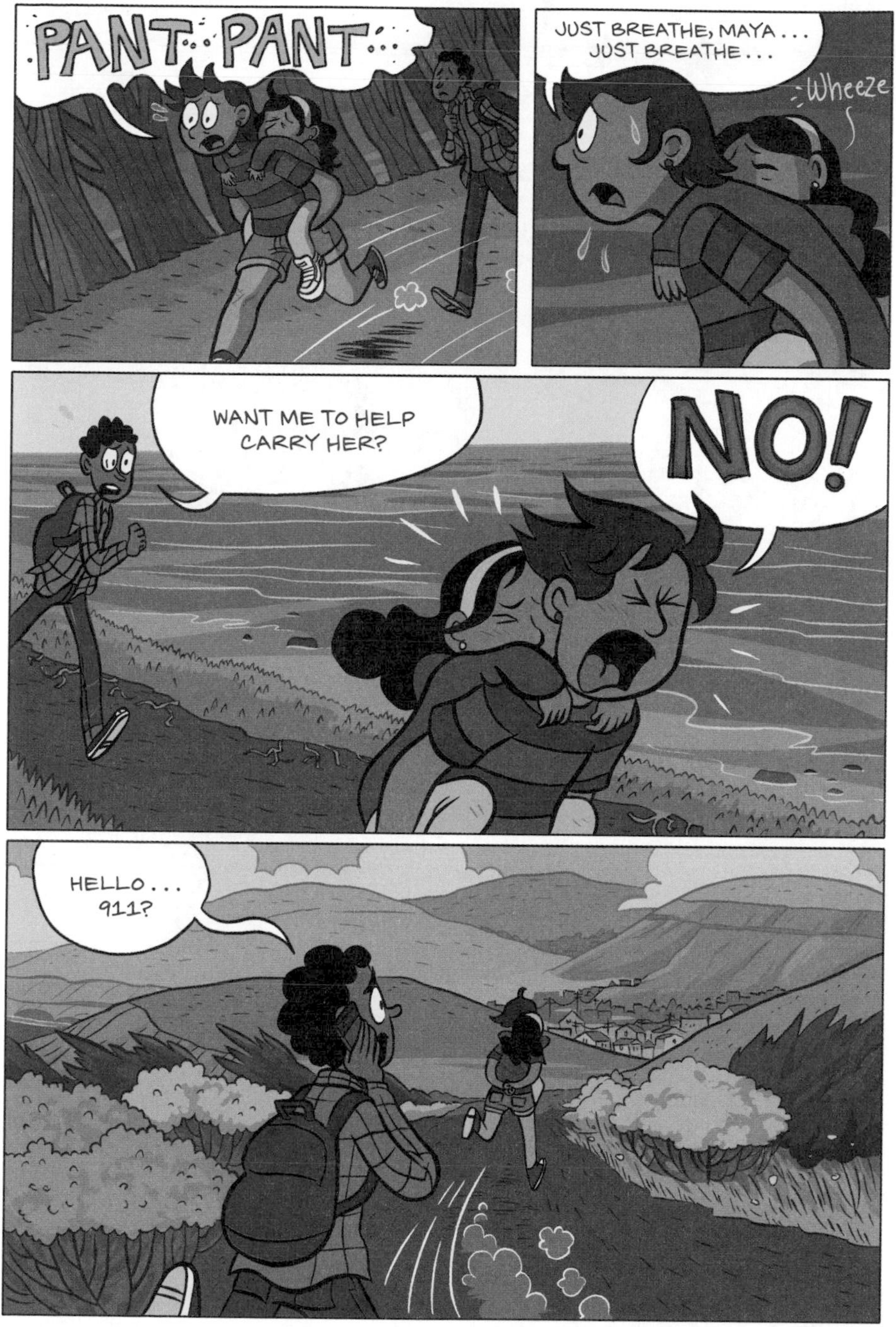
PANT PANT
JUST BREATHE, MAYA . . . JUST BREATHE . . .
Wheeze
WANT ME TO HELP CARRY HER?
NO!
HELLO . . . 911?

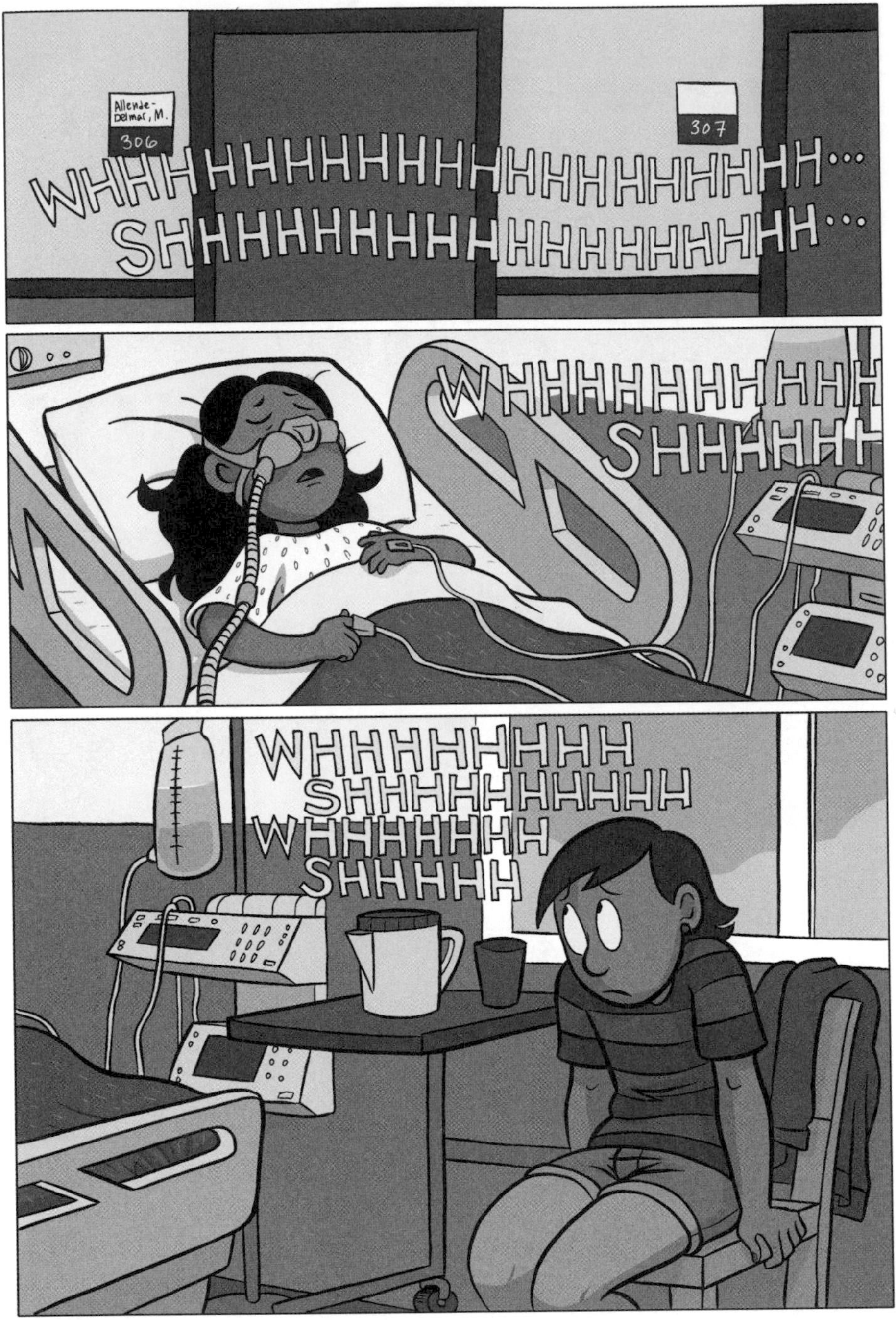
Allende-Delmar, M.
306
307
WHHHHHHHHHHHHHHHHHHHH...
SHHHHHHHHHHHHHHHHHH...
WHHHHHHHHHHH
SHHHHHH
WHHHHHHHHHH
SHHHHHHHHHHH
WHHHHHHHH
SHHHHHH

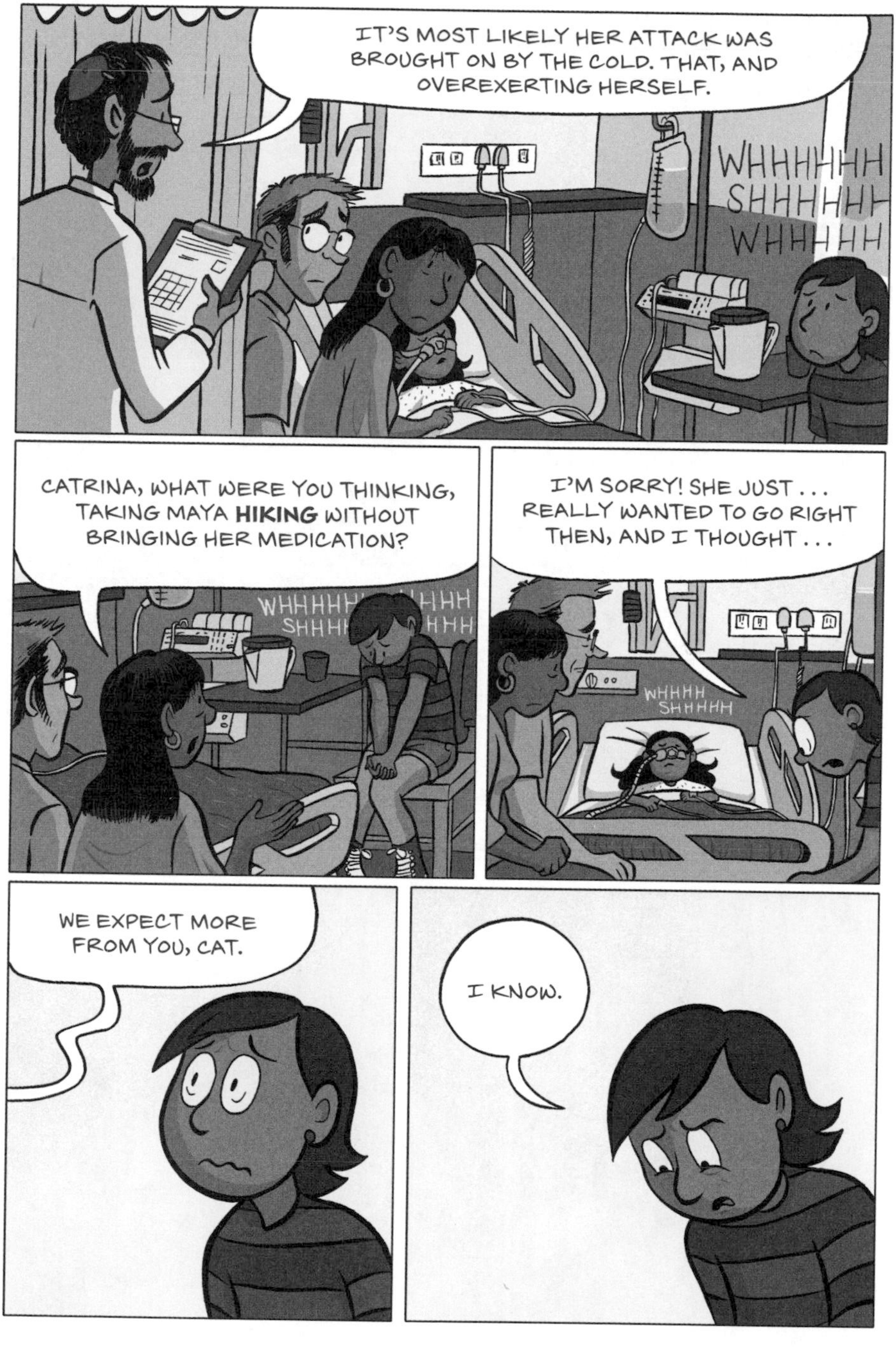
IT'S MOST LIKELY HER ATTACK WAS BROUGHT ON BY THE COLD. THAT, AND OVEREXERTING HERSELF.
WHHHHHH SHHHHHH WHHHHHH
CATRINA, WHAT WERE YOU THINKING, TAKING MAYA **HIKING** WITHOUT BRINGING HER MEDICATION?
I'M SORRY! SHE JUST . . . REALLY WANTED TO GO RIGHT THEN, AND I THOUGHT . . .
WHHHH SHHHHH
WE EXPECT MORE FROM YOU, CAT.
I KNOW.

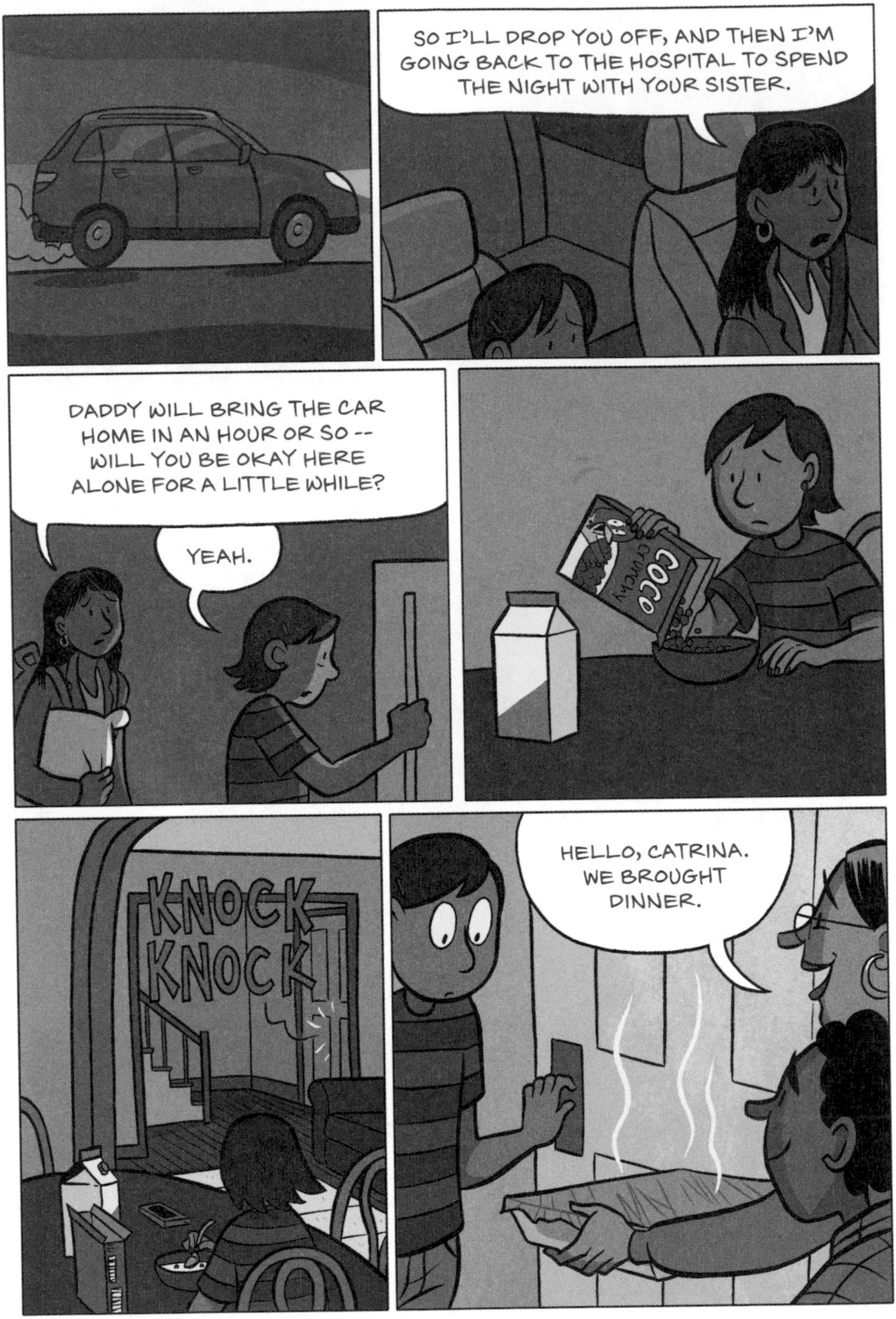
SO I'LL DROP YOU OFF, AND THEN I'M GOING BACK TO THE HOSPITAL TO SPEND THE NIGHT WITH YOUR SISTER.
DADDY WILL BRING THE CAR HOME IN AN HOUR OR SO -- WILL YOU BE OKAY HERE ALONE FOR A LITTLE WHILE?
YEAH.
COCO crunchy
KNOCK KNOCK
HELLO, CATRINA. WE BROUGHT DINNER.

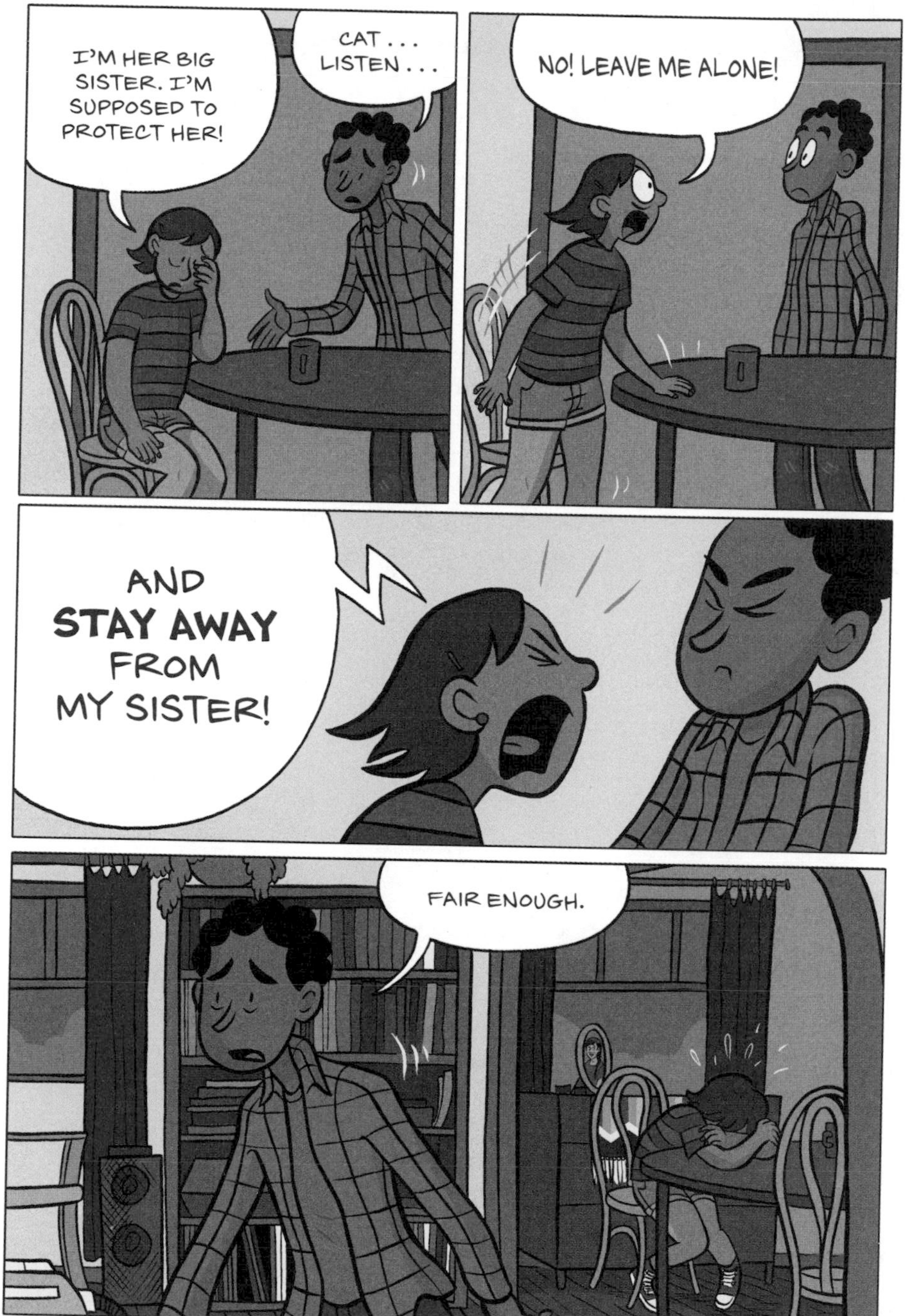
I'M HER BIG SISTER. I'M SUPPOSED TO PROTECT HER!
CAT . . . LISTEN . . .
NO! LEAVE ME ALONE!
AND **STAY AWAY** FROM MY SISTER!
FAIR ENOUGH.

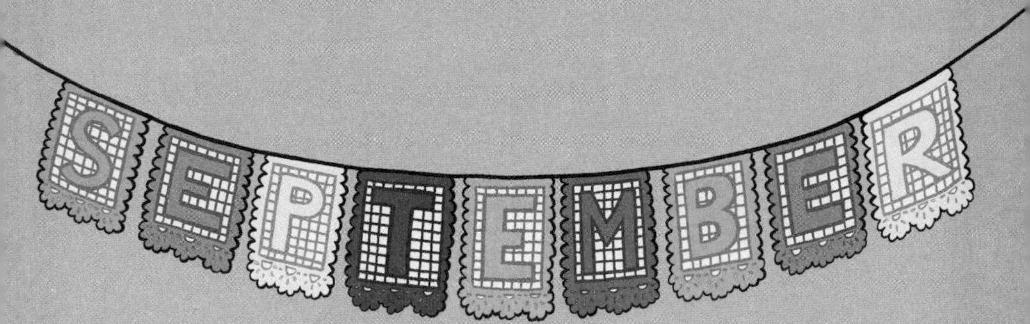
SEPTEMBER

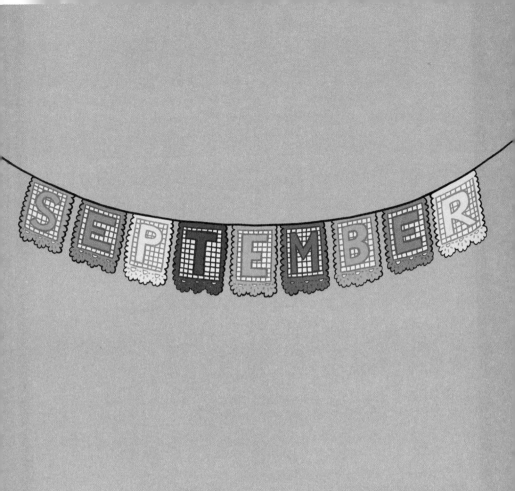

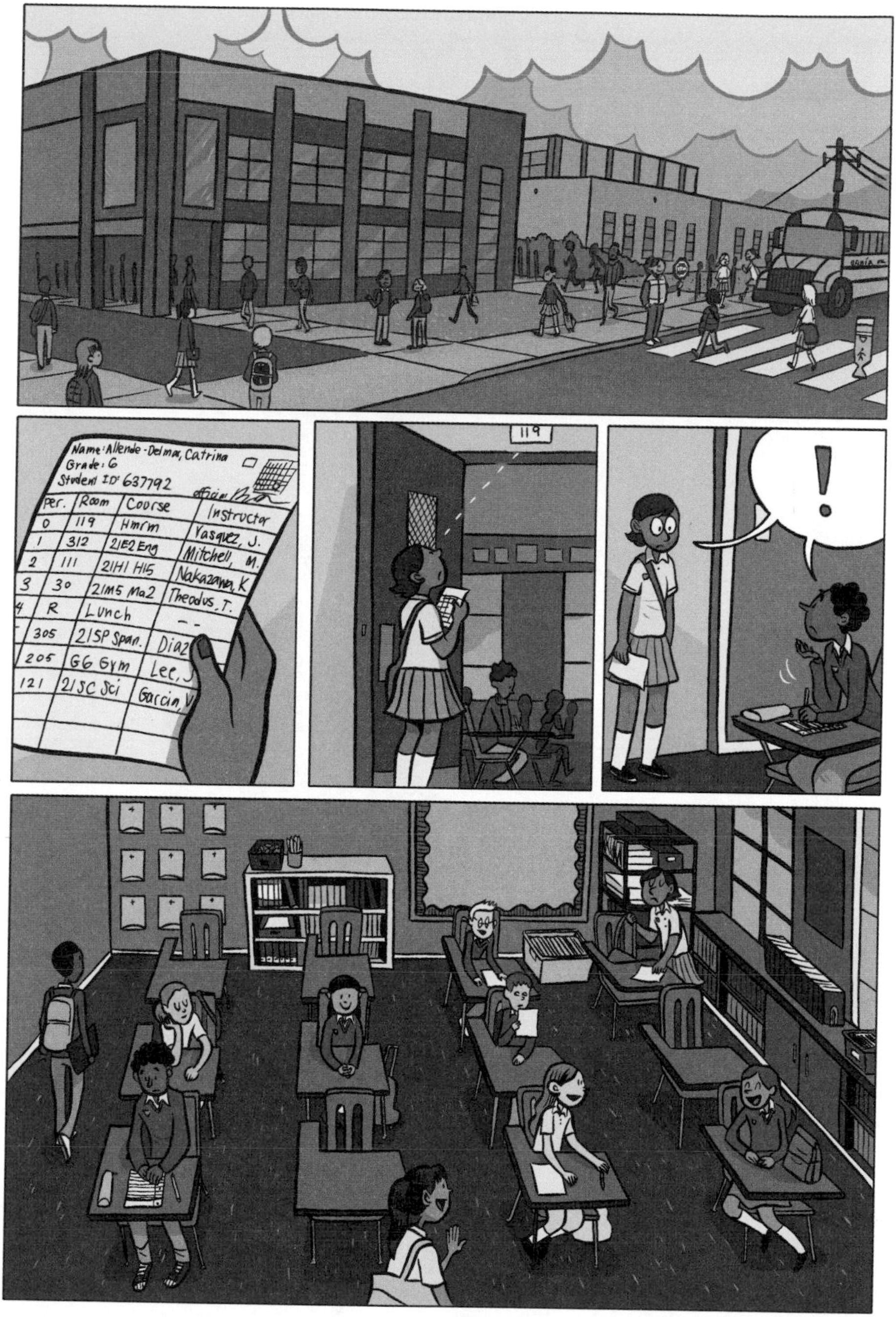
Name: Allende-Delmar, Catrina
Grade: 6
Student ID: 637792
Per. Room Course Instructor
0 119 Hmrm
1 312 21E2 Eng Vasquez, J.
2 111 21H1 HIS Mitchell, M.
3 30 21M5 Ma2 Nakazawa, K
4 R Lunch Theodus, T.
305 21SP Span. Diaz
205 G6 Gym Lee, J
121 21SC Sci Garcia, V
119
!

111

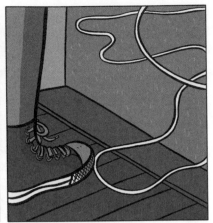

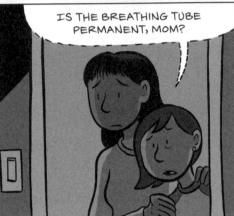

IS THE BREATHING TUBE PERMANENT, MOM?

WE'RE NOT SURE YET, SWEETIE.

YOU KNOW CYSTIC FIBROSIS IS DEGENERATIVE . . . SO, HER LUNGS WILL PROBABLY KEEP GETTING WORSE AS SHE GROWS UP. NOT BETTER.

UH-HUH.

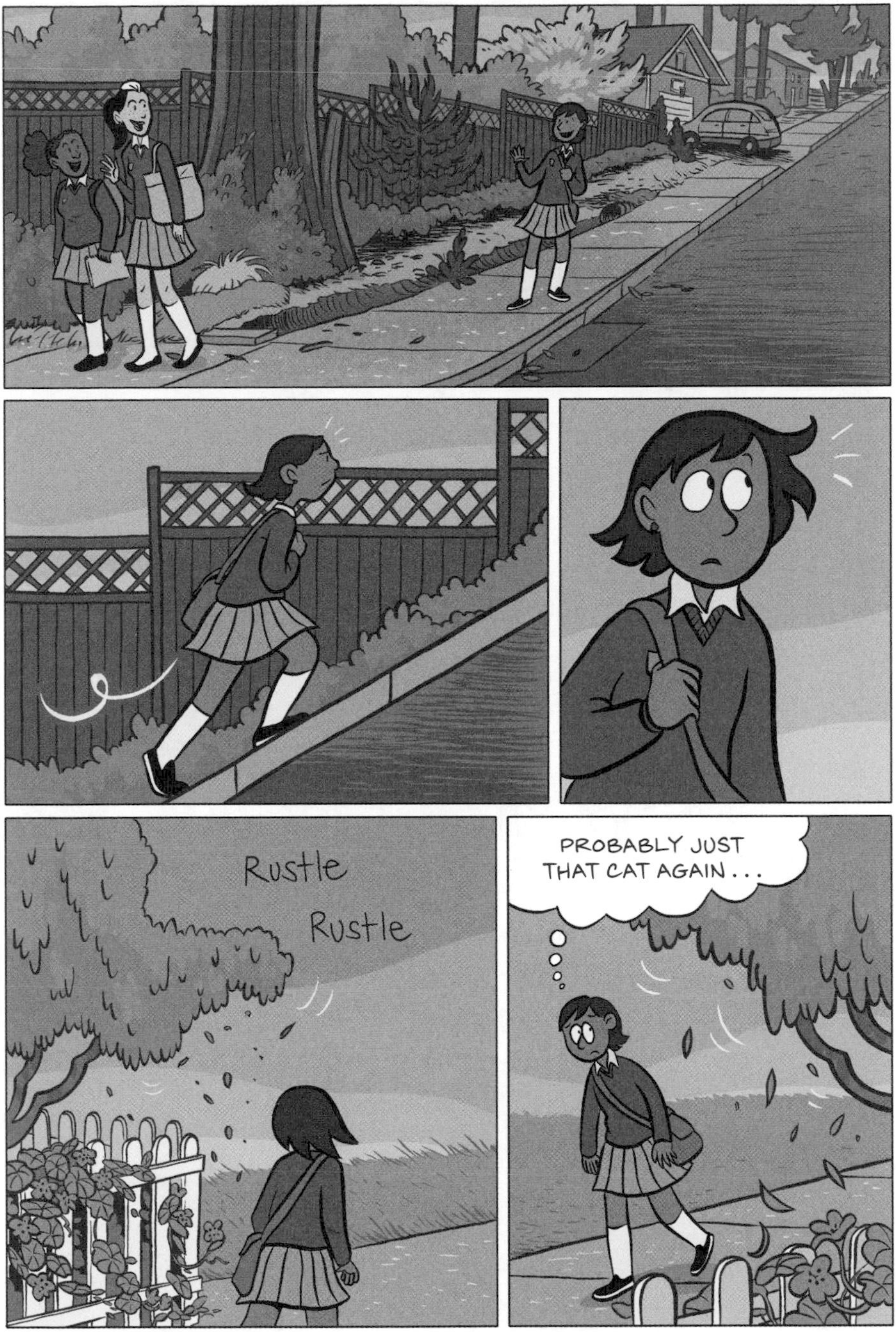
Rustle
Rustle
PROBABLY JUST THAT CAT AGAIN . . .

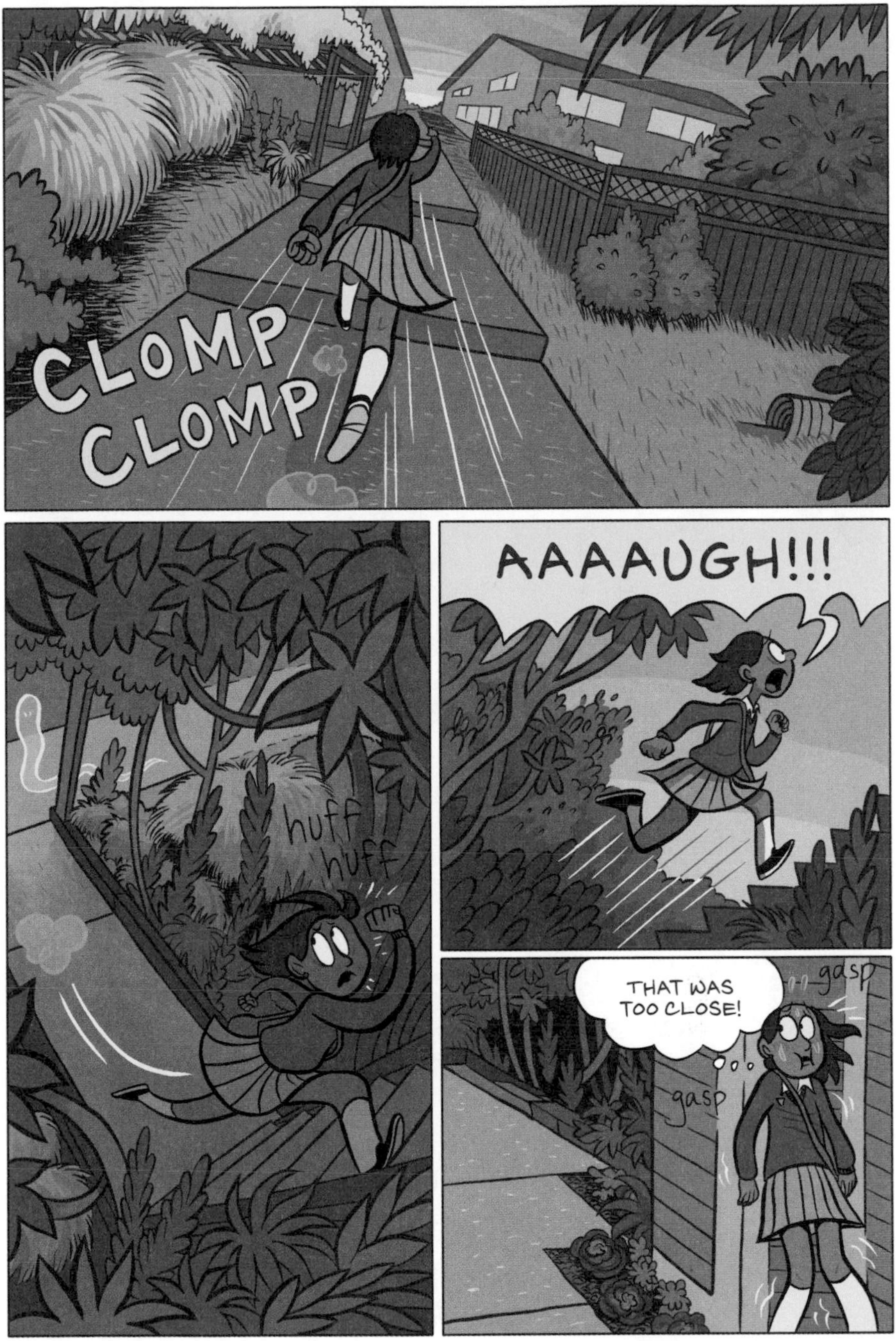
CLOMP
CLOMP
huff
huff
AAAAUGH!!!
THAT WAS TOO CLOSE!
gasp
gasp

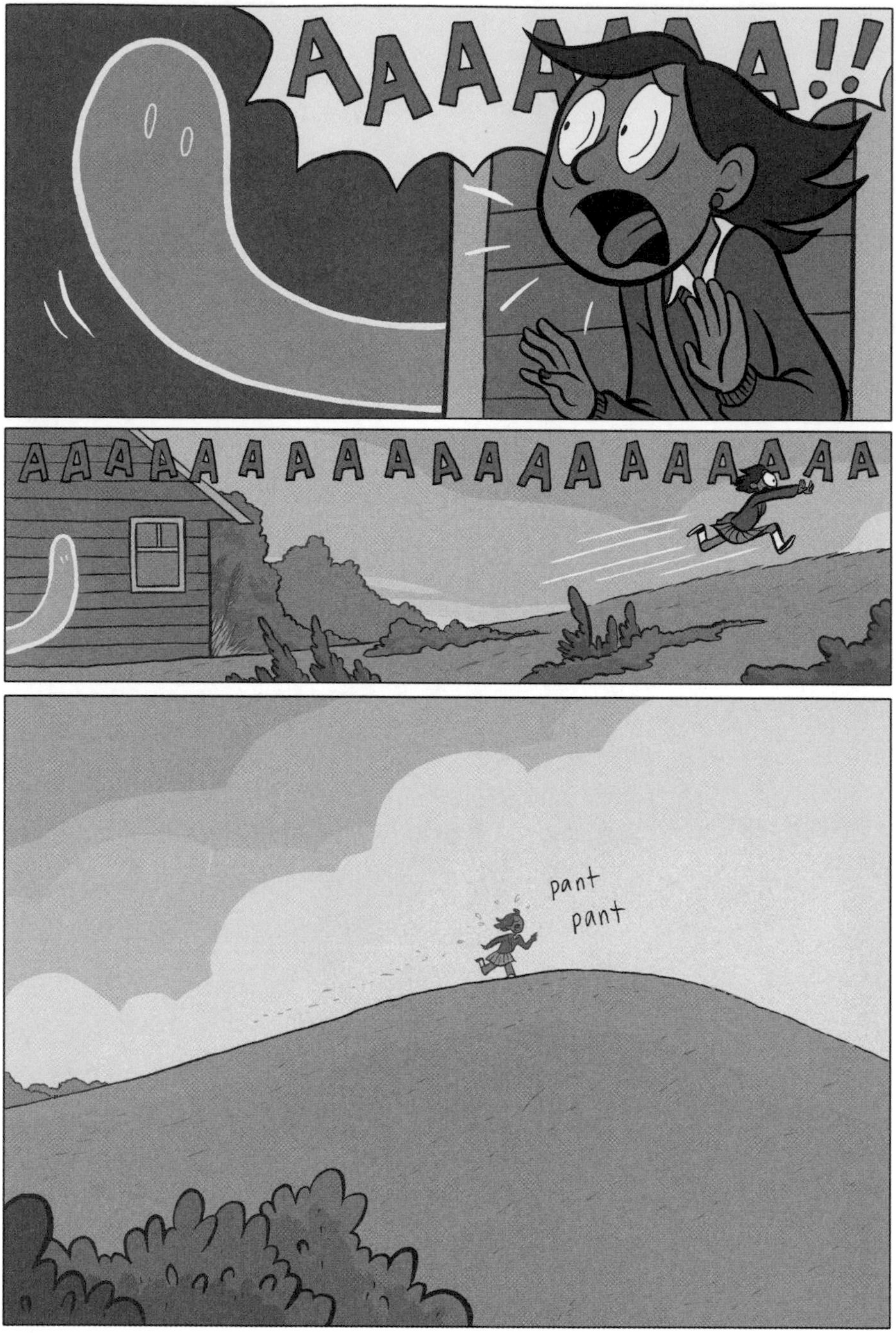
AAAAAAA!!
AAAAAAAAAAAAAAAAA
pant
pant

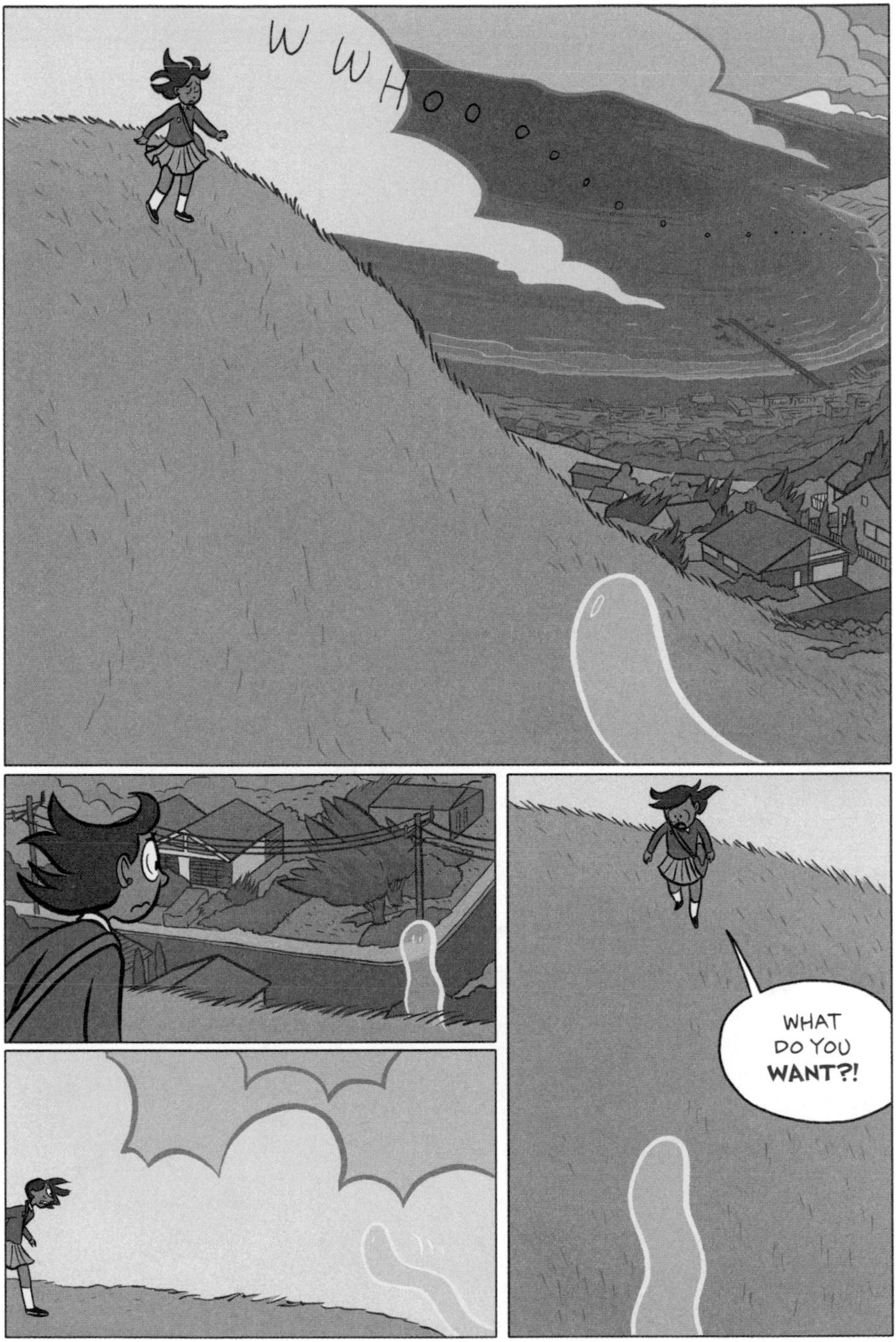
WWHOOOOOO
WHAT DO YOU WANT?!

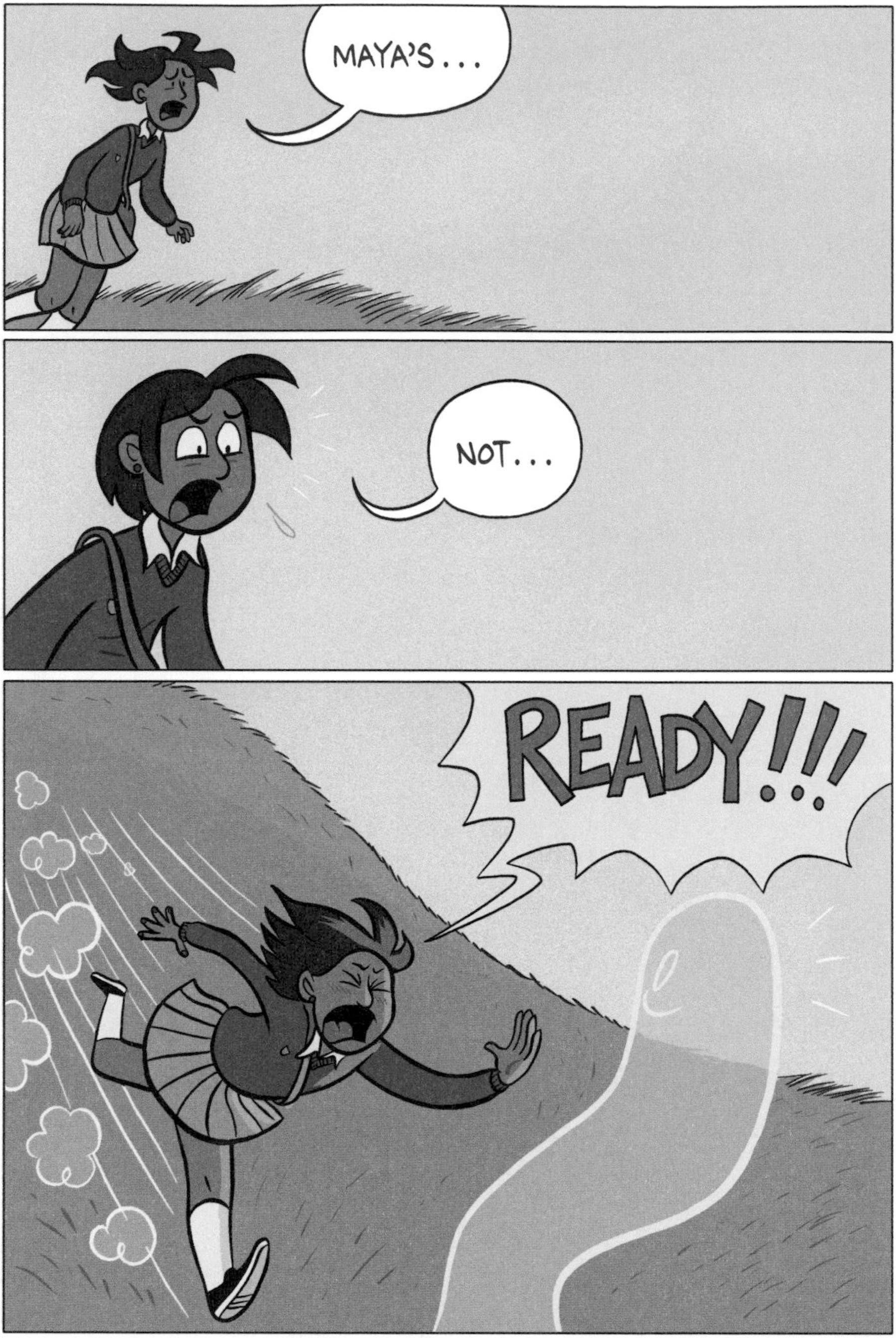
MAYA'S...
NOT...
READY!!!

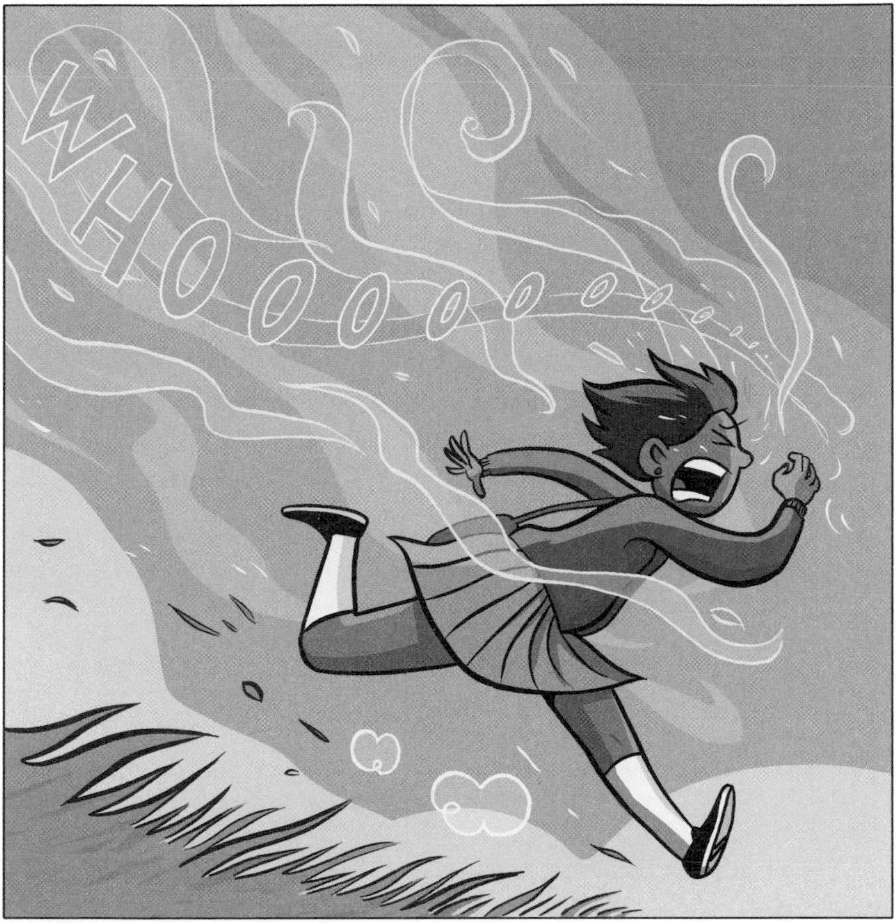
WHOOOOOOOOOO

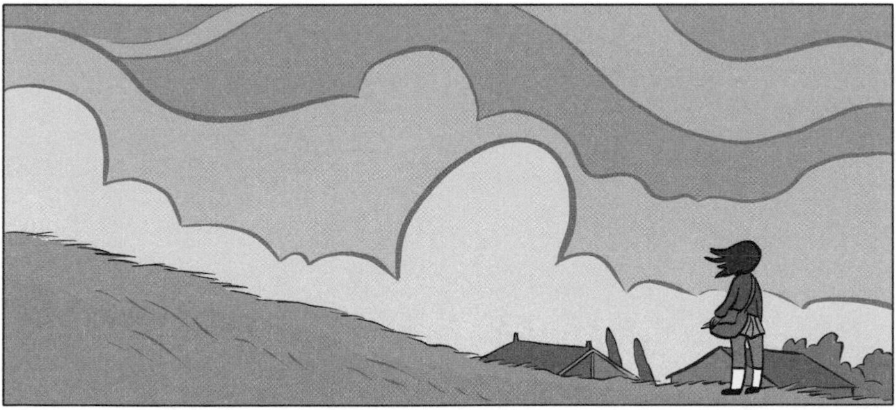

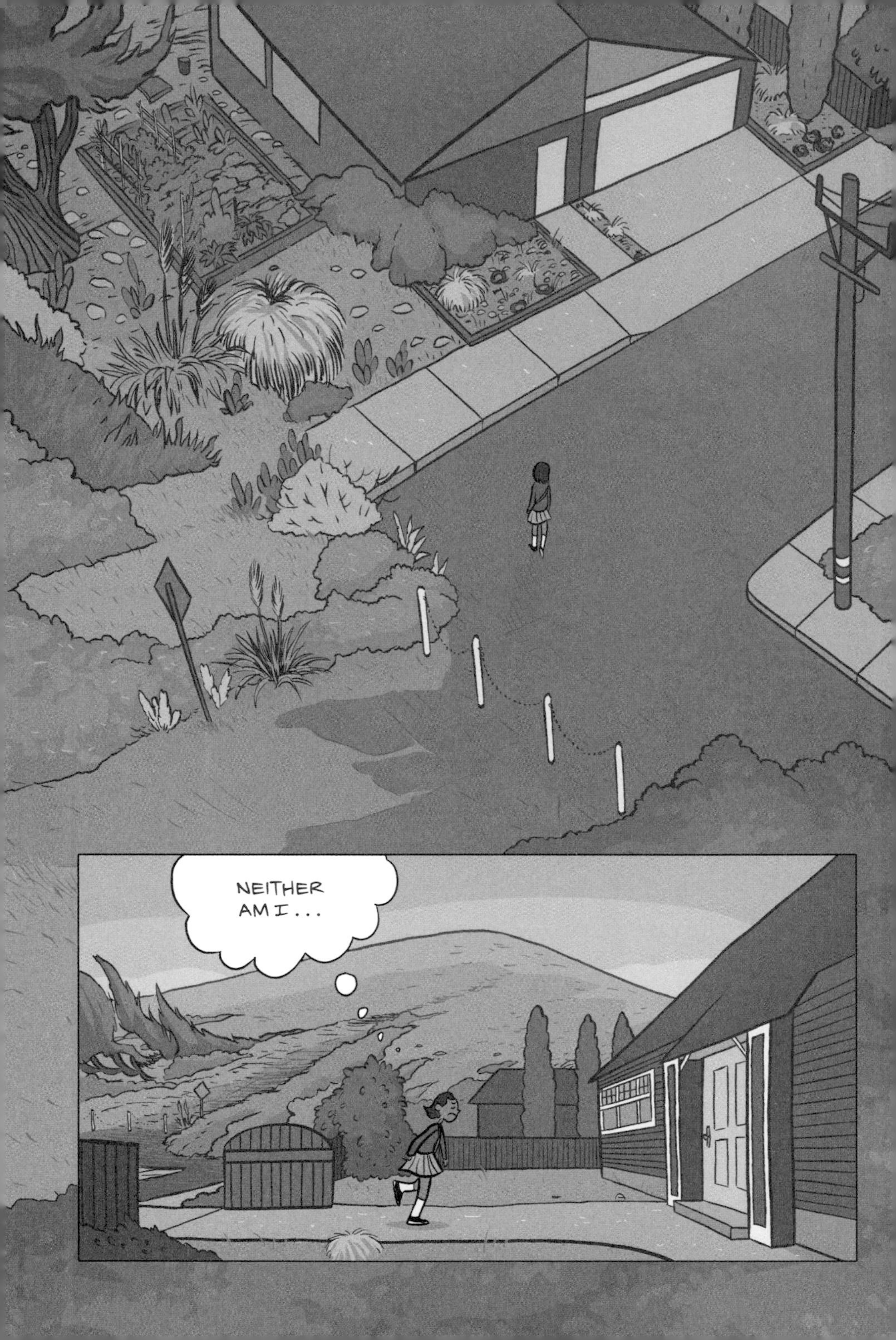
NEITHER AM I . . .

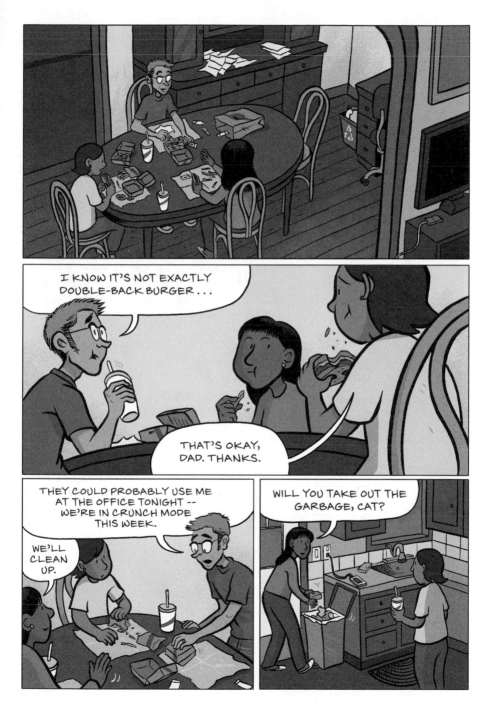

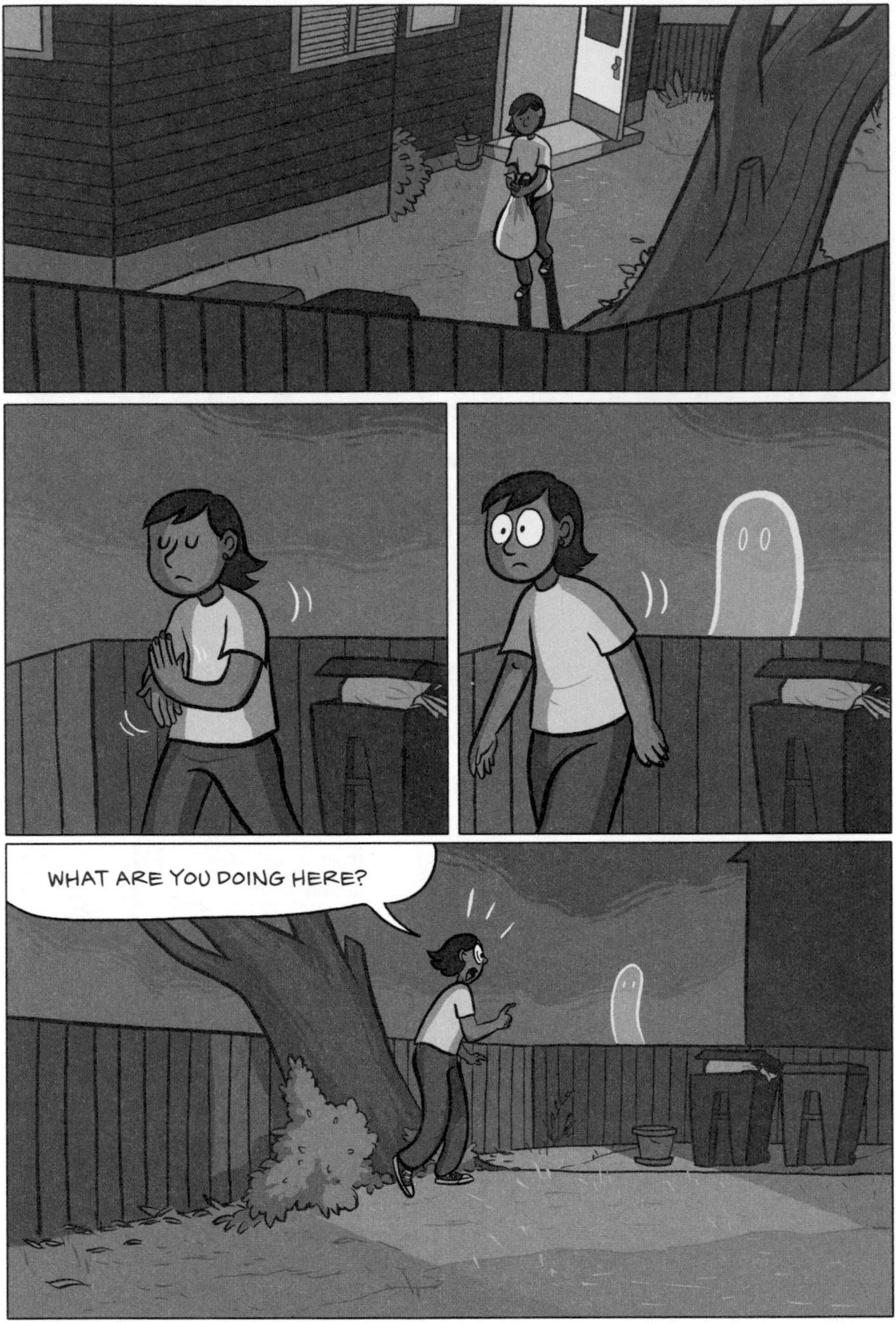
WHAT ARE YOU DOING HERE?

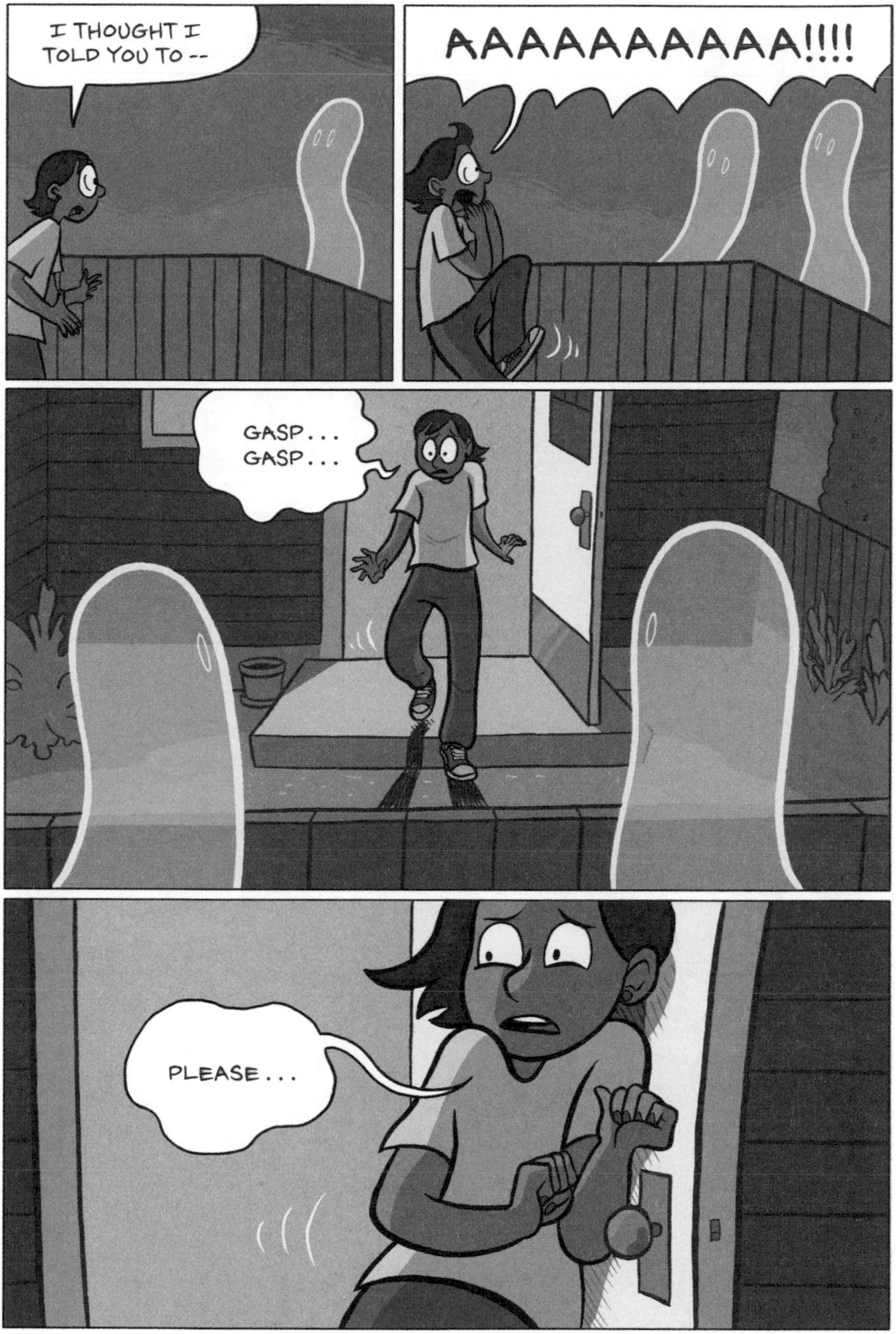
I THOUGHT I TOLD YOU TO --
AAAAAAAAAAA!!!!
GASP...
GASP...
PLEASE...

131

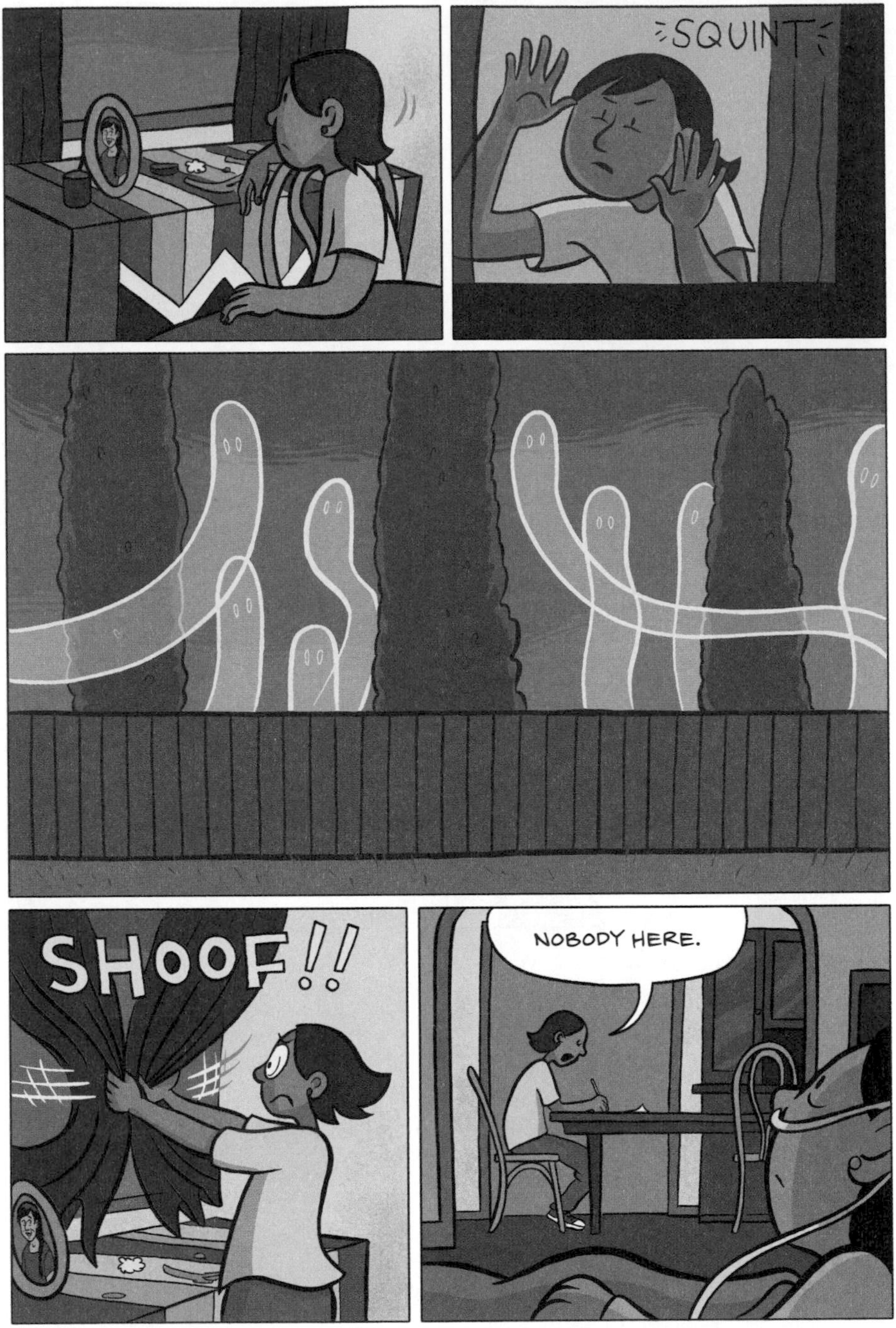
SQUINT
SHOOF!!
NOBODY HERE.

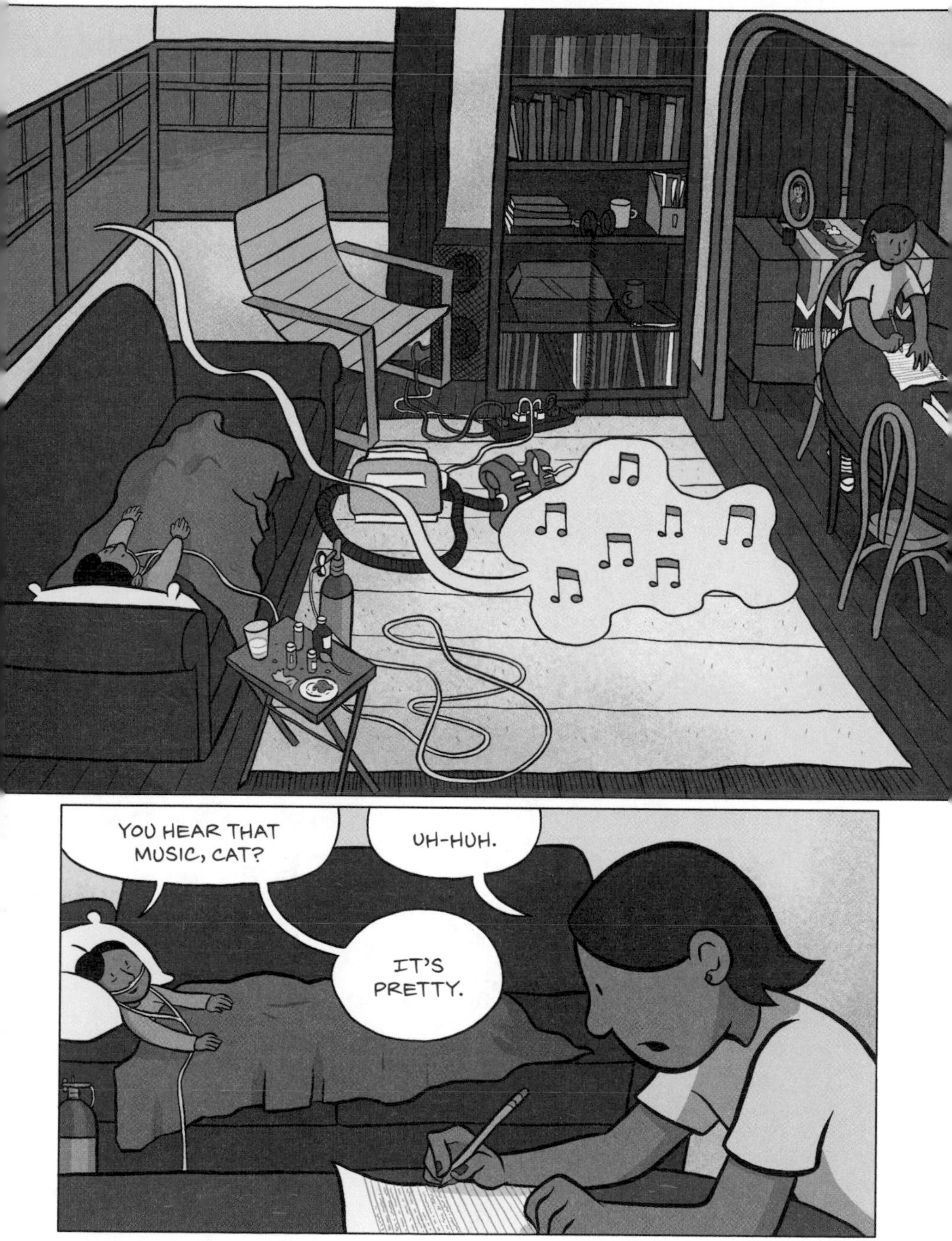
YOU HEAR THAT MUSIC, CAT?
UH-HUH.
IT'S PRETTY.

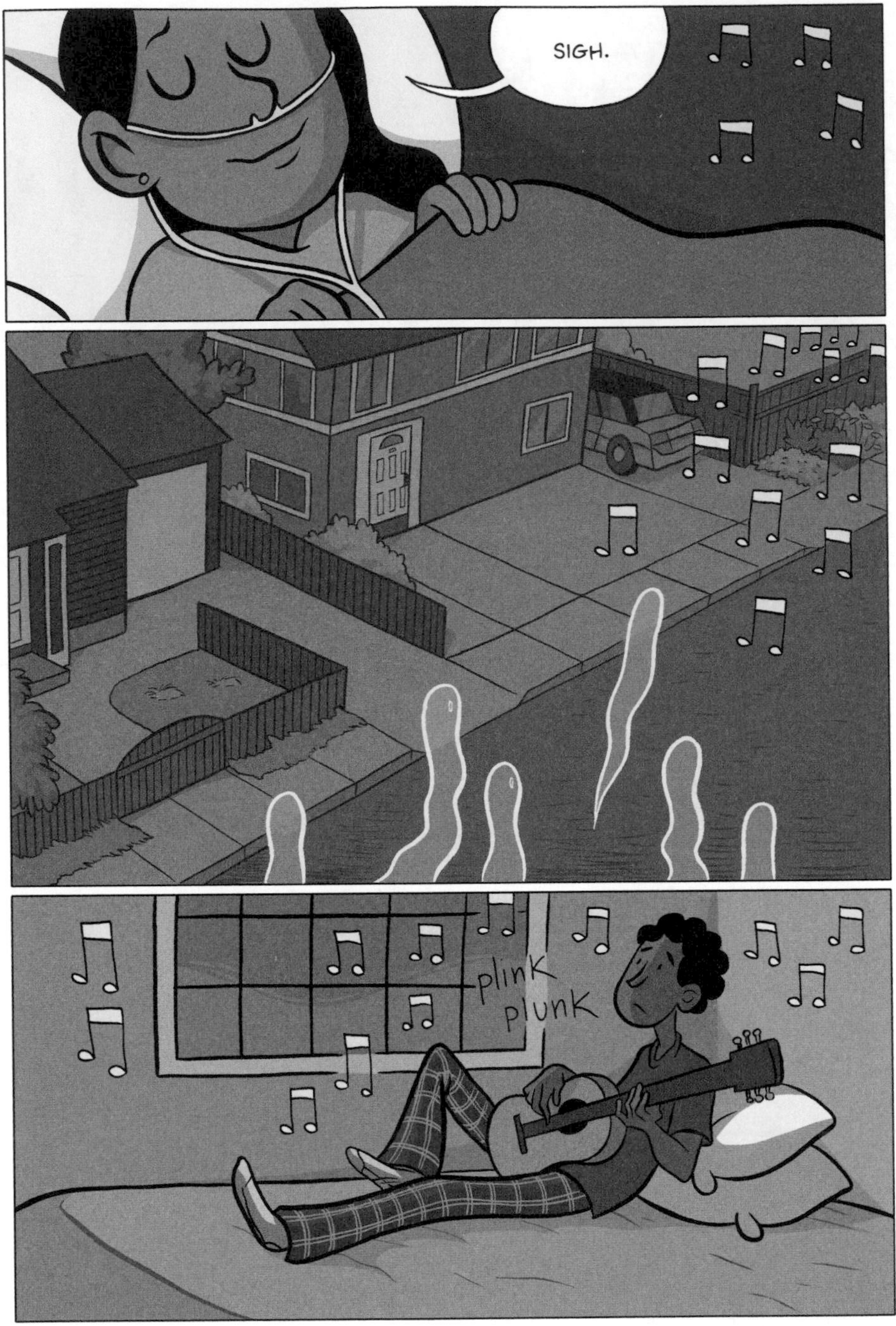
SIGH.
plink
plunk

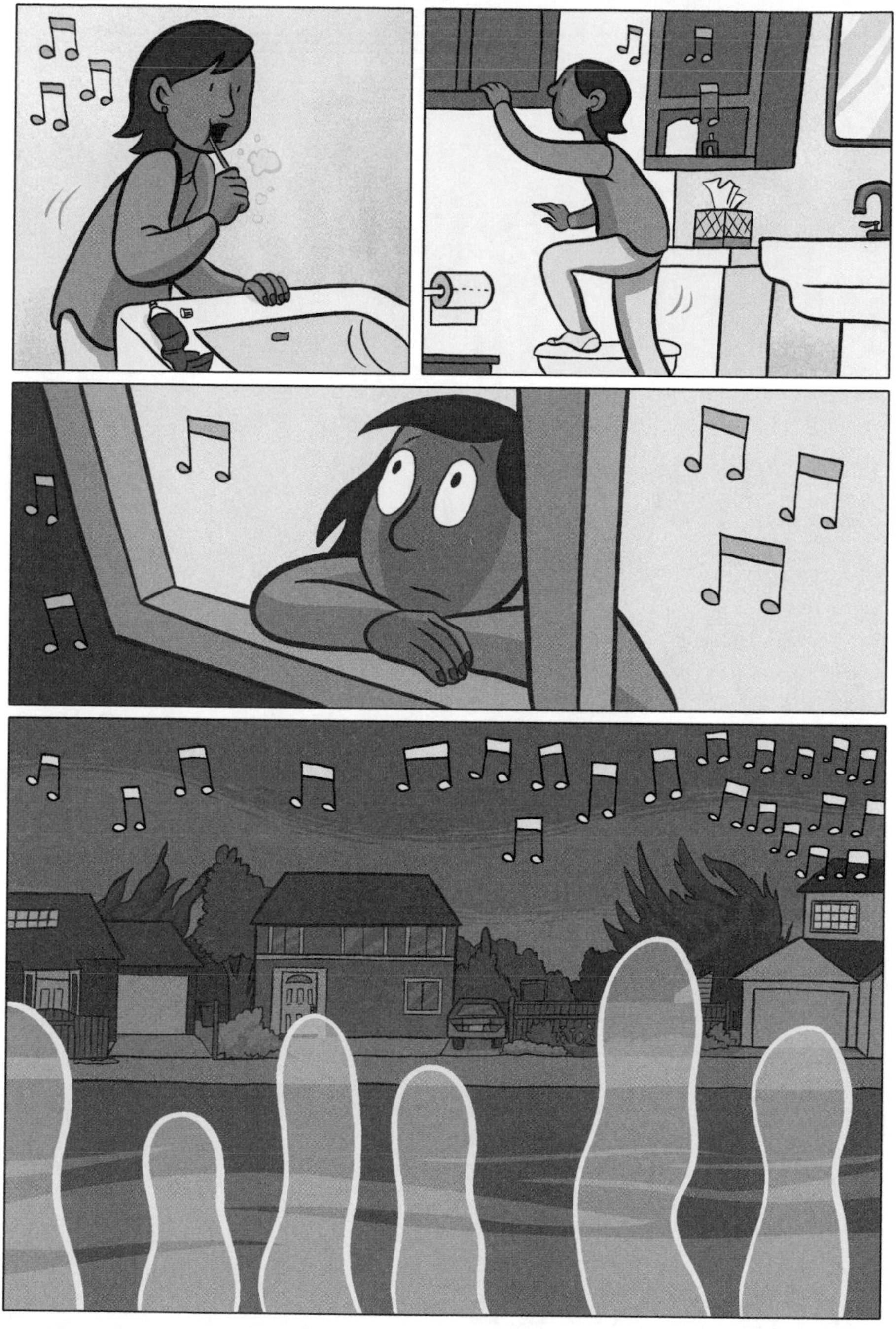

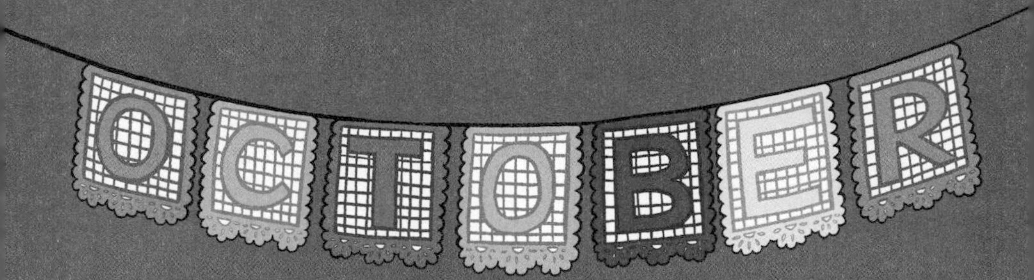
OCTOBER

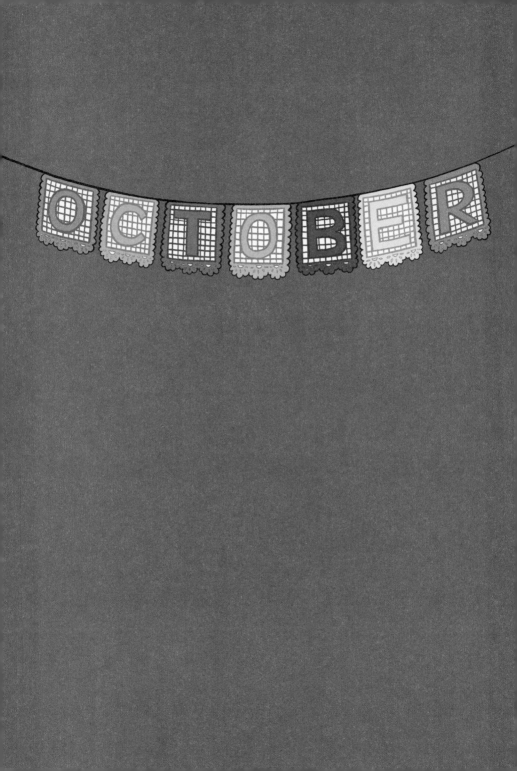

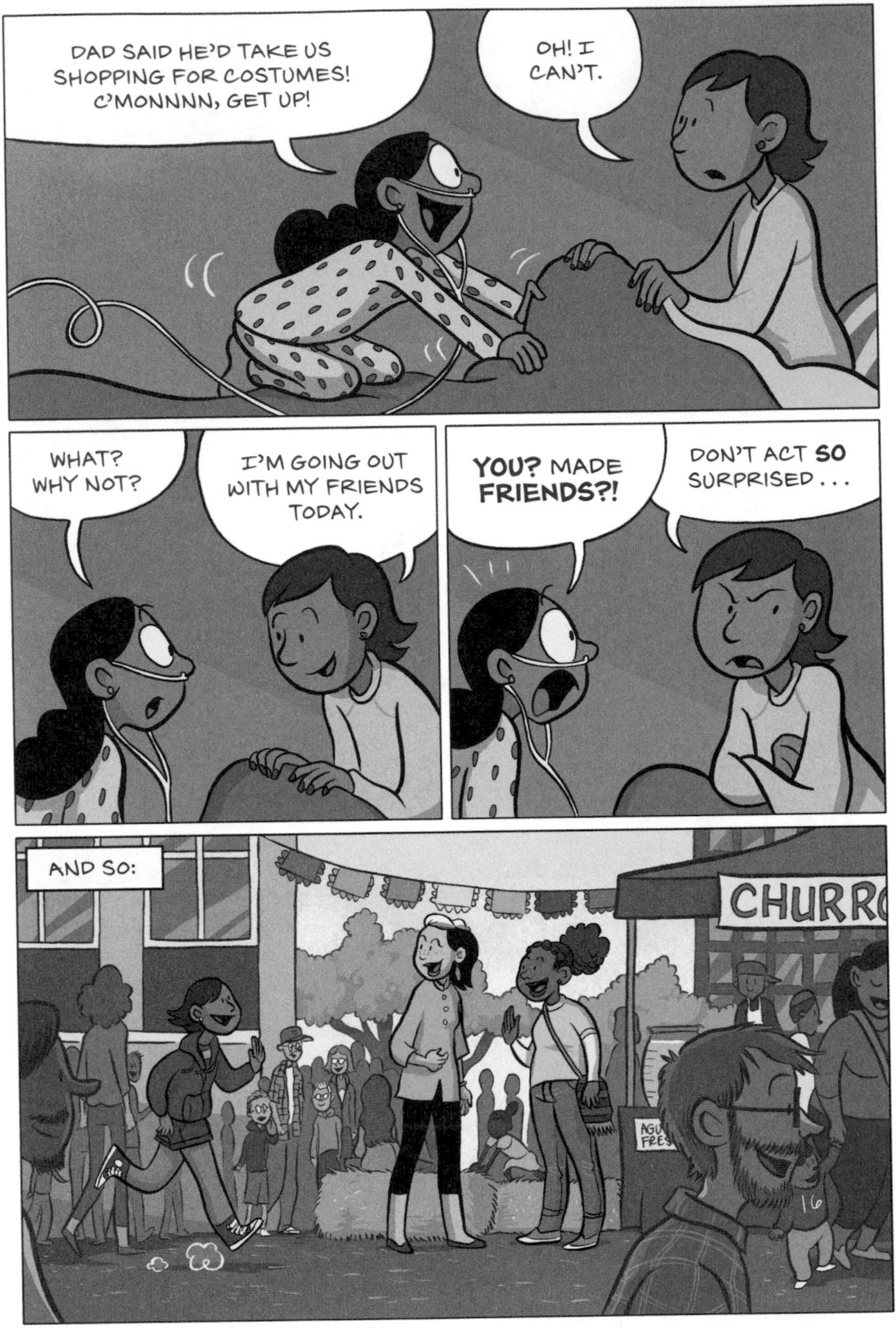
DAD SAID HE'D TAKE US SHOPPING FOR COSTUMES! C'MONNNN, GET UP!
OH! I CAN'T.
WHAT? WHY NOT?
I'M GOING OUT WITH MY FRIENDS TODAY.
YOU? MADE **FRIENDS?!**
DON'T ACT **SO** SURPRISED . . .
AND SO:
CHURRO

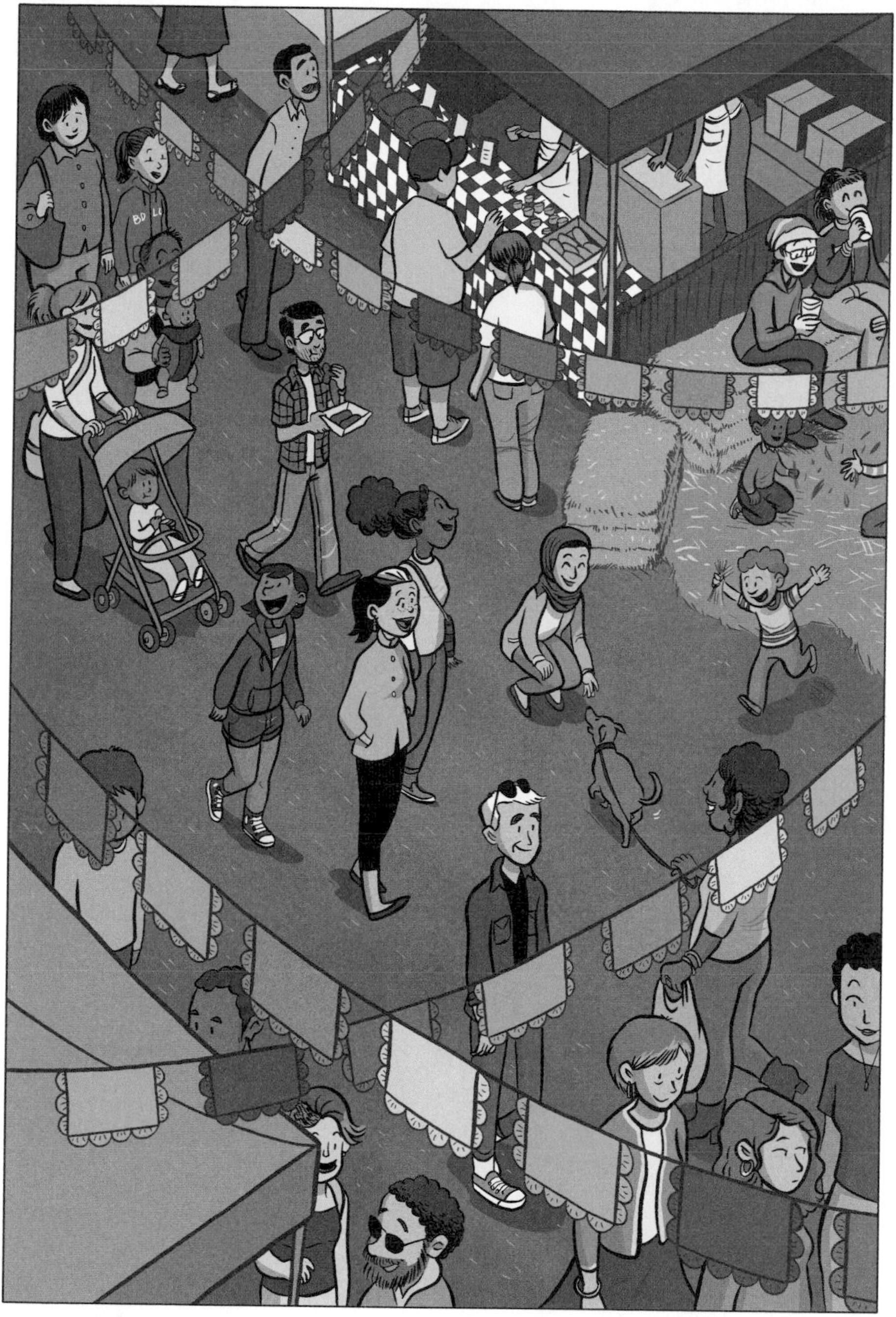

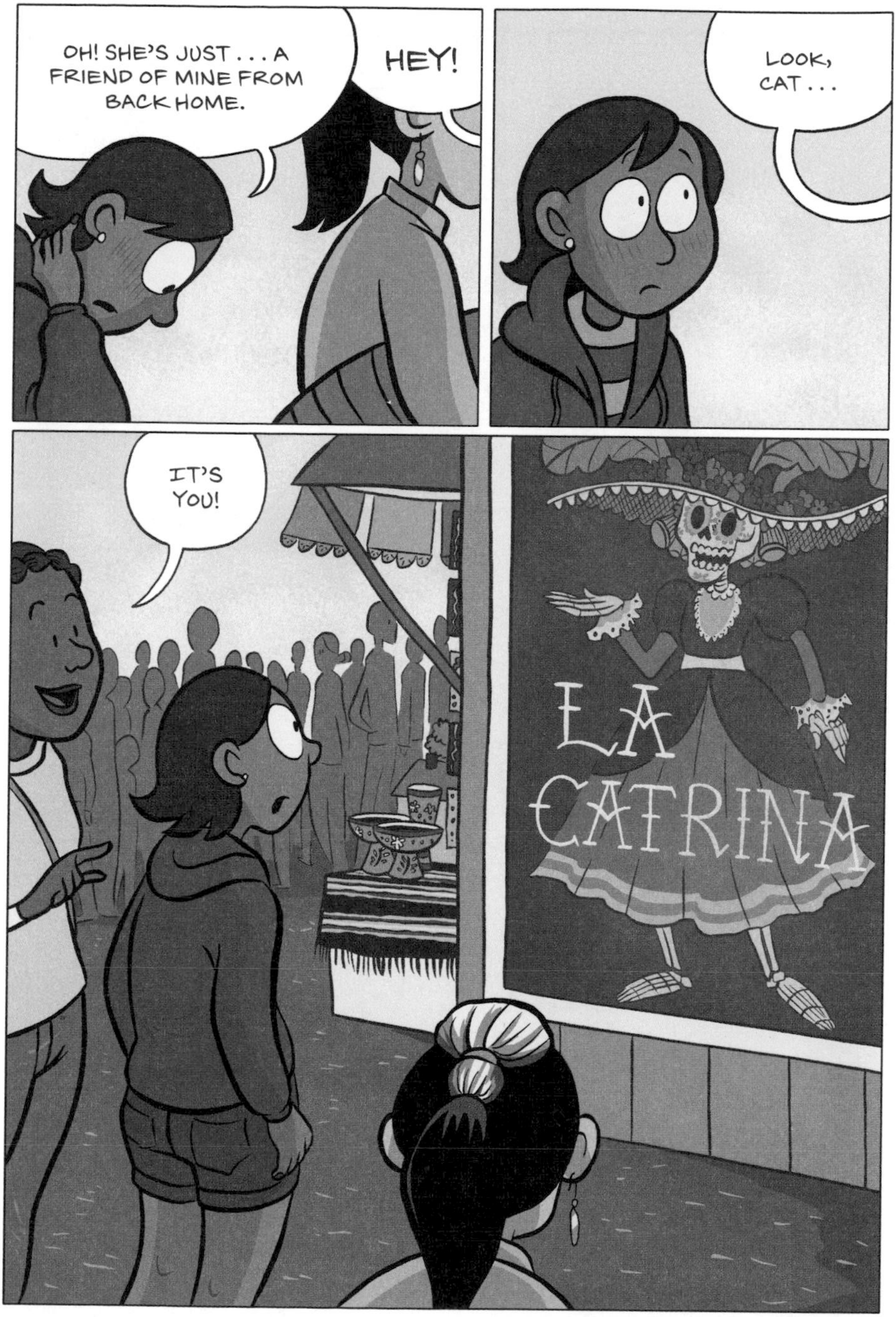

OH! SHE'S JUST . . . A FRIEND OF MINE FROM BACK HOME.
HEY!
LOOK, CAT . . .
IT'S YOU!
LA CATRINA

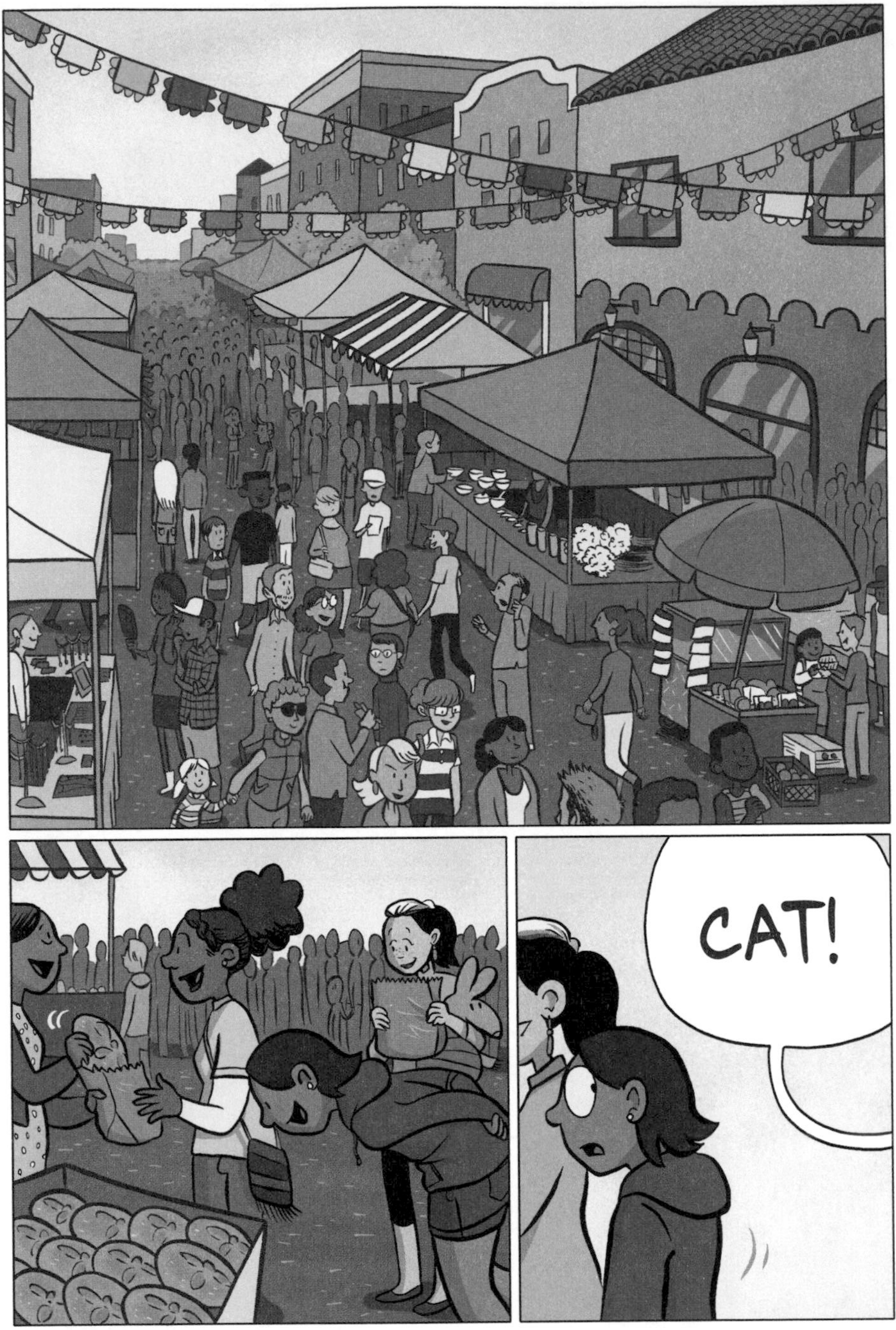
CAT!

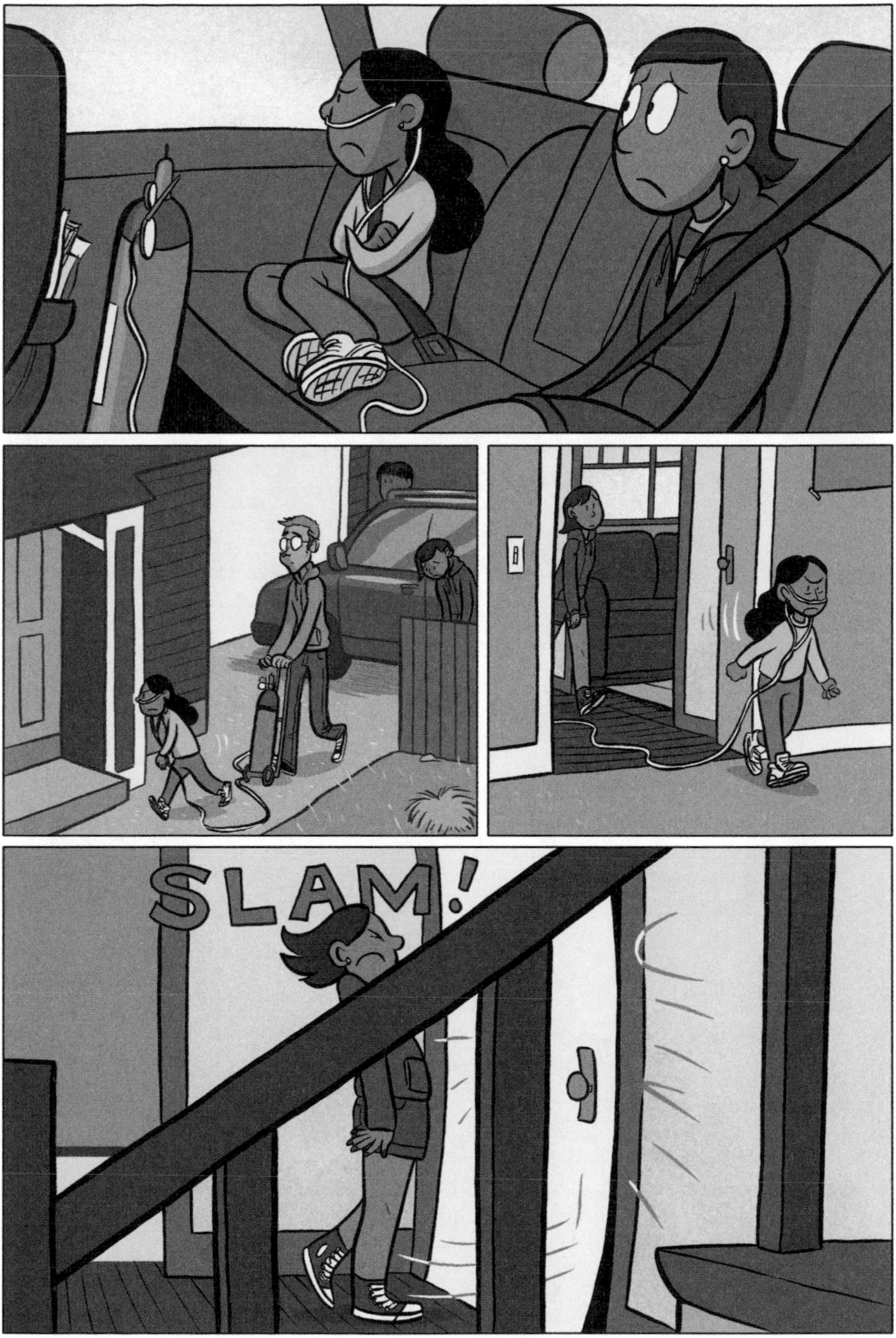
SLAM!

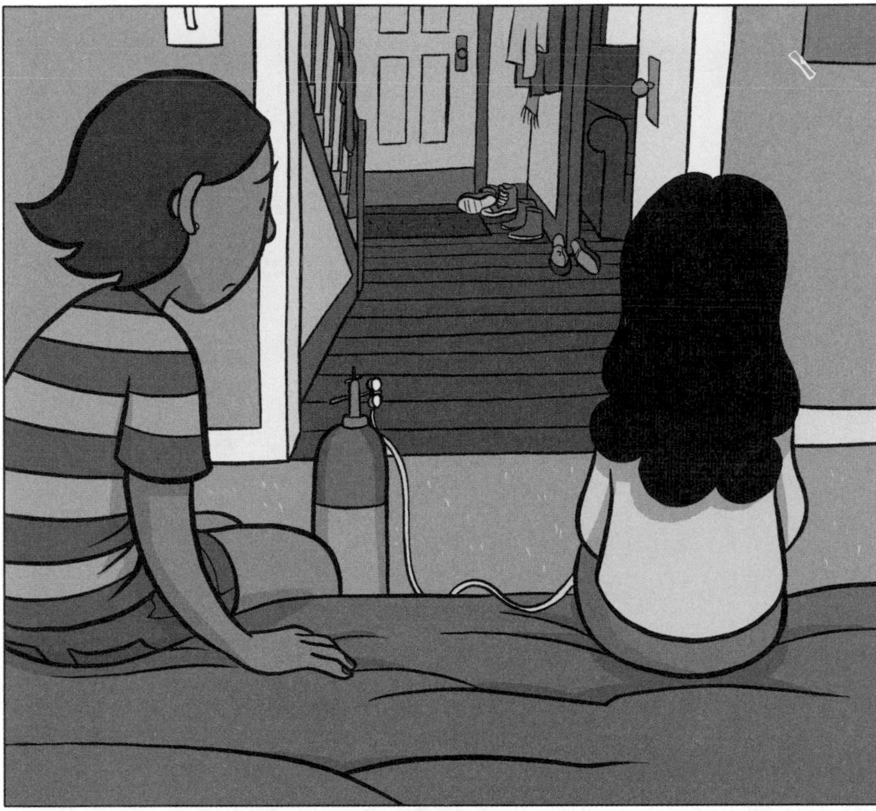

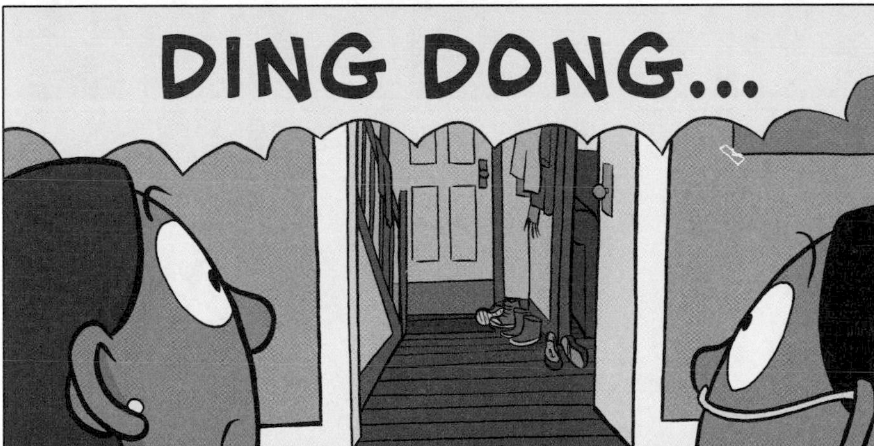
DING DONG...

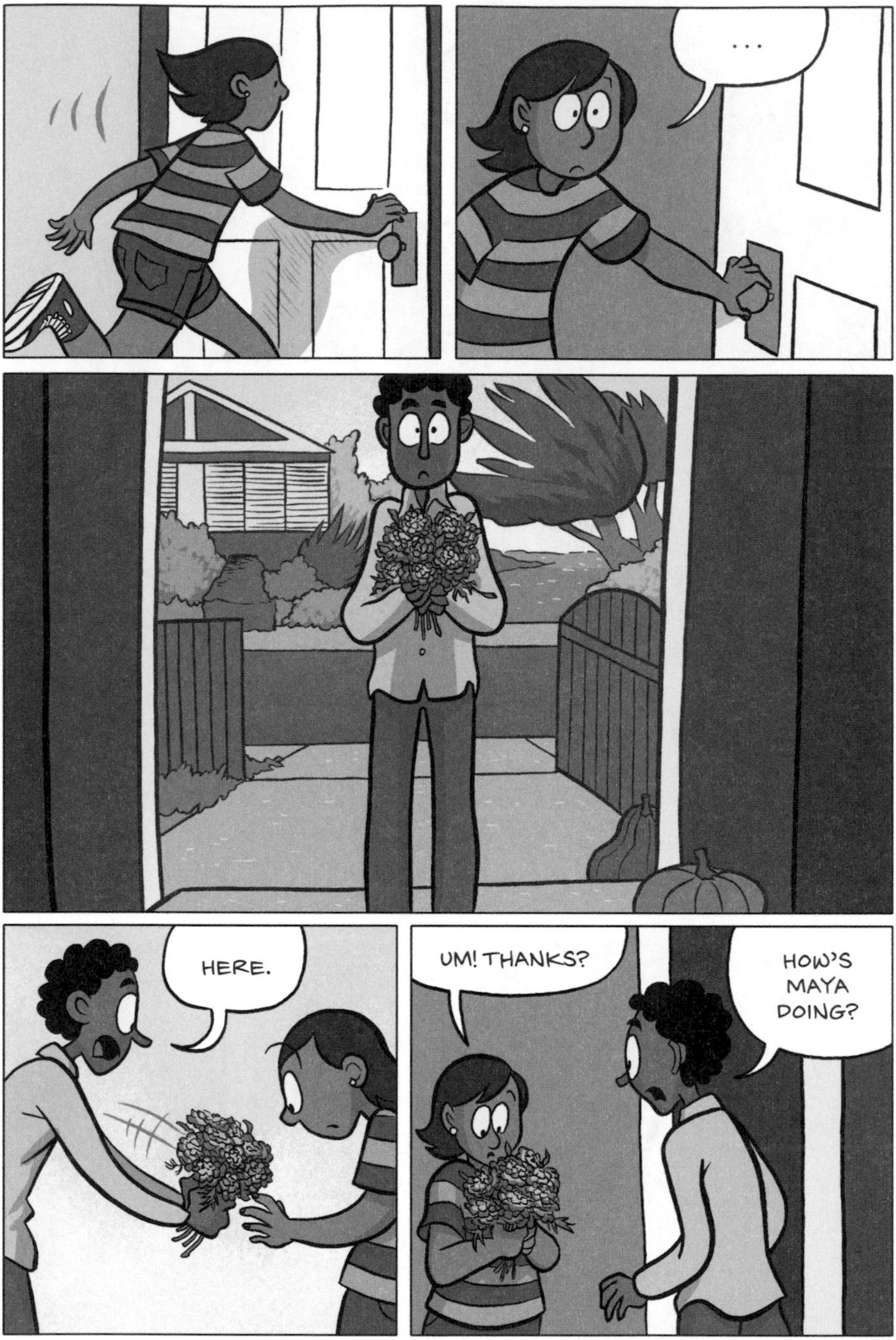
...
HERE.
UM! THANKS?
HOW'S MAYA DOING?

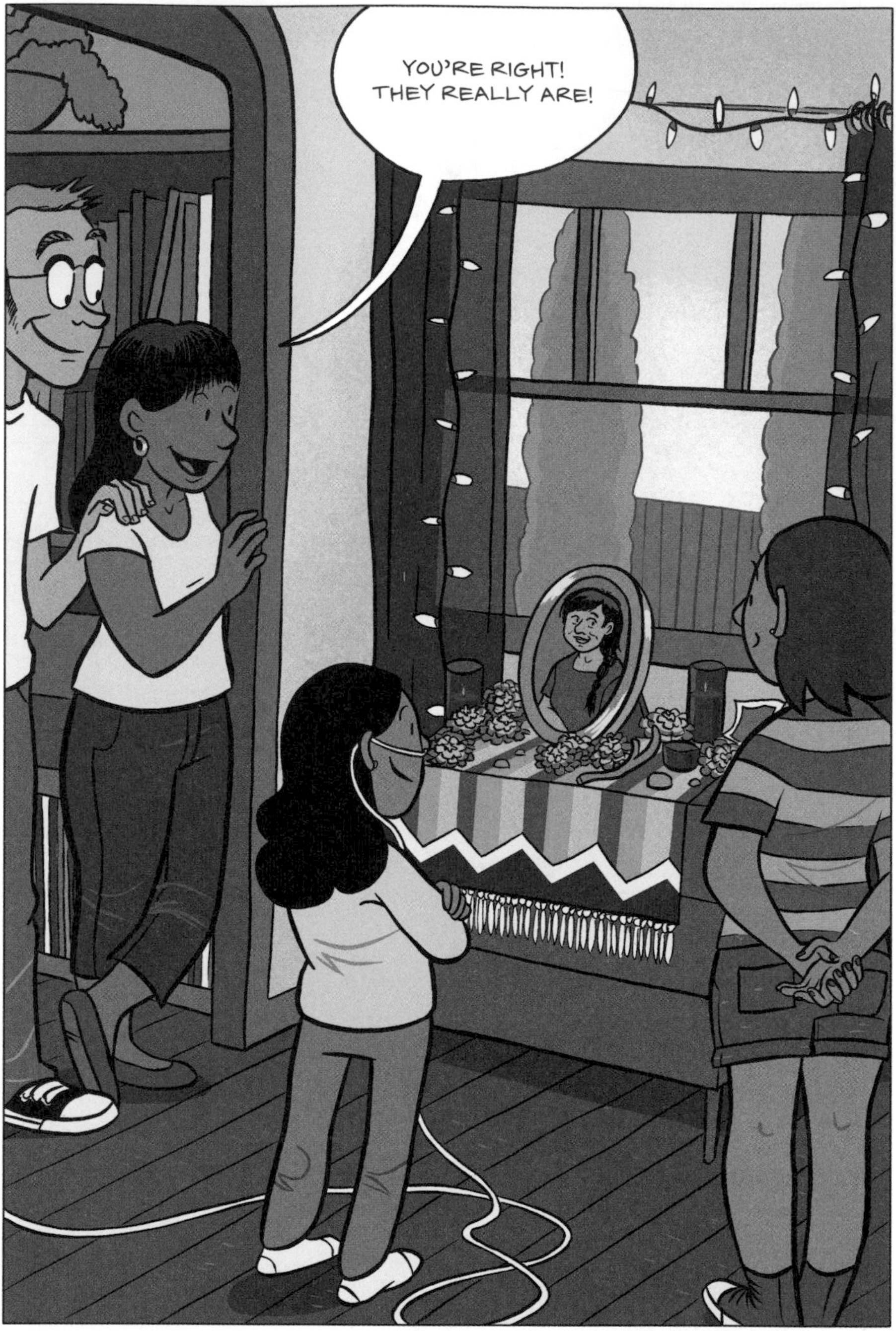
YOU'RE RIGHT! THEY REALLY ARE!

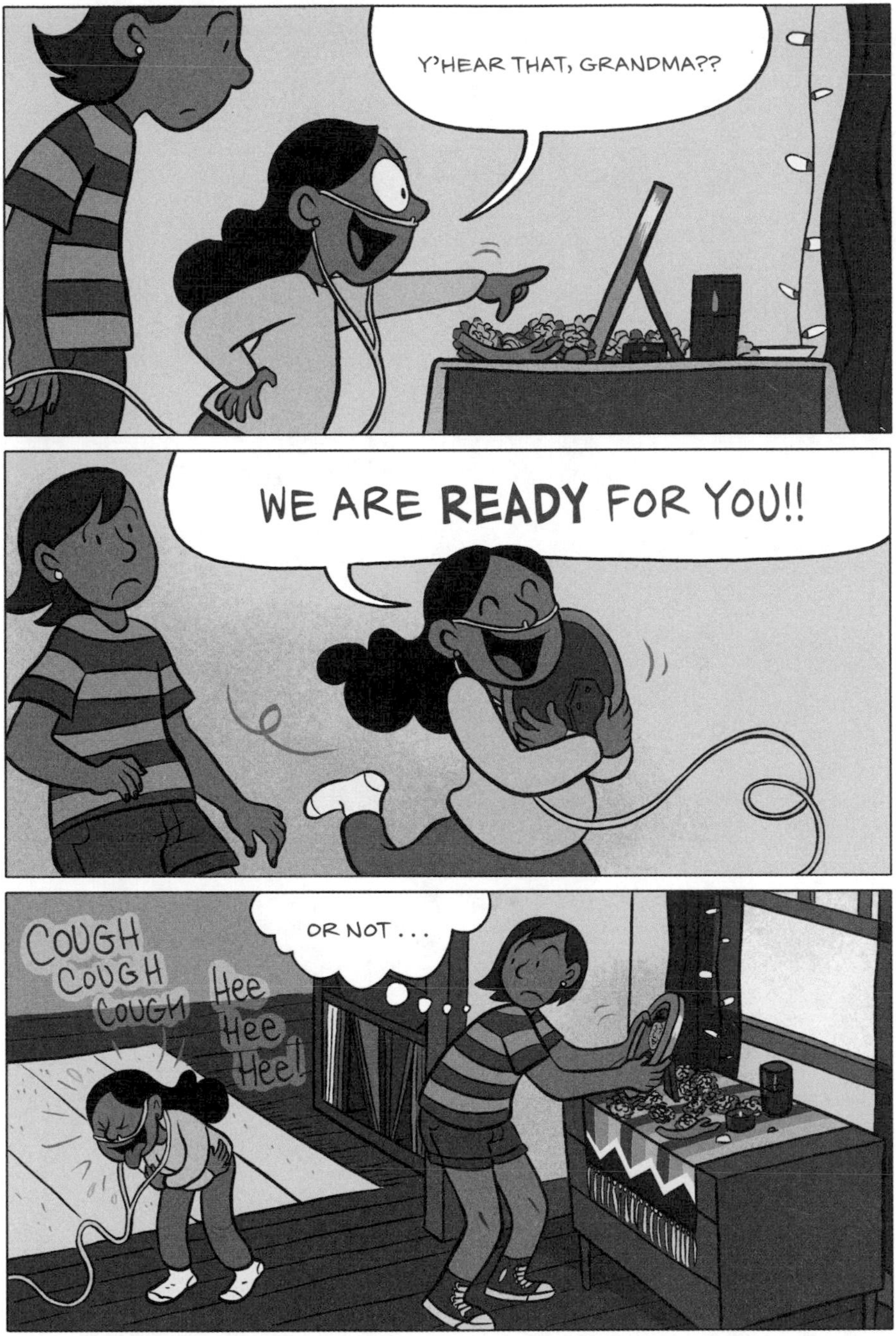
Y'HEAR THAT, GRANDMA??
WE ARE **READY** FOR YOU!!
COUGH COUGH COUGH
Hee Hee Hee!
OR NOT . . .

LATE OCTOBER

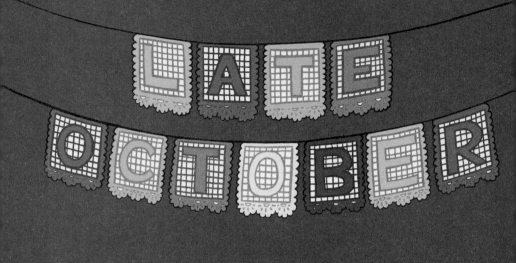

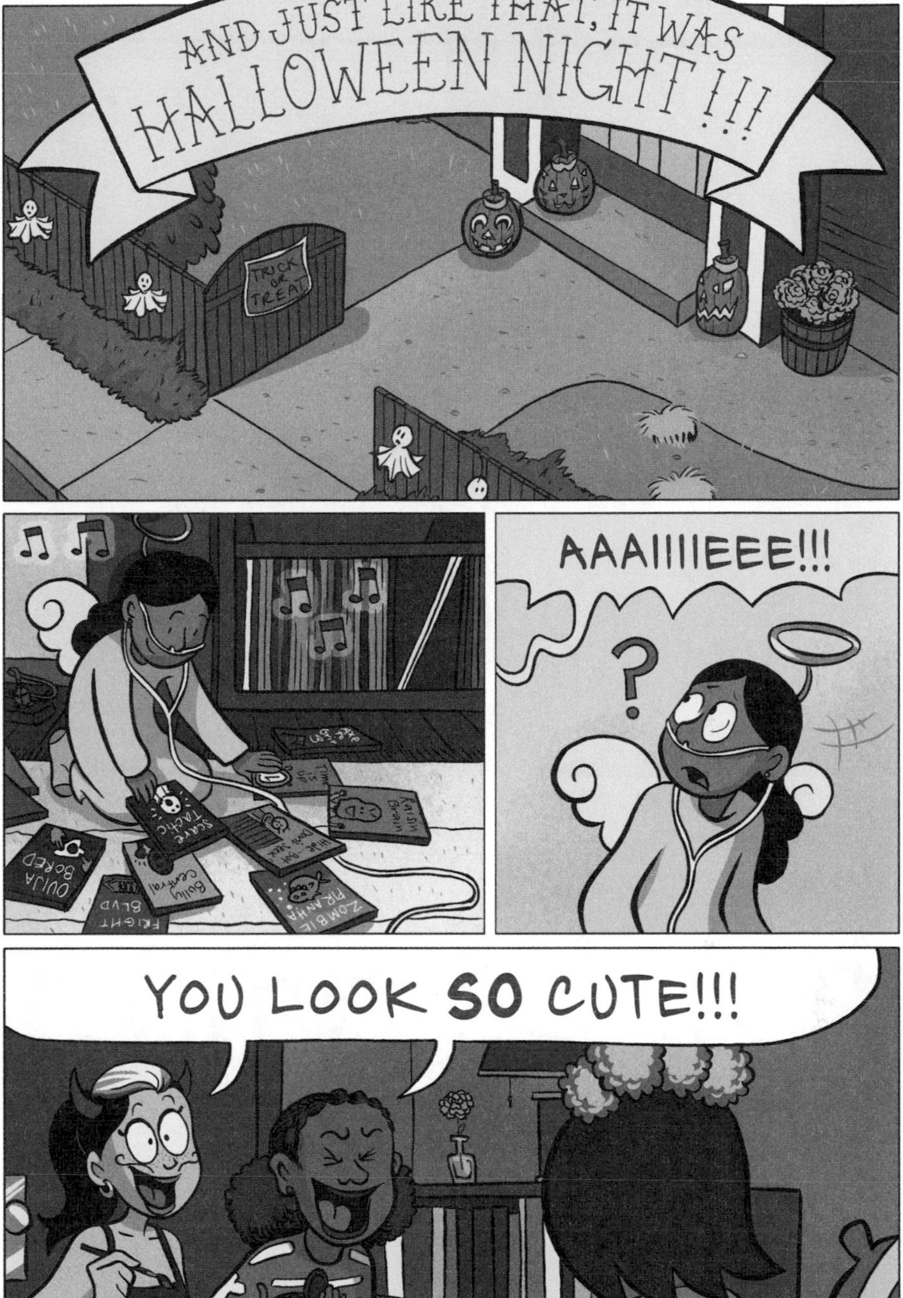
AND JUST LIKE THAT, IT WAS HALLOWEEN NIGHT!!!
TRICK OR TREAT
OUIJA BORED
FRIGHT BLVD
ZOMBIE PIR-ANHA
AAAIIIIEEE!!!
?
YOU LOOK **SO** CUTE!!!

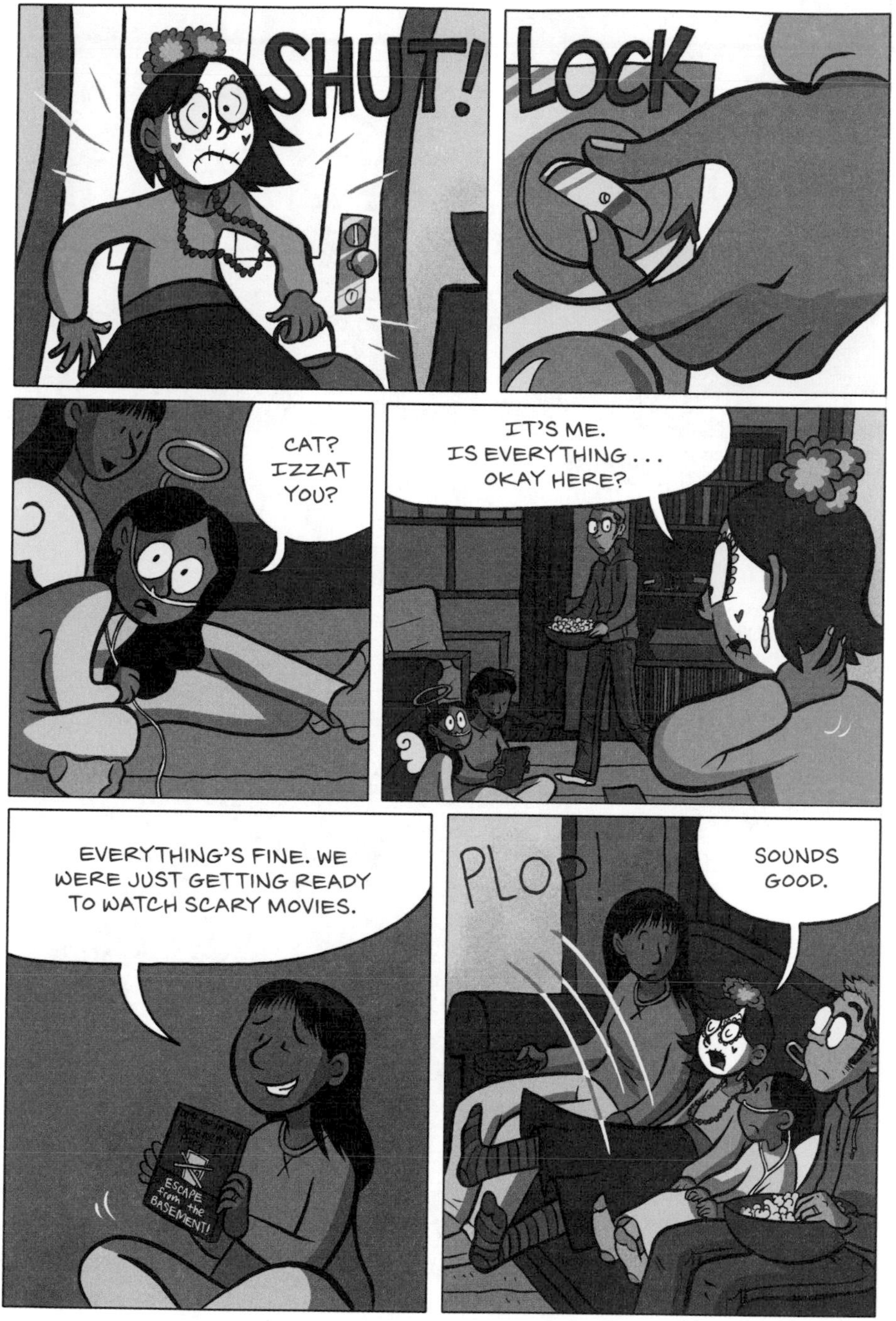
SHUT!
LOCK
CAT? IZZAT YOU?
IT'S ME. IS EVERYTHING . . . OKAY HERE?
EVERYTHING'S FINE. WE WERE JUST GETTING READY TO WATCH SCARY MOVIES.
ESCAPE from the BASEMENT!
PLOP!
SOUNDS GOOD.

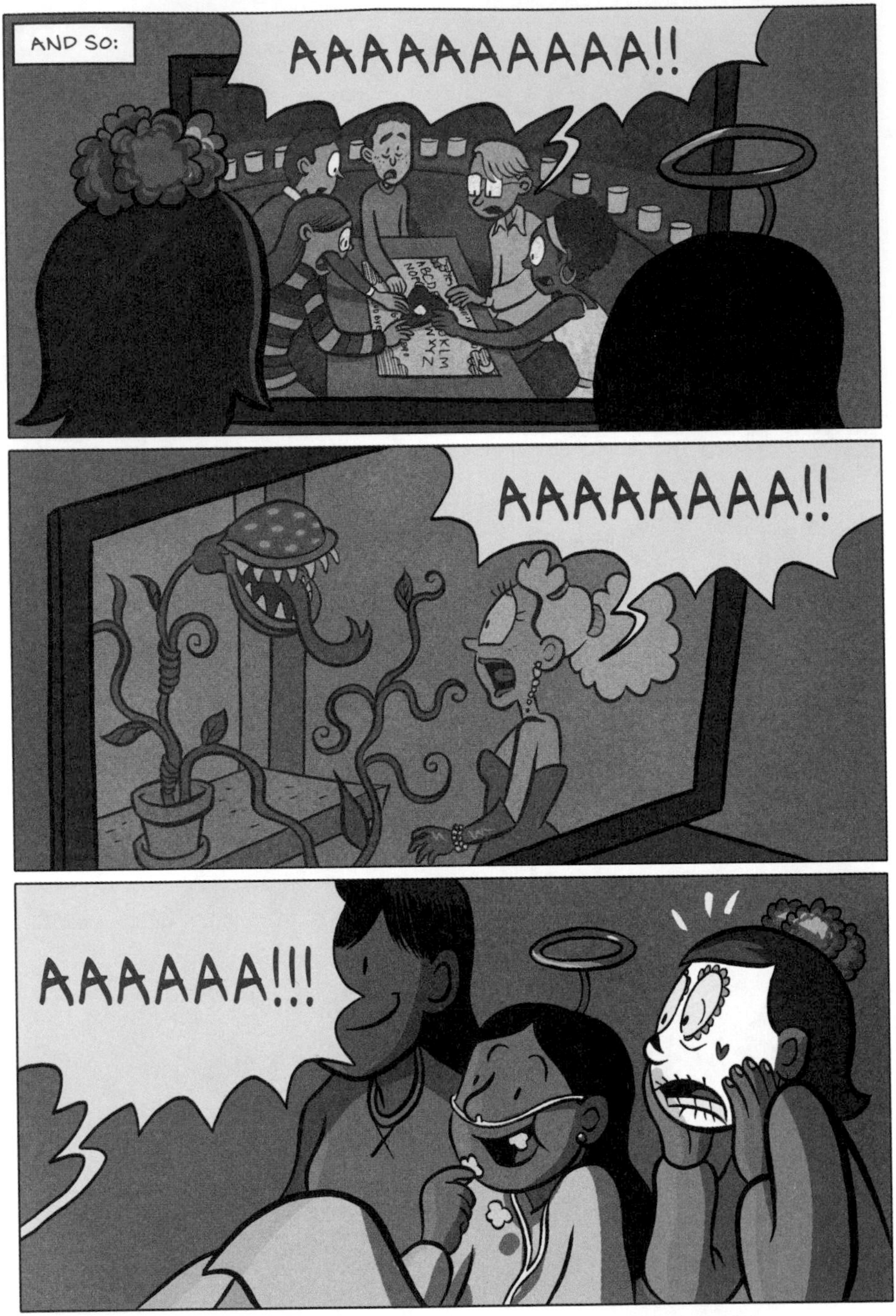
AND SO:
AAAAAAAAAAA!!
AAAAAAAAA!!
AAAAAA!!!

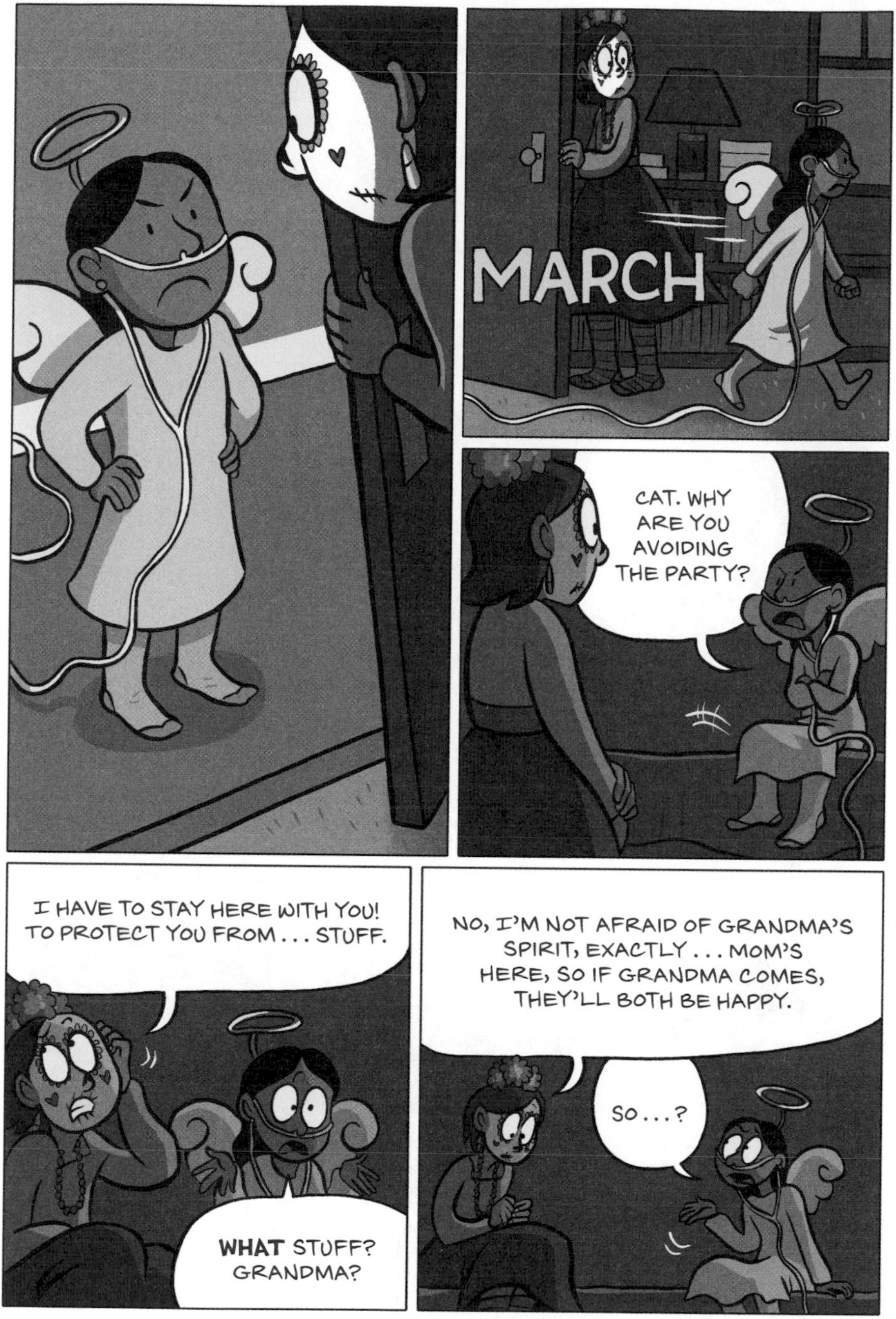
MARCH
CAT. WHY ARE YOU AVOIDING THE PARTY?
I HAVE TO STAY HERE WITH YOU! TO PROTECT YOU FROM . . . STUFF.
WHAT STUFF? GRANDMA?
NO, I'M NOT AFRAID OF GRANDMA'S SPIRIT, EXACTLY . . . MOM'S HERE, SO IF GRANDMA COMES, THEY'LL BOTH BE HAPPY.
SO . . . ?

176

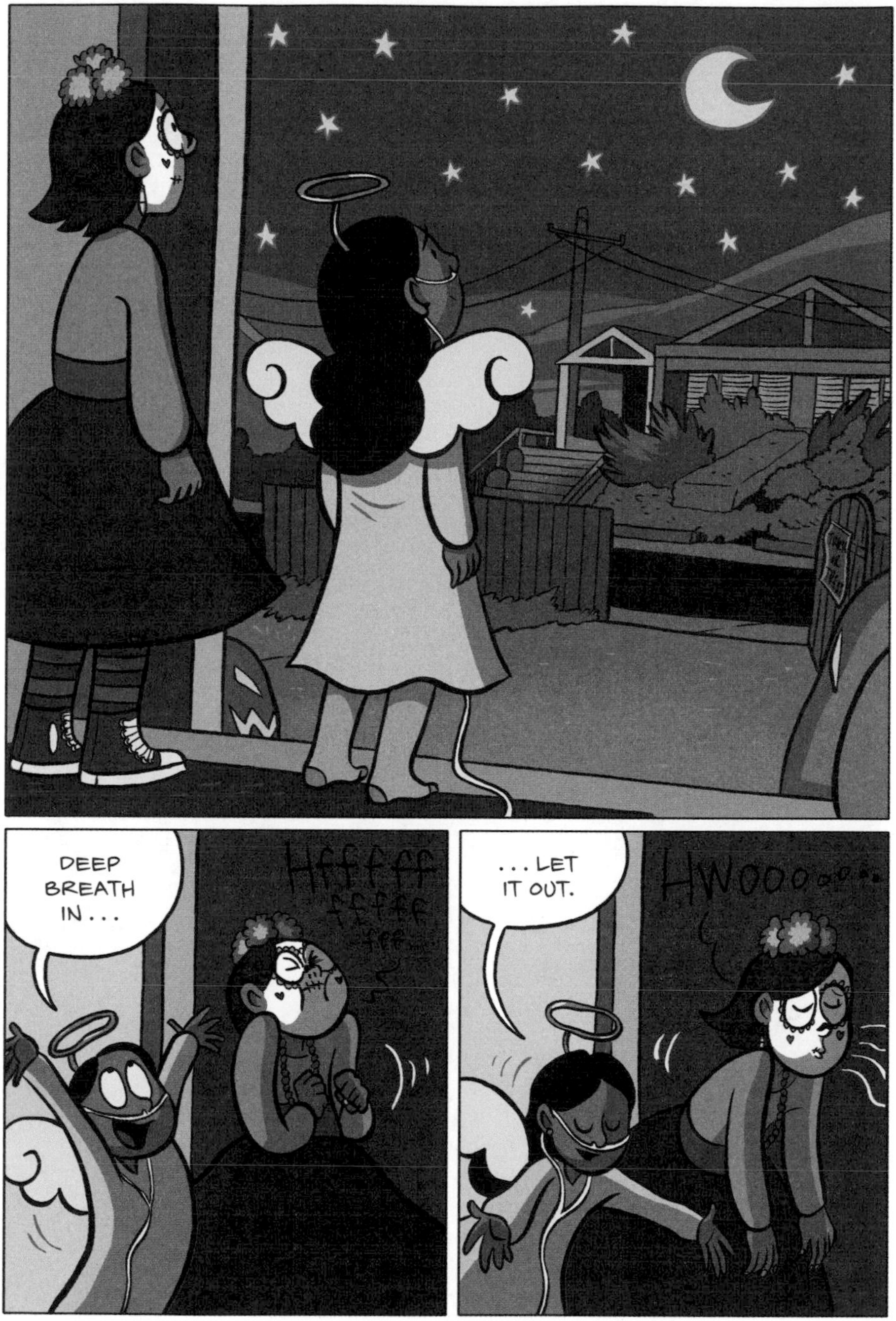
DEEP BREATH IN . . .
Hfffff fffff fff...
. . . LET IT OUT.
HWOOOooo..

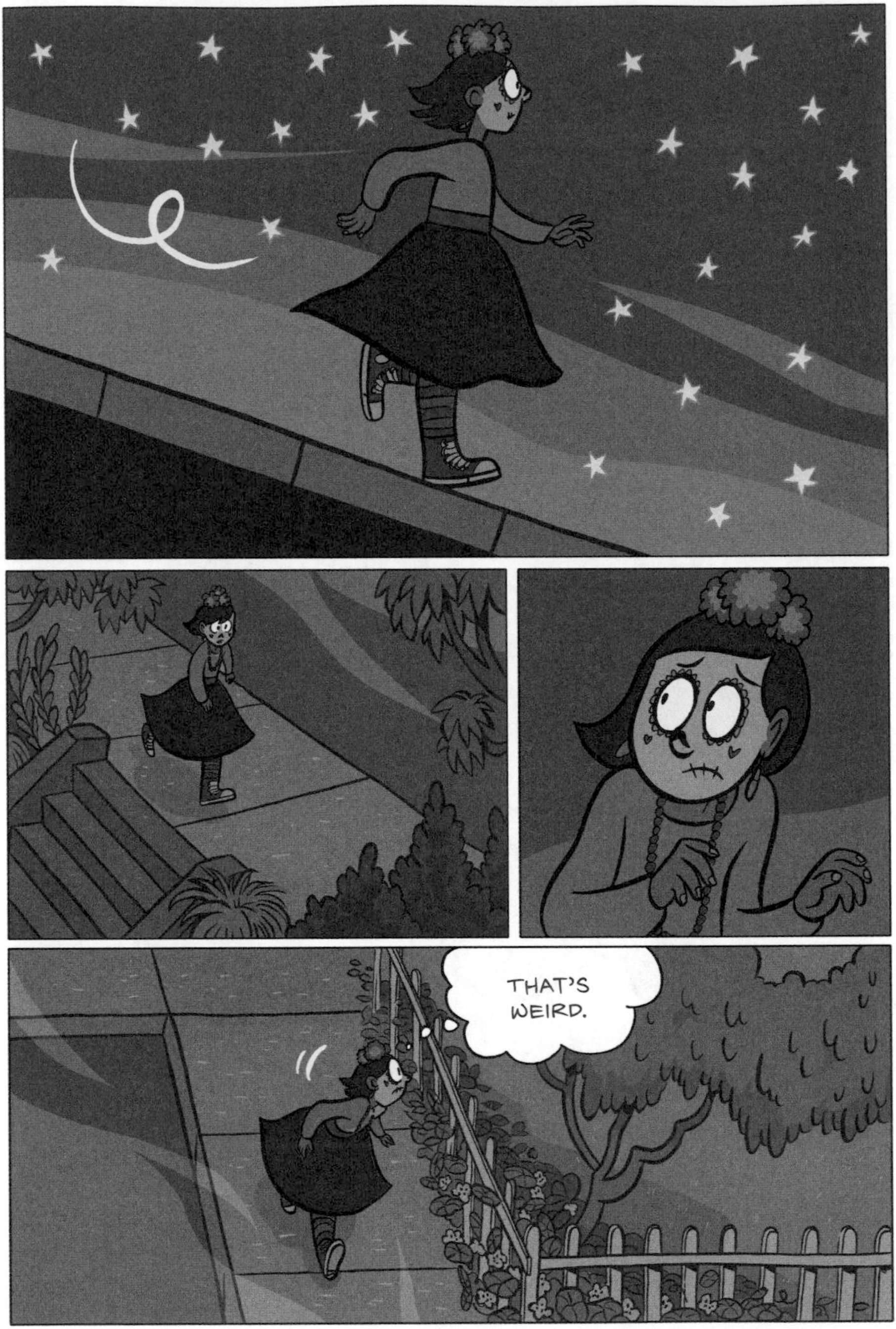
THAT'S WEIRD.

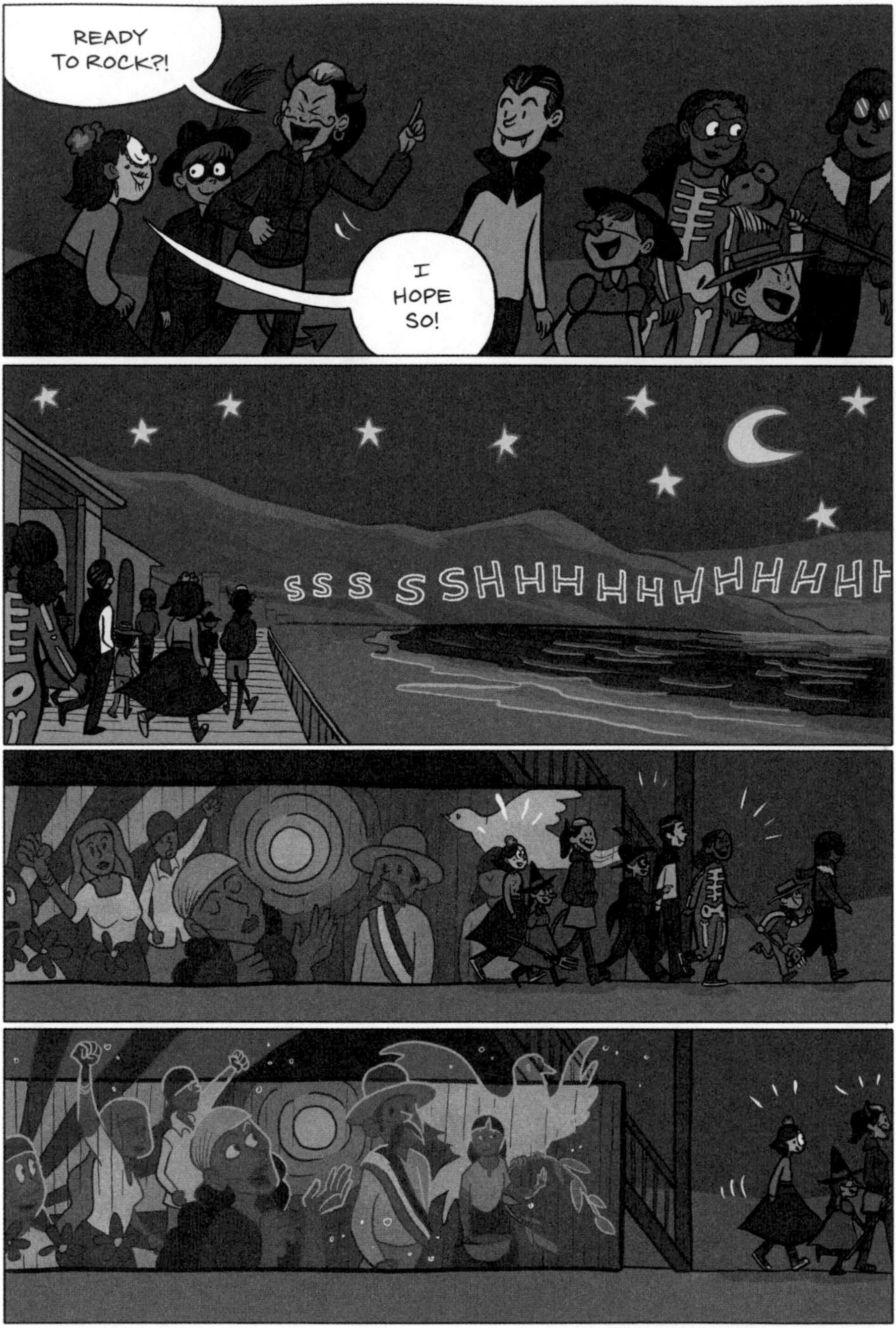
READY TO ROCK?!
I HOPE SO!
SSS SSHHHHHHHHHHHHH

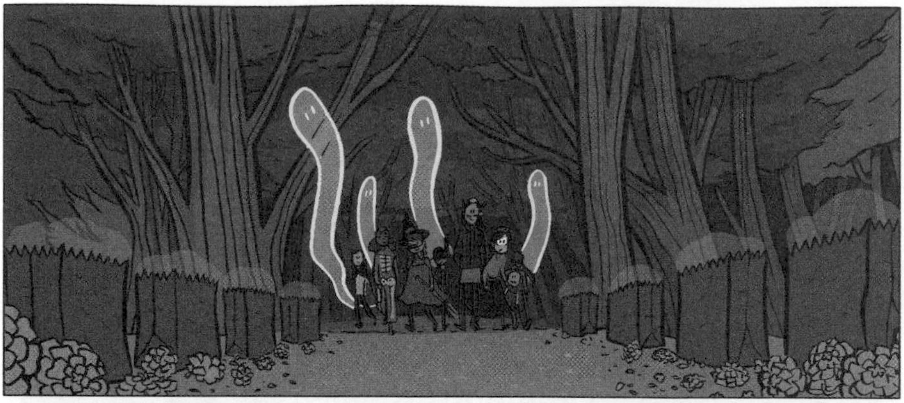

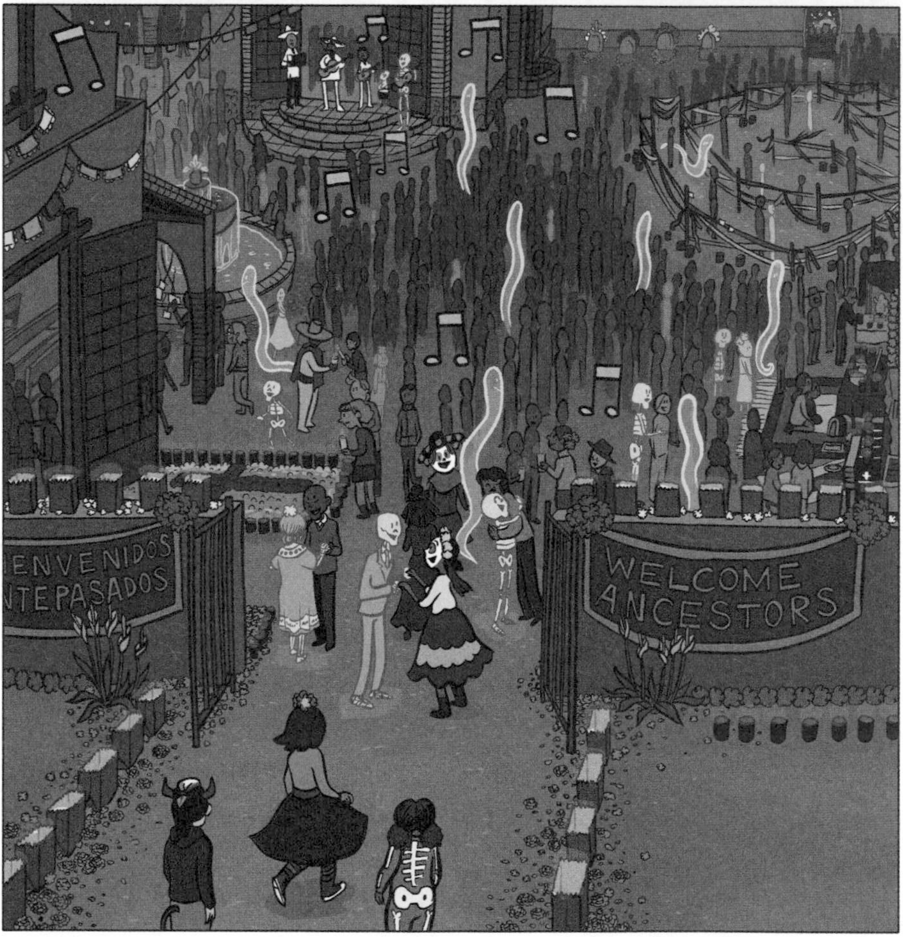

IENVENIDOS
NTEPASADOS
WELCOME
ANCESTORS

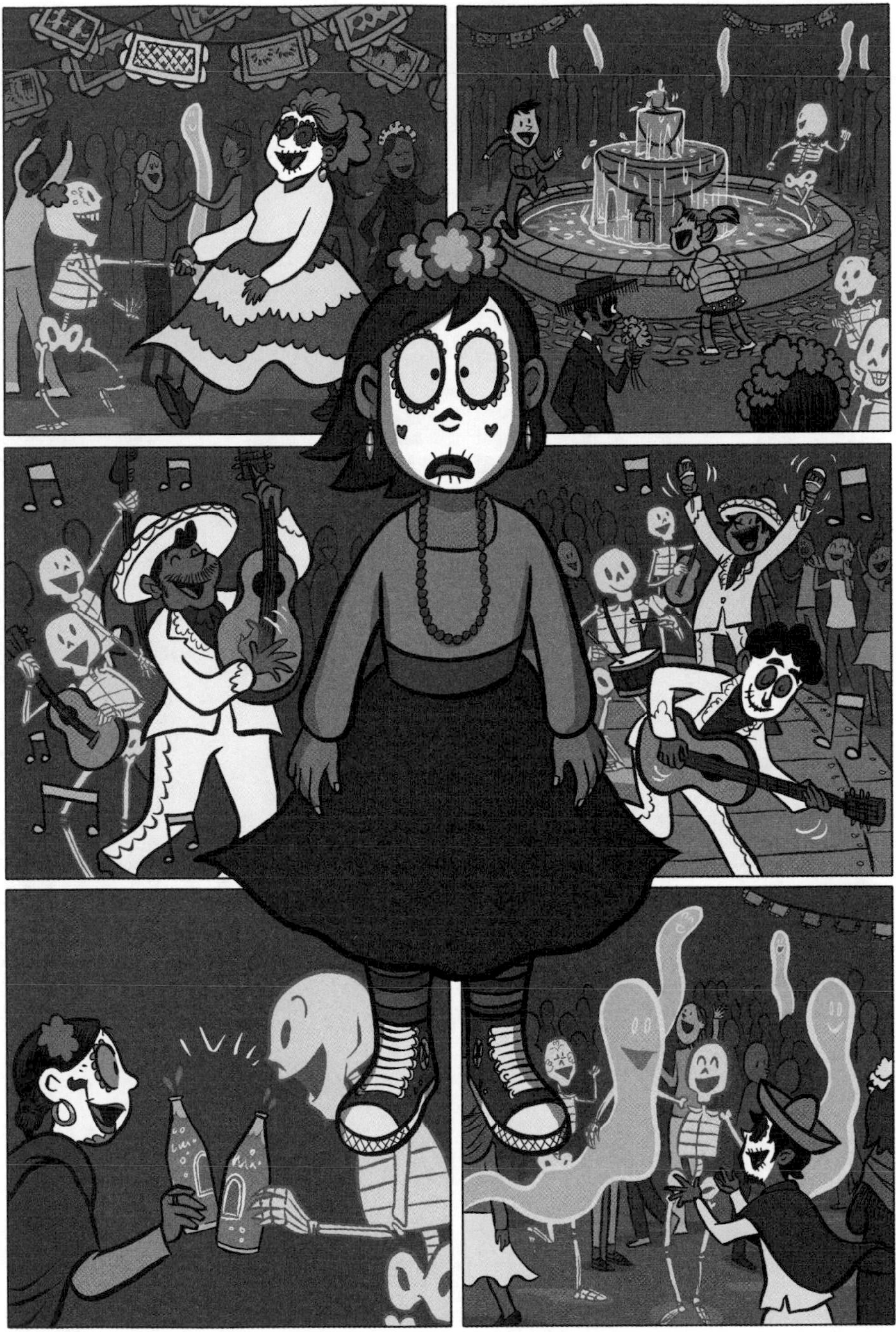

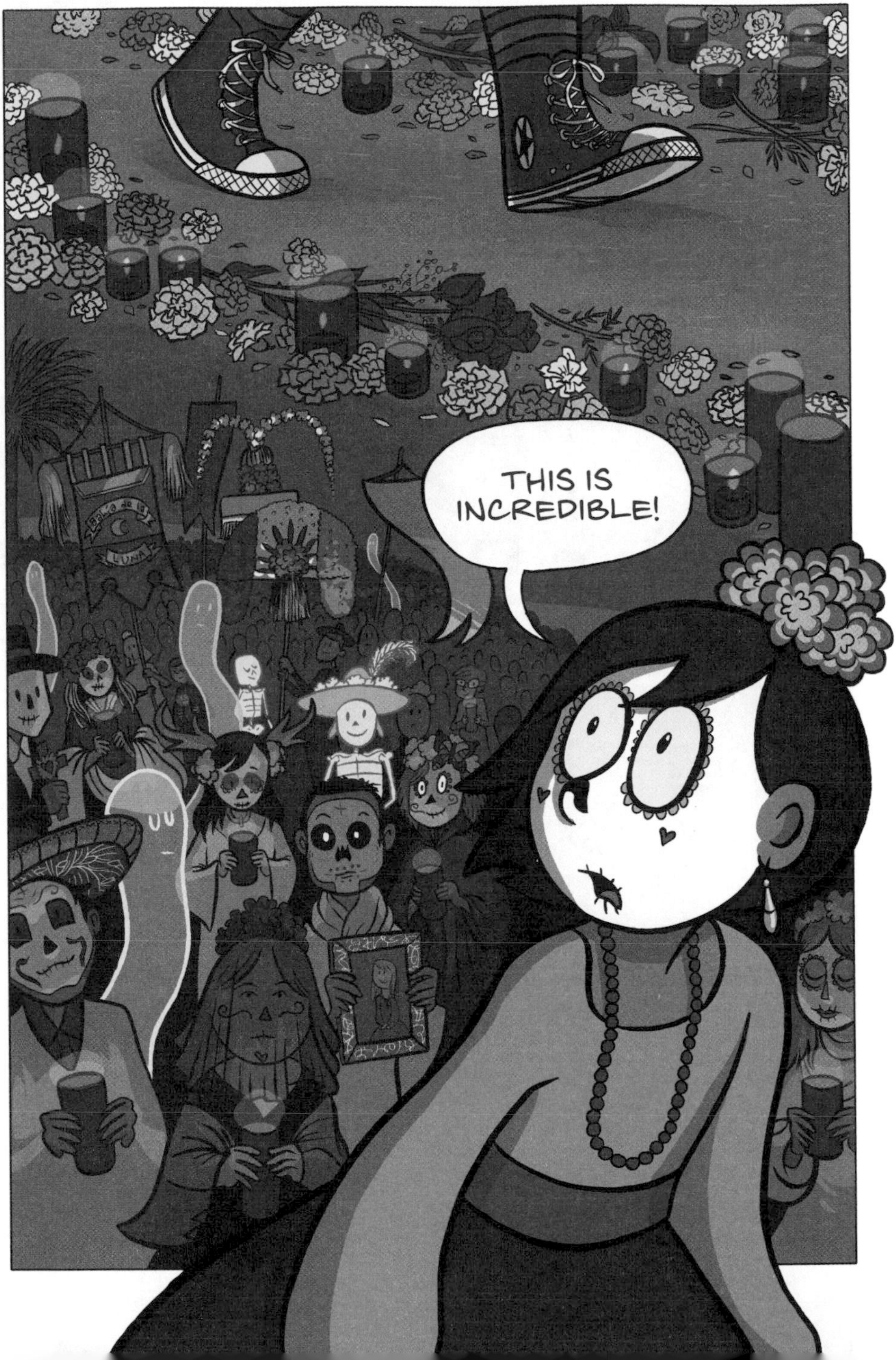
THIS IS INCREDIBLE!

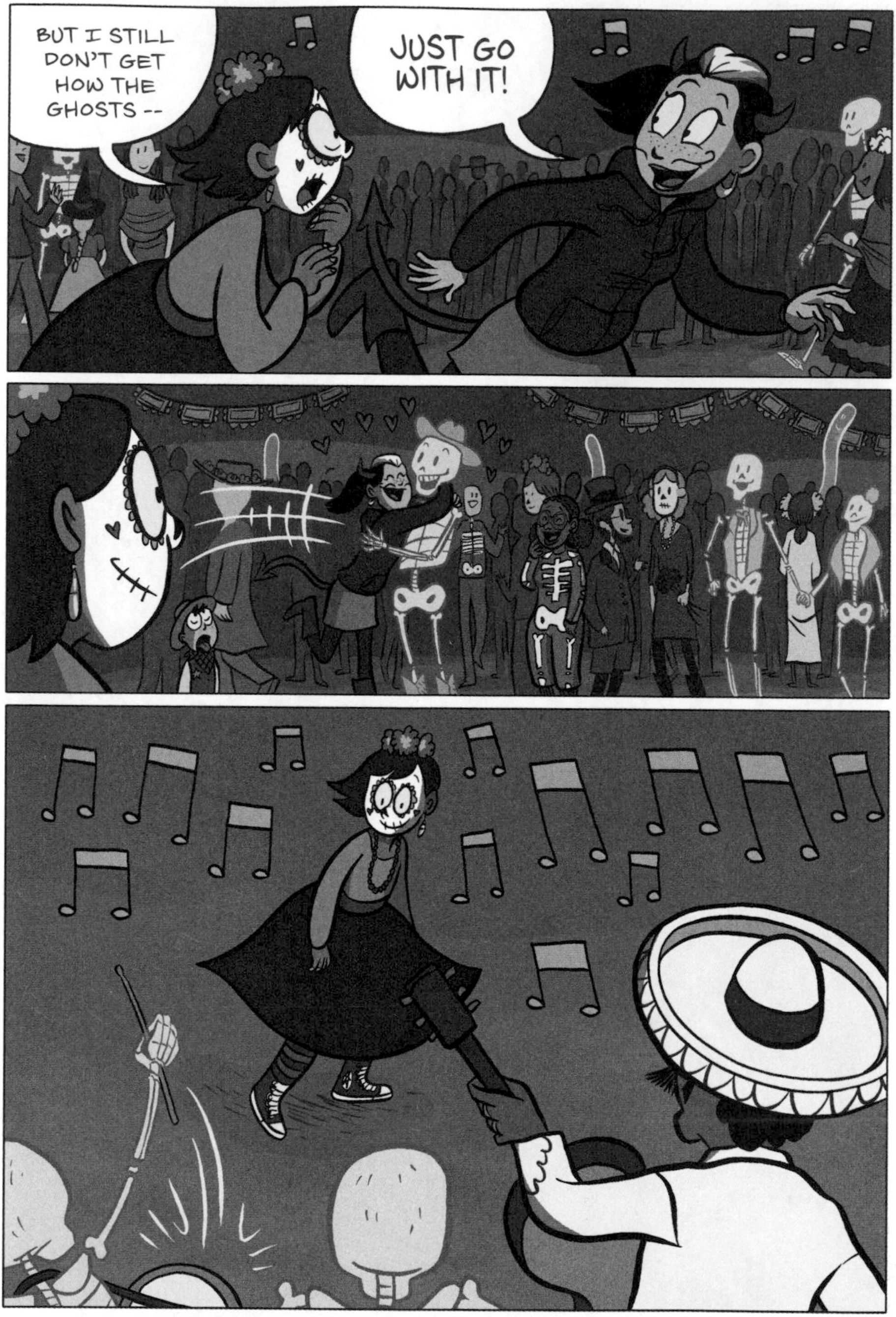
BUT I STILL DON'T GET HOW THE GHOSTS --
JUST GO WITH IT!

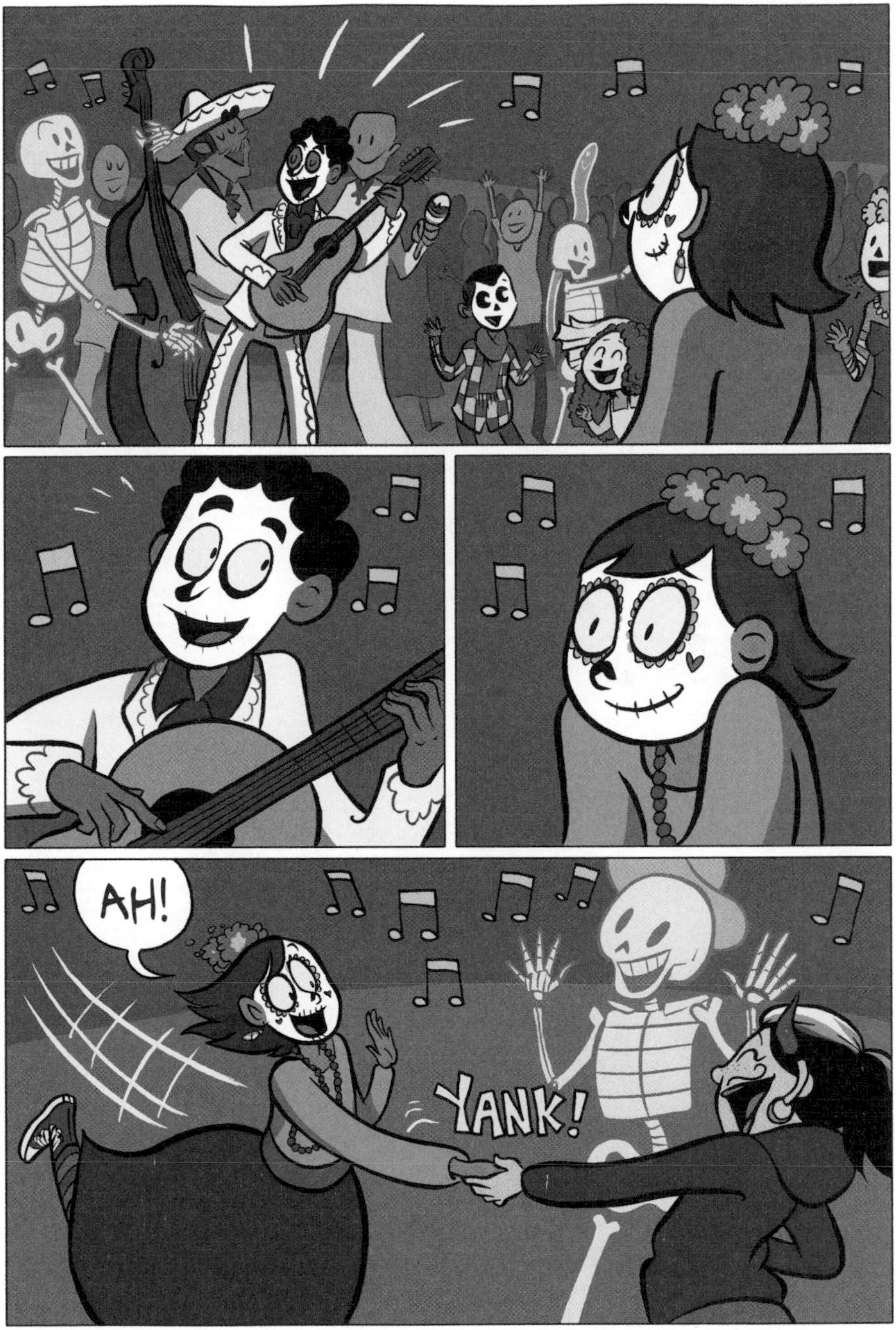
AH!
YANK!

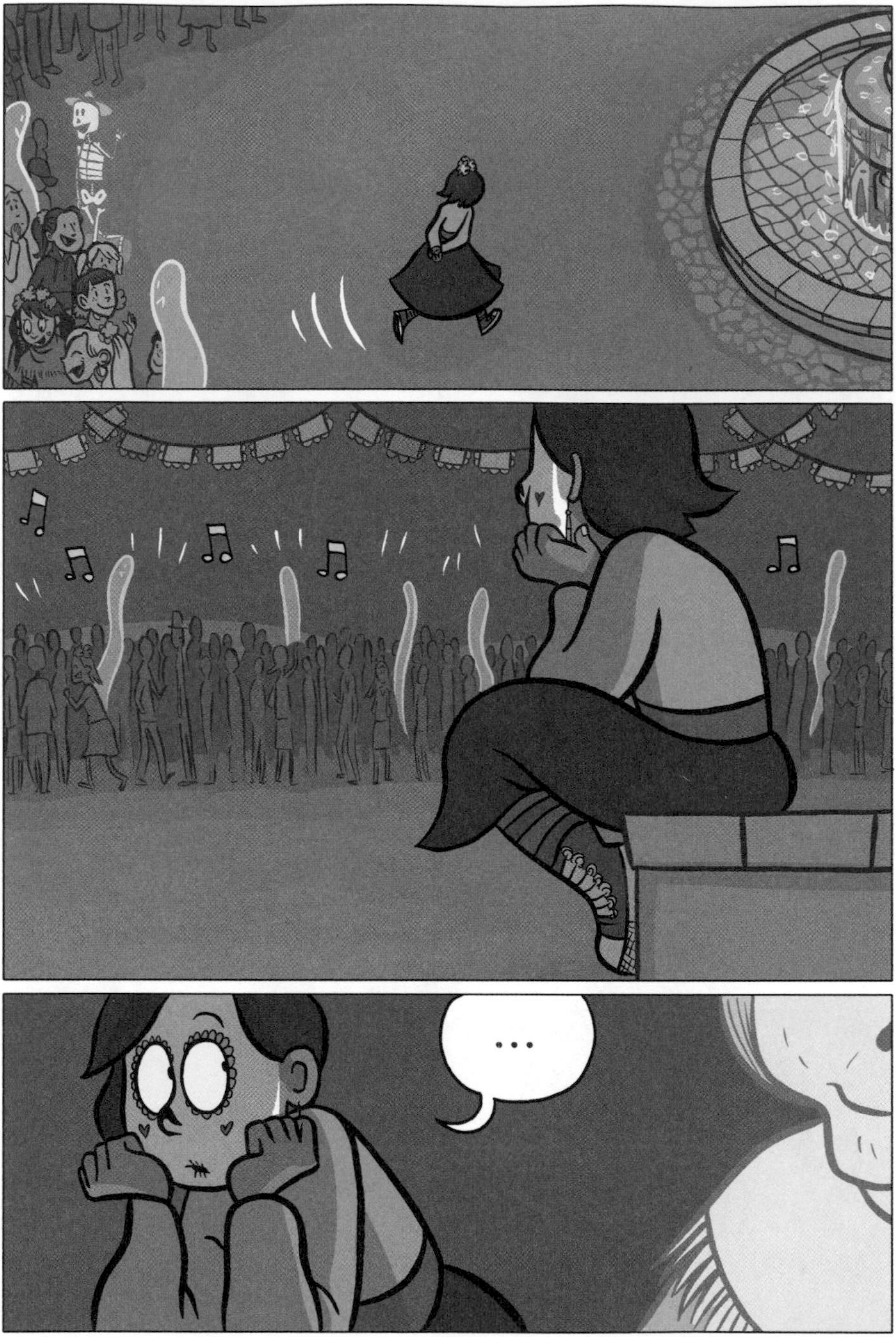
...

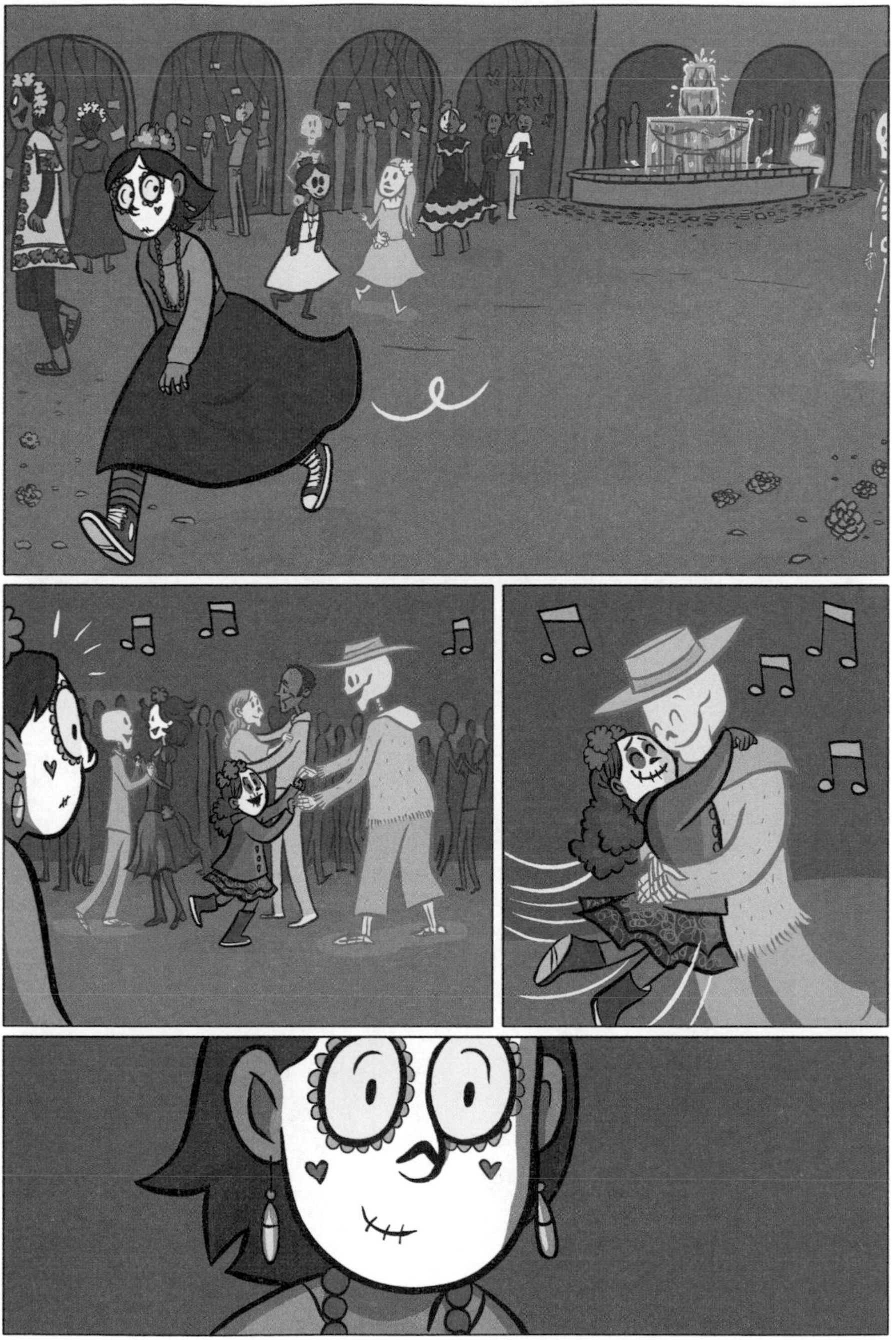

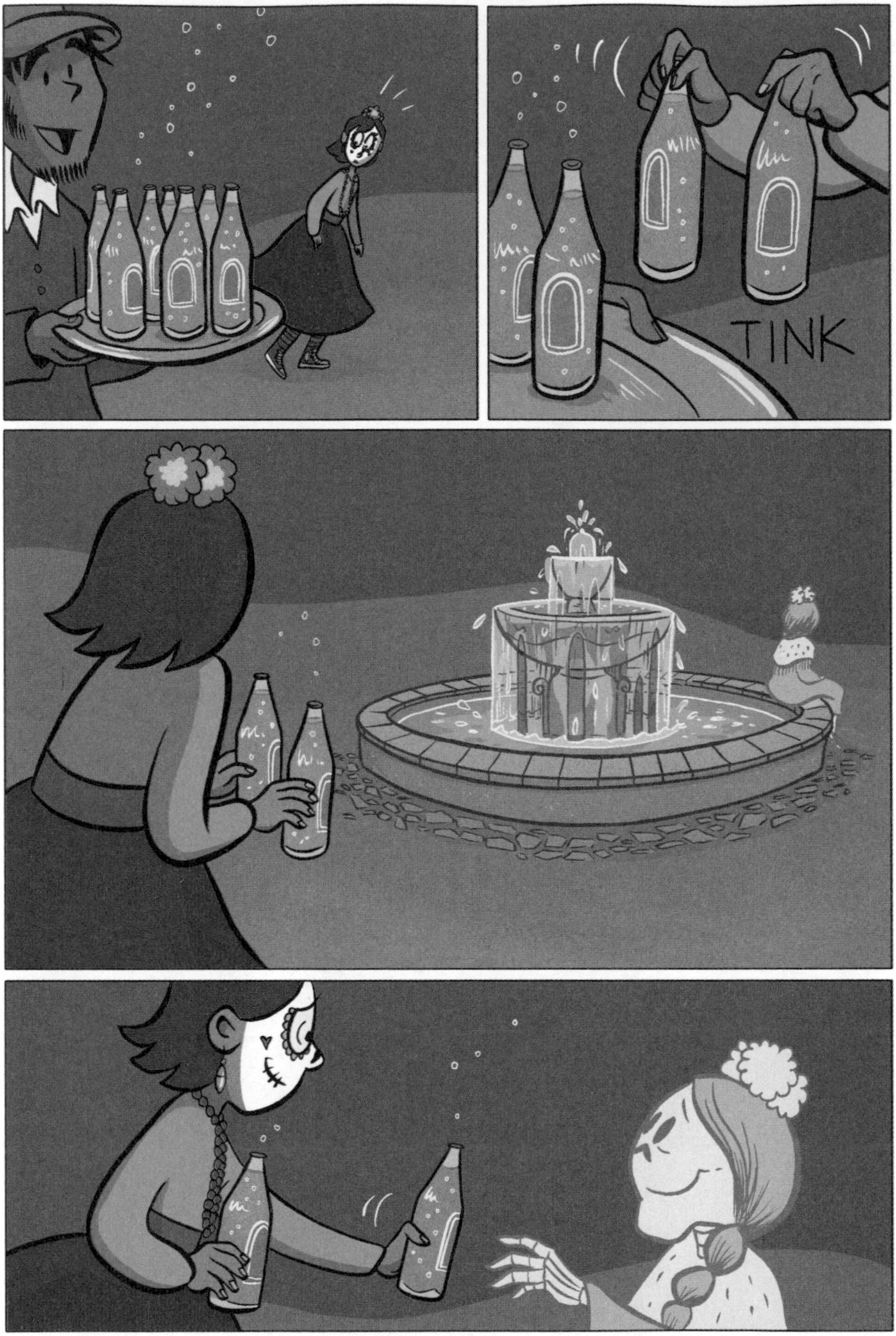
TINK

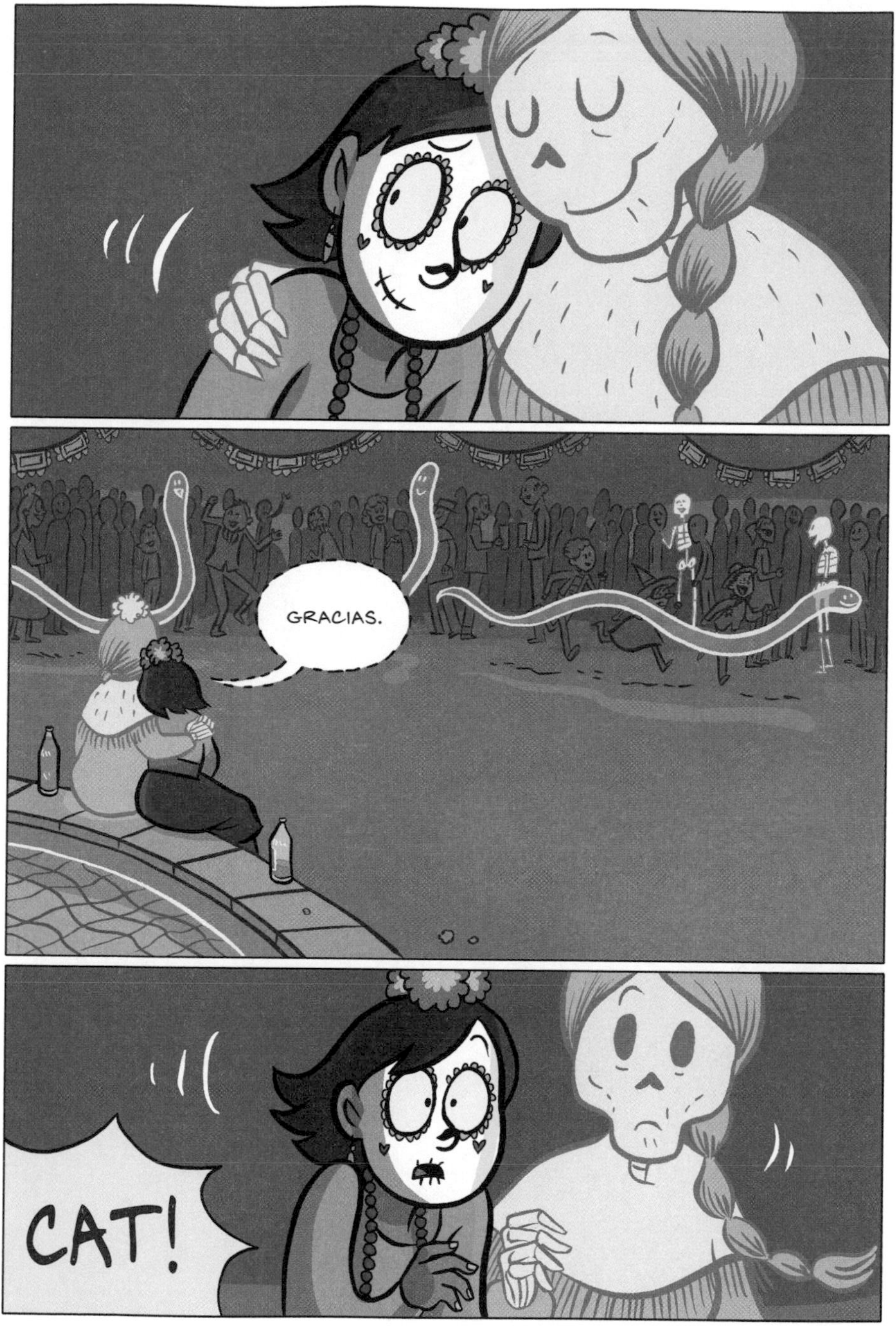
GRACIAS.
CAT!

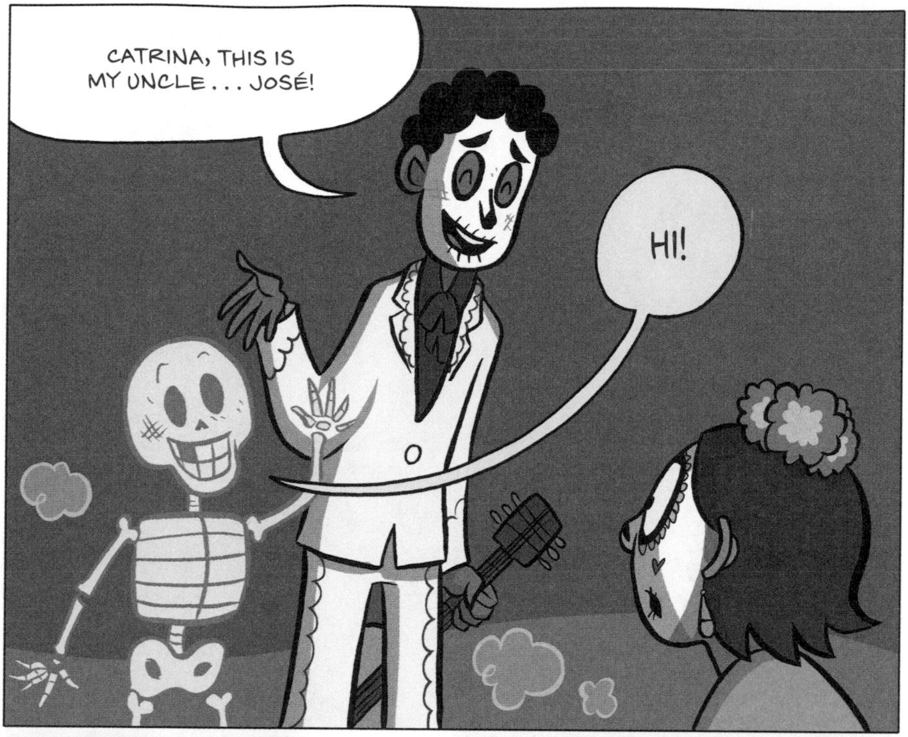
CATRINA, THIS IS MY UNCLE . . . JOSÉ!
HI!

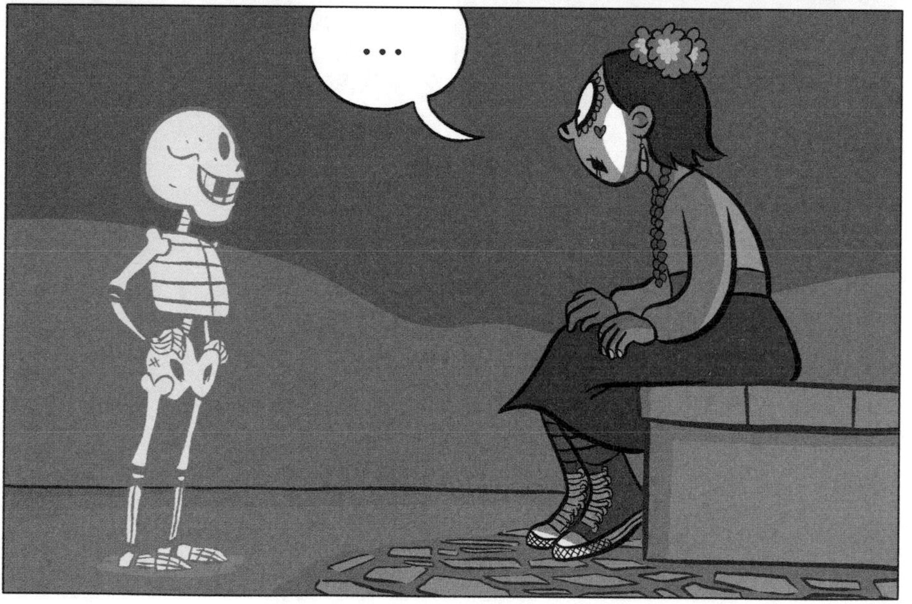
. . .

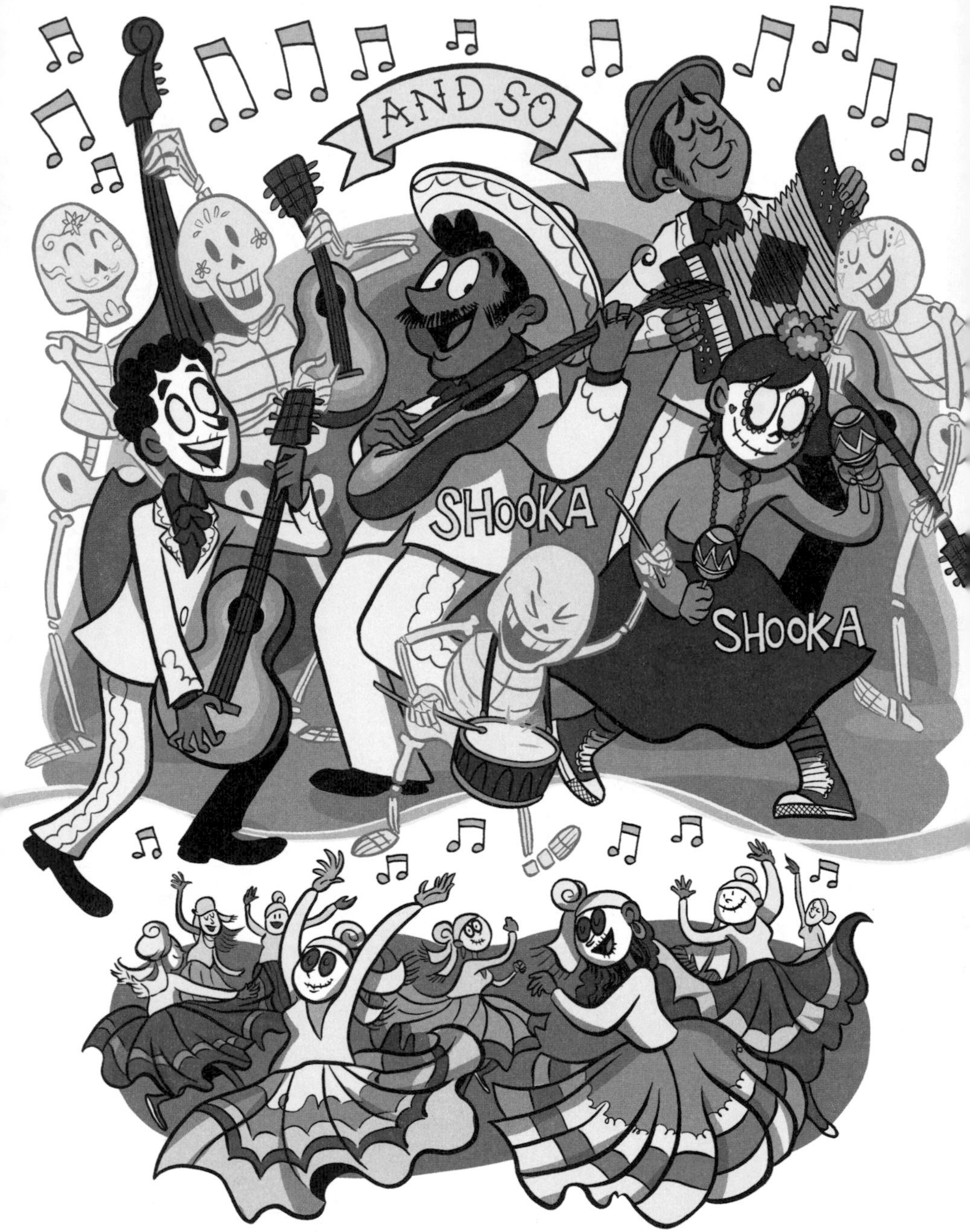
AND SO
SHOOKA
SHOOKA

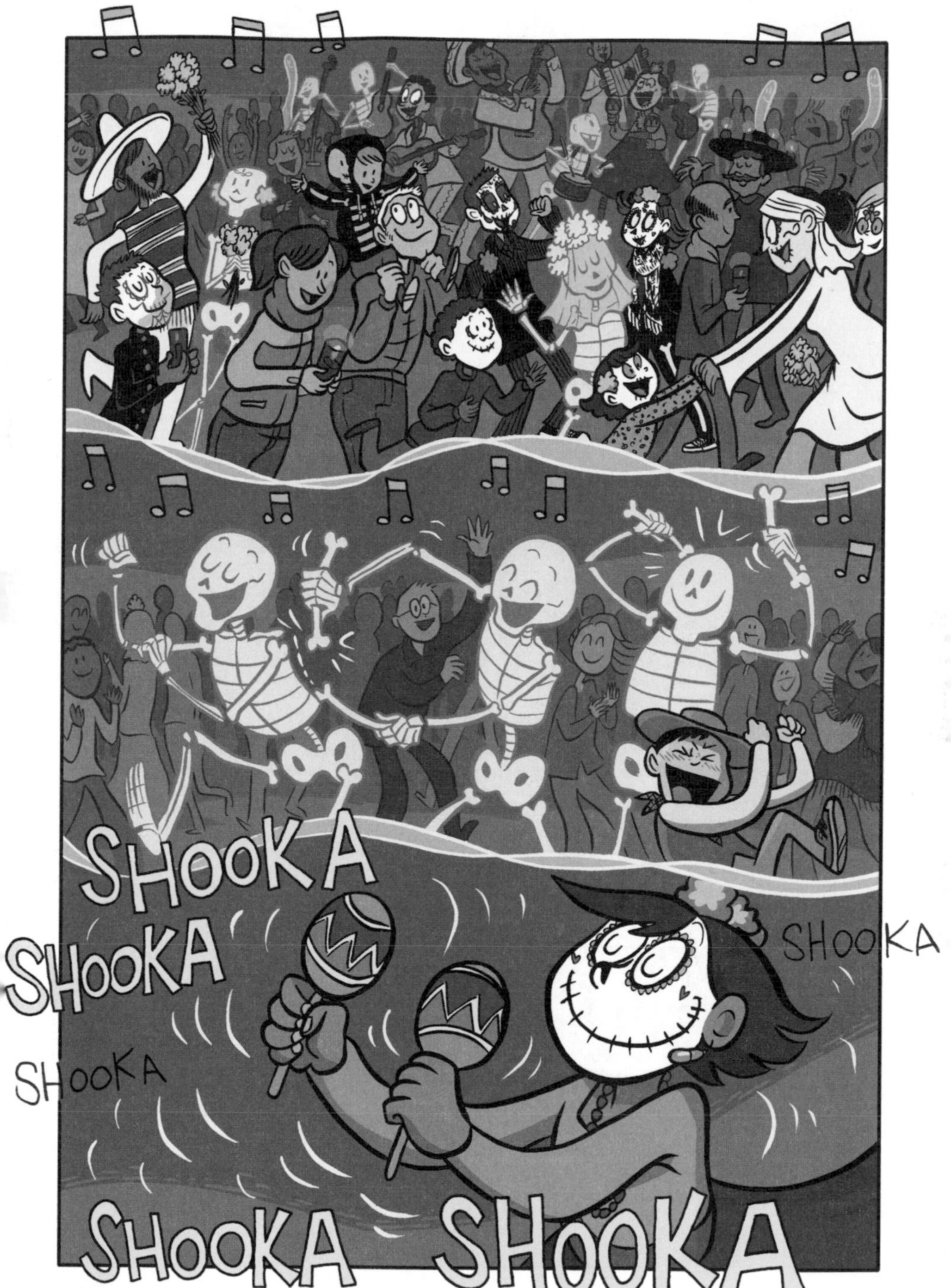
SHOOKA
SHOOKA
SHOOKA
SHOOKA
SHOOKA
SHOOKA

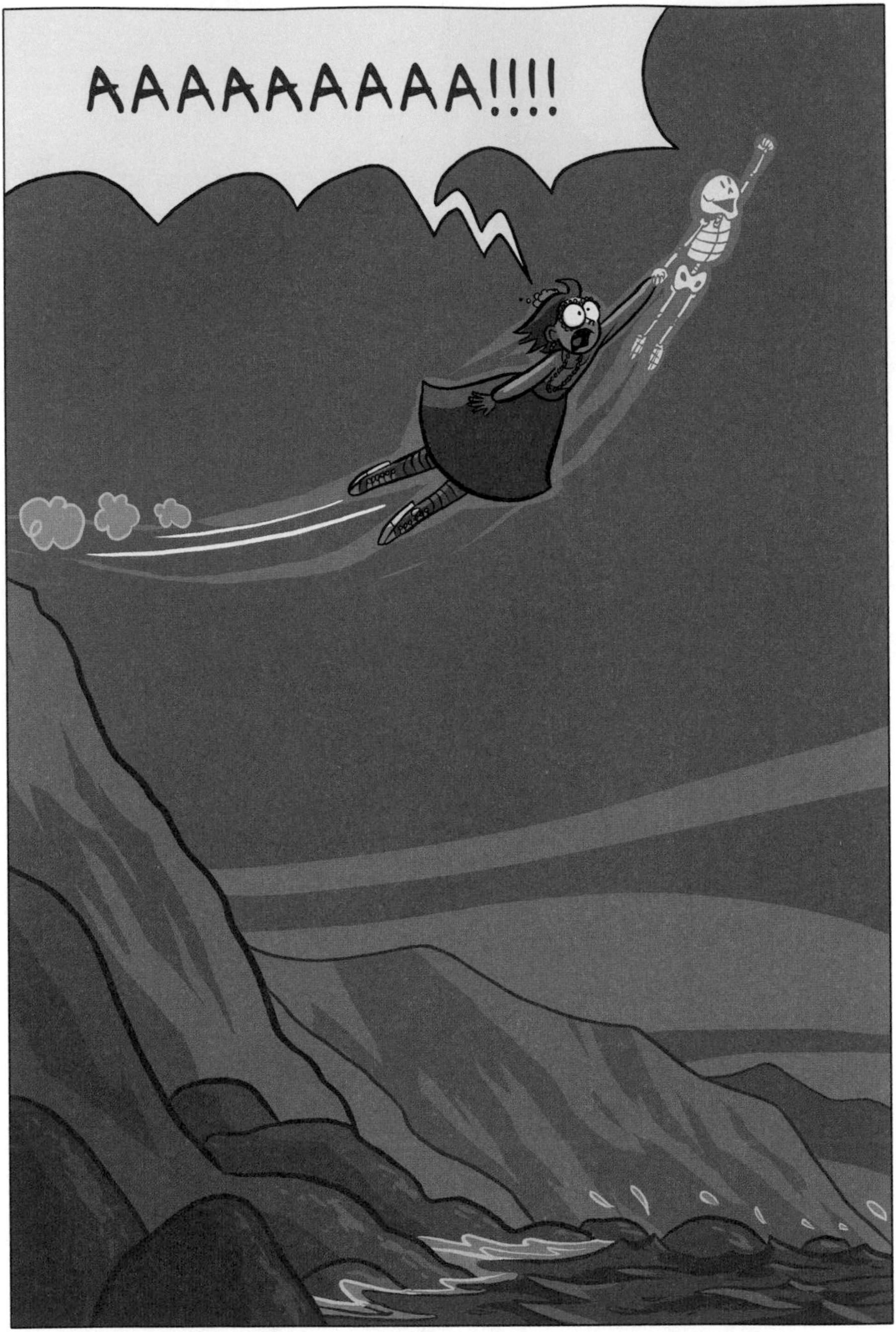
AAAAAAAAAA!!!!

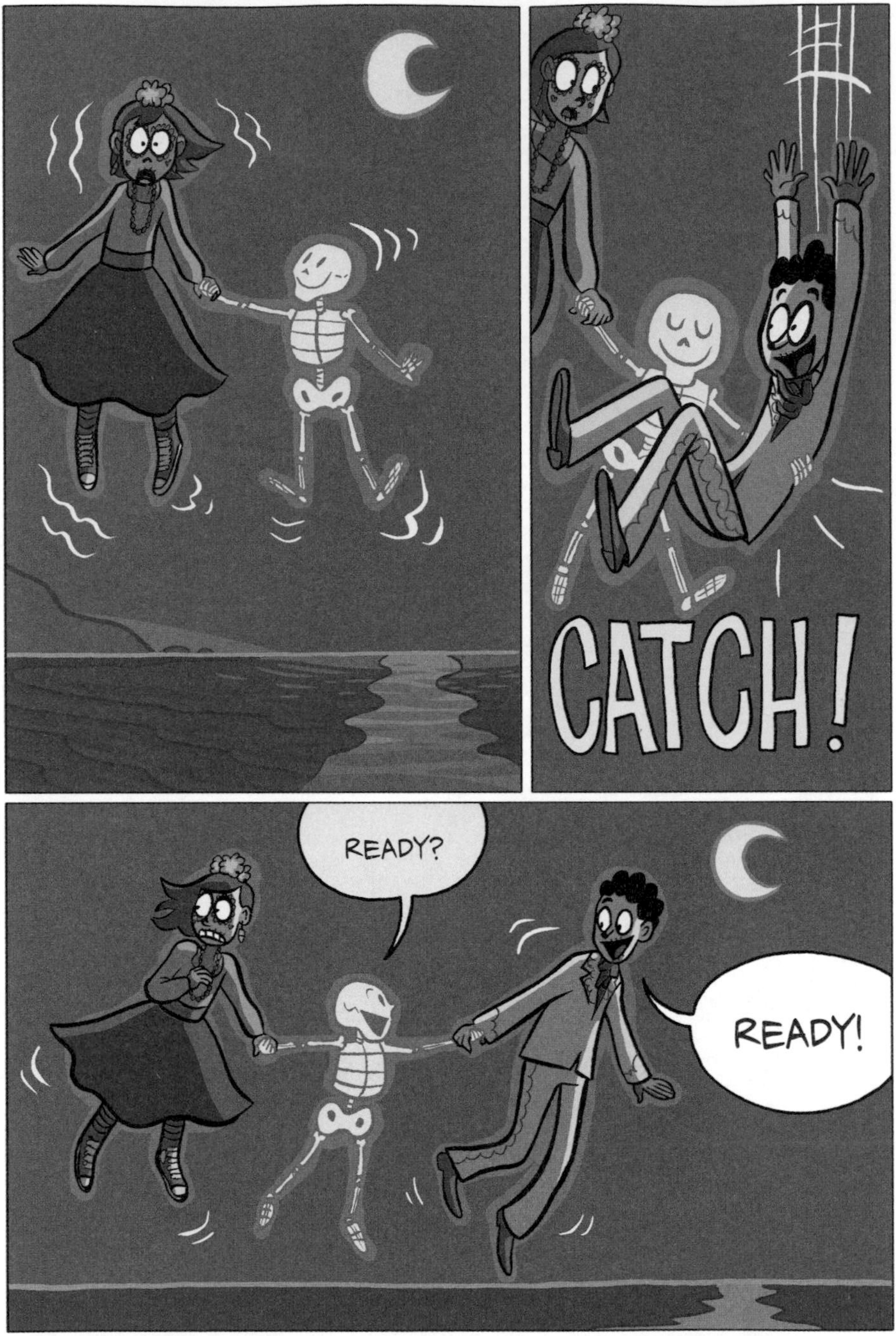
CATCH!
READY?
READY!

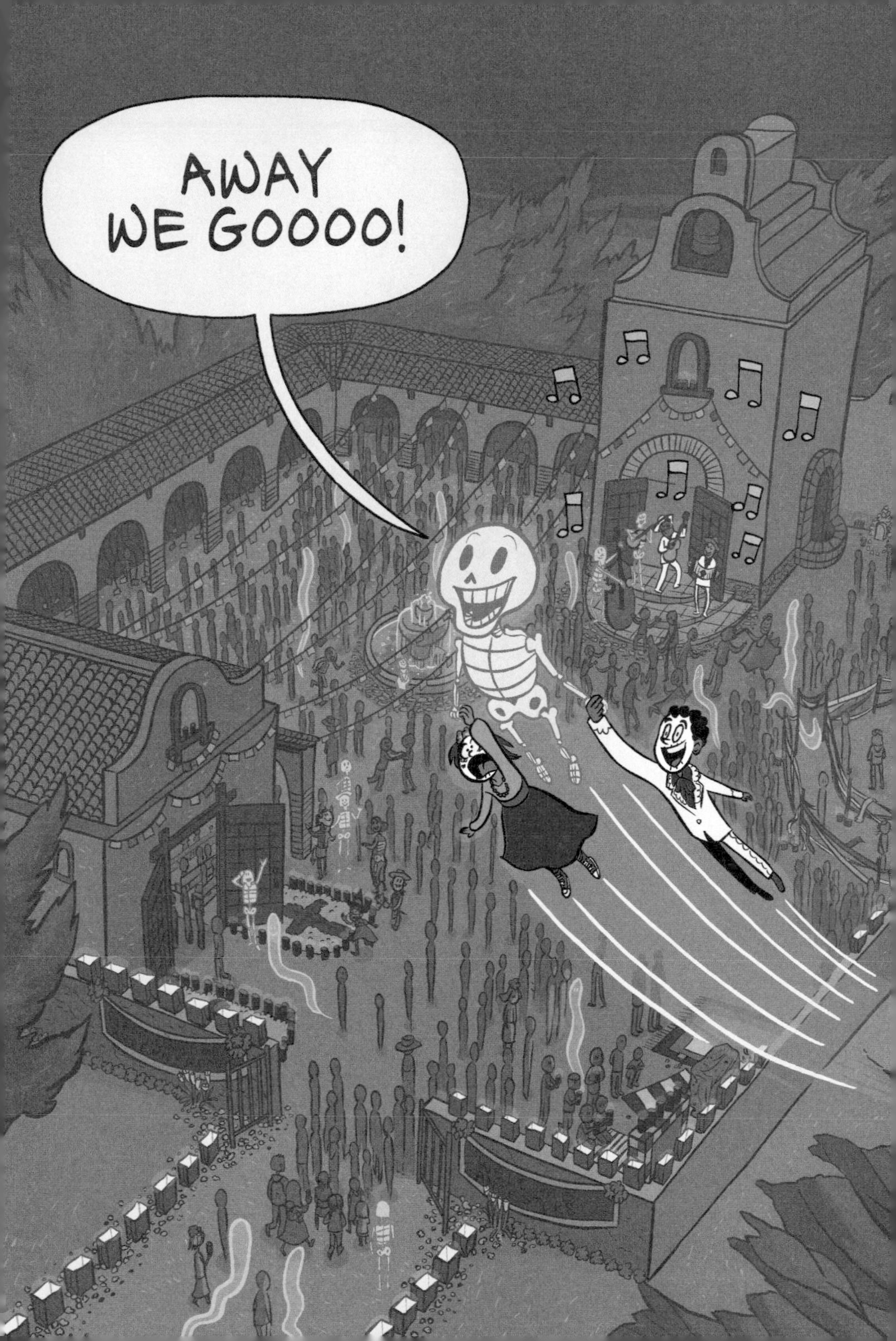
AWAY WE GOOOO!

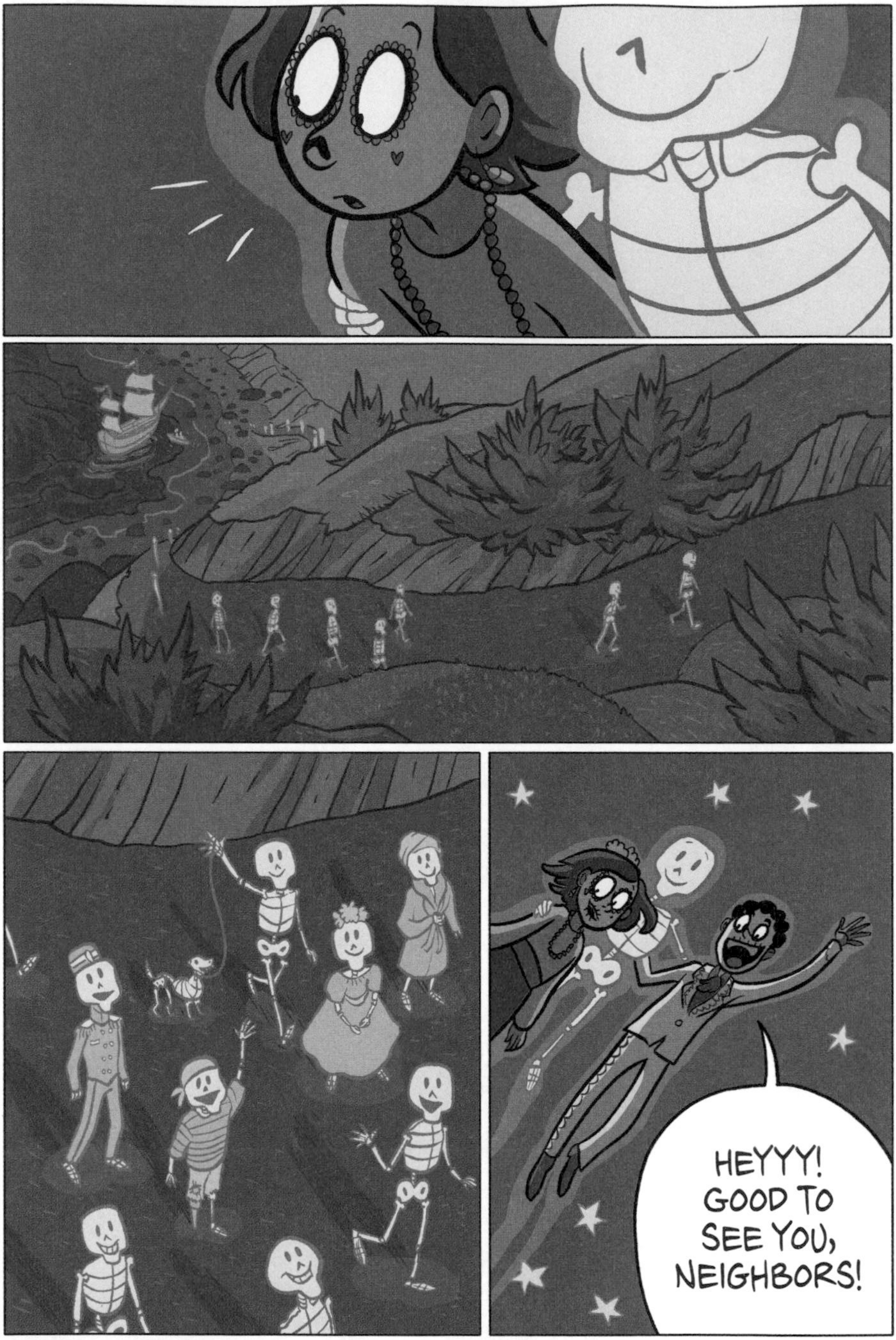
HEYYY! GOOD TO SEE YOU, NEIGHBORS!

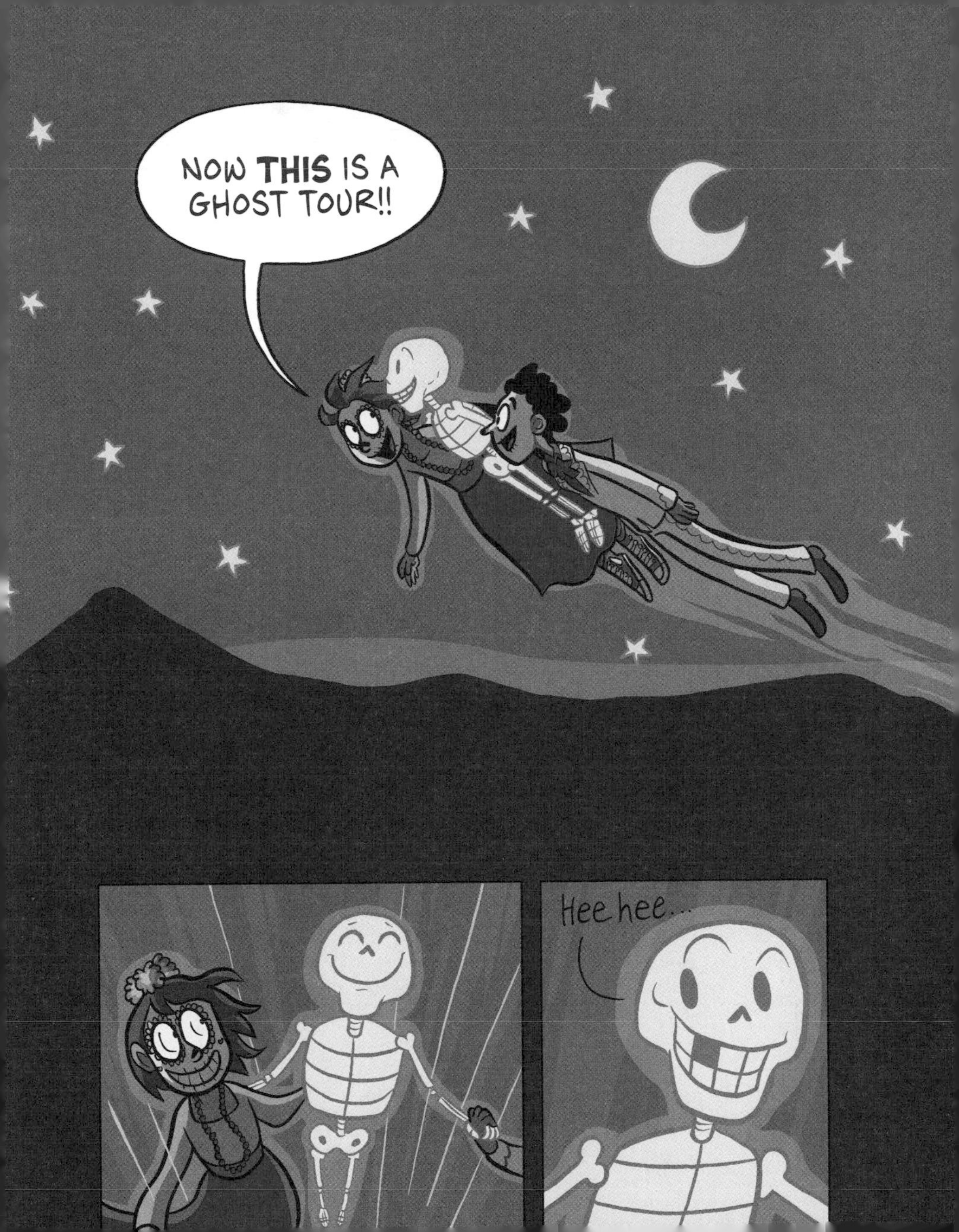
NOW THIS IS A GHOST TOUR!!
Hee hee...

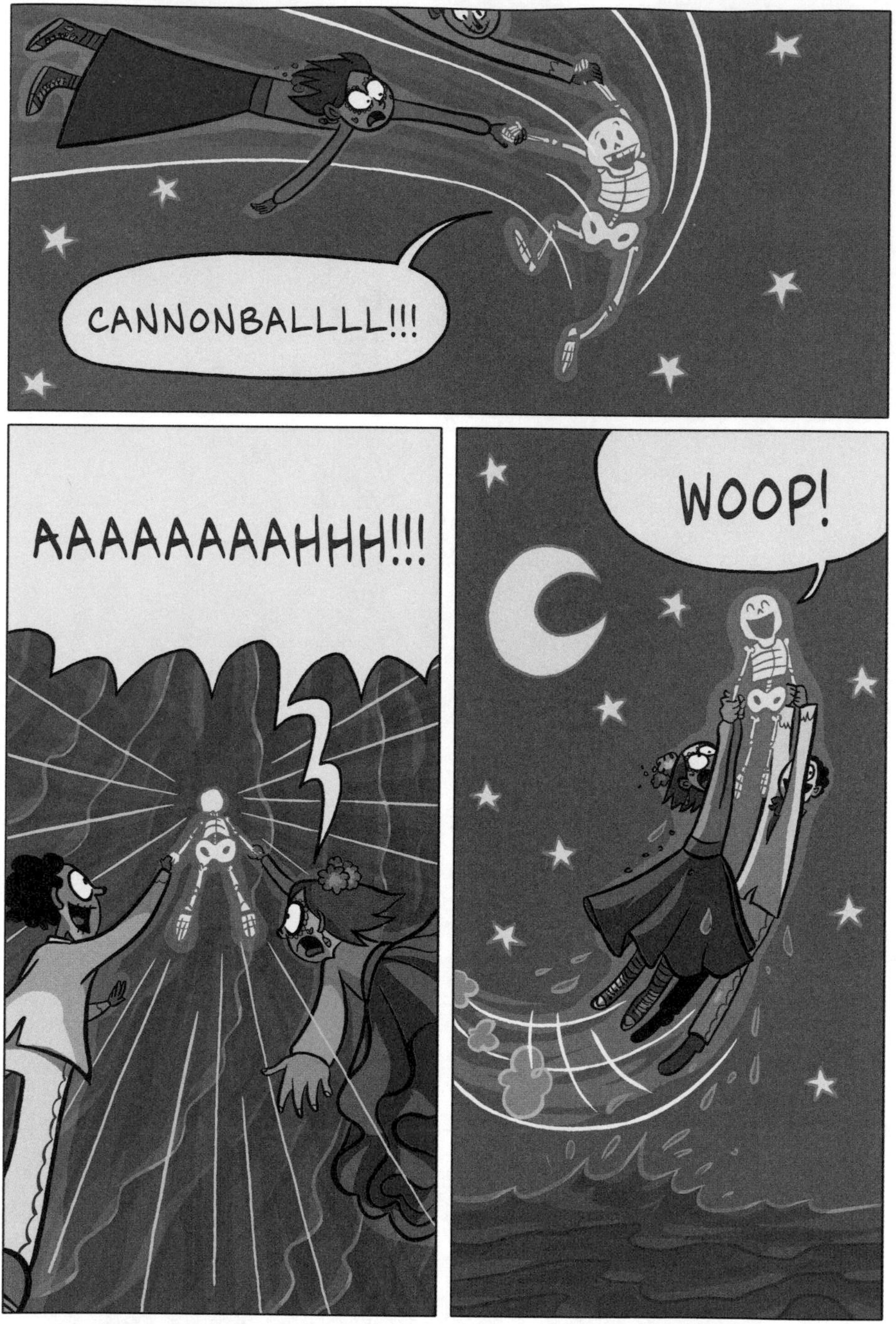
CANNONBALLLL!!!
AAAAAAAAHHH!!!
WOOP!

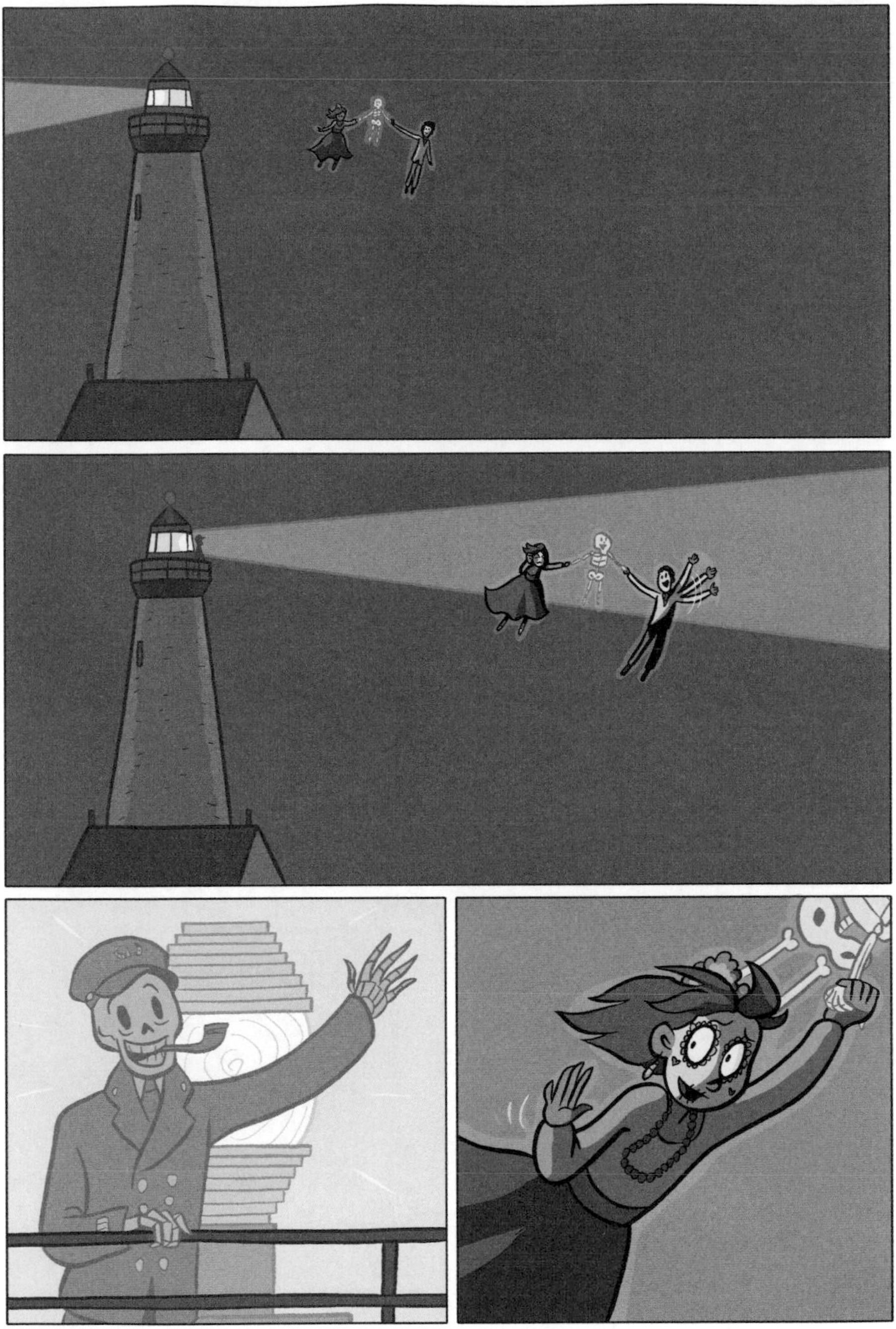

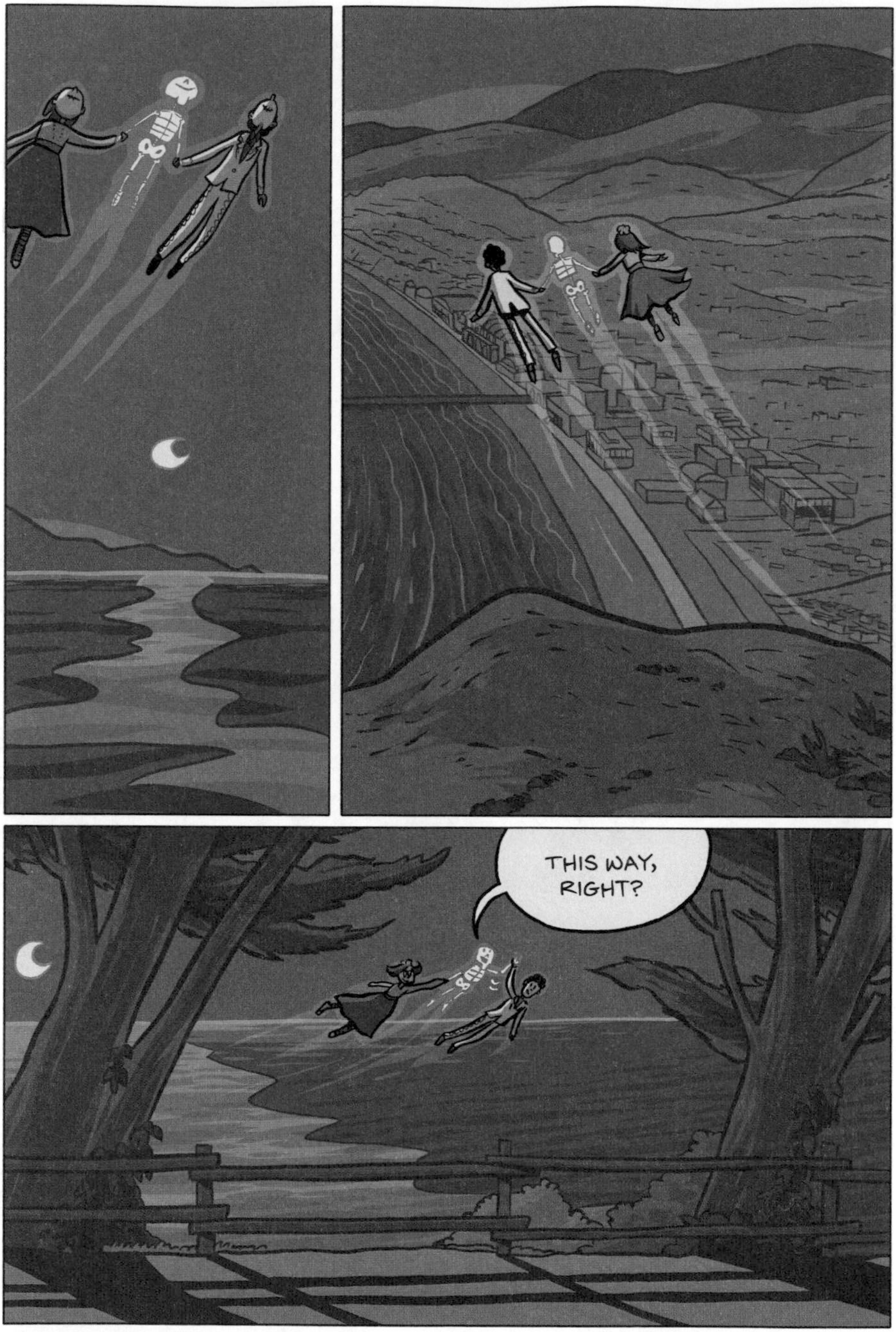
THIS WAY, RIGHT?

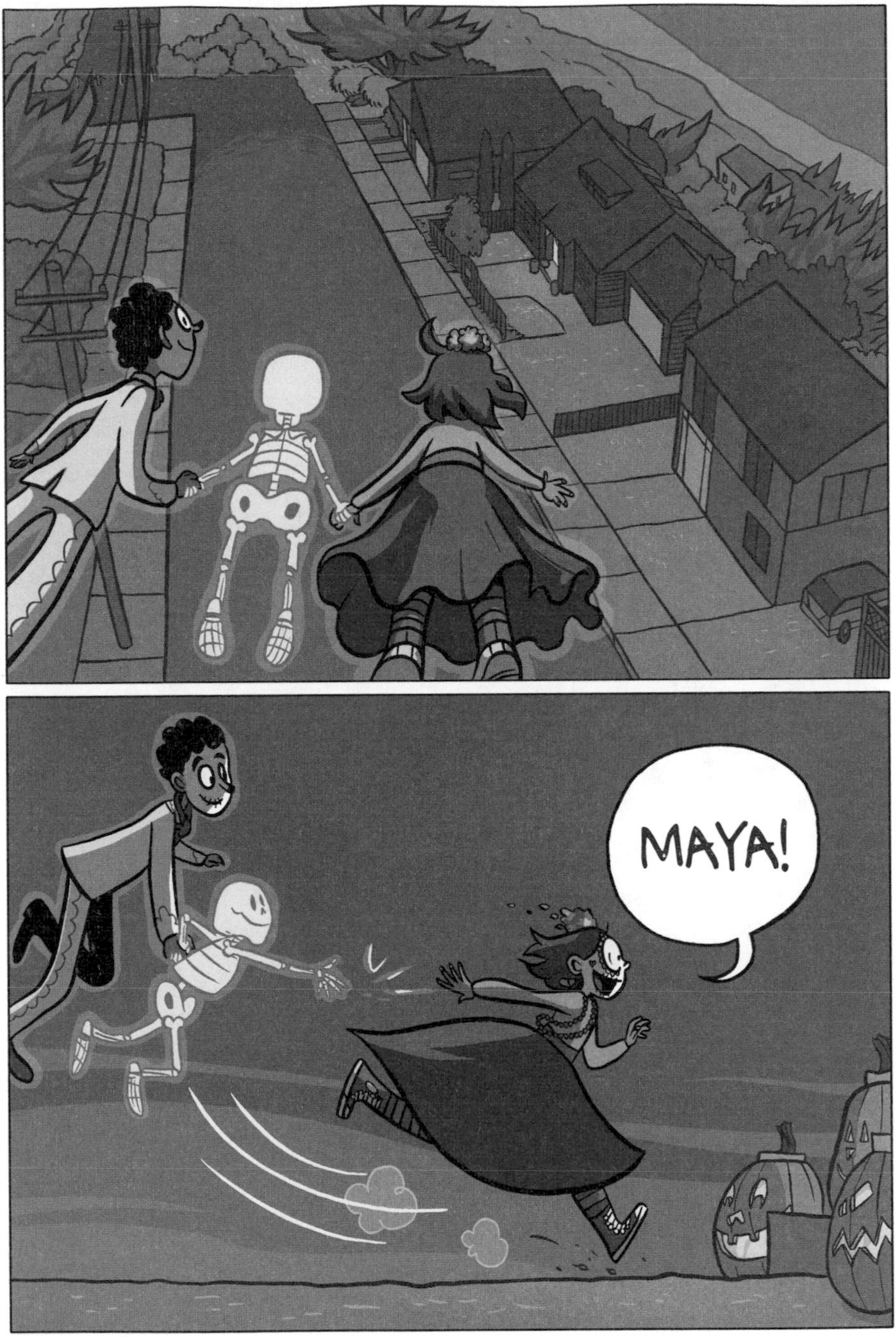
MAYA!

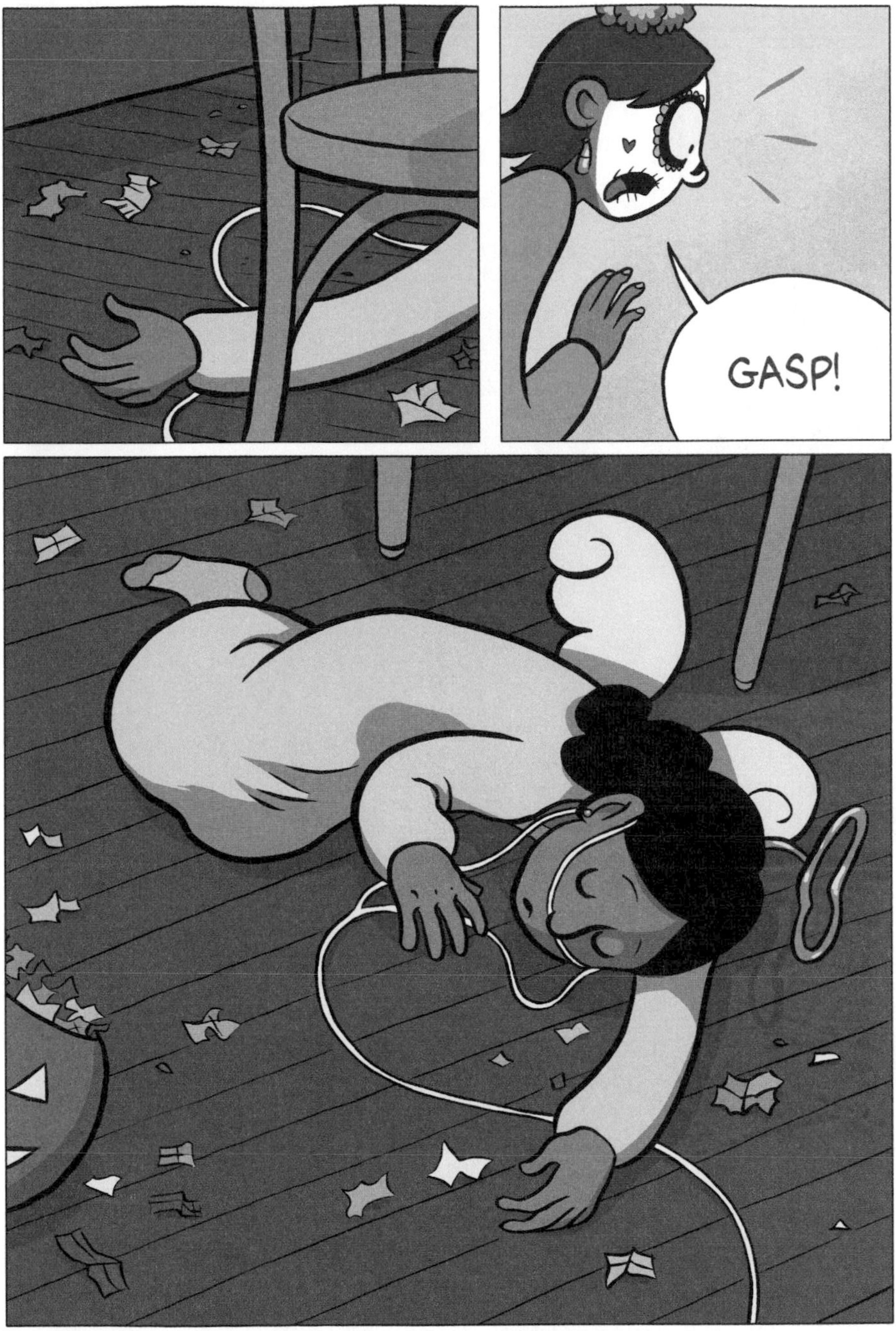
GASP!

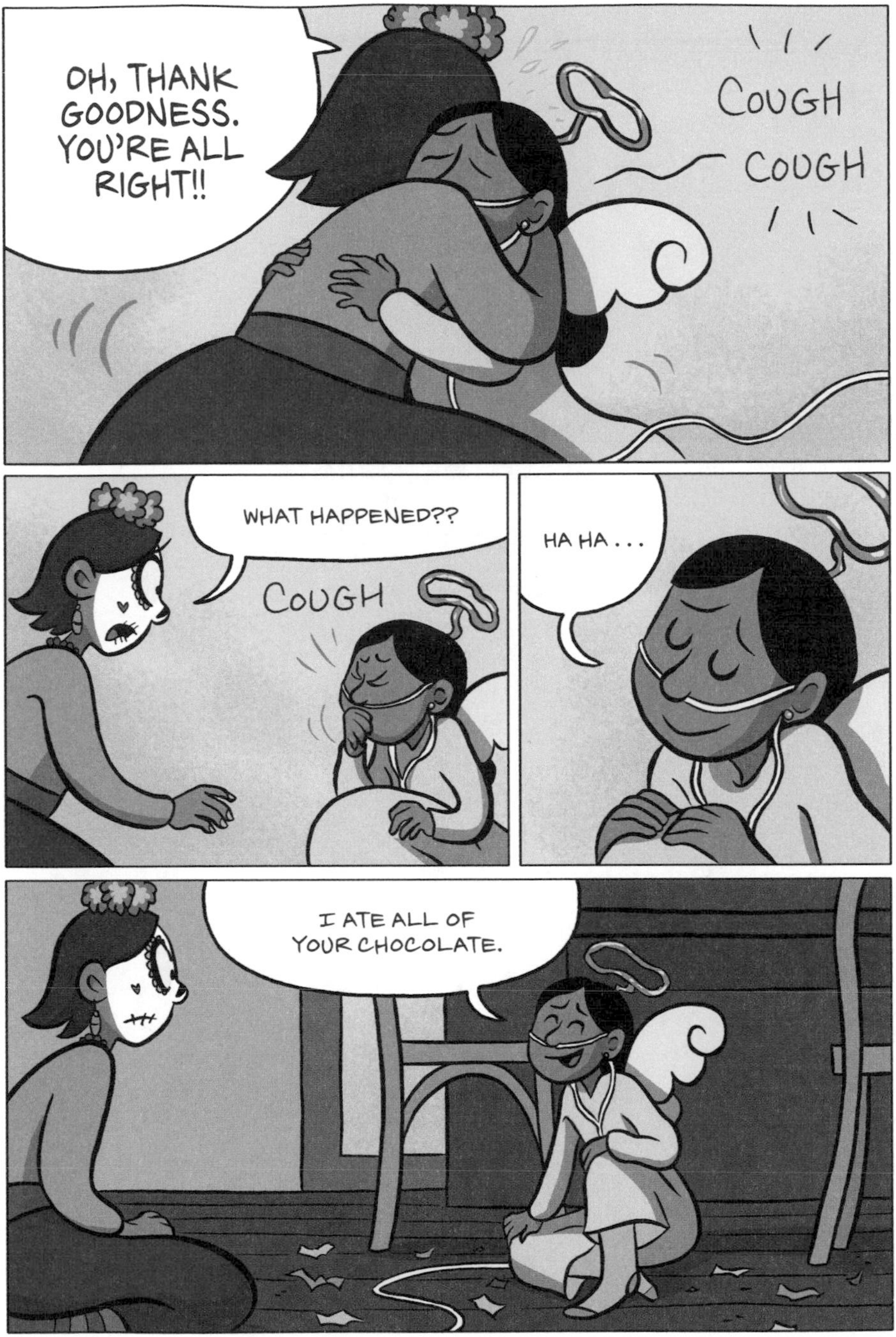
OH, THANK GOODNESS. YOU'RE ALL RIGHT!!
COUGH
COUGH
WHAT HAPPENED??
COUGH
HA HA . . .
I ATE ALL OF YOUR CHOCOLATE.

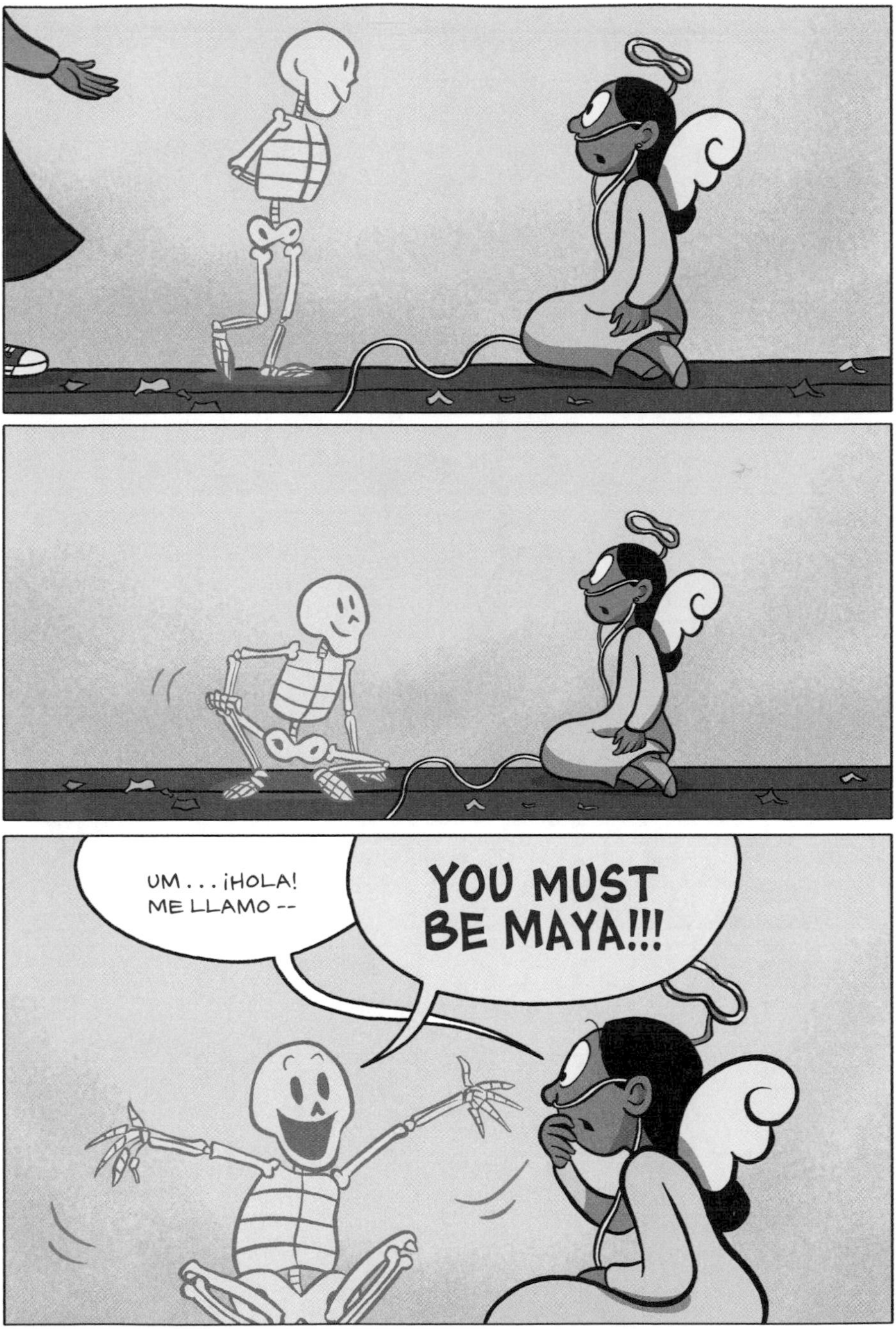
UM . . . ¡HOLA! ME LLAMO --
YOU MUST BE MAYA!!!

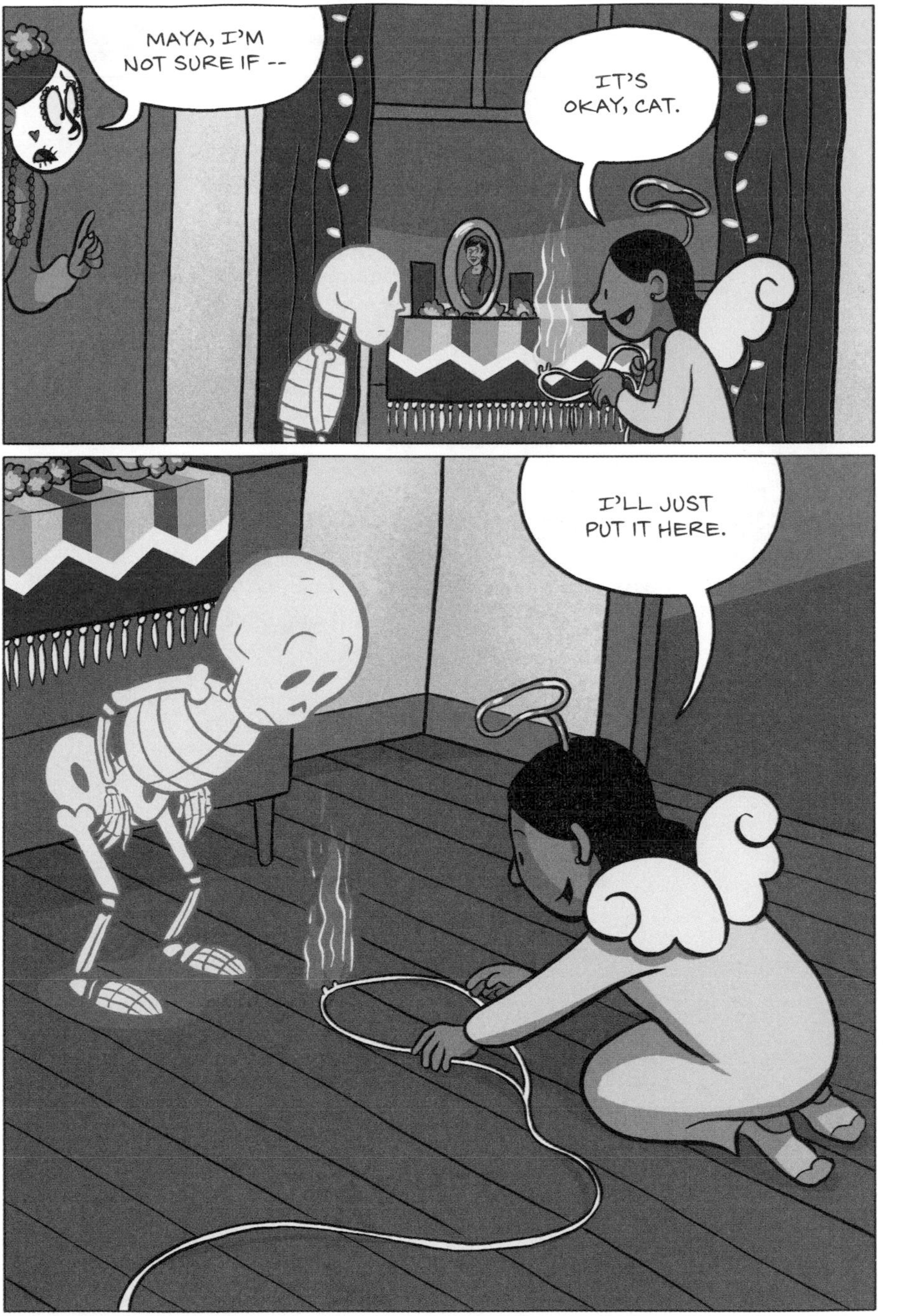
MAYA, I'M NOT SURE IF --
IT'S OKAY, CAT.
I'LL JUST PUT IT HERE.

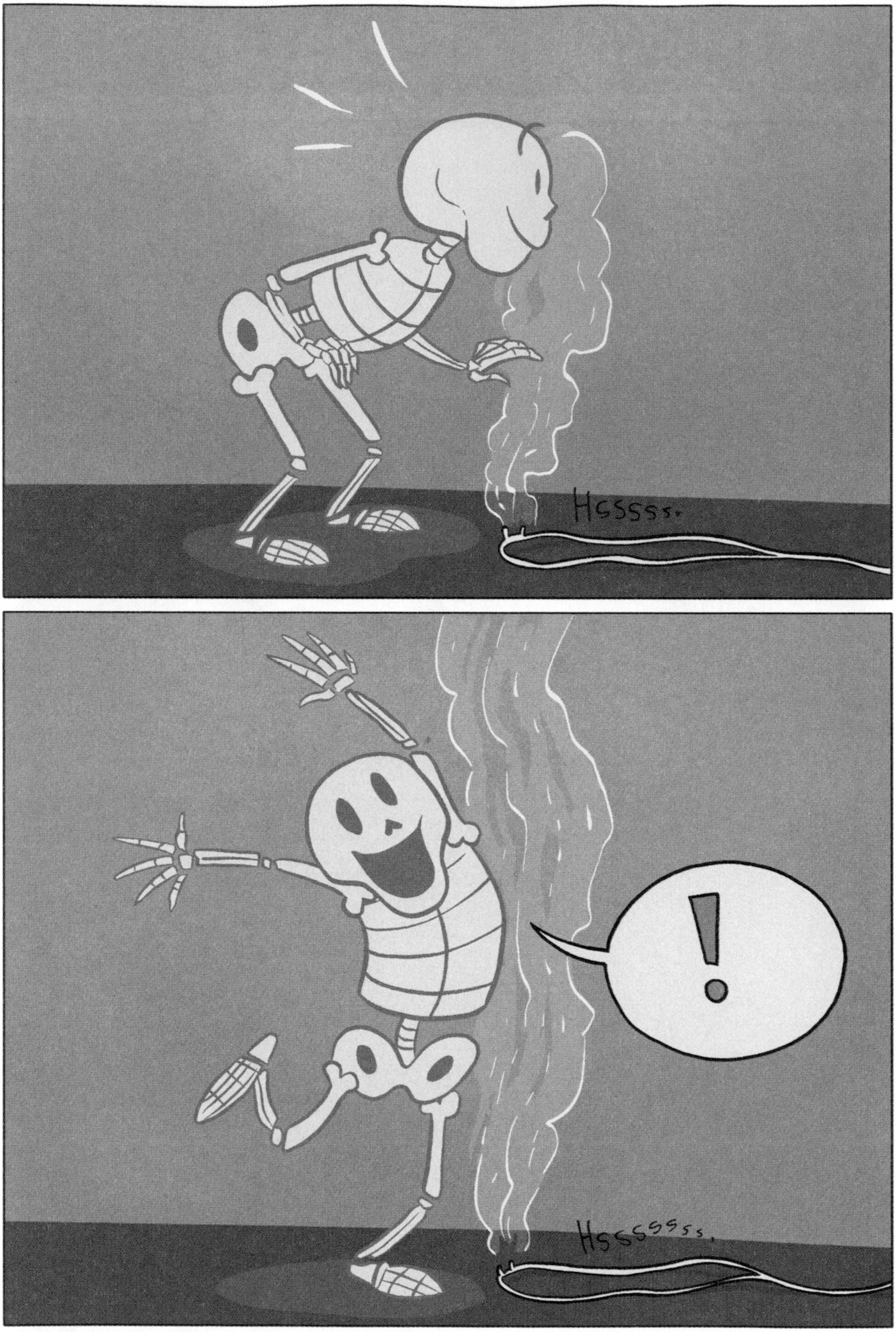
Hsssss.
Hssssss.
!

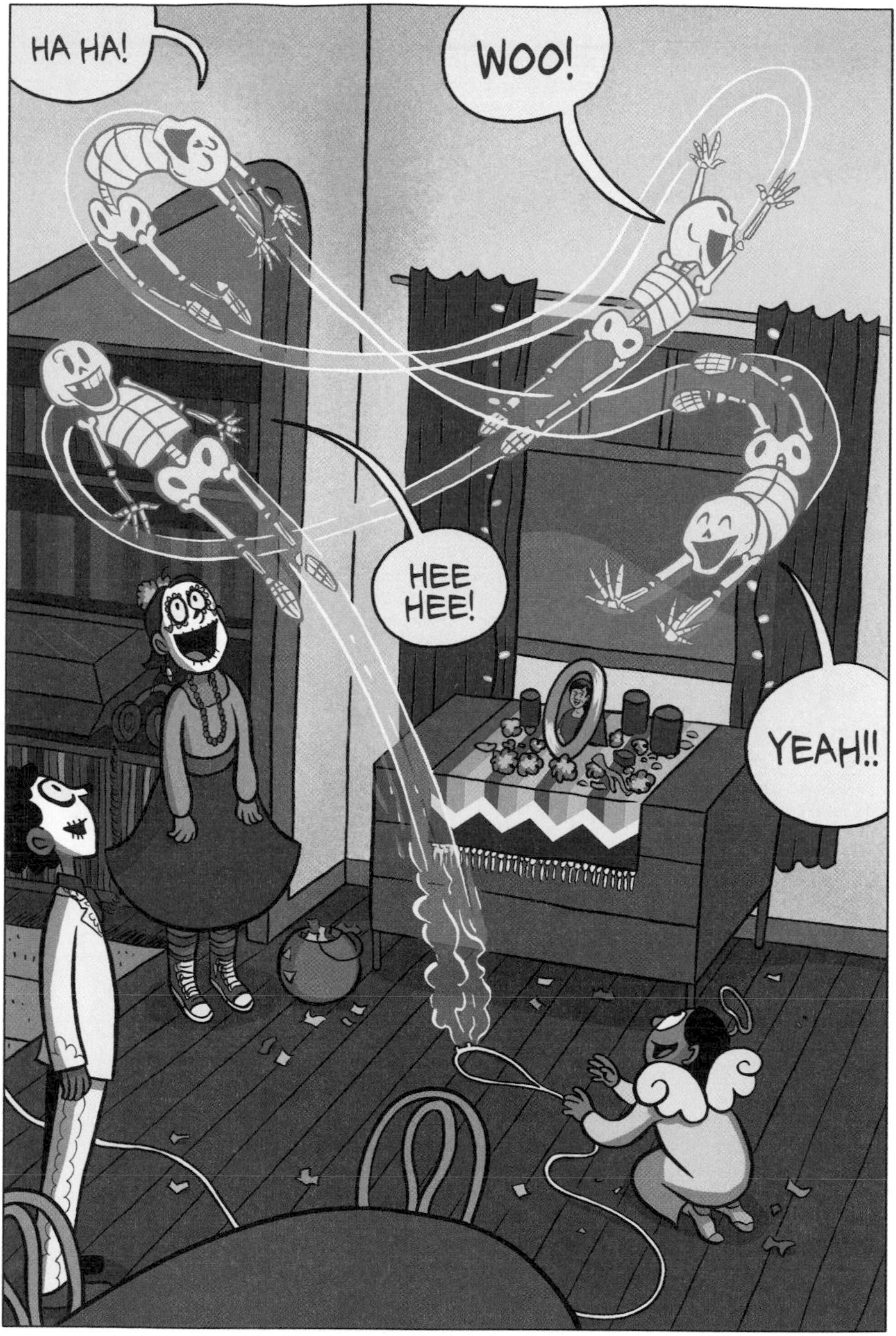
HA HA!
WOO!
HEE HEE!
YEAH!!

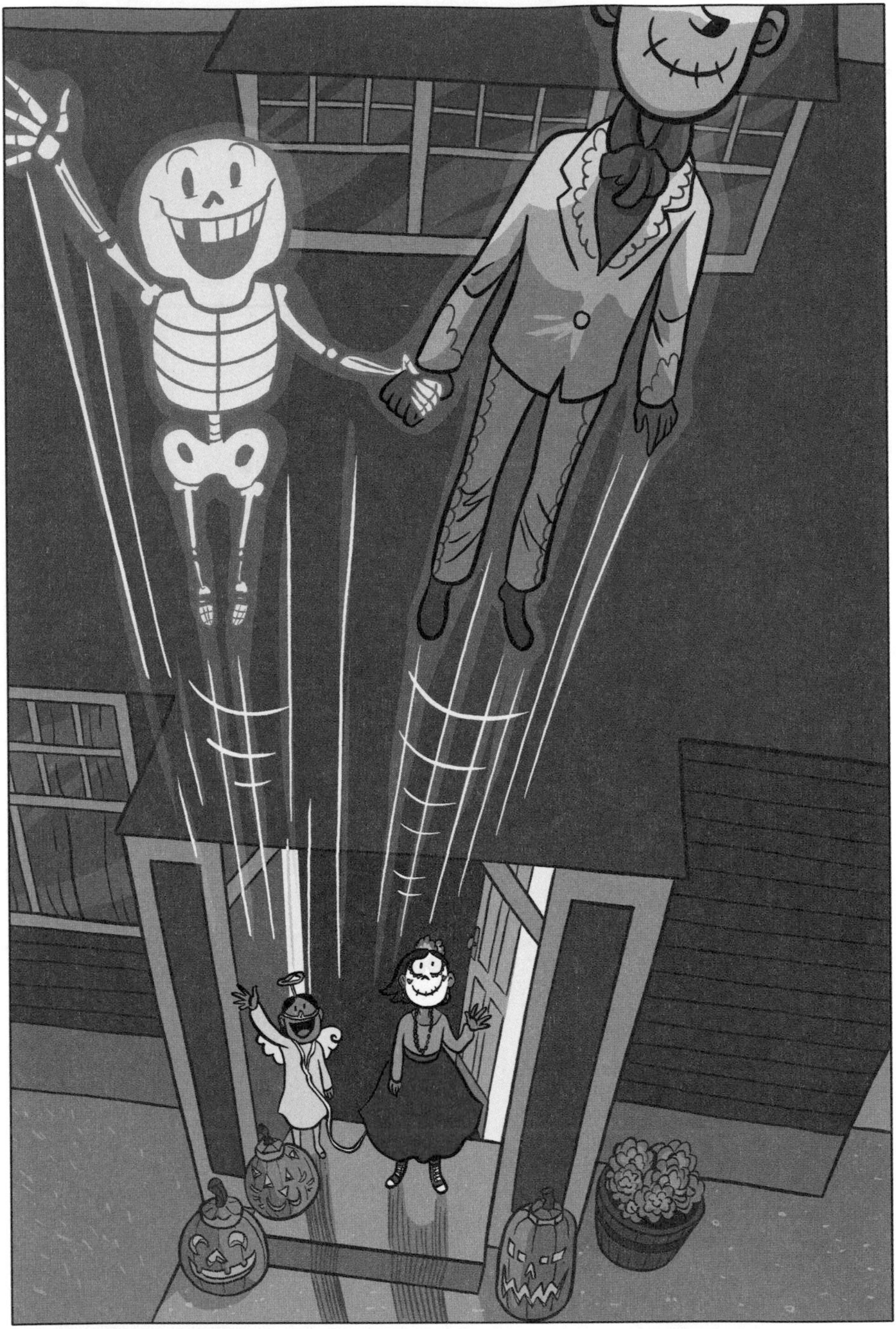

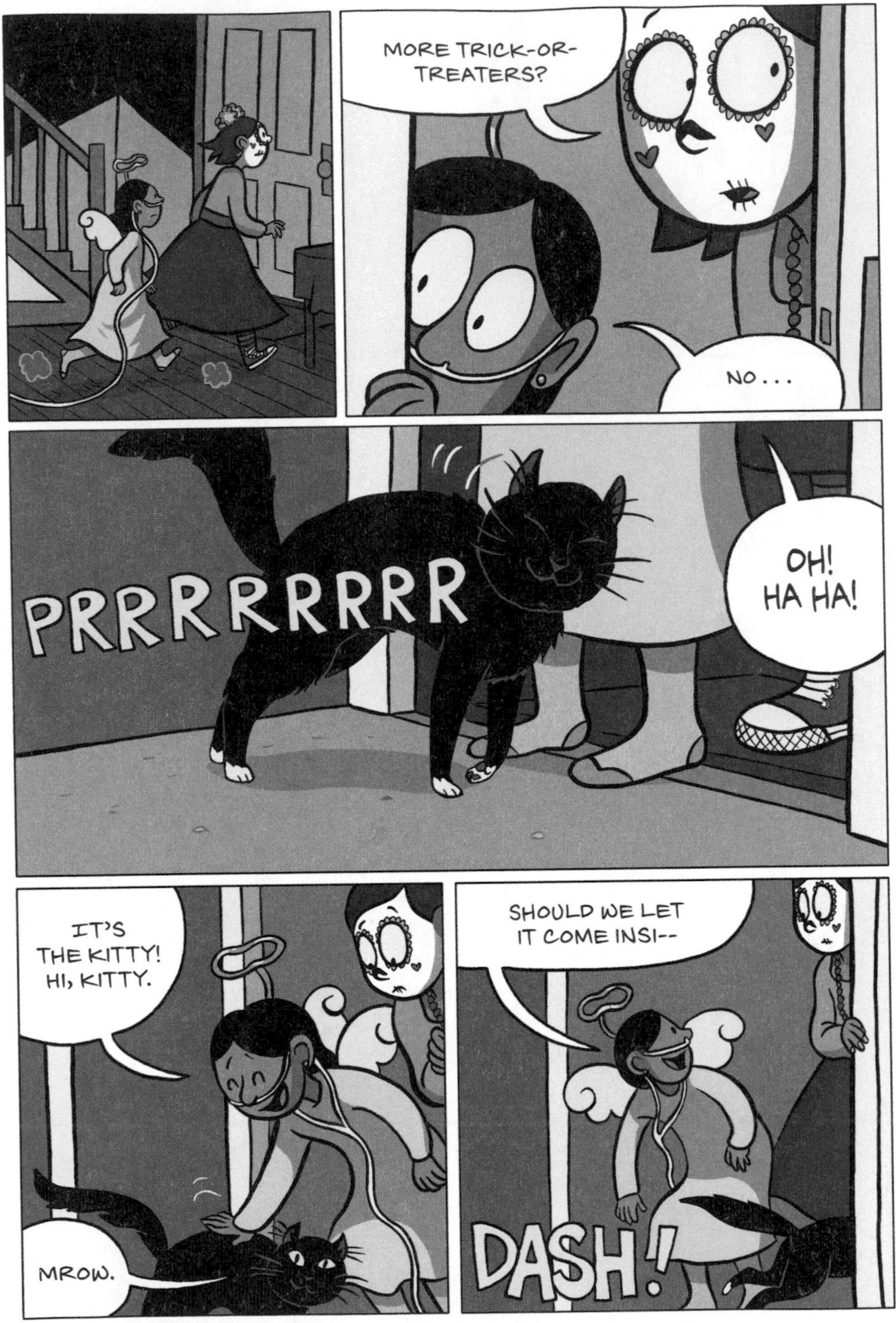

MORE TRICK-OR-TREATERS?
NO . . .
PRRRRRRR
OH! HA HA!
IT'S THE KITTY! HI, KITTY.
MROW.
SHOULD WE LET IT COME INSI--
DASH!

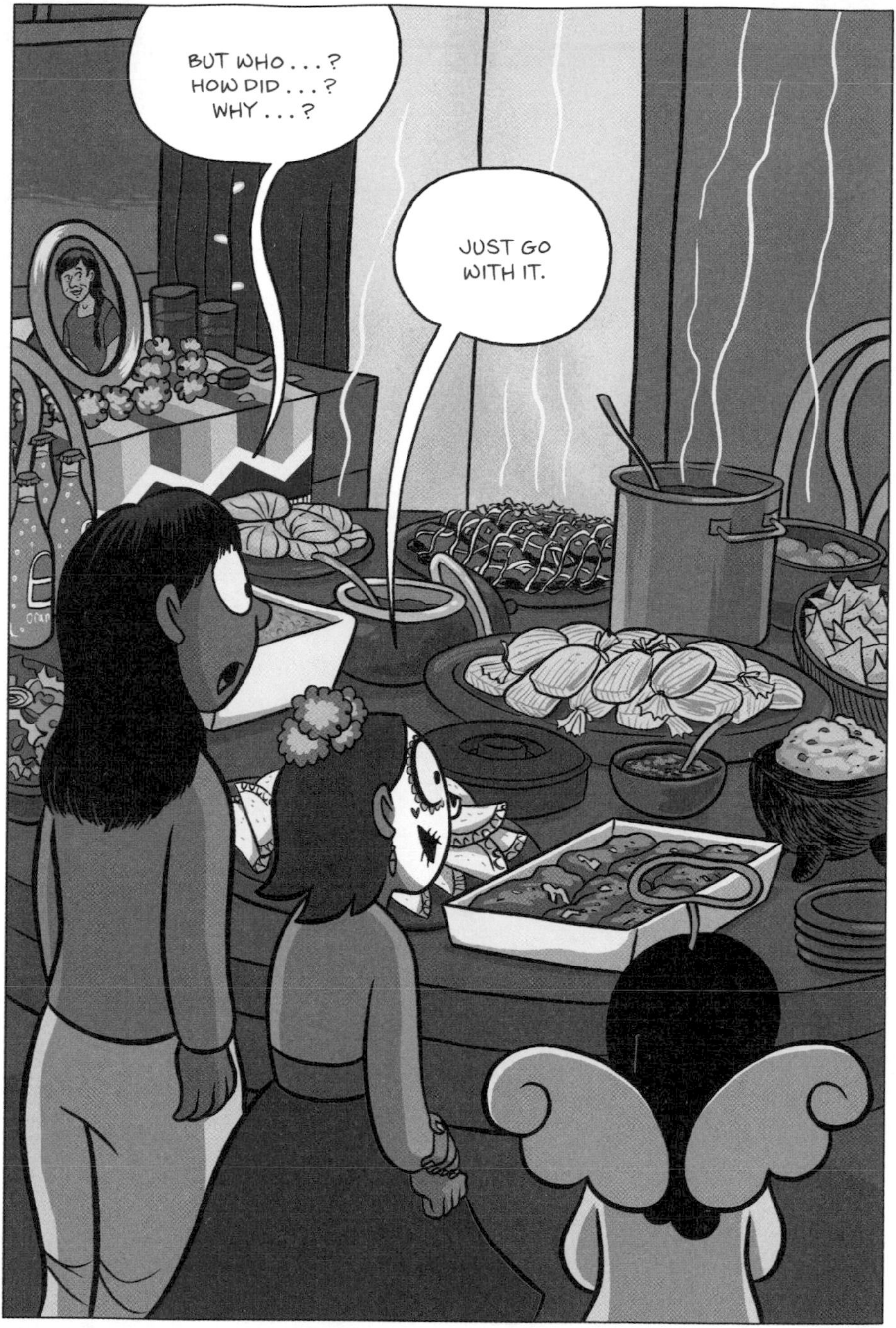
BUT WHO . . . ?
HOW DID . . . ?
WHY . . . ?
JUST GO WITH IT.

A FEW NOTES ABOUT
GHOSTS

BAHÍA DE LA LUNA

Bahía de la Luna was inspired by foggy coastal Northern California, where I grew up. I've always had an appreciation for the windswept coastline, the gnarly cypress trees, and especially the seaside town of Half Moon Bay, which is famous for its artichoke fields, pumpkin farms, and cheerful, laid-back Halloween vibe. I wanted Bahía de la Luna to feel like that, and the characters who live there to reflect the laid-back, gnarly, slightly haunted atmosphere.

DÍA DE LOS MUERTOS

Día de los Muertos, or Day of the Dead, is an ancient tradition that is now largely celebrated in Mexico and throughout the world. Instead of mourning the loss of loved ones, Mexican culture chooses to celebrate and honor the dead each year at the beginning of November, building altars (ofrendas) in homes, parks, and cemeteries, and decorating them with flowers, food, photographs, and other personal items. Although Day of the Dead represents the afterlife, there is something undeniably joyous about it!

I was very fortunate to attend San Francisco's annual Day of the Dead celebration during the course of creating this book. Thousands of people came together to dress up, build altars, light candles, and remember their loved ones. It was one of the most beautiful, respectful, and moving experiences I've ever had. Many of the visuals from the celebration scene in *Ghosts* came directly from that night, as I sat, sketched, and observed everything and everyone around me. The process of creating a book is not unlike letting go of the things that haunt your past. Making peace with your ghosts is as profound as the idea of life itself. And at the end of the day, love transcends life and death.

CYSTIC FIBROSIS

Cystic fibrosis is a genetic disease that causes thick, sticky mucus to build up in the lungs, making breathing difficult and leading to frequent infections. Some of the treatments Maya endures in this story are the vibrating vest designed to break up the mucus in her lungs (making it easier to cough out); extra nutrition delivered through a port in her belly while she sleeps; and, eventually, a breathing tube to administer more oxygen. Scar tissue can build up in the lungs following infections, reducing the space available for air to pass through. In some cases, CF patients need to undergo lung transplants. While there is no cure, improved treatments for CF have greatly extended the life expectancy of patients. I chose to write about cystic fibrosis because breathing is a huge theme in this story. Ghosts can't breathe, and Maya can't breathe very well herself. Cat has normal lungs, but she is often anxious and sometimes needs to be reminded to stop and breathe deeply. You can learn more about cystic fibrosis at www.cff.org.

SKETCHBOOK

These sketches were done in 2008, eight years before the publication of *Ghosts*! The characters, their story, and this environment have existed in my head for a very long time.

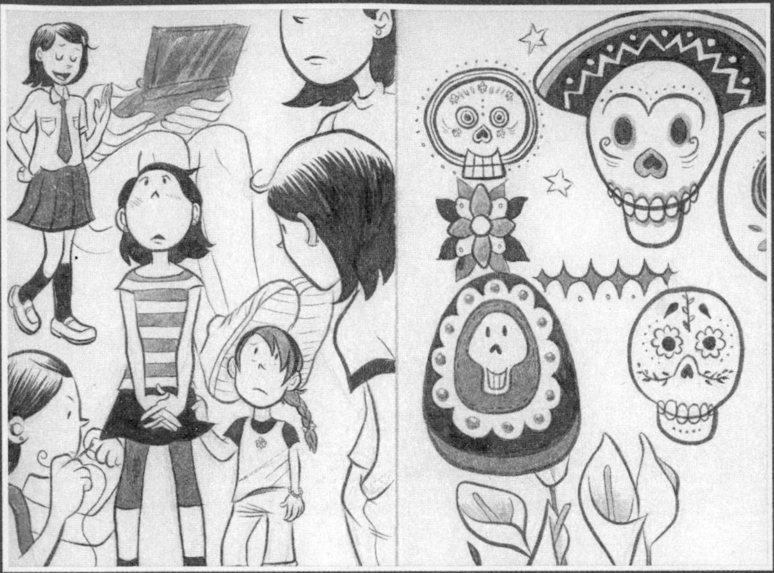

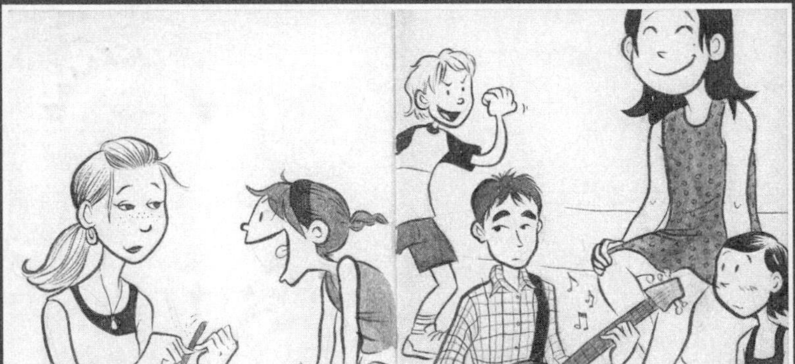

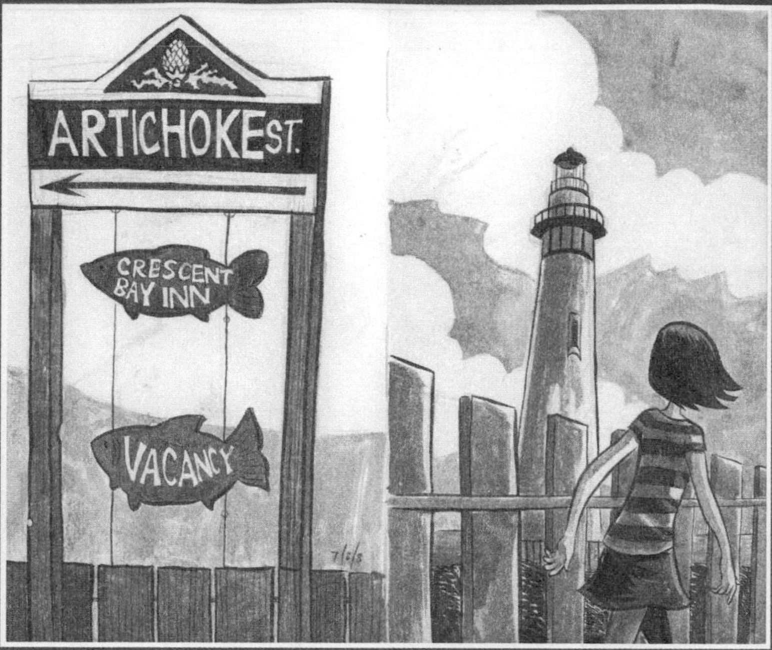
ARTICHOKE ST.
CRESCENT BAY INN
VACANCY

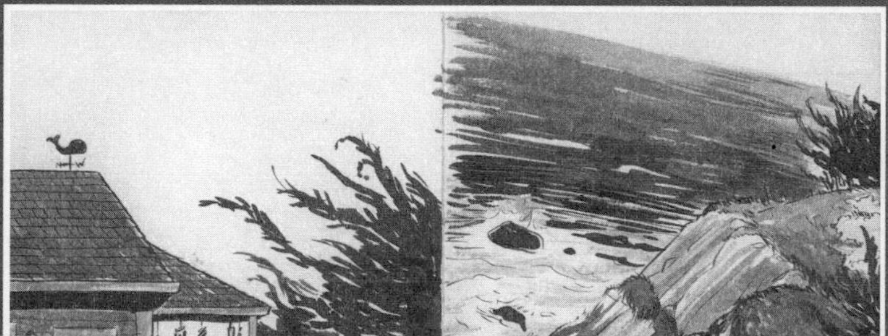

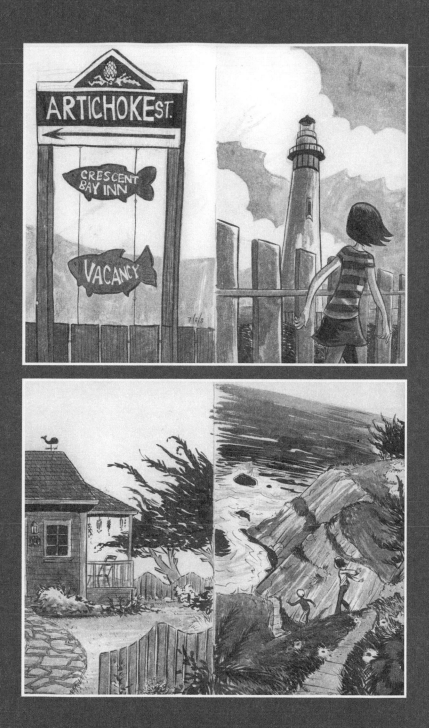

THANK

This book drew a lot of inspiration from my cousin Sabina Castello Collado, whom we lost to cancer when she was thirteen. Sabina was one of the most inspiring kids I ever met: spirited, joyful, and not interested in letting her illness define her or slow her down. She is greatly missed and will never be forgotten.

Sabina's parents, Suzanne and Dioni, and her siblings, Sophia and Adonis, also blew me away with the depth of their love for their daughter and sister. They are incredible people and I wish to thank them for everything they are and everything they do. Special thanks to Sophia for being one of the coolest big sisters I've ever known.

Thanks to Dave Roman and the Cuevas, Roman, Rigores, and Fernandez families for their support. Special thanks to Tammy Diaz Cuevas for talking tamales with me.

The cystic fibrosis community, especially the brave families who posted their stories online, was a constant source of inspiration as well as a great resource for understanding.

My editors, Cassandra Pelham and David Saylor, nurtured this project from the ground up and helped me down the winding path that leads from one ocean to another. I can't think of two better people with whom to wander the windy hillside that is creating graphic novels.

Thanks to Phil Falco, Sheila Marie Everett, Lizette Serrano, Tracy van Straaten, Lori Benton, Ellie Berger, Bess Braswell, Antonio Gonzalez, Caitlin Friedman, Michelle Campbell, Emily Heddleson,

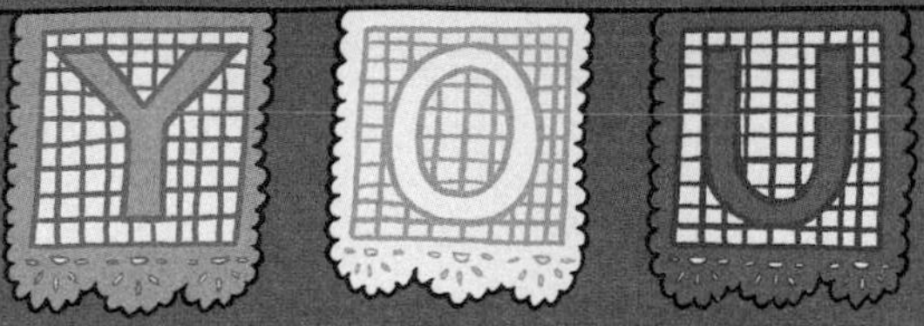
YOU

and the rest of the incredible team at Scholastic. I love working with all of you.

Braden Lamb deserves an extra-special round of bone-rattling applause for the coloring of my art for this book, translating my notes and reference for the atmosphere of Bahía de la Luna into stunning Technicolor. And muchas gracias to Braden's team of assistants, Shelli Paroline and Rachel Maguire!

Additional thanks to my studio assistants, Alexandra Graudins and Kristen Adam, for providing so much help, never-ending good cheer, and cookies; my wonder agent, Judy Hansen; ace letterer Jenny Staley; Sofia Vasquez-Duran, for talking health and medicine; Jewels Green, for her thoughtful insights on cystic fibrosis; and my friend in all things art, introspection, and skeletons, Ashley Despain.

Thanks to the authors, artists, filmmakers, and photographers who inspired me to think about spirits and magical realism and history and delicious food. Thanks to the librarians, booksellers, teachers, comics community, and everyone who has supported my work so wholeheartedly. Thanks to the state of California, my lifelong muse. Thanks to my family, who don't seem to mind living in the fog; I'll bear it if I have to, as long as you guys are here. Thanks to my friends, who are a continual source of love, support, and ideas. I'd be lost in the dark without them.

Finally, an orange soda toast to my readers, young and old, who are endlessly amazing.

–Raina

BIBLIOGRAPHY

While *Ghosts* is a work of fiction, I conducted many interviews with friends and family members, and referenced or participated in the following resources during the creation of this book.

BOOKS

Carmichael, Elizabeth and Chloë Sayer. *The Skeleton at the Feast: The Day of the Dead in Mexico.* Austin: University of Texas Press, 1991.

Greenleigh, John and Rosalind Rosoff Beimler. *The Days of the Dead: Mexico's Festival of Communion with the Departed.* Portland: Pomegranate Communications, 1998.

Hyams, Gina and Masako Takahashi. Day of the Dead Box. San Francisco: Chronicle Books, 2001.

Stavans, Ilan, ed. *Wáchale! Poetry and Prose about Growing Up Latino in America.* Chicago: Cricket Books, 2001.

Tonatiuh, Duncan. *Funny Bones: Posada and His Day of the Dead Calaveras.* New York: Abrams Books for Young Readers, 2015.

Winningham, Geoff, Richard Rodriguez, and J. M. G. Le Clézio. *In the Eye of the Sun: Mexican Fiestas.* New York: W. W. Norton & Company, 1996.

ARTICLES

Delsol, Christine. "La Catrina: Mexico's Grand Dame of Death." *SFGate.* October 25, 2011. http://www.sfgate.com/mexico/mexicomix/article/La-Catrina-Mexico-s-grande-dame-of-death-2318009.php#photo-1824635

Gawande, Atul. "The Bell Curve." *The New Yorker.* December 6, 2004. http://www.newyorker.com/magazine/2004/12/06/the-bell-curve

Trivedi, Bijal P. "Doorway to a Cure for Cystic Fibrosis." *Discover.* July 30, 2013. http://discovermagazine.com/2013/september/14-doorway-to-a-cure

Wineland, Claire. "Living Life from a Hospital Room." CNN. October 23, 2014. http://www.cnn.com/2014/10/23/health/cystic-fibrosis-clairity-project/

WEBSITES

Cystic Fibrosis Foundation: www.cff.org
Day of the Dead in Mexico: www.dayofthedead.com
The Marigold Project: www.dayofthedeadsf.org
Mexican Sugar Skull: www.mexicansugarskull.com
SOMArts: www.somarts.org

RAINA TELGEMEIER is the #1 *New York Times* bestselling, multiple Eisner Award–winning creator of *Smile, Sisters,* and *Guts,* which are all graphic memoirs based on her childhood. She is also the creator of *Drama* and *Ghosts,* and is the adapter and illustrator of the first four Baby-sitters Club graphic novels. Raina lives in the San Francisco Bay Area. To learn more, visit her online at goraina.com.

ALSO BY
RAINA TELGEMEIER